Noon

on the

Third

Day

JAMES HULBERT

Noon on the Third Day

HOLT, RINEHART AND WINSTON / NEW YORK

Published, August, 1962
Second Printing, August, 1962

Designer: Ernst Reichl
83811–0112
Printed in the United States of America

To Joan

The terms of the President and Vice-President shall end at noon on the 20th day of January, and the terms of Senators and Representatives at noon on the 3rd day of January, of the years in which such terms would have ended if this article had not been ratified; and the terms of their successors shall then begin.

—THE CONSTITUTION OF THE UNITED STATES OF AMERICA, ARTICLE XX.

Noon

on the

Third

Day

1

Senator John Burnett called down the stairs of his Georgetown house to the foyer where his wife Ellen and the maid, Leona Smith, stood.

"Ellen, is Leona here yet?"

"Just came in," Ellen Burnett said as she fluffed her gray hair and gazed at herself critically in the mirror with half-closed eyes.

"Good. Mr. Adamson and I could use a little more coffee."

"I'll bring it right up, sir," Leona said, "soon as I hang up my coat."

"I'm going to be out most of the day, Leona," Mrs. Burnett said. "Upstairs on the hall table I've left a list of things to do. Get as much done as you can. And I've also left a ten-dollar bill and a list of things to get at the store. Get anything else we need if there's any left over."

"Yes, ma'am."

"Let's see. What else? I guess that's all. I can't think of anything else now. If I do, I'll call you." She drew on her white gloves and gave herself a mildly approving glance in the mirror. She turned and patted Leona's arm affectionately. "If I'm not back before you leave tonight, I'll see you on Friday." She stepped into the bright sunlight and shut the door behind her.

Leona put her purse on the closet shelf, from which a moment before Mrs. Burnett had removed her own. Slipping on a plain white apron, she went into the kitchen and tested the temperature of the coffee with a sizzling flick of her forefinger against the pot. She took the metal pot upstairs and set it on the marble-top table beside the library door to save herself a trip. She rapped lightly on the open door.

". . . that's the way I and many, many others see it, John," a man was saying.

"I'll get some more coffee," she said.

"Good morning, Leona," the Senator said. "If you would, please."

Leona entered and picked up the silver pot. "Leona, I'd like you to meet Mr. Adamson. Mrs. Smith."

"How do you do, Mrs. Smith," said the man, rising from his chair.

"Mornin', sir," Leona said. "Excuse me, I'll get the coffee." She hurried out, shut the door, and filled the silver pot from the kitchen one. She wished the Senator wouldn't do that. He was a good man, but she wished he wouldn't introduce her to people that way.

". . . you have no idea how valuable it is, Claude," Senator Burnett was saying as she came in again, "for me to get the benefit of your thinking . . . thank you, Leona . . . it's so easy to get out of touch with things here in Washington, you know, and I do appreciate your taking the time to come here, particularly at this inconvenient hour."

Leona closed the door and went to the hall table. Glancing at the list of tasks, she saw that Mrs. Burnett had attempted, by numbers, some sort of priority system, but had abandoned it, leaving only "guest room" numbered one and double underlined. The grocery list lay beside it with a ten-dollar bill paperclipped to it.

The Senator emerged from the library with his arm resting fraternally on the smaller man's shoulders. "You can be certain, Claude, that I'll reflect most carefully on our conversation of this morning. And please give my regards to . . ." he checked his mind for a fraction of a second ". . . your lovely wife, Lucy."

"Pleasure to talk to you, Senator. Damn considerate of you to ask me out. And I hope you see my point. Something's got to be

12

done about these monopolistic labor unions. They've got the bit in their teeth, and they'll wreck the whole economy if they're allowed to continue. In St. Louis it's a terrible situation, I'm told. They come in there with their goons, and throw bricks through plate-glass windows, and beat people up and scare the liver out of them. And the police stand idly by and do nothing. They're intimidated. The police are intimidated. That's a shocking thing. But they get away with it. And the salaries they demand are just ... ridiculous. You can't run a business and make a profit paying salaries like that. And if they run you out of business, then what? No businesses and no jobs, that's what. Right?"

"Perhaps," said the Senator.

"It's vicious," Adamson continued. "They think they're a law unto themselves. And somebody's going to have to stand up to them, or, mark my words, we're going to have a labor dictator in this country. . . ."

The Senator nodded thoughtfully.

"Small businessmen like us out there in Missouri may not be big fat cats like General Motors," Adamson said, "but, *in toto*, there are a hell of a lot of us. And if we stick together, they'll sit up and take notice here in Washington. You know, Senator, there are four and a half million small businesses in this country. That's nothing to be sneezed at, Senator. I mean, that's a force to be reckoned with. . . ."

"It surely is," said the Senator.

"I'll tell you frankly, Senator," Adamson said confidentially, "there were some of the boys down at the Chamber that felt it would be a waste of time talking to you. Hell, he's a pinko—I mean that's what they actually said—you're not going to get anyplace with him. His mind's closed. But I said to them, let me try. There's nothing to be lost by trying, and Senator," he said, firmly grasping the Senator's hand and holding on to it, "I mean to tell them about the fine reception I got here."

"I appreciate that, Claude."

"And I mean to tell them that I got you to thinking about an aspect of the problem that you hadn't considered before, and that I think I made some progress with you."

"It was most interesting and I learned a good deal," the Senator said. "Thank you for coming, Claude. Can you find your way out?"

Claude laughed dryly. "Well, I didn't expect to bring you around in one sitting," he said. "And I don't expect an answer. Politicians never give straight answers. No offense intended." He started down the stairs. "Keep in mind there's a lot of us small businessmen out there, Senator, and we'll be interested in seeing what you do on this labor bill."

"I'll do that, Claude. It's still in committee, and it won't be coming to the floor for a while yet. Thank you again for coming." Mr. Adamson disappeared down the stairs, and the front door clicked shut.

"Tedious," the Senator muttered, "most tedious. Early start for me today, Leona. Business before, during, and after breakfast. How's the family?"

"Oh, we're gettin' along pretty good."

"Arthur doing all right?"

"Oh, yes, he like his job all right. Only thing is the hours is bad."

"I meant to tell you. I spoke to a couple of people down at the Post Office about Arthur. Things are tight down there right at the moment, but they assured me that Arthur will get first consideration for a job in his classification. I wouldn't be surprised to see that happen in a couple of months, maybe sooner, if this so-called economy drive blows over."

"I'm much obliged."

Outside a horn sounded.

"There's my cab," the Senator said, starting down the stairs. "No dinner for me here tonight," he said hollowly from the downstairs hall as he took his hat from the closet shelf and set it on his head carelessly. "Having dinner downtown with some constituents who are in town." The door slammed vigorously.

Leona decided to have a cup of coffee before starting to work. She filled one of the fancy cups and sat down.

It was funny how times changed, she thought. Now she lived out in the suburbs, and all the white people lived in Georgetown. Forty years ago, when she had been a little girl, she had lived with her family in Georgetown, below M Street, in a crowded house owned by her uncle and aunt. Her uncle had sold the house in 1934 for twelve hundred dollars, and he thought that he had made a killing. In those days, the houses in Georgetown seemed to be slowly collapsing. Nowadays they sold them for forty, fifty, sixty thousand dollars each. They fixed them up, of course. Put new glass in the broken windows, unplugged the toilets, straightened the sagging shutters and painted them. But they were still huddled together, with back yards not big enough to whip a cat in. Patios they called them now.

She had bought her house in the suburbs with a check for ten thousand dollars, her first husband's Government life insurance. A gray asphalt-shingled house with green-and-white trim on a plot 60 by 120 feet. All of the other houses in the block, most of them owned by white people, were equally neat and well kept. Her second husband, Arthur, had worried about moving into a mixed neighborhood, but the neighbors did not pay any attention to them.

Finally she told herself it was time to get to work. She rose languidly from her chair and prepared to go downstairs to wash the breakfast dishes.

2

In his cab on the way to the Senate Office Building, the Senator was thinking about the labor bill on which Claude Adamson had just expressed his vehement opinion. His breakfast conversation with Adamson was now being sorted, correlated, and cross-tabulated with the stuff of thirty-five years in politics: a million facts, statistics, emotions, impressions.

That bill was going to be a problem for him—one of the bills on which his vote would satisfy no one, including himself. It was, in fact, going to be a problem for almost everybody. Management, riding the crest of public feeling aroused by the committee hearings on labor racketeering, was determined to avenge twenty-five years of wrongs. Labor, for centuries an underdog, was just as determined to accept no bridle, least of all one fashioned by its enemies.

His mind began to accelerate, seeking a solution, but it did not work as he was accustomed to have it work—smoothly, like a piece of electronic equipment. Now, somehow, it could not make the final step, provide the final answer. It was as if some crucial gear had been stripped toothless, and was whirring silently, failing to drive any machinery beyond itself.

As the cab stopped in front of the Delaware Avenue entrance to the Senate Office Building, the Senator hauled himself forward by the side strap and dropped change, which included a liberal tip, into the driver's palm. As he passed through the bronze doors, a police officer nodded deferentially.

"Good morning, Senator."

"Morning, Bob. Did you get that days-off problem settled?"

"That I did, sir, and thanks for your help in the matter."

"Glad to do it."

He nodded to the Negro porter, who feinted at tipping his cap. "Edward, how's the leg?"

"Mendin' all right, Senator, mendin' all right."

"Good. Take it easy and give it time to knit."

"Intend to, sir."

He stepped into the elevator and spoke to the operator, Ernest Smeekins, who had held his job for the last five years at the Senator's pleasure. He was from, and voted in, Missouri.

"Ernest, how's Elma this morning?"

"Complainin'."

"Her back giving her trouble again?"

"Her back's givin' her trouble, and her mouth's givin' me trouble."

"You marry for better or worse, Ernest."

"I know. I know. No way out. We need a law to protect men from women."

"Impossible to draft, Ernest, and hopelessly impossible of passage."

"True," said Ernest. "Political dynamite."

The door slid open, and the Senator strode briskly down the hall, noting with satisfaction that it was two minutes before nine-fifteen. Several times he had tried to explain to his staff that a Senator's hours were long and irregular. Often he was up late at night and thus he would occasionally be late in the morning. But it seemed hopeless. For a short time after one of his lectures, they arrived on time, but slowly, almost imperceptibly, they drifted beyond the official opening time. At first they offered excuses—traffic, automobile breakdowns, and other more ingenious reasons—but finally even these ceased and nine-thirty, by popular usage, became the accepted arrival hour. Dick Goetz, of course, was there.

"Good morning, Dick. My gosh. That's a stack of mail."

17

"We have now crossed the thirteen thousand mark on labor mail."

The Senator shook his head incredulously.

"Sixty-eight letters and cards in the first delivery," Dick Goetz continued. "About fifty against, eighteen or so for. But the fifty are almost all alike. Obviously inspired. Same words and phrases we've been getting all week. Probably rounded them up at some labor meeting and gave them the word."

"How about the eighteen?"

"Well, it's actually more than eighteen, since one is a petition. Eighty names or so. Chamber of Commerce. *They* obviously rounded up everybody at the weekly luncheon and had them sign it as they left. Then there's a long letter from Fred Eaton."

"Eaton. What does he have to say?"

"The usual. America stands at the crossroads. Free government versus labor monopoly. Freedom versus totalitarianism. Class against class. Et cetera." Goetz handed him the letter.

"I'll never understand what this man is doing in the Democratic party," the Senator said, glancing at it. "I once suggested to him, you know, that he join the Republican party, and you'd have thought I had hit him across the face. 'Oh, I could never do that,' he said. But he was never able to give any reason. I don't think he has any except that he doesn't know anybody on the other side. He feels comfortable with us, even though he's almost one hundred per cent against anything the party ever does, or tries to do."

"It takes all kinds."

"I suppose it does. If the Democratic umbrella is wide enough to cover Negroes and segregationists, I guess it's big enough to cover Fred Eaton. Anything else?"

"Long letter from Father Kelly. God's against the bill."

The Senator was annoyed. "God's always against whatever Father Kelly's against."

"They are remarkably consistent, those two," Dick said.

"I'm a little tired of Father Kelly. He has no wife, but he hands out all sorts of advice on marital relations; he has no children, but lots of advice on raising them; and he has no labor

18

problems, but he sure does know just how those who do have them should solve them."

"He has some good points," Dick said.

"Oh, I'm sure he does. He's read everything that was ever printed on the subject, as far as I can tell. It's just that superior attitude. He always equates Christianity with his point of view, and heresy with any other. I'll have to stop in and see him next time I'm in St. Louis. Anything else?"

"Note from the President, thanking you for your support on the budget bill. Nothing special. Everybody got one. They've been doing this regularly since Alfie Warder took over congressional relations."

"Good politics," the Senator said. "It's about time they got on the ball up there. It still produces the intended warm glow, no matter how much you discount it. What's on the list today?"

"Virgil Akers is coming in for lunch, you remember."

"Bearing tidings of no great joy, I suspect."

"I thought we'd better make sure it was private, so we're going to meet him in his room at the Congressional. We can have lunch sent up."

"Fine."

"Judge Russell has been trying to get an appointment to talk to you about the labor bill. I've been stalling him off. . . ."

"Good. Not today. Sometime next week. I'm not quite ready to talk to Liberty Electric about that bill just yet."

"From eleven to twelve, you're booked to chair the minimum wage hearings. They're splitting it up, so the chairman requested that you be prompt in relieving the previous senator."

The Senator grimaced. "That cussed old goat. All right, I'll be there. What else?"

"They expect a roll-call vote on the Rivers and Harbors bill, probably around three o'clock. If Shoten doesn't talk all afternoon. Otherwise it will be tomorrow, first thing. So be sure and let me know where you are."

"That all?"

"No, the senior senator from New Mexico requested that you drop by sometime today, at your convenience. He didn't say what he had in mind."

19

"I know what he has in mind. Campaign funds. He's chairman of the Senatorial Campaign Committee. He wants to get his hands on the money so that he can spread it about on handbills, posters, superfluous office help sitting here in Washington, and other useless bagatelle. He will leave me twenty-five cents on the dollar to try and get myself elected."

"Seems like a silly way to handle it," Dick said. "Why don't they leave it where it will do the most good?"

"Asinine," the Senator agreed. "They feel that I get more money than I need, and they would like to spread it around among the needy. The welfare state in action," he said wryly. "I guess I shouldn't complain."

"One more item, before you run off," Dick said. "Dinner tonight with the Shannons."

"Oh, yes. Who's coming? The whole clan?"

"Just about. Shannon and Anne. Daughter Pamela and husband. Son Herbert Junior, and his wife, Luisa. She's one of the Gorens, isn't she? Pretty potent group," Dick observed.

"You don't know the half of it," the Senator said. "Their family tree is more complicated than the Windsors. Tentacles like an octopus throughout the whole state. Fortunately, a quiescent octopus," he added.

The Senator went into his office and skimmed through a stack of letters three inches high, which had been culled from the original stack six inches high, scribbling notes of instruction to his staff in the corner of each. He called in Mary and dictated certain letters which required his personal touch. Actually, Dick Goetz had become so expert at imitating his style that the Senator often could not be sure whether he himself had dictated the letter when it came in for his signature. He picked up the previous day's *Congressional Record* and skimmed through Shoten's statement, which, in fourteen pages, "briefly summarized" his views that the labor bill passed by the House of Representatives represented mass enslavement of the working man, a one-hundred-and-eighty degree departure from the traditional American principles of freedom of speech, press, and assembly, and an ill-concealed attempt to sever labor's jugular vein, among other things. At one time, Senator Burnett and his colleague had agreed on most things, but in the last few years, Shoten had veered off course. He seemed to be afflicted with a form of paranoia, in which he saw himself the last trooper at the barricades, holding off the surging mob of rapacious bankers, corporation presidents, and big interests.

The Senator spent his assigned hour in the minimum wage hearing. He appeared alert and interested, making periodic notes, and occasionally asking the witness a question, but his mind was actually turning over other problems, principally those concerning the labor bill.

In front of him the witnesses droned on, reading their thick, dry statements word for word. And as always, the arguments were the same. The Chamber of Commerce, the NAM, and business groups argued that any increase was inflationary, would upset the delicate balance of the free enterprise system, and would result in mass unemployment of marginal workers who would no longer be worth the new minimum wage. Indeed, they added ironically, it was surprising that unions had any interest in minimum wage legislation. The unions had become so powerful and monopolistic that they had the power to raise wages to dangerous levels, far above any Government minimum. In addition, the entire idea of the law was un-American, having been foisted on the American people during the depths of the depression when the Government was in the hands of radicals. In summary, after forty pages, no changes in the law were necessary or desirable.

Union spokesmen took the stand, and were incredulous that the paltry projected minimum wage, which was insufficient to sustain life, could be opposed by anybody. It could be doubled, even tripled, and it would still be niggardly. They embarked on long case histories of families of six or eight, squeezing out a pitiful existence, even at the proposed minimum. Our interest in the matter, they said, is, of course, altruistic, because everybody in our union makes more than the minimum wage.

Thus it went, on and on, day after day, with the senators splitting up the assignments so that each could sit, to the limit of his patience, nodding and asking a question here and there to indicate sympathy and interest. And all for nothing, because it had already been decided that minimum wage legislation would not be considered in the session but would carry over to the next session, when new hearings would undoubtedly be held.

At noon, the Senator adjourned the hearing and met Dick Goetz. They walked to the Congressional Hotel together. Virgil Akers was waiting for them in his room. Little in Akers' appearance suggested that his principal interest in life was the manipulation of people. Angular, graceless, with a thin, ascetic face, and rimless glasses, he looked more like a bloodless accountant than the Senator's chief of staff in Missouri.

"Good trip, Virgil?" the Senator asked, as Akers poured them drinks.

"Fine. Left St. Louis in the rain, but it cleared up by the time we got here."

"What are our dissident Democrats up to?" the Senator said, sipping his drink.

"The usual. They're going to try to knock us off again, just like last time."

The Senator spat out an oath. "This isn't a political party. It's a goddam hothouse for prima donnas. We raise them by the bushel in the Democratic party." He paced the room, shaking his head in incomprehension. "I swear to God you'd think they'd have better sense. They took a solid licking last time. We kicked hell out of them in that primary. And they have nothing on which to base a campaign. Nothing. We've cut the ground out from under them on issues. We've thrown out all the people they called crooks. We've neutralized every argument they had last time. I can't think of a single issue from last time that will cause us problems this time. Not a single one. They don't have a man in office with the single exception of Weston Walls. They're starved for money, starved for appointments, starved for insurance business, legal business, everything. Yet the scraggly group pulls itself together and calmly plans to try it all over again, as if nothing had happened."

"I have no doubts at all," Virgil said, "that we'll give them a sound beating again."

"Nor have I," the Senator said. "None whatever. But it will be a bitter fight, a hell of a bitter fight. It will be closer than last time, and that means, inevitably, mud. I'll go up against the

Republicans in November looking like I just came out of the tar pits."

"It might not be so bad, Senator," Dick Goetz said. "Last time it wasn't so bad, as political campaigns go."

"That was last time, and the situation was quite different. We were virtually certain we were going to win, for one thing. It's easy to be generous under those conditions. Secondly, we were up against a group of political greenhorns. So we held our fire, waited for them to make mistakes, which they made, by the bucketload. But they're no longer green. They'll make a few mistakes, but nothing like the boners they pulled last time. And they'll be wise to some of our tricks, for that matter."

"I still think we'll whip them."

"Of course. So do I. But it's going to take some doing." He sat down in a chair, heavily, and passed his hand across his eyes. "I'm sorry, boys. But this just means a campaign for the primary and another for the general election. Six solid months, and I can't say that I'm looking forward to that prospect. No rest for the weary . . . or is it wicked?"

"We'll give you all the help we can, Senator," Dick said.

"I know you all will, and I appreciate it, but there's only so much you can do. Unfortunately, there is no acceptable substitute for the candidate on many occasions. Virgil," he said, fixing him with a cocked eye, "any possibility of a deal?"

"I'd say they'll make a deal. They've intimated as much to me and several other people."

"A realistic deal?"

"Not very. They want the moon."

"What's the price?"

"Too high for my money. They want something like an even split on appointments, roughly half-and-half split on elective jobs, a chance to run some of their guys in some of the Congressional districts and for the legislature without our opposition and . . . one of the two top jobs."

"You mean the Governor's or mine."

"Right."

"Not interested."

"That was my reply."

"They don't want much, do they? Just for us to turn the state over to them on a silver platter."

"We'd retain the machinery and the voting control, of course," Virgil said.

"For how long? Until they solidify their position? That's nice of them."

"This is their asking price," Virgil said. "They'd take a lot less. But the one thing I think they'll stick on is one of the two top jobs. They're desperate for a name."

"Well, that's out. They're trying to split Ross and me, that's apparent. I assume the Governor feels equally adamant on the matter."

"He says so."

"He says so, but does he?"

"I think Ross is a little scared. I think he's not so sure they won't win as you are."

The Senator rocked back in his chair so hard that it creaked. "What have they offered him? Another term as Governor and a shot at Bell's seat next Senatorial, or a shot at my seat now?"

"That's approximately it."

"And what are his inclinations?"

"Well, this is all just by guess and by God. I size it up about this way. When the offer was first made, he turned them down flat, as you would expect Ross to do, considering all that he owes you. Then a doubt began to eat at him, and he began to think a little more about his own skin. You can be sure that they pointed out to him that if he ran for Governor and then ran for Bell's seat, he'd have to survive two elections to get to the Senate. While if he ran against you, he'd make it in one jump. But he respects you, and somewhat fears you. He still has some loyalty and grati- tude to you for what you've done for him, although I don't think we can count on that. On the other hand, he knows that Bell hasn't been in the Senate as long as you have, and that he doesn't have nearly the popular strength. But Bell is making a pretty good record, and in four years he may be a tough man to beat. Further, Ross has a good record now, after four years as Governor, and I'm sure he has some doubts that it will be any better after eight years than four. The only other factor, I'd say, is the Democratic tide. He's not sure yet whether it's going to be running strong enough to suit him next November."

"Ross reads too much Shakespeare. He's always waiting to seize that tide that leads on to fortune, but he's never quite sure that this is the time."

"Right. I think his indecisiveness will be a help."

"So do I. I haven't talked to Bell. I held off until we had a little more definite word on their intentions. It's a damn awkward subject to discuss with him."

"Is Bell interested in sitting in the Senate for the rest of his natural life?" Goetz asked.

"Apparently. At least, he's been careful to mention no other ambition to me."

"There is one other factor here. Our favorite Attorney General, Bill Milano," said Akers.

"He may be a problem all right," the Senator said. "He wants to be Governor so bad he can taste it. That means he's likely to be pushing Ross to move up, and failing that, he's likely to end up on the other side. It's awkward too, because Wilson is the logical candidate. He's Lieutenant Governor, he's earned it, and he's been down the line for us."

"Sure," said Akers. "But you know as well as I do that he's no vote getter. He'd coast in with a strong ticket, but I don't know how much of an asset he'd be in a party fight."

"Some," said the Senator. "He's thought of as honest, a quality much prized by the voters."

"I think Milano has something up his sleeve. I'm not precisely sure just what. But I have an idea it may be a well-timed investigation of some sort. He got a taste of that sort of thing in the bank case, and he liked it. I'd guess he's planning some rip-roaring, attention-grabbing investigation, with radio and television and his name smeared on every front page for a couple of months. It could be anything of high interest, of course—racketeering, gambling, prostitution. Although it will probably be something with a high-minded twist."

"If that's so, we'd better move to nip it in the bud," the Senator said. "We may want to offer Milano something, but we want to offer it; we don't want him to appropriate it by force." The

Senator pursed his lips. "How does this sound to you? It's a diversionary tactic of sorts. The idea is to get him so tied up that he can't extricate himself to conduct some damaging investigation without appearing to be promoting his own interest over the public interest. I'm thinking of an investigation of State-chartered insurance companies. It's so terribly complicated he would have to spend a couple of months just reading background material. And it shouldn't provide any sensational copy. It's been pretty thoroughly gone over. A little favoritism. Perhaps the costs are a little too high. But that's about all. Yet, with a little management, we can make him think he's on the verge of uncovering something big. The first step is, I think, to plant a couple of newspaper articles hinting about some scandal. Then some editorial support. A panel show or two can be arranged on TV through the Shannons. We'd turn up a few abuses and hint at more. A little later, Ross could announce that he was disturbed by the reports; subsequently, he could recommend that the Attorney General begin an investigation. I'll back him up on that. Bell might even be inveigled in. He has a stake in this too. What do you think?"

Akers rolled an unlit cigarette between his fingers. "Good. Provided the timing is right. If Milano got wind of what you were up to, he'd kick off his own investigation of something else before you could get started."

"I agree with you there. Well, think about it, Virgil. I trust your judgment, as you know. One other thing about Milano. Can this fellow Conner in his office be trusted to be honest with us?"

Virgil spread his palms, with a quizzical expression. "So far as I know, he can. He's been candid with us so far."

"Funny, but I've never entirely trusted him," the Senator said. "Those beady eyes bespeak ambition. I'm sure he sees himself as a potential Attorney General." The Senator laughed and shook his head. "That's the way it is, and always will be, I suppose. He probably has an assistant who's panting for *his* job, and the office boy is waiting to move in as assistant. Well, I've got to be going. I think I'll plan to come out next week, probably on Thursday. I'll want to have a talk with Ross, if you would arrange that. Set up a date with Father Kelly. And I suppose with

26

Fred Eaton too. And I think you ought to get somebody preparing the insurance stuff—just some quiet preliminary digging around. I'll be in touch with Bell, and I should have a pretty good line on him by the time I come out."

"Senator, I hate to rush you, but we'd better get going. I checked, and they expect the Rivers and Harbors vote at about three-thirty," Dick Goetz said.

"Right. Virgil, good-by. Have a good trip back, and I'll see you sometime next week, unless you hear from me to the contrary."

As Dick Goetz and the Senator walked back to the Capitol, Goetz said, "It's a shame you have to spend so much time on things like this."

"I agree. Frankly, I once thought that by the time I reached the U.S. Senate, somebody else would handle these matters. But it didn't take long before I realized that it was not to be so. With my left hand I influence the domestic and foreign policy of a nation of one hundred and seventy million. And with my right hand I fight a nickel-and-dime rear-guard action against my enemies, and, sometimes, my friends. And I have to perform the latter feat by remote control, as you observed at this lunch. Time is divided about equally between them, and that, of course, is ridiculous and uneconomical. But there is no other way. At least I haven't discovered one."

"Doesn't it make you nervous to be forced to rely on somebody else's judgment the way you're forced to rely on Virgil's, even though it's good?"

"Yes, it does, of course. But you used the key word. Forced. I suppose it's not too unlike the problem involved in running any large enterprise. The boss has got to delegate and rely on his subordinates. More than one business organization has failed because the founder just couldn't bring himself to let his subordinates make decisions, and then accept the mistakes they made. He could do the same job, without mistakes, and he just can't resist doing it himself. The secret of success, I'm convinced, is to rely on people, even in the shifting sands of politics. You've just got to pick good people, that's all."

"But you pick them, and then they turn on you. Look at

27

Ross, flirting with those bastards. It makes my blood boil. I don't see how you can be so calm about it."

"I'm not calm about it, let me assure you. But in politics you learn to look at your fellow man with the cold eye of reality, Dick. To look at him sentimentally, or in any other distorted way, is sure political death eventually. One lesson you learn early is that every person is extremely interested in one thing, himself. If you remember that, it will explain most of the activities of our friends we discussed this noon, or, if it won't explain them, it will at least make them predictable. Which is more important. The greatest asset a politician can have is foresight. A politician, after all, deals almost never in the past. Most of his time is spent anticipating. By observation, experience, intuition, he's got to be able to predict the probable actions of people. Which is—and I speak as one who has had considerable experience—goddam difficult."

They had reached the Senate cloakroom, and stood talking in its lush Victorian interior. "Boy," said the Senator to one of the pages, "how soon is the roll call?"

"About five minutes, sir."

"Good, we just made it." The Senator went through the frosted doors onto the floor, as Dick Goetz sat down on a leather sofa. It's a tense business, Dick thought. They always have to keep their guards up. Funny how most people think of them as bumbling, wishy-washy, softheaded. On the outside, they appear that way. On the inside, most of them are like Burnett, tough as steel. A steel framework, covered by a soft, amorphous, inoffensive mass—the political man. But a driving, tough man underneath. Burnett's really a practical idealist, which is a funny combination. Trying to do what he thinks is right, but willing to compromise if he has to, to get something done.

The Senator came back through the swinging doors. Dick fell in step with him as they headed for the subway to the Senate Office Building.

"Dick, there is one matter I'd like to proceed on. I'd like to fill the second job in our office as soon as practicable. Things are moving somewhat faster than I had anticipated."

28

"Fine. I assume you have some deserving soul in mind. A contributor's son, or something?"

"I don't have a specific person in mind, but I have the qualifications pretty well in mind. First of all, of course, we need somebody with a labor background who can write well. But we need more than that. Maybe a research man, or at least one who can lay his hands on the facts. He should be strong on detail, and have ability to analyze and digest our usual run of material. He doesn't have to be a public relations man—that I am leaving in your hands—but he should have a pleasant personality. Also, he should be a Jew."

"A Jew?" Dick said in surprise.

"Thought that would bring you up short. Yes, I think so. It's quite important for us to have a Jew on our staff. Our dissident friends are a liberal group. Jews are among its leaders, which is a natural thing. I'm sure if I were a Jew there would be a few things about the world that I would like to change too. And while you and I may not be conscious of who's a Jew and who isn't, Jews are very conscious of it. They know what writers are Jews, what composers, what entertainers; and what few Jewish politicians there are, they are always aware of. And, inevitably in these campaigns against liberal groups, the question of anti-Semitism is raised sooner or later. I don't know who starts it. I don't think Jews do. I think probably politicians raise it, knowing how strongly Jews feel on the subject. At any rate, it's almost inevitable. It was done, you know, in the last campaign. Never gained much currency, because I think most people knew that such a charge against me was patently false. But it will be raised again. And I intend to have a good living argument against it, even if it means discriminating against some poor white Protestant who is better qualified for the job. And we will none too subtly advertise the fact by selecting a Jew with a Jewish name. I'm not interested in a Miller or a Green. I want a Steinberg or an Epstein."

Dick scratched his head. "This won't be too easy, you know, with all these qualifications."

"You'll find it easier than you think. Talk to Lou Greenfeld over at the NLRB. Actually, Lou is just the type of man we want, but he wouldn't be interested in the job. Lou is an old friend of

29

mine, and I think you can speak frankly with him, just about as frankly as I have spoken with you. Just tell him we're looking for a younger version of himself. You might ask his opinion about this, incidentally. I've gotten good counsel from Lou over the years, and I'd trust his opinion on this. I think he'll agree with me."

"O.K.," said Dick, "I'll get to work on it."

The subway reached the end of the line and they stepped off and stood in the basement rotunda.

"I'm going up and have a talk with our friend Bell. See if I can draw him out on this matter. I'll drop back by the office before I leave."

"You remember the date with the Shannons."

"I do. I'm meeting them at the Senate entrance at . . . what time . . . six?"

"Right."

"Fine. I'll see you later."

The Senator entered the elevator, and pondered just how he would handle the conversation with the junior senator from his own state. Bell had been one of his protégés in Missouri, and during his first years in the Senate, he had consulted John Burnett on almost every major vote. In the last couple of years, he had drawn away somewhat, and Burnett had not attempted to maintain any sort of sovereignty over him, feeling that in the long run it was impossible. Bell still remained friendly, but now he made his own decisions without aid, at least without John Burnett's aid.

He entered Bell's office. "Ladies," he said gallantly, shaking hands with each of the secretaries in turn. He made the kind of light talk that caused them to titter to each other, after he had gone into Senator Bell's office, about what a charming man he was.

"Delighted you dropped by, John. I was going to come by your office today or tomorrow," said Les Bell, extending his hand over his desk.

"Well, my secret service tells me things are beginning to pop in our favorite state, so I just thought I'd drop by and compare notes."

"Good. Like to do it."

"It looks like they're going to put up a slate against us."

"So I'm told."

"Nobody's just sure how it's going to shake out. Apparently they're not quite sure themselves. But the basic decision has been made."

"Needless to say, I hate to see it," Bell said. "It can only result in a weakening of the party. And we've all got a stake in that. All the quarreling, backstabbing, and elbowing that takes place. It's bound to weaken the party."

"Well, you can't reason with these people. God knows we've tried. But they are determined to have their own narrow way, and nothing else."

"That's always been one of my objections to the group," Bell said. "It seems to me a political party is a large umbrella under which you try to herd more than fifty per cent of the people. You broaden your principles to take in as many people as possible. Yet they are always purging people who don't precisely agree with them. As liberals, they pretend to extreme tolerance, but they're tolerant only as long as everybody espouses militantly liberal causes as they think they should be espoused. If you don't, they turn totalitarian and boot you out. Which is, I think, the principal reason they will never gain control of the party. Maybe we are too flexible in trying to please a majority. But they never try. Thus, they're doomed ever to be a minority."

John Burnett was surprised to realize how closely Bell's views coincided with his own.

"You're right, of course," he said. "Let's hope they're ever doomed. One thing you can say for them is they don't think they're doomed. They certainly are persistent. They never give up."

"They'll always be a force to be reckoned with, but never a majority force. I still say that."

"Would you say they had a chance to become a majority force if Ross went over to their ticket?"

Bell bit his lower lip and shook his head. "I've heard that Ross is thinking that over. I think he would be grossly ungrateful, not to say stupid, to do such a thing."

"He would run against me, of course."

"And lose."

"Let's hope so. Needless to say, Les, the prospect of a knockdown primary is repugnant to me. Physically, I'm not anxious to take the punishment. And I think it would hurt us in November against the Republicans. I don't know what your thoughts are, but it looks to me as if the Republicans are going to run pretty strong come fall. And Carpenter is shaping up as a formidable candidate."

"You think it'll be Carpenter?" Bell asked.

"It's almost got to be," the Senator said. "The Old Guard will scream and carry on of course. Carpenter's much too liberal for them. But he's young, vigorous, and attractive. And he's shown signs of being a vote getter. He wants it, and I think they'll have to go with him. Besides, the Old Guard has nothing to offer but a sure loser."

"I think you're probably right," Bell said.

"So, with that facing me, I'd just as soon not get involved in any bloody intramural civil wars."

"John, let me go on record, here and now. You will have my complete and unequivocal support, both privately and publicly. I'll do anything and everything I can to secure your victory in this primary."

"Well . . ." said Senator Burnett. "I'm gratified. I really am, Les. And somewhat surprised. Naturally, I hoped that you would back me, but I didn't come here to ask you outright to do it. I know the problems involved. . . ."

"I know you didn't. You came to sound me out. See which way the wind is blowing. But I'm willing to commit myself right now. No need of holding back."

"Les, as a politician you know what a pledge like this means when you're going to be involved in a dogfight."

"I do, and I'm happy to give it."

"I don't want to push my luck too far, but would you be willing to indicate your support publicly . . . soon?"

"Whenever you think it would help the most."

"My own announcement, followed by strong support from you, might be enough to scare Ross off. You know . . . I suppose you're aware, Les, that if we scared him off the Senate race this time, he'd probably run for governor again, and take a shot at your seat next time. . . ."

"I am aware of that. I would hope, in such a situation, you would see your way clear to give me your backing."

"Without question." A smile flickered across his face. "You must be pretty sure I'm going to win."

"I am. I'm confident you'll win by a good margin. That, of course, as you imply, plays an important part in my thinking. But that is not all of it. I think it's a matter of choosing between an experienced, farsighted man, with a record for getting important things done, as against a lightweight—a pleasant, ambitious lightweight, who seems to spend most of his time examining his profile in the mirror for any new wrinkles. It's apparent that I have never liked Ross. That's neither here nor there in politics, of course. I've backed plenty of people whose guts I hated. But it is a pleasure to be able to back somebody you respect, and oppose somebody you don't like, and satisfy your own conscience, all at the same time. That's something of a rarity."

Senator Burnett rose and ambled toward the door. Les Bell left his desk to join him.

"John, we haven't been as close in the last couple of years. I think you're aware of that. It's been my doing, primarily. I felt that I was falling under your shadow. You're quite influential and persuasive, you know. I just felt that I needed to establish a political personality of my own, rather than turn out to be a carbon copy of you. With some experience under my belt, I think that I've been able to do that. And I intend to work with you more closely, if you're willing."

"I'd like to, Les. I'd like to very much."

"On one condition. Senator to senator. Not senior senator to junior senator."

"Senator to senator it will be. And if I get too grandfatherly, you have my permission to kick my ass."

"Right. Any time on this public statement. I'll wait to hear from you."

"Thanks again, Les. I think you know how much real gratitude is packed into that short word 'thanks.' "

Senator John Burnett walked down the corridor with considerably inflated spirits. There were some honest people left in the world. He would stake everything that Bell was playing square with him. It was a good feeling. It restored him somewhat, after a cynical day.

He dropped into his own office. Two of the girls, about to leave, were gathering up their purses. "Good night, ladies. I'll see you in the morning." They wished him a musical good night. He went into the inner office and sank down in a chair in front of Dick Goetz's desk.

"Well, Dick, things are slightly improved since I left you. Bell will back us to the hilt."

"Fine, fine," said Dick, his chair screeching as he leaned back.

"Bell's a good man. He's developed much more, frankly, than I ever thought he would. He's turned into an effective senator, and, I'll admit, right under my nose without my realizing it." The Senator got up, stuffed his hands in his pockets, walked to the window and looked out. "It's nice to have friends, Dick, especially powerful friends. Actually, Bell's support will be more crucial than I realized. A while ago, when I thought I might have to fight it out alone, I downgraded him a bit. But his name will help. And I'm sure he'll be willing for his staff to pitch in. He's got some strong supporters back home, who are only lukewarm toward me. And access to certain people that I don't have. Yes, the clouds are lifting slightly, Richard. Well," he said, bringing himself up short, "don't want to hold you up. It's quitting time. There'll be plenty of long hours ahead, so you had better clear out on time while you have the opportunity. Give my regards to Edith, and tell her I expect to call on her organizational genius with the ladies' clubs, come summer."

"She's ready, even eager," said Dick, rising. "Claims it brings her into contact with the real world, instead of the grubby world of houses and children."

"That's the real world, doesn't she know that?"

"It's too real, I guess."

"Good night, Dick."

"Good night."

The door clicked shut. The Senator looked at the Capitol dome, glowing pink in the western sun. It really is the greatest gentlemen's club in the world, he thought. Nothing like it.

He went into his bathroom, washed his hands and face, and rubbed himself briskly with a towel. Thus refreshed, he thought, the senator begins a new day. He went down the stairs and through the revolving door. Herb Shannon's black Cadillac was punctually parked outside.

He had known Herb Shannon for twenty years, and in that time he could not recall an interesting observation the man had ever made. Shannon was pleasant, bland, and empty. He rode the vicissitudes of life, those few which affected him, like a cork on the ocean, carried gently by the rollers, never inundated, unaware of the desperate struggles going on in the depths below him. Probably if a Communist revolution took place, Herbert Shannon would emerge somehow untouched, as a commissar in charge of his own factories, and continue to live his shallow, peaceful life, unaware of the dead in the streets.

Perhaps the Shannon line was petering out, unraveling into the nothingness of Herbert. Herbert's grandfather had been a buccaneering monopolist, who fought his way to the top, grinding down competitors and friends by any means necessary. Fighting politicians, driving his workers, suspicious to the last day of his life, which ended in his eighty-seventh year. Could this soft, unseeing man, his grandson, be of the same blood? Or was he to preside over the slow disintegration of the arduously assembled properties, the factories, the newspaper, the television and radio station? Certainly, nothing would indicate that it was about to happen. Each one of the properties, year after year, as they had for the past half century, produced a good profit, which was dutifully spread among the growing number of descendants of the old man.

Perhaps the key, the Senator thought, is the fact that the family has never produced a black sheep: a wild, dissolute spender with a sense of guilt, a drunkard, a bohemian artist, or a compulsive woman chaser. Herbert himself had never caused his family a qualm. He attended Harvard College, rarely missed a class, graduated with a solid, if undistinguished, record. When he married, he joined his fortune to the considerable fortune of a newspaper and radio station owner.

Herbert's son had followed the same undeviating path, graduating from the same college with a similar record, and marrying, at the proper time, the daughter of a farmer who had inherited enough rich bottom land to be called a landowner. Luisa had just turned eighteen when Herbert III married her.

Herbert's daughter, Pamela, was a dabbler in the arts, and directed the family's cultural activities. She had married Houghton McMillan, son of a famous family, now an assistant professor at the University of Missouri.

McMillan had been a diplomat of the type who made friendships, on foreign assignments, exclusively with the thin upper skin of royalists, old families, and rich merchants. An untimely event had brought an end to his career with the State Department. A rather bloody revolution had taken place in the small Central American country to which he had been assigned. He had never, in his four years in the country, mentioned to Washington that such a thing might occur. When it did, and the Embassy was suddenly swarming with people of all sorts seeking asylum, rugs were rolled up and people slept, as in a military evacuation hospital, in rows on the marble floors in the library, the reception room, and the dining room. But not on the second floor, to which the Ambassador retreated, with selected members of his staff. His State Department career did not end with this episode, but it was shadowed with the hardest to bear of all criticism, ridicule.

This was the closest, so far as the Senator knew, that any member of the Shannon family or its related entourage ever glimpsed life as it was led by most of the earth's inhabitants. Houghton had been recalled, and shortly thereafter resigned, taking the post of assistant professor of fine arts at the university. At forty-one, still a bachelor, he had married one of his postgraduate students, Pamela Shannon, some fifteen years his junior.

The Senator was not surprised that all of the Shannons were scheduled for dinner. They always traveled like this. They vacationed in Europe together. Two or three times a week, they all gathered for cocktails and dinner at the patriarchal mansion, purchased around 1920, and called simply, "Trees."

Their talk was always well modulated and about nothing. For years they had been saying the same things over and over to one another.

"Good evening, John," said Herbert pleasantly, as the Senator slipped into the air-conditioned Cadillac. "Delighted to see you again."

"My pleasure, Herbert, I assure you. I always look forward to dining with the irrepressible Shannons." Herbert acknowledged this truth with a genial smile.

"Things must be quite busy for you at this stage in the session. We are all delighted that you could find the time to join us."

The Senator was about to repeat his previous statement, but instead said, "When things are important, you just move other things about and make the time."

"That's most kind of you, John. Is Ellen in good health?"

"She's fine. As I mentioned to you earlier, she won't be joining us this evening. She was quite upset when I told her you were going to be in town, but she had accepted an invitation of long standing to address the Women's Democratic Club of Montgomery County—that's an adjacent Maryland county."

"Sorry that she can't be with us. But I'm sure she'll do well. A remarkable woman."

"That's true," said the Senator. The Senator inquired into the health of the Shannon family, meticulously descending the ladder by age until he had reached the newest grandchild. Herbert was obviously impressed with the performance.

"It's a pleasure, John, I might say reassuring, to know that we have an able man such as yourself representing us in the Senate."

"Well, thank you, Herbert. That's most kind of you. As you know, I value highly the judgment and support of people like yourself."

"You can always count on it."

"Good," said the Senator. Let's hope so, he thought.

"There they are now," said Herbert, indicating a small crowd of people on the sidewalk in front of the Mayflower. They were soon joined in the car by a somewhat jumbled group of Shannons: Herbert's wife, Anne, and Herbert's daughter and her husband, the McMillans. Houghton McMillan handed a piece of the Shannon money to the doorman and pulled down a jump seat for himself.

In deference to Houghton's highly developed epicurean tastes and long experience abroad, he was asked to select a restaurant. After a deprecatory prologue about the paucity of eating places in the United States, and Washington in particular, he grudgingly selected France's, in Georgetown. Herbert III and Luisa were given directions, and set off in their own car. Herbert guided his enormous craft over the cobblestones, and cocked it against the curb on the steep hill. Herbert III and Luisa were waiting for them on the sidewalk.

They entered the courtyard and went up the stairs to the little balcony porch and into the old mansion. "Charming," said Herbert, who had apparently never been there. The high ceiling of the old room flickered in the candlelight. Several people sat on the antique chairs, having cocktails.

They had a large and expensive dinner, preceded by cocktails, accompanied by two kinds of wine, fussily chosen by Houghton, and followed by rich desserts and brandy. The Senator wondered, uncomfortably, if all Shannon evening meals were like this. Apparently as an aid to digestion, conversation during the meal had been determinedly lighthearted. After dinner, Herbert all but rapped for order and turned the talk to "serious matters." First, the foreign situation was examined, and each issued a shallow and uninformed opinion of what needed to be done, all more or less in agreement. Houghton McMillan did not offer an opinion, referring obliquely to his former position, which he alluded would not permit him to discuss, much less criticize, American foreign policy. Next, domestic politics were taken up and disposed of in the same easy fashion, with the Senator listening and indicating by his expression that he was being exposed to new ideas and fresh thinking which would bear further reflection. State politics were next on the list. A gentle argument moved back and forth as to whether Ross MacKenzie should be nominated for a second term as Governor when his term expired, or whether "new blood" was required. The Senator was glad to hear that there was no mention of the possibility that Ross might run for the U.S. Senate. Apparently, there had been no public discussion, although it was possible that the Shannons might never have heard of it, if there had been. Houghton suggested that a certain professor of world politics at the university, although without practical experience, was "sound" and would make an excellent candidate. The Senator suggested again, as he had many times before, that Herbert run for public office. Herbert declined, with a pleased smile, as he always did.

Carefully, the Senator guided the conversation to his own future. The Shannons had assumed without question, of course, that he would be nominated and re-elected. The thought that he might be opposed in the Democratic primary had never occurred to them, and for the moment he intended to leave it that way. He wanted to make sure that the usual Shannon contribution to his campaign would be forthcoming—a contribution he valued above all others. First, it was large. Second, none of the Shannons appeared to have any political ambitions or to be seeking appointive office of any sort. Third, it gave him the support of a highly respected group in the Missouri community, whom scandal had never touched, and the support of the newspaper they controlled. Fourth, the Shannons gave him the money and relied on his judgment. They never questioned a vote he cast. "John Burnett has never failed to act in the interest of the people of this state and the people of this country. He is unable to act in any other manner," Herbert once said to a critic. The Shannons seemed to have a vague, almost collegiate, desire to be associated with liberals and intellectuals, and they were proud of him, although none of them followed his record in any detail.

"I firmly hope," Herbert said, "that you intend to continue to represent us in the Senate. I might say that we all feel that way."

"We certainly do," said Anne.

"Herbert, I'm not sure you know how much I value your support and the support of the Shannon family. Capitol Hill is slippery; friends come and go, and often turn out to be unfriendly in the end, and enemies remain forever implacable enemies. It's reassuring to know people like you at this table. We've been friends for twenty years, and I don't think that we've ever had a serious disagreement. I value your friendship greatly, and I hope it will continue as long as we both live. As for myself, I certainly don't see any point in concealing matters with my oldest and closest friends, though this is, of course, not for publication. If there is an indication that I can still be useful, I do intend to make the race."

A little wave of polite applause swept the group. "Excellent, excellent," said Herbert. "I was certain that you would do it. We're proud of you, John, and I think that I speak for all of us when I say that. And I might add that we will, as usual, back up our convictions with action."

"That's gratifying, Herbert. I know that the family has always considered it part of its duty to participate actively, and I, for one, appreciate it."

"It's the only thing to do," said Herbert. "Otherwise the Government would fall into the hands of rogues." The political discussion ended with a toast to the nomination and election of John Burnett.

For the next two hours, the conversation drifted from American writing, which Houghton pronounced to be at a tedious garbage-can level—he called for the rise of a modern Henry James—to modern art, which he found equally depraved, to modern music, which he felt was strident and discordant.

The Senator asked questions, nodded wisely, and contributed a homogenized opinion now and then. He might have been a member of the family.

Finally, at midnight, they left France's, and the Shannons dropped him at the door of his house, which was not far away. Tedious but very worth while, he thought as he climbed the brick steps. A ripple of pleasure swept over him as he swung the door open and saw his wife, Ellen, glancing in her birdlike way through the evening paper.

"Well, my dear. Delighted you're still up. How did the speech go?"

"Not a speech. Just a talk. A speech is read, and a talk is just given. You look tired. It went quite well. I'm really surprised, sometimes, that I am able to do this sort of thing at all. Remember when I slaved over a speech, couldn't eat, memorized it, and then read the whole thing anyway? Now I toss them off like after-dinner drinks."

"There's nothing the typical human being likes better," the Senator said, sitting down in his wing chair, "than to stand up before a group of human beings and talk. His only worry is that he won't do it well. Once he becomes convinced he can do it well, you can't keep him down. That is a general observation about the entire human race and not directed at you in particular."

"Well, I'm not at that advanced stage yet. Would you like a drink?"

"God, no . . . thank you. I've been plied with bourbon, wine, and liqueurs for the last six hours."

"Coffee?"

"Better not."

"How are the scintillating Shannons?"

"They're all fine, as usual. Some wise man once said that a politician must bear the company of fools gladly. But I'm only awake eighteen or so hours a day. Six hours is a lot of time to spend with them."

"They were as dull as usual?"

"Easily. I really have no basis for understanding those people. I don't know how they keep their minds alive on the pittance of new material which is permitted to filter in. They're good hearted enough, and these days I suppose we shouldn't ask for more. But most of their opinions, if you can call them that, have no basis in fact, and they're the same ones I've heard for years. I shouldn't really talk this way about Herbert, because I really like him. He's naïve, simple, and good, which is more than I am. No telling what he would be like, in the unlikely event he ever had to face a real crisis, where people were tearing at one another. He'd probably turn out to be as beastly as the rest of us. Anyway," he said, easing off his shoes and squeezing the balls of his feet reflectively, "it was worth while, I think."

"Did you have something definite in mind?"

"I did. I'm thinking of asking Herbert to be my finance chairman."

"Oh, John, you know he won't. He'll never do anything but give money."

"Don't underrate that. But I may need him. I may have to force him to."

"Why should you force him to? Are you worried?"

"No, not yet. But Virgil was in for lunch today, and it looks fairly definite that there will be a primary fight.

"Why that's silly. Who have they got who could possibly run against you and have a chance?"

"Oh, Don Wood, perhaps. He ran a good race on their ticket last time. Ross only beat him by fifty thousand votes."

"But he has no experience, and he did lose, and further— maybe this is woman's intuition—but some of the gloss has gone from Don Wood. I don't think he'd run as well this time."

"I think you're right. The candidate might also be Ross."

"Ross!"

He knew that this would upset her. She was unable to maintain his detachment from the emotions involved in shifting political alliances. During the course of a campaign, she became fiercely loyal to his friends—and fiercely hated his enemies. "Ross . . ." she repeated, as if to get used to the name as an epithet. "I just can't believe that."

"I've always thought it might be possible. In politics, every friend, particularly those you bring along as protégés, may turn out to be Frankenstein's monster. You take a calculated risk every time."

"Ross won't do it," Ellen said.

"I suspect he might," the Senator said. "Our militant, liberal friends are apparently determined to have another go at it. They don't have the over-all strength to take us if Ross, Bell, and I stick together. Thus, they're trying to break us apart. They've had feelers out to all of us."

"But why should Ross go over to them?"

"Ambition," the Senator said. "He's had his eye on the Senate ever since he got into politics."

"John, I give up. I can't get involved in this race. My feelings are too mixed up. . . ."

"Lester Bell told me this afternoon that he would back me to the hilt."

"I've thought he was growing," his wife said thoughtfully.

"But you may have to face the fact that our politically adopted son may run against me."

"It would be a stab in the back. You brought Ross along. He owes everything to you. He worked in your law office. You got him made magistrate. You made them take him as attorney general when they were adamant against it . . . well, I don't need to tell you—it would just be inconceivable, that's all."

"Well, my dear, you can be sure that Ross is having similar thoughts, and probably much more agonizing. Let's go to bed. We'll know soon enough whether conscience or ambition wins out."

3

Ed Flowers gazed at the Capitol dome, which rose out of the trees several hundred yards beyond his picture window. He rolled his cigarillo, which had cost fifty cents, between his finger tips, and languorously exhaled the smoke with satisfaction. They had criticized him for this building, especially when it became apparent that it was going to cost four million dollars—one million more than had been originally estimated. But it was worth it. It could certainly hold its own with any corporate building in Washington, and it looked excellent reproduced by line drawing on all union stationery. Unpolished white marble on the outside, terrazzo and ceramic tile inside, crisp with modern furniture, it contained the best of everything.

Ed's own office was traditional, despite the fact that the building was stark modern. The interior decorator had been right about that. The Oriental rug, the solid mahogany and green leather furniture, and the mahogany paneling had produced a sense of hushed dignity. It spoke to anyone who entered that it was occupied by a man of importance, the president of a union of consequence.

"You're nuts, Ed," they told him, "they'll never put up with it."

If union officers are going to get over their inferiority complexes, he told the doubting vice-presidents, they have got to live on a scale similar to corporate executives. They've got to have decent offices, big cars, and nice houses. They've got to pick up the check once in a while. Otherwise, the executives have a leg up on you, and you never escape the category of a poor relation or, worse, the aura of boss-employee.

The union vice-presidents were certain that such high living would cause resentment among the rank and file. Ed said that it would not, and it had not. The members, in fact, were quite proud that their man earned forty thousand a year and had an expense account, like the company executives. As Ed said, it made them feel, in small part, that they too were as good as anybody. "I drive a Cadillac and smoke fifty-cent cigars," he told the members at a convention. "You pay for both of them. If you ever feel that you're not getting your money's worth, get a new boy." They cheered him for that remark.

Shortly thereafter, Ed joined the Metropolitan Club and the Congressional Country Club; and he began having his suits tailor made for $175. There was not a ripple from the membership.

Flowers' election as President of the American Electronic Workers six years before had been something of a surprise. The former president, dictatorial and dogmatic Dan Gault, had died suddenly, as almost everyone thought he would, of a heart attack brought on by a choleric rage. No successor was available, since Gault had refused even to discuss the subject. Shortly after his death, a factional battle broke out among two strong groups. One group consisted of hot-eyed rebels with a thousand radical ideas for changing the union, changing the Government, changing the world. Energetic and tireless, they made heroes of their leaders and dismissed all others with contempt as stupid or evil.

The second group had no use for "ideological crap." They were largely satisfied with the world, and had only a few minor suggestions for improving it. Their main interest was to keep the raises coming regularly, to protect their work from the encroachments of others, both union and non-union, and to insure that the union was to be run by the older senior members, not by newcomers.

A deadlock resulted. On one side of the abyss sat a patriarchal workman with forty years in the union; on the other side, the volatile leader of the rebels.

The union shivered and almost cracked apart, until the moderates had moved back and forth, like couriers through the lines, and had, at last, brought about a truce.

The uneasy search for a compromise candidate began.

Three specifications were agreed to—the last unspoken. The new president must not be allied with either group; he must not have offended either group; he must be the type of man that both groups felt they could manipulate.

Ed Flowers was one of the few who could meet these requirements. He had been a regional vice-president for only eighteen months, not long enough to have made an appreciable number of enemies, but long enough to have made quite a few friends. He had been president of a large local in Fall River, Massachusetts, which he ran like a social club, with emphasis on parties, softball teams, square dances, card playing, and beery good-fellowship. He was immensely popular with his members. Ideology and politics never interested him and they played little part in the operation of his local. When he ascended to a regional vice-presidency, which carried with it a seat on the executive council, he followed the same pattern as he traveled from city to city. Local presidents looked forward to his coming, because it meant late nights on the town, girls, and gaiety, in which they feared to indulge unless they had the excuse that the international vice-president was in town.

The selection of a compromise president had proceeded, not by winnowing out the candidates to find the best man, but by eliminating the men with controversial records or traits. One by one the strong men, the leaders, were crossed off the list. The eleventh name to be considered was Ed Flowers. No one had anything substantial against him, and when Ed's old local heard that he had a chance, they vociferously backed him. He was offered, unanimously if unenthusiastically, the presidency of the AEW. A little weak, perhaps, the other vice-presidents told one another, but a very pleasant guy, who was easy to deal with. Under him, it might be easier to reverse the lamentable tendency toward centralization that had occurred under Dan Gault, and to restore vice-presidents to their proper places of influence.

Life had offered Ed Flowers a number of these pleasant surprises. People liked his easy, calm personality. He was untroubled by principle or consistency, and never agonized with his conscience. He did not like controversy and avoided it whenever possible. It seemed to him that all problems could be solved if everyone would make an effort to be pleasant and reasonable. In his local and his region, he had solved problems that arose on a personal basis, accepting temporary solutions and postponing final decisions. Conditions could change, and some problems might even disappear.

The drawn-out, bitter haggling of negotiations he left to his tough subordinates, appearing only in the newspaper picture when the matter was settled, smiling and congratulating his bargaining team and that of the company for concluding a contract that was fair to both. During negotiations he rarely appeared, and then only when his negotiators felt that his jollity might advance a point.

For this, Ed was acclaimed a genius and a statesman. A national business magazine ran an article on him and the principal companies with which his union dealt: "Ed Flowers of the AEW—Responsible Unionist." The article pictured the company presidents as efficient and able, and all of them had a good word for Ed, with whom none of them had ever had a serious argument. He was pictured as an affable, soft-spoken genius-of-sorts who could have succeeded in business had he been persuaded to follow that higher calling.

Neither Ed nor the company presidents seemed to be aware that they were caught in a vast economic tide which swept them jointly from triumph to triumph. For the great majority of his AEW members were engaged in making machines to control other machines. From both private industry and Government there seemed to be an unending demand for these machines which could replace men. Every one of the companies had backlogs of orders, worked long shifts, and pirated workers from one another. To avoid strikes, they gave generous wage increases, and still retained large profits. Thus, the presidents of the companies were acclaimed as brilliant by their stockholders. Ed Flowers was a union statesman and a man who brought home the bacon to his growing number of well-paid union members. Amity reigned. Wages and profits were high and promised to go higher; the number of jobs was expanding. Ed and the presidents of the companies exchanged compliments on the ease of working together when the other side was reasonable and pleasant.

His secretary buzzed and announced that the meeting at the National Federation of Labor headquarters would begin in fifteen minutes. He belatedly stuffed a few things in his attaché case, not because he thought he would need them, but because everyone else brought a well-filled case. He took a cab over.

In the executive council room on the top floor, his fellow vice-presidents were swinging their cases to the tables with thumps, while others set them beside their chairs and began to rustle through them importantly. Ed wished that he had been able to bring along one of his staff, in case it was necessary to express an opinion, but the president of the Federation had complained that the last meeting was too large and had asked that the member unions confine themselves to a single representative. The large room quickly filled up, and, shortly, Ernie Kane, the President of the Federation, shuffled in, his thick fingers gripping a cigar. He was a strong but graceless man.

"O.K.," he said loudly into the microphone, "let's cut out the chatter and get to work. Lots of work to get done here today, and not enough time to do it. I'm going to let Frank take over and explain what we need to do about this goddam bill." He sat down, and clamped his cigar between his teeth, his duty fulfilled.

Frank Raeder rose, gave the group an insincere smile, and began to speak in his characteristic rapid manner. His tone was that of a no-nonsense schoolteacher talking to his pupils. As always he had all the facts, figures, charts, graphs, and arguments well in hand. He was, in fact, unanswerable, as some of the older vice-presidents had learned. His ability to make fools of people had earned him respect, but with the exception of his circle of intimates, he was disliked by some, hated by others. Only because of his acknowledged ability and his willingness to work hard was he grudgingly permitted to lead.

The industry from which Frank Raeder drew his union strength was depressed. The presidents of the companies were purchasing the machines made by Ed's union members to replace union men. Entire production lines in new plants were operated by one or two men, from a spotless, button-filled booth above the production floor. Membership in Raeder's union had fallen two hundred thousand in the past four years, and further drops, he glumly foresaw, were on the way. There were long lines of unemployed in cities where his union was the strongest. His strength in his own union and in the NFL was diminishing, despite his extreme and desperate efforts to preserve it. There had been four major strikes in five years, and relations between the companies and the union were in a continual state of violence and bad temper. He hated the presidents of the companies, and they hated him. To appease his restive members, Raeder had to speak harshly and advocate extreme and impossible courses of action, which chilled the blood of the Republican press. They made him their chief example of what was wrong with unions and accused him of a shocking disregard for the public interest which was close to treason. Occasionally, a barb was thrown directly from the White House in irritation. Raeder felt that life was treating him and his talents unjustly; and with savage arrogance, he made other people, and himself, pay for it.

"Gentlemen," he began, "you're all aware, or you should be by now, of the provisions of the union-busting bill passed by the cynical coalition of Republicans and Southern Democrats who control the House of Representatives. We discussed them in detail at our last meeting, and I won't go over them again. I have a mimeographed analysis of the bill here, for those of you who didn't pick them up after the last meeting. Please be sure that you have one. The bill would never have gotten this far if we'd done our job right, but we didn't, and it has. The bill is now in the Committee on Labor and Public Welfare in the Senate. We have been in close touch with our people on the committee, and they are doing what they can to weaken or eliminate many of the provisions which management has inserted in the bill to destroy unions. We do not know, for sure, at this point, whether they will be successful in watering down the bill. I do not like to be a pessimist, but it looks as if the chances of doing that are not too good. There is a feeling on the committee, even among some of our own people, that the bill should be merely transmitted to the Senate floor, to permit the Senate as a whole to amend it, if they so desire. That's a shirking of responsibility on the part of the committee, in my opinion, and I've told them so. Nevertheless, it looks as if the bill will come to the floor substantially as it was written by the House. Such a bill would be completely unacceptable to us, and we would attempt to have it amended. Failing that, of course, we would do everything in our power to defeat it.

"That means, gentlemen, that we have only a short time to blunt this vicious anti-labor attack. Here is our situation: Nineteen real friends in the Senate we can count on; thirty-three senators who claim to be liberals but who have deserted us on several important issues in the past; on the other side, there are twenty-four who are hopeless. There are twenty-one more who have voted more often against us than with us. Pratt is dead, and it is unlikely that his successor will be appointed in time to vote. Two senators, Willliken and Cortez, are in the hospital, and there is almost no chance that they will vote.

"I'm sure you have all had enough arithmetic to see what the story is. There are about fifty-five men who may go either way, who need to be told the story of what such a bill as this would do to the house of labor, and what an effect their support for such a bill might have in their constituencies.

"Now, here is the plan of action." He flicked a finger to two lackeys who began to pass among the group, distributing papers. "I'm having mimeographed sheets distributed to each of you. On them you will find the line-up in the Senate as I have just given it to you. We will visit every senator. Opposite each senator's name there are the names of one or more of you people. This is in accord with our agreement at the last meeting. Where there is more than one man assigned to a senator, you should take the responsibility for co-ordinating with the other people who are to see him and make mutually satisfactory arrangements for the visits. As you know, we've drawn up this list based on your member strength in the state. In addition, we have considered the personal acquaintances and obligations you indicated on your questionnaires last time.

"In the mimeographed section marked "B," there is a list of questions which we feel each senator should answer. In section "C," there is a digest of our position on all major points, and our reasons. Any questions? All right. Please try to complete your calls in the next two weeks and report back to Arthur Lempkin on the results as soon as possible. He will serve as co-ordinator. We are not anxious for these lists to fall in the hands of the press, so hang on to yours. So much for procedure. Any questions?

"One last thing . . . we've all got special problems, we've all got unique situations, we've all got little deals here and there. But gentlemen, I emphasize to you—this is no time to air your personal problems. When you get into that senator's office, you should represent fifteen million organized men and women. You represent the united labor movement. You're speaking for all labor when you talk to them. Don't, gentlemen, all of us beg you, don't get involved with your special problems, and muddy the issues. It can only sow disunity at a time when we are beset from all sides with powerful forces which seek to destroy us. The reactionary management forces are united as never before, because they smell the kill. They're pouring in money, influence, lobbyists by the dozens. These hearings and investigations have damaged us seriously, and the press has trumpeted our troubles to the heavens. We must not let occur what has occurred so often before—the ranks of labor to be split and internal squabbling to destroy our effectiveness."

Raeder set aside the papers on the rostrum and leaned forward earnestly.

"Gentlemen, I've walked the picket lines until my feet ached. My head has been smashed in by police billies. I've fought with clubs against scabs and imported torpedoes. I've served time in jail for things that are no longer illegal. So have many of you. And I just want to remind you—this is war. It has been for centuries and it will be for centuries more. These are our natural enemies. They do not rest. They are always there, probing for an opening, waiting for a chance. I think this bill demonstrates that. Greedy management and owners are looking for higher and higher profits, no matter what the cost in terms of jobs, in terms of people. Our people. We stand in the way of that objective. Thus, they want to chain us down, make us weak sewing circles who won't give them any trouble. This bill is only the first step. If they succeed here, they will be back again, I can assure you of that. And the next time, if this bill passes, we won't be quite as strong. We won't be able to resist quite as much. Slowly we will be split apart, weakened, destroyed.

"So, the future of the labor movement, in a sense, depends on this bill. If it passes, you're going to lose people, and you're going to find it difficult to sign new ones up. Unions are going to slip in membership, in dues, and in influence, until the day comes when they are such easy pickings they will be destroyed entirely.

"That's all I have to say, gentlemen. Go to it. Your own fate may depend on how good a job you do. Good luck."

Frank waited for the applause, and it came, politely, dutifully.

The meeting broke up with a rumble of conversation and sliding chairs. Ed glanced at the list and saw that he was to visit three senators. By himself he was to see Burnett in the "sure" column. Marchant and Bruder, in the "leaning favorable" column, he was to visit in the company of two other union heads.

"So how do you like being a messenger boy?" growled a voice in Ed's ear. It was Fritz Meuhelbach of the Shipworkers.

"Frank gets a little carried away," Ed agreed.

"I'm getting damn sick of these meetings," said Fritz, "where they sit you down and Frank tells you what to do. I got a head. I can think. I got a few friends on the Hill too."

"Frank is hard to take sometimes, but he's a bright guy."

"Too bright. Listen to me. I know what I need to get into this bill and I know what I need to get out of this bill for the benefit of my boys. And it gets lost with the 'united labor' crap. It's forgotten. Who gives a damn. Nobody but me. If I don't say it, nobody does. I'll tell you this, I'm gonna talk to the senators about my problems whether Frank and Ernie Kane like it or not." He stuffed papers into his brief case vigorously. "And I'm going to see a hell of a lot more senators than the two they got me down on this list for." He snapped his brief case shut decisively. "Frank

52

don't pay my salary. My guys do. They pay it as long as I deliver. And I'm going to."

"I see your point," Ed said.

"You're damn right," said Meuhelbach. "See you later."

Ed left the meeting and had lunch with a couple of other Federation vice-presidents in the dining room of the Hay-Adams. He dawdled over lunch as he often did when he had an unpleasant task to face in the afternoon.

His meeting that afternoon was apt to turn into an argument because of the bitter bickering between the AEW field representatives and the staff in Washington. The organizers were, for the most part, tough, tight-lipped men, bare-knuckled veterans of a hundred picket lines, who were now more tense than usual because they were working the unrewarding South. Although most of them had only a high-school education or less, they were necessarily shrewd and voluble arguers. They were often frustrated, sullen, and given to violence. There were few among them who hadn't spent nights in jail on one vague charge or another. Their jobs were not easy. They traveled constantly, living, because they represented the proletariat, in second-rate hotels, and spent their days trying to persuade more than half the men that a union was a good thing. Then they had to allay their fears and get them to stand up for their own rights; hold them together under the drumfire of intimidation and threats from management until an election was held; then hammer out a rough agreement with men who did not bother to conceal that they hated you and considered you lower than vermin. Their lives were one long fight, and their personalities eventually reflected this.

The Washington staff consisted mostly of intellectuals. The field representatives considered them, variously, eggheads, footnote readers, pencil pushers, and pansies. They were mostly college graduates who regarded the field representatives as "nuts and bolts" men or as philistines. Many had come to the union directly from college, although most of them had, for the record, served some time on a picket line. They had studied Labor Economics at Cornell, or Collective Bargaining at NYU. Among themselves and in learned periodicals, they argued such subjects as "Keynesian Employment Theories—Has Time Invalidated

Them?" They all ended up in staff work, in research and administration, contract analysis, or working on some project which they had convinced Ed would be a valuable contribution to the world's knowledge. Often these projects were so esoteric that no announcement was made of the precise work they were doing. Their major interest was the over-all, long-range goals of the labor movement and labor's proper place in the social order and how that social order should be changed to accomodate their recommendations. They followed labor legislation with great interest, and in their usual fashion, argued obscure points well into the night. They were interested in all sorts of other activities which seemed somewhat odd to the field men: plays, art galleries, philosophy, politics, in fact, almost everything.

The staff men regarded the field representatives as useful and necessary, but of limited importance in the long run. The field representatives looked on the staff men as the muddy foot soldier looks on the impeccable General's aide. Ed good-humoredly moderated disputes between the two groups, generally giving each side part of what it wanted.

Ed's own inclinations were toward the staff group, for they represented what he himself would like to have been if he had been better educated and his wit sharper and more cutting. He enjoyed sitting with them and having drinks in the council room in the late afternoon, or drinking beer with them in the second-class downtown bars which they preferred because it demonstrated their ease with the working classes. He was amused at their wildly disputatious arguments which so often ended with shouting finales.

Most of all he enjoyed the trips to New York, which he occasionally made with a group of the staff. He justified such trips on the ground that they were tense people who worked hard, never quibbled about long hours, and thus deserved, and physically needed, an occasional period of relaxation. Usually the trips were spontaneous. Five or six of them, drinking beer in a bar at midnight, would decide, with a whoop, to make the trip. Hilariously, they would climb into Ed's Cadillac, arguing and talking as they raced past the silent skeletons of the steel mills, gas plants, and the ghostly factories of New Jersey, arriving in New York at dawn as the city was just beginning to stir. They slept until after noon and then set out on the rounds of an endless number of places that his staff seemed to know about. They ate and drank in bars and restaurants in the Village, in Harlem, in the Bronx and Brooklyn. They listened to jazz, watched night-club shows, and occasionally went to the theater. No diversion was too odd. They attended a night lecture by a Socialist at NYU, a slide lecture on the universe at the Hayden Planetarium; they joined a picket line in the garment district, taking their places in the lines of drab and suspicious Italians, Jews, and Greeks. They went to parties and met writers, TV people, and actresses. They went to museums to see exhibits of modern paintings, photography, architecture. They were in a constant state of excitement, loping from one amusement to another at the first suggestion. On Sunday evening about six o'clock, they wearily began the drive back to Washington. The drive home always began with a babble of conversation which slowly became a trickle and, at last, ceased altogether. Finally they slept, carelessly piled on one another, as Ed, red-eyed, guided the land yacht along the dull turnpike at seventy miles an hour listening to the radio.

Later that night he would slide into bed beside his wife.

"Good time?" she would mumble sleepily.

"Satisfactory," he would say. "Got to do it occasionally. Part of the job."

"Uh," she would grunt, dropping off to sleep again.

It was the last trip to New York, about a month ago, which had caused the trouble. Somebody had bragged about it, blabbed to the wrong person, and there had been a perceptible wave of criticism among the field representatives. It was almost simultaneous, although they were spread far apart geographically. There had been an immediate increase in the expenses of field representatives, as if they dared anyone to object. Ed judiciously decided that he would not raise any question about it.

In one way or another, the subject was bound to come up at the meeting that afternoon. That unpleasant subject would be joined to another equally unpleasant—Airython Manufacturing. Airython Manufacturing laid on Ed's mind as a dull, unceasing rebuke. And the difficult decision now had to be made—whether to give up the attempt to organize the plant, which would be a serious psychological blow to the field representatives, or whether to continue to pour increasing amounts of money into another attempt which might well fail, as had the last. The feeling among the organizers was clear: it must be done. But the Washington staff had calculated that they had already spent fifty-six dollars a man in trying to organize the plant. Almost a year's dues per man. Let it sit, they agreed. It was not all that large or important. Why kill yourself and spend all that money when it could be spent more fruitfully elsewhere? Airython would fall into their laps eventually, anyway.

It was two-thirty when Ed returned to the office. He had an hour before the meeting. He settled down with the report titled "Airython Manufacturing," which had "confidential" stamped in the corner. He had a slightly guilty feeling for not having read it over the night before, but it had been an unpleasant task and he had postponed it.

For six years, the Airython case had hung over him like a storm cloud. In the thirties, Airython Manufacturing, under its crusty old president, Peter Hillstrom, had fought the AEW tenaciously, finally succumbing after a seven-year battle. Even after the union had won and organized the plant, the running battle continued, and there seemed to be no prospect that relations would ever improve, that the union could ever relax, until old Hillstrom left the company. Finally, in 1947, the old man died, but his successor, Peter Hillstrom, Jr., was another in his image, and the battle and sniping continued. In 1951, the company suddenly announced that the main plant, then seventy-five years old and located in Fall River, Massachusetts, the seat of Ed Flowers' home local, would be closed, and a new plant would be opened in western South Carolina. The union fought to forestall the move, through the NLRB, the courts, and political influence, then to postpone it; and when this was obviously not possible, to get workers moved, with moving expenses paid by the company, or severance pay for those left behind. It suffered complete defeat. Peter Hillstrom at last had his revenge. The company refused any concessions and finally, in a storm of shouts and threats, closed the Massachusetts plant, paying only accrued vacation pay. A thousand men were left without jobs, and with serious doubts about the value of a union—a punishment that Peter Hillstrom, Sr., would have felt was approximately equal to twenty years of extortion.

Dan Gault had sworn that if they actually carried through the threat to close the plant, he would organize the South Carolina plant if it was the last thing he ever did; but when he died, the plant was still non-union. When Ed Flowers became president of the AEW, the Airython case had become a holy cause among the staff and leaders of the union. In his maiden speech to the union convention which made him president, he had told the cheering delegates that the first order of business in his regime would be the organization of the notorious Airython plant. For six years the union had tried, but Peter Hillstrom, Jr., proved as tough an adversary as his father. It was still non-union and stood as a blot on Ed Flowers' record.

Hillstrom had been resourceful. The first union organizers to appear in Spartanburg were arrested for attempting to organize without a license. This was, of course, insupportable in the courts, but for six months the injunction stood. When the union began again, the organizers were arrested for loitering and vagrancy. A few months later one of them was beaten by assailants who were never found.

Finally, the union organizers felt that they had a majority, and the AEW petitioned the NLRB for an election. Five months were expended in getting the matter through the ponderous machinery of the Board, with company attorneys contesting every step. At last, the election date was set. For weeks before the election, the company fought its case skillfully within the law, using arguments, innuendo, subtle threats, and gossamer promises. The union lost the election and was, under the law, prohibited from participating in another election for a year. Now a second attempt was under way and had been for nearly a year, and it was slow going.

Ed took his seat at the head of the conference table, nodding to Phil Heffner, Vice-President for the Southern Region, Al Horwitz, Secretary-Treasurer, and Harold Berg, of the Research Department. Don Harrack, the field representative in charge of organizing Airython, had come up from South Carolina to report.

Ed began. "Don, why don't you lead off, and fill us in on where we stand."

"All right," said Harrack. "It's too early to tell for sure. We're picking up a little strength week by week. I don't see calling for an election now. It would be premature. We need another three months, maybe longer."

"Another three months," said Harold Berg. "It's been damn near a year already."

"That's right," said Harrack, "so . . . ?"

"Well . . . why," said Berg, opening his palms questioningly, "can't we move any faster?"

Harrack eyed him coolly as he drew on his cigarette. "Why, Mr. Berg? Well, for one reason, the company has some damn smart lawyers, who know all the ins and outs, every possible delay and excuse, every possible argument. They don't make things exactly easy. Then there has been quite a turnover in the labor force since the last election. The company has brought in quite a lot of people who don't seem to think that unions are such a good idea. Pure chance, of course. And the company has managed to fire, under one pretext or another, half the leaders we had last time. They've also managed to promote non-union guys and strike breakers, and hand our people the dog work. And people who are open supporters of the union find that it's suddenly very hard to get a bank loan on a new car or a mortgage on a house. And the bank vice-president tells them that he certainly hopes they don't get a union over there at Airython. Frankly, the guys see all of this and they wonder if unions are all they're cracked up to be. They know all about the Fall River plant and a thousand guys who were left without jobs. They also know we've tried and failed before. Then day in and day out, Hillstrom hammers away on the big-brother theme, how they're all one big happy family and part of the team which will share the fruits of their labor sometime in the future, if they'll just be patient. They also say we're a crooked union, a Communist-dominated union and that we're nigger lovers. That, if the union ever came in, they'll have Negro foremen because the union will force it. I've left out a few things, but that's approximately the problem, Mr. Berg."

58

"Where do they get that Negro stuff?" Ed said. "We've soft-pedaled that since Gault died. We haven't opened our mouth on that subject for six years."

"But the Federation has," Harrack said. "Contributes to the NAACP. They make a big thing out of that. And they have long memories down there. The company reprints speech quotes, with no dates. So what if they're eight years old. Who's to tell them but me. And when I tell them, they're still suspicious."

"Well, that's a hell of a note," Ed said. "We can't afford another licking down there, Don. I don't want to go ahead until we're sure of winning."

"In that case, we can forget an election."

"I'm not with you," Ed said in puzzlement.

"I mean this. I can't see, in the foreseeable future, that we're going to muster much more than a bare fifty per cent of that vote. At best. If we win at all, it will be a squeaker. When it's this close, you know as well as I do that there's no such thing as being sure you're going to win. Any little thing—a bad break, a rumor—just before the election, and you're dead. So I say, if you're going to wait until you're sure of winning, you'll just never have any election."

"What's the alternative then?" said Berg. "Close up the books on the whole matter and write off the thousands upon thousands of dollars that have been poured into it already?"

"All right, boys, we're all friends," Ed said.

"Did I say that, Mr. Berg?" Harrack said.

"Well, it seems to me that you implied it."

"I did no such thing. I merely said that we can't wait until we're sure, because that day will never come."

"I see your point, Don," Ed said. "We've got to push ahead as best we can."

"All right," said Don, "glad to get your backing on it. Now, there are a couple of other nasty little problems—like money, for one."

Al Horwitz whistled in exasperation. "Man, I don't see how we can afford any more than we're giving you."

"Well, I hate to break the news to you, Al, but it's going to take about twenty-five grand more."

"My God," said Al, "are you kidding?"

"I don't kid about money," Don said. "We've got to have handbills, some newspaper ads, and probably some radio time, maybe TV time, just before the election. The company will flood them with it, and we're dead without it. I've got to have beer at the meetings. They don't donate the beer in Spartanburg, you know. And a rally the night before the election. There's a hell of a lot...."

Ed chewed his fingernail thoughtfully. "It's going to be difficult to find that much money, Don," he said. "We're running in the red. This building is eating us up. We haven't found a tenant for the first floors yet, and the contract and research staffs here have been expanded."

"I know," Don said, "money is never easy to come by. But look, this whole election is a razor-thin proposition. We've spent years of blood, sweat, and tears on this bastardly outfit. Now that the time has come, let's not hold back for a few dollars. Let's give it everything. I tell you this: If we miss by a hair and I think we could have made it by spending a few extra bucks, I'll be ready to quit the damn union." He snubbed out his cigarette. "I think you know I wouldn't ask for it unless I needed it. After all, I'm not spending it on liquor and broads, I assure you. I live very modestly in a flea bag called the New South Hotel."

"No, no," said Ed, "we know that. It's just that I don't see how I can promise you money that I don't have and don't see any prospect of getting."

"For godsakes, Ed, this union takes in ... how much? Several million dollars a year. Can't something be cut? Can't you find a measly twenty-five thousand somewhere in those millions? Maybe like cutting down on travel," he said, looking Ed in the eye, "trips to New York, things like that...."

"I'm with Don," Phil Heffner said. "If he says he needs it, we'll just have to find it someplace."

"O.K.," said Ed, "we'll try to find the money someplace. I don't know where."

"Thanks for your kindness. Now, one more thing. I need another man. Things are beginning to move and I just can't get to everything myself. Bob Light is fine, but I need a guy like Burroughs, preferably a Southerner, starting right now."

"It's damn hard to break away a man now," Ed said. "I'll just have to see. A month or so before the election, perhaps earlier if we can manage it, we'll send down Burroughs or somebody."

"A month is not time enough. He wouldn't even get to know people, let alone get them to trust him in that time. A month is useless."

"We'll do our best, Don," Ed said.

"I'd hate to lose it on that account."

"You won't lose it," Ed said, "we're counting on you."

"O.K.," said Don, "I'll count on it. Burroughs by the middle of next week—and twenty-five G's."

"Whew," said Harold Berg, "at this rate we'll be out of business before Christmas."

"If we don't get people organized, Mr. Berg," Harrack said, "we'll all be out of business. Including you and the vital job of research."

The meeting broke up and Ed returned to his office with a feeling of relief. It had not been too bad. A few barbs, but no shouting arguments. Still, he was glad it was over. He felt like a little celebration.

"I'll be leaving a bit early," he said to his secretary as he went into his office. "You can go too, if you want to," he added. He put a call through to Barbara Merideth, and a second call to his wife.

"Agnes, sorry to call you so late. Several things have come up. I'm not going to make it. That doesn't cause any major problems, does it?"

"No, that's all right," said the toneless voice at the other end of the line.

"Dinner isn't half cooked, or anything like that?"

"No. Hasn't been started. Are you going to be very late again?"

"Looks like I might be. Hard to tell. Some of these guys get enchanted with the sound of their own voices. You know how it is. . . ."

When he hung up, he was tense, as he always was when he was lying, but he quickly cleared his mind of the matter.

He left the office, went to the basement garage, picked up the Cadillac, and drove out to WRC-TV, humming to himself. He parked the car at a careless angle in the circular driveway, went inside and asked the receptionist to let Barbara know that he was there. He sat down in one of the flat, hard, modern chairs to wait. He lit a cigarette and turned through a trade magazine called *Broadcasting*. It made no sense to him, and he soon laid it aside. He drew on his cigarette and smiled to himself, remembering a phrase he had read someplace: "The inimitable thrill of the chase." He was stalking Barbara Merideth with the infinite care of an experienced big-game hunter. Over fifteen years he had developed a pattern of approach, which he varied, of course, according to the personality of the girl involved. Slowly, never hurrying, he had revealed to each of them, in turn, the many facets of his character.

For the first month, with a new girl, he was merely gay and likable, good company, without a care in the world. In the next stage, he became thoughtful, somewhat philosophical, in a confidential way, leaving the impression that he could not share his deeper thoughts with many; in fact, she was one of the few people he could really talk to. At last, he revealed, several layers below, the depth of his sadness. That was the point at which he usually told them that he was married.

4

The untroubled face of the clock clicked off another minute: 11:02. Another minute older, another minute of life gone, another minute nearer death, an hour since his coffee break, another hour before lunch. Without turning his head, Sidney Bronstein made sure that his office mate had not noticed that he was watching the clock. He pulled the next fat brown file folder from his IN basket. The wad of onionskin papers slid out, falling into the wastebasket and sailing across the floor, leaving him holding the empty folder.

"So leave them in the wastebasket," said Milton Greiner. "Nobody will be the wiser."

"Good idea," said Sidney, "but it's like the Army. It might take them ten years, but somebody would eventually be the wiser. Someday I'd get a memo saying, 'We have a record of file WX 29999999 entering your office, but no record of any action on it. Please prepare a report in quadruplicate on the matter.'" He gathered the papers from the floor and began to sort them by date. "I'm making the natural assumption that ten years from now, you and I will still be sitting side by side, doing the same challenging work, in the same cream-colored office."

"It's a living," said Milton, in his irritating imitation of a Yiddish accent.

Sidney bent over the papers, trying to make himself push forward the dull and ponderous work of the Division of Wages and Hours of the United States Department of Labor. The first papers in the case, dated a year before by a Wage-Hour Inspector, had at last resulted in an overtime claim against a small employer. It was slowly grinding its way to a conclusion.

Sidney smiled wryly to himself. The "Great Crusade" was now so dull and routine, lifeless in the hands of the bureaucracy, of which he was now a part. It hadn't been that way in the beginning. He remembered that his father had told him of the Massachusetts textile mills of his own youth, where small girls darted back and forth tending the looms at ten cents an hour, for twelve hours a day, six days a week. The Fair Labor Standards Act of 1938, one of the last great Roosevelt New Deal laws, under which the Government extended a helping hand downward to the masses, was supposed to cure all that. And it had. Such things had now passed away. The law marked the achievement of an elusive millennium: the end of the sweat shop; the end of crushingly long hours at starvation wages; the end of the oppression of his people, the Jews from the old country, who worked desperately in their shabby apartments, under the light of a bare bulb, far into the night on a piece rate, only to have the rate lowered when they got their speed up. It marked the end of competition for work among laboring men—competition so fierce that it drove the wages of labor ever downward as men offered themselves for less and less. It was a law that announced the common man was at last in control, through his chosen instruments, Franklin D. Roosevelt and the Democratic party. Twenty years ago, Sidney Bronstein, aflame with the excitement of the new crusade, fearing that it would all be over before he could get the college degree his father insisted he take, joined the Wage and Hour Division as an inspector, with a clear-eyed determination to flush out evil employers—a determination to see that the common man, the man who, after all, produced all of the goods, was given his fair share.

He had been assigned to the Boston office, where he worked with vigor and dedication. He took a dry pleasure in seeing the New England employers become tight-lipped with hatred when he caught them in the complex tentacles of the law, which they refused to accept or understand. He endured abuse and contempt. He was, in their eyes, a marauder attacking basic freedoms, a precursor for communism, and most often, though usually unspoken, a Jew son of a bitch. These assaults never shook him; he knew that he was in the right, and he pursued the offenders with a holy zeal. Within eighteen months he was responsible for the collection of more back overtime than any other man in the Boston office.

Suddenly the war came, and he was swept up in it for three years in the U.S. Navy Supply Corps. He never left the United States, except for one short training cruise to Cuba. He read with retching horror of the fate of his people in Europe.

When he returned after the war, Sidney went back to his old job, but he found it impossible to work with the same driving zeal. In the frantic prosperity of the postwar years, the Wages and Hours Act fell into unimportance. There were other things, more important things, to be done. More important rights to be defended. But he was married, with a small child, so he submerged his doubts and set about to make himself an expert on the Wages and Hours law and its complex interpretations. He was advanced from the grade of inspector and brought to the main office in Washington. The thrill of participating in matters on the policy level near the seat of power was sufficient for a time, but after a while he became dissatisfied. The excitement, the battles, and the causes worth fighting for seemed to have passed him by, leaving him in an unsatisfactory little backwash of technical activity, outmoded by the passage of time.

After six months of cautious inquiry, he managed to arrange a transfer to the main Labor Department. With the new job, his old drive returned, and he began to work with single-minded concentration. It was quickly apparent, to him and to his superiors, that he was the brightest and quickest of the young men in the department. He was seen in his office on Saturdays, and as the department emptied at 5 P.M. and the lights clicked off one by one, discomfited young men noted that his light still burned. Reluctantly, some of them answered the challenge to work late. When he left the office, his brief case was sloppily jammed with reading material for that evening.

He became unpopular, and one after another the young men challenged him. Sidney responded by becoming more articulate, most positive in his arguments, more confident of his own abilities.

In arguments, whether public or private, his objective was to win, to crush the opposition with facts and dialectic. One by one, he silenced them, but he mistook the silence for conversion.

With his superiors, he was forced to adopt a more conciliatory tone, although from time to time he was helpless to conceal his contempt for their ignorance and caution.

His ability was recognized, and he moved up rapidly, for government, to become the chief aide to an under secretary.

Occasionally, he became aware of his grating personal relationships with others, when some dispute flared into the open. When this happened, he applied rules from some human relations book that he had read. But he applied them mechanically, without sensitivity, and his patronizing attitude invariably showed through.

The election of a Republican President gave his enemies their chance. For two years, they made their case. He was an ultraliberal and a parlor pink. Admittedly, he was knowledgeable and worked hard, but because of his personality problems, he was difficult to work for and impossible to work with. In the end, he created more problems than he solved.

In time, he was asked to head a field office in Witchita, Kansas. The suggestion shattered him: to leave Washington, to go to a small-town Siberia in the Middle West. He pleaded with his superiors to stay in Washington, in any job. They were pleasant, but firm—there were no other jobs available in his classification, and his present job was being telescoped with another. Finally, they suggested obliquely that if he wanted to stay in Washington, perhaps some assistance could be given in finding him a place in another division, since no openings existed at the moment in main Labor which exactly suited his talents. Indeed, a job was finally found—his old job in the Wage and Hour Division, which, in utter despair, he finally accepted.

When the telephone rang at 11:14, he had been working quietly there for four years.

"Mr. Bronstein?"

"Yes."

"Mr. Bronstein, this is Dick Goetz. I'm administrative assistant to Senator John Burnett. I was just wondering if you might be able to spare a couple of hours off this afternoon to drop by our office?"

Several minute bubbles of perspiration burst forth on Sidney's upper lip.

"Well . . . could you give me an idea of what it's about?"

"I'd really rather not, over the phone. If you're tied up today, perhaps we could make it tomorrow."

"No, I'm not tied up," said Sidney. "But if I could just have some idea of what it's all about."

There was no answer.

"I mean," he continued, "if it's something to do with legislation, or a Congressional committee, that's out of my bailiwick. I'd be stepping out of line if I took it on myself. . . ."

"Nothing like that," the voice said. "Would two-thirty be O.K.?"

"Two-thirty? Well, I guess so. But if I knew what you wanted, I could bring along any necessary papers."

"No, no papers are required."

"What did you say your name was again?"

"Dick Goetz. Richard Goetz. We're in Room 4537 in the Senate Office Building. I'll see you at two-thirty. Nice to talk to you."

"Thank you," said Sidney as the phone clicked. He remained holding the receiver until he noticed Milton Greiner's quizzical stare. He quietly replaced it on the cradle and returned to the file before him.

"The President?" Milton said.

"Nothing important."

After arranging to take several hours of annual leave and breaking his lunch date, Sidney went off to a worried, solitary lunch. He strained to think of any possible reason why Senator John Burnett's administrative assistant would want to see him. If it was an attempt to worm from him some information about the operation of the department, or some individual in it, he resolved to say nothing. Maybe they wanted him to give testimony of some sort, turn informer. He would refuse. He finally concluded that it must be something personal, something about him. Perhaps Burnett was going to crucify him before a committee. It was certainly unlikely that a liberal like John Burnett would do that. Perhaps he was going to be warned. Some other senator or committee was about to crucify him. Perhaps one of the Senator's constituents was tangled in the web of the Wage and Hour law. But why would they come to him? He was of no great importance in the division. Surely they realized that he had no power to quash an investigation. Certainly a senator would go directly to the Secretary on a matter of that sort, or at least to the Administrator.

Very slowly, he chewed his egg salad sandwich and drank his glass of milk. His ulcer ached. With a sense of doom, he slid off the drugstore stool and took a bus to the Senate Office Building.

His heels were noisy on the terrazzo halls of the building. He opened the door to 4537, and was greeted by a handsome girl. He waited for a moment in the outer office, which was filled with stacks of printed bills, large cardboard boxes filled with thousands of envelopes, fat books, piled half a dozen high, or open on desks. Angular fluorescent lights guarded them like giant praying mantises.

Dick Goetz came out and shook hands. "I apologize for the mess," he said. "We're sloppy around here, but this is worse than usual." Goetz led him into an adjoining high-ceilinged office filled with antiquated overstuffed black leather furniture, the walls lined with books.

"Sorry if I sounded mysterious over the phone this morning," Dick Goetz said. "I just thought it might be helpful if we talked the matter over personally. There is really nothing mysterious about it. We have a job open here, and we'd like to talk to you, among others, about it."

"I see."

"Obviously we don't know, at this juncture, whether you would fit into our operation here; nor do we know if you'd be interested. I just thought that we might explore the matter a little bit, with the understanding on both our parts that neither of us is committed to anything."

"Yes," said Sidney in a controlled voice. "Yes, I'd like to very much."

"Fine. Well, first let me outline, in a general way, the kind of a background we're looking for. I'm sure you're aware of the Senator's interest in labor and social legislation. He's been in Congress for twenty-six years. Four terms in the Senate, and a previous term in the House. He's been involved in almost every major piece of legislation in this area enacted in the last twenty years."

"Yes, Mr. Goetz, I admire the Senator. In fact, I think he's one of the great liberals of our time."

"We all do. So you can see, first and foremost, we are interested in a man who has worked in these areas, and is well grounded in them."

He opened a file folder and picked up a Government form. "I have your Form fifty-seven here, and certain other records. I suggest that we use these as a basis for discussion. Graduated Columbia, 1938, with honors. Major: Labor Economics. Went to work as a Wage Hour inspector, Boston office. Approximately four years there. You were given a top evaluation, you may be interested to know. Three years in Navy Supply. Then an M.A. at Columbia, under the G.I. Bill. Thesis subject: The Economic Justification of the Fair Labor Standards Act of 1938. Back to the Wage Hour Division, rose to a GS-9, transferred to Washington, 1948. From 1948 to 1954, Department of Labor, Office of the Secretary. Then, '54 to the present, back in Wage Hour. In a paragraph, I assume that accurately describes the last twenty years of your life."

"It seems like such a little."

"It's correct?"

"Yes."

"Good. Let's look at the precise work that you have done. That's important to us." For thirty minutes, Sidney was closely questioned about his work. He controlled his eagerness and strove to answer the questions factually.

Then Goetz eased into a series of questions that Sidney found very difficult to answer. He stumbled about, half trying to please his questioner, half telling the truth. What do you do in your spare time? Do you read? What books have you read recently? Which of the jobs that you have held did you like best? Which least? In each case, why? What do you want out of life? If you had no money or family considerations, what career would you choose? Why? Sidney had become nervous, and before Goetz stopped, his palms were slick on the leather chair arms.

"Cigarette?" Goetz said finally. He lit one himself. "It's pretty clear, I guess, that you have a background and job history that interests us. Let me tell you a little about the precise job we have in mind here. We need a man who could handle some research. Somebody who knows sources, and can find material quickly. He's also got to be able to draft legislation and explanations. That can be learned, and we have technicians we can call upon, but he should have a facility for it. He's got to be able to analyze bills, and believe me, that takes patience. And we'd consider it a great bonus if the guy were a good enough writer to handle speeches. You've had some speech-writing experience, haven't you? For the Secretary and others?"

"Yes, I drafted about a dozen or so."

"I have here," said Goetz, drawing a sheaf of papers from the folder, "a draft of a speech you wrote for the Secretary." He tossed it across the desk. "The final speech, of course, was liberally sprinkled with gobbledegook and governmentese, but this draft is really quite good. As a matter of fact, it's what singled you out from the crowd. You have a nice touch. You turn a nice phrase, without bogging down in purple prose."

Sidney studied the speech. It was the speech of a Republican Secretary of Labor before the NFL, a good mixture of technical matters, propaganda, and humor. He remembered it well.

"Don't be surprised that I have it. The Government never throws anything away," said Goetz. "They have warehouses all over the country full of nothing but paper. It dwarfs our farm surpluses. Have you any idea how long it took you to write this?"

"Oh, I don't remember exactly. But usually it took me a couple of weeks or so. Not working full time on the speech, of course."

"Would you need a couple of weeks?"

"No, I think I could turn out something like this in two or three days."

"How about one day?"

"One day! Well, I suppose I could, if I had to. If somebody else handled the research."

"Would the pressure of getting it done in one day bother you?"

Sidney paused. He knew that it would bother him. "I've worked under pressure before and I've managed to survive."

"Well, I think you should give that matter some thought. We don't always have to turn out material like a high-speed rolling mill, but a good part of the time, things move so fast we barely have them under control. Sometimes we don't. And there may be no letup for quite a period of time. Three or four months of punishing physical and mental activity. Long hours. Saturdays, sometimes Sundays. It's not a nine-to-five job. It's like harvesting hay. You've got to get out there and cut like hell before it rains. Otherwise, there's no point in it."

"That would be all right with me," Sidney said.

"As you can see from what I've told you about the job we have here, all of us wear many hats. We are constantly in the position of trying to get organized, but as long as I've been here, we've never made it. Unfortunately, it's been a matter of doing whatever needed to be done, whenever it needed to be done. The pace is fast, and there is never enough time to do anything right. I just want to give you a fair picture. Working for a senator is not all glamour."

"I understand that," said Sidney."

"And you would be amazed at the things the governing body of this country sticks its nose into. Everything from brassières for the wards of the Republic on Guam to seventy-billion-dollar budgets, and everything in between.

"And it's sometimes frustrating. You're working for a senator. He takes the credit, and, incidentally, the blame. It doesn't matter if you know the answers or could say it better. You rely on him. We're a little like a boxer's seconds. When he's out in the ring, he's on his own. There's little you can do to help him, no matter how much of a beating he's taking, except sponge off his face between rounds."

"I'll tell you frankly," said Sidney. "For the last couple of years, my work at Wage Hour has not moved fast enough to suit me. This sounds like a tonic to me." A life preserver, he thought, thrown to a drowning man.

"That brings me to another question I must ask. I would be remiss if I didn't. Why did you leave an apparently interesting job to go back to the Wage Hour Division?"

Sidney sat, paralyzed, for a moment. Goetz was quick, penetrating. He had more information in that folder on his desk. He had been talking to many people. Sidney decided to tell the approximate truth.

"To be honest, it wasn't an entirely voluntary move. I wasn't fired, but I was made to feel unnecessary, superfluous."

"They didn't offer you a transfer, or something like that?"

"Yes, to Wichita. But it wasn't a transfer. It was exile."

"Why was that necessary?"

"It was my own fault. I've come to see that, although I didn't realize it at the time. I thought I was about the smartest guy that ever turned up in the United States government. I was aggressive and ambitious. My eye was on success, and I saw nothing more." Sidney caught a look of sympathy in Goetz's eyes, and he felt a sudden urge to tell him everything. Start with a clean slate.

"I'm Jewish, Mr. Goetz. I doubt if anyone who is not Jewish knows what that means. Part of the problem goes back hundreds of years in the history of my race. They admire learning and scholarship. The greatest ambition of every uneducated father is for his son to go to college. To become a professional. A doctor, or a lawyer. And those who succeed in the Gentile world, are noted, talked about, and admired. A Jewish kid learns early what the standards of value are, and he is forced, especially if his father came from Europe as mine did, to compete, to surpass, and to succeed. The emphasis is on mental development, not physical as it tends to be with the Irish, for example. So he tries. He's rewarded with smiles, favors, and attention if he succeeds. Contempt if he fails. Or worse yet, just dismissal as a *yehupetz*. He pays for the fact that he succeeds, that he studies his lessons.

72

Every Jewish kid I know has endured the slurs, sneers, and repeated challenges to fight for some trumped-up reason. Some Jews curl up. They isolate themselves in tight little societies of their own. They live together, eat and socialize together. They own and operate businesses together, and they mix very little with the Gentile world. Some choose the other way. They strive to excel in the unfriendly Gentile world. They grow a shell over themselves to shield themselves from the barbs, and blindly drive ahead. They don't like the world as they know it, and they are determined, by their industry, to change the world. I was one of those in the latter category. I shut my eyes and started to climb. I didn't pay any attention to anybody else. And if I stepped on a few people, so what? That was the way the world was. Besides, they hadn't been very solicitous of my feelings either. They didn't deserve consideration. The hell with them." Sidney realized that he had been walking around the room, gesticulating wildly.

"You did pretty well for a while," said Goetz, "then you found too many enemies to conquer."

Sidney's words began flowing rapidly, as if a cork had been pulled from the bottom of a full barrel. "Yes, I did. But I also learned some things. That's not the end of the story. When they tried to exile me, and then dumped me back in Wage Hour, I went to pieces. I was never irrational, or anything like that. But I didn't care about anything—myself, my wife, my family, my job, or anything at all. I was so depressed I seemed to be slipping into melancholia, with a touch of paranoia. Finally, when I thought that I was really losing my mind, I went to a psychiatrist. I went to him three times a week for eighteen months. When he got through, he had not put me back together the way I was, which is just as well, but I'm put back together, and for that I'm thankful. I've learned to accept things—the world and my place in it—a little better. Oh, I still have occasional periods of acute depression, like everybody else, but I come out of them. I've even come to accept the dull job I now have—" He stopped talking suddenly, conscious of the damning confession. "Well, I just wanted to tell you that if you hired me, you wouldn't be getting one of those smooth-as-cream, well-adjusted people. Because

I'm not." He finished weakly. "I suppose that closes the interview."

Dick Goetz stared at his pencil intently as he rolled it between his fingers. "No, I wouldn't say that. I knew that you had been under psychiatric care. No details, of course." He paused. "Sidney, we can put up with a certain amount of temperament if the work is good. But it can never come to a point where it threatens the work of this office or the career of the Senator. Tell me this: After what you have told me, do you honestly believe that you would work out in the job?"

"Mr. Goetz, I give you my word of honor, I would try to make it work out."

"O.K.," said Goetz, nodding his head. "One other question, and I know of no other way of asking it, other than straight out. I'm ashamed to ask it, but we have no other choice. One of the unwritten charges made at the Labor Department was that you were a liberal—very liberal. No involvements with any subversive groups, I assume."

"No."

"Good. And one last thing. You haven't asked any questions about money. You're now a GS-12. We'd kick the salary up a bit to put you on a level with people doing comparable work here."

"I'd come for less money."

"Don't sell yourself cheap. Why don't you wait a few minutes? I'd like to talk to the Senator if I can get a few words with him, and have him talk to you, if he has time."

Goetz disappeared through the massive doorway, and Sidney found himself wandering about the room, looking uncomprehendingly at the inscriptions on the pictures and plaques. His soaring happiness was deadened by the fear that he would not get the job. If they didn't give it to him now, after being so close. . . . He feasted on the idea of working for Senator John Burnett. Of escaping from Wage Hour. How proud Sylvia would be. And his father. What would his neighbors in Wheaton say when they heard it? They would be awed. No other word would do—awed. To think of getting up every day to come to a challenging job.

"Sidney," a voice interrupted, "would you step into the Senator's office?" He entered, and Dick Goetz introduced him to the Senator.

74

"Dick tells me that your background fits well with what we have in mind."

"From what he told me about the job, it appears to, sir."

"Have you got a taste for politics?"

"A taste? Well, sir, as I told Mr. Goetz, I'm not essentially diplomatic, if that's required. But I've always been fascinated with the subject."

"The only diplomacy absolutely necessary around here is with constituents. We can tear each other to shreds within the house and usually do, but courtesy to constituents is an inviolable rule. How do you react to working in a group? Seeing your ideas or your speech melded into a whole, or changed?"

Sidney paused. The truth had gotten him this far. "Frankly, sir, I don't like it. And probably I'd argue until everybody was ready to throttle me, but I think my years in the Government have conditioned me to accept this. After all, everything in the Government is the product of group effort."

"A man's not worth much though," the Senator said, "if he doesn't resent combining his work with others. You'd also be anonymous, in most cases. You'd do the work, and I'd get the credit. Some people need more personal recognition than this job will provide."

"The work sounds so fascinating that I think I wouldn't mind that," said Sidney.

"Sidney, we're interested in your background and the types of things you do well—Dick has gone over that ground pretty thoroughly with you—but I'm frankly interested in how we would get on together. Dick tells me that you would probably be a hard worker, thorough, reliable, and conscientious, and could probably turn a pretty good hand to many jobs. That's a valuable trait here. But he also tells me that you would probably also be argumentative, irascible when you didn't get your own way, and sometimes so moody and depressed you would be most unpleasant to have around. . . ."

Sidney felt as if a scalpel had laid him open. He rose to his feet to defend himself, but, instead, hung his head like a schoolboy. "I'd say Mr. Goetz has stated the case fairly."

"Mr. Goetz views people with a terrible clarity that I couldn't

75

tolerate," said the Senator. "I prefer my view to be slightly fuzzy and pink. Nevertheless, I've found he's usually right. Sidney, I don't think there's need to further examine your id. Dick recommended that we hire you. I'm prepared to offer you the job."

Sidney rose and looked at the Senator through watery eyes. "Senator, I'd consider it the greatest honor I could ever hope to have, to work for you."

The Senator almost made a light remark to bridge the embarrassing silence, but he saw the sincerity in Sidney's eyes and said instead, "I'm sure we'll both learn many things. You'll have to learn the art of compromise, and it won't be easy for you. A senator strives for a public image of no compromise. Yet we all must; those who don't, become useless curiosities instead of the heroes they want to be. This is going to be difficult for you. You're going to see many things that need changing, many injustices that need correcting, and you're going to want to do it all immediately. I've found that changes can rarely be brought about quickly by a dramatic stroke of a few men in the Senate. Rather, they are brought about by the abrasive activity of a few of us who push things along a little bit at a time. It always seems as if you compromise away everything and accomplish so little. Actually, if you look back over a period of thirty years, you see that you've come quite far. Well," he said, abruptly, "that's about enough lecturing. We're delighted to have you with us, Sidney. I know that it will be mutually beneficial. Dick will introduce you to the rest of the staff and familiarize you with the details of office procedure."

"I can't get over this," Sidney said, "it's all happened so fast."

"Not so rapidly as it appeared," said the Senator. "We've been doing some checking and talking to a few people. All that remained to be done today was to look you over."

Shortly thereafter, Sidney left the Senate Office Building, and stood looking at the majestic Capitol dome against the drifting sky. Incredible. Incredible luck. Sent, perhaps, as partial recompense for the dreary years of bad luck. Almost an act of God.

He spent the bus ride home, usually so hot and dreary, spinning soaring fantasies. He tried to bring himself back to earth by mumbling that there were bound to be disappointments, bad times, but he didn't really believe it. Several times he chortled to himself, drawing the attention of his seat mate and two matrons who were sitting in the seat in front of him. When they looked down their noses at him, he gave them a blinding smile. When they finally reached their stop, and got up to leave, they both stole glances at him.

"The man is insane," said one as she stepped off the rear treadle door.

"Drunk," said the other.

Deliberately, he had not telephoned Sylvia in advance. He gave her his usual kiss, but she sensed something and demanded to know what the trouble was.

"I quit today," he said airily.

"You quit!"

"Yes, I've had enough." He saw the look in her eyes and could not continue the cruel play. "Sit down," he said. They sat down on the couch, she sitting tensely forward. He told her. For an instant it seemed to her a joke, but she saw the serious delight in his face.

"I can't believe it," she said. "Why, I just can't believe it. Senator John Burnett! It's just too good to be true. There must be something wrong with it." Tears ran down her cheeks; he told her it was silly to cry, but she said she couldn't help it. They sat talking for an hour in the twilight as the dinner got cold. Then he saw a shadow cross her face.

"I know what you're thinking. The answer is no. He asked me. I said nothing." She looked at him fearfully, unconvinced.

"Sylvia, they checked everything. They had all my old records from the time I went with the Wage and Hour Division in Boston. They knew about the treatment I got when they threw me out of the Secretary's office. They knew about my trouble, and they knew I'd been to a psychiatrist. It was the most thorough check I've ever had. They hired me. That's final and conclusive proof as far as I'm concerned."

"And you didn't say anything?"

"No," he barked in reproach. "I did not. Syl, when I realized that I might get this job, that I might be liberated from that damn dull job, I just couldn't do it. I told them everything else.

If I had told them that, with all of those other things against me, I wouldn't have gotten the job. I'm convinced of that."

He was annoyed that she sat looking at him without saying anything.

"Syl, do you know how corroding it can be to a man's soul to drag himself to a job he hates every day? Have you ever seen some of those people who have been there twenty or thirty years? They're anesthetized. They're no longer conscious of the pain. For forty hours every week they're numb. After a few years, it extends outside their jobs, and they go through life half alive. And that was me. When I left for the office this morning, that was me. That was my prospect. I'm forty-one years old; that would mean nearly twenty-five years more there. Think of that. So I don't care what you say, or anybody else says. Say whatever you please. Say I'm dishonest, selfish, a liar, anything. I don't care."

"I'm not saying that, Sidney." She patted his arm. "I'm so proud I could explode." That was true, he realized, but he also knew that the nagging worry that he had shut out of his mind by sheer force of will, was lingering in hers.

78

5

Paul Finch contemplated his large new office in the Liberty Electric Company's Washington headquarters.

He shook his head and smiled to himself. It was odd how your life took sudden changes in direction. It was not like an elevator which you stepped on and rode straight to the top. You moved in a zigzag fashion. And the zigs and zags came when you least expected them. Seven years of white-collar grubbing in the offices of Liberty Electric. Suddenly, unexpectedly, it was all over and a new life began.

He remembered vividly the black mood that had settled on him that night only a few weeks before as he drove home from the office. He had engaged in contentious maneuvers with other drivers on the road and had cursed them under his breath. He had driven his usual route. Although it was somewhat longer, he preferred it because he liked to examine the fine old Federal houses of Georgetown, the mansions along Foxhall Road, and the spacious houses of Spring Valley, weighing one house against another, deciding which he would eventually like to buy—a gracious Georgian brick, a half-timbered English Tudor, a French chateau.

That night the houses depressed him. He had been brooding about his age, which was thirty-six. Not too old, perhaps, if you were making some progress, but he was not. His salary had increased, but he was no nearer to buying one of those houses now than he had been seven years ago. His expenses had gone up, and the prices of the houses had gone up. No gain. He seemed condemned to everlasting mediocrity in job, salary, house.

He had picked a fight with Jean that evening, deliberately. Raged against Liberty Electric, against his boss, Judge Russell, against his job, and finally against himself.

His wife, who had heard it all before, did not respond.

"Dammit, *will* you put down that book."

She sighed and let it sink into her lap.

"It's always the man and his glorious career, isn't it? That's all anybody is supposed to think about." The room vibrated with silence.

He remembered distinctly what he had next said to her. "I'm a failure and I might as well admit it now as ten years from now. And I'm becoming a cranky old man, just like all the other cranky old men who never got anyplace in the world. A precious human life, one to a customer, and I spent mine on nothing. Nothing but a gold watch from Liberty Electric."

And yet, at 4:08 that very morning, his life was changed, yet unknown to him. The Vice-President of Liberty Electric in charge of Washington affairs, Robert "Judge" Russell, suffered a stroke, was taken to the Washington Hospital Center, and placed in an oxygen tent.

Russell had suffered a massive coronary attack, and for several days he lay near death. The tough old man survived and finally was permitted to leave the hospital in a wheel chair some weeks later, under strict orders that he was to rest completely for several months.

Shortly after the attack, Rex Hance, Senior Vice-President of Liberty Electric, had called Paul and asked him to assume the responsibility for the company's Government relations office in Washington, during the emergency. A few weeks later, Paul was called to New York. It had been determined, Hance told him, that the Judge would be unable to continue his duties. Liberty Electric was appointing Paul Finch as manager of its Washington office, with a salary increase from $10,000 to $15,000 a year. The decision had been carefully considered. It was a great responsibility and a great opportunity. Hance intimated that there would be a vice-presidency in the job eventually.

Paul plunged into his new job with surging enthusiasm, convinced that at last, after seven years, he had climbed out of the junior executive class. He had his foot on the ladder of top management. The bottom rung, to be sure, but it was there. Above him lay the sweet rewards business bestows on the successful—an eventual salary of $50,000 a year, a practically unquestioned expense account, and the status of a big corporation vice-presidency. If he made it.

Paul was startled by the sharp sound of the unfamiliar buzzer. It was the receptionist in the outer office. "Judge Russell is on his way in," she said when he picked up the phone. "He just rolled right by me, and I didn't have a chance—"

"Didn't take you long to move into that desk, young man," said the Judge. He glowered from his wheel chair. Paul half rose from his chair in shock. He knew the Judge was recuperating satisfactorily, but with the rapidly moving events of the last few weeks, the Judge had receded from his mind. Paul had pictured him sitting in his garden, covered with a blanket, sunning himself. Yet here he was, glowering and irascible, looking fiercely displeased with the imposter who sat in his office chair.

"Scat," he said to the nurse wheeling his chair. She disappeared like a shadow when the light is turned on.

"Well, Judge, it's good to see you. You look fine."

"Horseshit," said the Judge. "I'm a cripple for life, but my brain is as good as ever, and that's pretty damn good."

Paul laughed. "I see you've got your spirit back."

"Never lost it. Ridiculous." He glanced around his office, noting a few subtle changes: a different family picture on the desk, a few accessories changed. "How old are you, boy?"

"Thirty-six," Paul said.

"Ridiculous," said the Judge. "So what are they calling you?"

"Well, sir. They made me manager of the office. I guess they waited to see whether you would be able to return or not. . . ."

"Well, I have. I can't gallivant around Capitol Hill, and I can't live it up socially, or drink. One drink a day, but that isn't drinking. But otherwise I'm as good as ever. Better probably. A trip to the brink and return is bound to wise up anybody. I'll just have to depend on the telephone, and hold down my contact work to just the most important people. Just a matter of working out a little different *modus operandi*."

Paul had a sinking feeling that there had been a misunderstanding. The Judge was to be given a consulting position for the next three years, until he was eligible for the company pension plan. But the understanding—at least he thought there was an understanding—was that this arrangement was for tax purposes, and there was no hint that the Judge would again be active.

"You'll have to handle some of the leg work. You'll do for some of the contacts with the younger men on the Hill. I'll handle Goar of Rules, the majority and minority leaders and whips, and committee chairmen."

Paul realized that his next statement was crucial. Either he acquiesced, or raised an objection, or perhaps he pretended to acquiesce and let time work things out. But the Judge might be around for another ten years.

"I had planned on operating with a little wider scope, Judge."

"Nonsense," said the Judge. "You can't. Hampton Goar has been in Congress for forty years. He came to Congress before you were born. You think he's going to listen to you?"

"Well, perhaps—"

"Well, do you?"

"Yes, I think he will, in time."

"In time. How much time? Five years? What does Liberty Electric do for Washington representation while waiting five years for you to grow up?"

"It won't be waiting. . . ."

"How about the majority leader? Do you know him, do you even know what he looks like?"

"Of course, I know what he looks like. I don't know him, but . . ."

"I've known him for fifteen years. Now don't be absurd, boy. Who's the better man to talk to him about a delicate matter?"

"Well, as of right now, you are."

"Of course I am. How about the Speaker, how about the minority leaders. You don't know a single one of them, do you?"

"I know Wilson, and I've met the others."

"You've met 'em. So have fifty thousand other people. That's their business, to meet people."

"Look, Judge. You're an ex-congressman. You're somewhere over sixty years old. You've been in Washington working for Liberty Electric for twenty-five years or so. I don't claim to have your knowledge or your wide circle of contacts—not yet. It would be impossible for me to have. You're one of the best acquainted men around Washington. But don't you think New York knew that? Don't you think they realize it will take a little time to bring a man along to the point you now are?"

"New York doesn't know its ass from a hole in the ground sometimes, and this is one of the times."

"Thanks."

"Don't get sarcastic, boy. You're too thin-skinned for this work. I make a couple of statements, which are true incidentally, and you get your back up. In this work you take all sorts of kicks in the teeth, and you smile. It's the principal requirement for the job. Glad to see you've some gumption though. I always thought you were pretty wishy-washy. I certainly wouldn't have recommended you for the job they've handed you. But they didn't ask me."

"Judge, I know this is hard. To let go of the reins after so long."

"Let go of the reins, my ass," said the Judge. "Physically I can't run around the way I used to, but my brain is sharp as ever. And I don't make many mistakes. After twenty-five years with this company, I know when you charge and when you run for cover. And I know who to talk to and how."

Paul didn't reply. He wanted to avoid an open test of strength with the old man. "We'll see how it works out," he said evenly.

"It will work out all right, boy. You'll see. I'm going to have lunch with Goar. This labor bill has gotten to the crucial stage." He wheeled his chair around and bellowed for his nurse. "You'll hear from me," he said as she rolled him out the door. Paul sank into his chair and listened for the quiet hiss of the elevator doors.

"What was that all about?" said his secretary from the doorway.

"Tell you about it sometime, Susan."

"He's far from dead, isn't he?"

"Far from it. Would you get me Rex Hance, please. And would you close the door."

He sat in the solitude of his office, drumming his fingers on the desk, waiting for the telephone call to be put through to New York. After a long time, the buzzer sounded and he picked up the phone.

"Mr. Hance is coming on."

There was a clicking. "Just a moment, Mr. Finch, for Mr. Hance."

"Hello." Rex Hance's voice boomed over the phone. "Paul?"

"Yes, Rex, how are you?"

"Can't complain. How are things going?"

"Well, Rex, they've been going just fine. We're getting things organized. I've just had a rather surprising visit—from the Judge."

"Oh. How is he feeling?"

"Full of piss and vinegar."

"Good. Well, I'm glad to hear that. I know he's slipped somewhat physically, but mentally he seems just as alert as always."

"Yes, I'd certainly say that's so. He's in a wheel chair."

"I heard that he was. A shame."

"We had an interesting little talk. He says that he intends to continue in a fairly active capacity here in Washington."

A noncommittal sound issued from the phone.

"Naturally, I'm interested in just what sort of work he will be doing."

"Of course."

"I know you mentioned that he was being retained as a consultant here, but I had the idea that he would be inactive."

"Yes. Well, Paul, we thought we would use him on a spot basis. On some of the things where his contacts cannot be duplicated. At least, not at this stage. But you proceed as we discussed here. What else is happening down there in that holocaust?" Hance asked, closing the subject. They made abstracted conversation about some of the problems then confronting Liberty

Electric in Washington. Finally, Hance said, "Glad you called, Paul. I'm only a minute away on the phone, you know, if you ever have any problems. One other thing. About the Judge. Just ride along for a while. One of the principal tasks of a Washington man, you know, is to get along with people. This is very important, very important."

"Yes, Rex, I know it is."

"Good. Call me any time, Paul, that's what I'm here for."

They hung up, and Paul tilted back in his swivel chair and stared out the window, biting his lip. Should have realized this. Too good to be true. Things are never undiluted. Always those strings that you never see but which slowly become apparent over time. Well, I'll tell you one thing. I'm not going to slip back to being a lackey and office boy to Robert M. Russell. If he wants a fight, he'll get one. I'll fight him subtly. Never lose my temper. I'll just outlast him. It won't be easy. He's as tough an old coot as they come. And smart. But I'm younger, and he's handicapped in getting around. I'll run the legs off him. By God, I'll run the legs off him.

6

The Senator returned to his office from a meeting of the Labor Committee, which had considered the prickly question of how to handle the labor bill. Dick and Sidney were working at the long table, which was strewn with papers.

"How did it go?" Dick asked.

The Senator sat down in his swivel chair, turning his back to them to face the window behind his desk. "Badly," he said.

"They're not going to soften it?" Sidney asked.

"No, I'm afraid not."

"Why not?" Sidney said. "I thought committees were supposed to come up with something palatable."

"They're not, for the simple reason that they have nine votes for transmittal to the floor as it stands, and we have six for modification."

"You mean nine of those senators have no changes whatsoever they want to make in that bill?" Sidney said.

"No. Most of them do. But the pressure has been terrific, and they don't want the blame for softening the bill to focus on them. Thus they're going to send it to the floor so that the blame can be spread around widely enough not to be too damaging to anybody."

"Cowards," Dick said.

"I've told them that, not quite in that pungent language. But the lines are set. You can't budge them."

"So it has to be done on the floor," Sidney said.

"It has to be done on the floor," the Senator said, "if it's to be done at all. And it won't be easy."

His buzzer sounded and he picked up the telephone. "Have him come in," he said, and hung up the receiver. "Flowers is here to give us a lecture on this wretched bill."

"Ed," said the Senator, standing behind his desk and extending a hand forward to Ed Flowers as he came in, "it's good to see you. I don't think I've seen you since I made a speech before the Federation at their convention two years ago."

"I think that's right, sir," said Ed Flowers.

"I've taken the liberty, if you don't mind, of asking Mr. Goetz and Mr. Bronstein to sit in on this meeting. I'll be discussing the matter with them, and I thought it might be helpful if they had a chance to get the background."

"No objections at all, Senator."

"All right," the Senator said, "the floor is yours."

"Well," said Ed, "you know why I'm here. I'm representing not only my own electronic workers, but the Federation as a whole, and I come to urge you to fight against the labor bill." He paused. "It's probably silly to make this pitch to you, of all people, Senator, but we're trying to cover the water front."

"I heard that was being done," the Senator said.

"This bill is a raw deal, Senator. They're trying to crucify the labor movement as a whole for the sins of a few. They've been laying for us and they think that this is their chance."

For a few minutes, Flowers lectured them on the magnificent achievements of unions and the iniquities of labor's enemies.

"Now about the specifics." He paused briefly to consult his mimeographed sheets. "The clauses on boycotts and picketing violate the traditional rights of labor, rights that we've enjoyed for hundreds of years. We think these clauses violate the First Amendment to the Constitution. We feel that the Supreme Court will overturn them, if the law gets passed and these boycott and picketing restrictions are brought before it. But that might take years. In the meantime, we'd have to live under them, and that would do us irreparable damage. Also, the bill is one-sided. There were plenty of employer abuses uncovered in the hearings, and this bill practically ignores them. Yet there are six pages of fine-print rules and regulations for the internal affairs of unions in the so-called bill of rights section. That whole matter was discussed thoroughly in 1947 when Taft-Hartley was passed, and it was decided, rightly, that the Government shouldn't reach its hands into the labor movement and regulate everything it did. If it's going to do that, why doesn't it reach into business and regulate all of its affairs too? Why just us?"

"I've read that argument," the Senator said, "and, Ed, if you'll forgive me, I don't think there is too much merit in it. We have regulated business. They operate under the Sherman Act and the Clayton Act. There's the Pure Food and Drugs Act. The SEC oversees the handling of stocks and bonds, and the Federal Trade Commission looks into advertising and business practices. We have the FCC, the ICC, and others. Business is regulated in lots of ways. I don't think that labor should feel that it is being singled out."

"Maybe you're right, Senator," Ed said. He launched into another argument from his mimeographed sheets. "But why take this meat-ax approach and weaken the whole labor movement— when you are trying to get at only a few? If you must pass a law, why not write one that is aimed specifically at evils found, instead of this sweeping approach, which we feel is unjustified by the evidence uncovered at the hearings? Well . . . that's about how we feel about the matter, Senator, and we sure hope that you'll not only fight against the bill—I mean, we know that you'll do that—but that you'll also try to swing a few other people with you. You know, the waverers."

"Tell me, Ed. I'm sure that all of those reasons you gave are good ones, but let's focus down from the broad generalities. Tell me about how this bill would affect you and your union."

"My union?" said Ed. "Well, in all those ways that I've just said. . . ."

"Now would it?" the Senator said. "You're a clean union from everything I've heard. Is there anything in the section pertaining to union financial reporting requirements, or in the so-called bill of rights for union members section that would really bother you?"

Ed sat, puzzled for a minute. "Well, no, I guess those sections wouldn't, too much. I mean, there's nothing in that section on rights that we don't already do. We elect a president in an open convention every four years, and we don't have trusteeships and all those things. Our pension money is handled very carefully, and independently audited. In the financial area, I suppose there might be a little more paper work."

"Yet, you can see that this is the guts of the bill as far as cleaning up the Truckers and some of the other outfits is concerned."

"Yes, sure."

"And there is no way to write it, that I know of, so that different unions meet different requirements. Now what about the boycott sections? Does your union use boycotts?"

"No, I can't think of a time we ever did," Ed said. "You see, our contracts are with big manufacturers—a lot of big defense stuff, things like that. I mean that's practically unboycottable. So is the automatic control gear that is sold to the big companies. And even the consumer stuff, well, hell, we can't follow every pocket radio around the country trying to persuade people not to buy it. We'd go broke in a month. Besides, all the big guys we deal with are unionized anyway."

"Now, the picketing restrictions do, I suppose, clip your wings a bit."

"A little, maybe," said Ed, "although we don't try to organize from the top like the Truckers. The picketing restrictions wouldn't do us any great harm."

"Well, it seems to me that there isn't a lot in the bill that would really do you and the Electronic Workers much harm. In fact, there are a few sweeteners for the unions in the bill. Like strikers voting in elections. All things considered, you might come out ahead."

"Senator, maybe you're right about us in particular. The bill probably wouldn't hurt us much one way or the other, but. . . ."

"And you're a clean union. The question is: Are you unaffected because you're a clean union?"

89

"Well, there are other unions that will have lots of problems. . . ."

"Clean unions?"

"Well, yes, some of them. Most of them."

"Tell me, Ed," the Senator said, "do you honestly believe this bill is going to weaken or destroy the AEW?"

"Well, we're a little different."

"Or any other clean union? Or the Federation?"

"It'll cause problems for some people," Ed said stubbornly.

"Honest people?"

Ed eyed the Senator in bafflement. "Senator, you're acting very funny about this bill. As if you're for it. You're not for it, are you? You couldn't be."

"I'm trying to explore it thoroughly in all of its ramifications, with those who will be affected most by it. That's supposed to be an essential part of the legislative process, although I have to admit that things are sometimes rushed through without thorough examination."

"Good," said Ed. "You just sounded so, well, anti-union."

"Certainly didn't mean to," said the Senator. "I don't think that anyone could accuse me of that."

"No offense intended, Senator," Ed said. "I understand."

"Ed, I want to thank you for coming by. This has all been most enlightening, both for me and my colleagues. I wonder," he said casually, "if you might leave us those notes you spoke from. We didn't take any, and they would be most helpful to us . . . unless you'd rather not."

Ed glanced at the mimeographed sheets, decided there was no harm in it, and handed them over with his compliments. They shook hands all around and stood talking for a few minutes before Ed departed.

"Gentlemen," the Senator said, when Ed had left, "what do you make of that?"

"I understand he makes forty thousand a year," Dick Goetz said. "Isn't that incredible?"

"He has that elusive quality of personality," the Senator said. "And he's a fine-looking fellow. Just looks as if he ought to be president of something."

"But he has no brains," Goetz said. "No depth whatsoever."

"He did look like he was reading all of that stuff word for word," Sidney said.

"He was, pretty much," said the Senator, scanning down it. "I make this out to be the work of Frank Raeder. I know that touch. Probably everybody on the Hill is hearing these same reasons for rejecting the bill. They're pretty good reasons. A lot better than they seemed when our friend Flowers presented them."

"Well, I can't figure it out. How that guy ever got to be the forty-thousand-a-year president of that big union is beyond me," Goetz said.

"Politics, my boy," the Senator said. "It doesn't always result in the survival of the fittest. Sometimes it's the survival of the most malleable."

7

The engines' whine rose in pitch, and Sidney's fingers contracted into a ball, as if there were some connection between the two. The Senator laid a large hand on top of Sidney's. "One of the hazards of modern living, Sidney."

"An airplane is something I'll never learn to live with, I don't think," Sidney said. "I once thought I'd get over this if I understood just how this monster of several hundred thousand pounds, loaded with a hundred people, ever stayed up in the air. So I read something about it, and I understand it perfectly. But it was no help at all. I'm still scared to death. It's emotional. Pure fear."

"Still, you ride in them. A triumph of the rational over the emotional. It's surprising what the mind can will, even in the most fearful situations."

"No triumph in my case. I just hope to hell I survive."

"It's odd how things affect people differently. This particular situation, airplane riding, reduces you to jelly. Some situations, which reduce other people to jelly, you'd be able to face calmly and courageously. Like dentists, for instance. Do you mind dentists?"

"Oh, not particularly."

"You see. I fear them beyond belief. I am constitutionally unable to make myself go to the dentist. I cancel appointment

92

after appointment. When I finally bring myself to go, I go with sweaty palms. Risking my life in this airplane bothers me not in the least, but risking that dentist hitting a nerve undoes me. The human mind, which is the seat of rationality, is totally irrational."

Sidney relaxed as the plane reached cruising altitude. "Now I don't mind this. I feel no sense of danger at all. I might be sitting in my living room, looking at television. It's about the same size as this window. It's the take-offs and the landings."

"Magazine?" said the stewardess with a bright smile.

"No, thanks, dear." The Senator opened his case and drew out a copy of his speech which was scheduled for that evening. He leafed through it slowly, his lips moving and his eyebrows rising in emphasis here and there. Occasionally he penciled a change. "This is a good speech, Sidney. The kind I hoped you would be able to turn out."

"Thank you."

"The flavor is right. Serious, but not pedantic. Prose is simple, not too ornate. Humor in the right spots."

"Well, Dick was very helpful. He has a humor file."

"Yes, it's a good speech. I like the simplicity. Politicians naturally drift toward the pompous if they're not careful. It's natural when you've been assistant God for twenty-five years, I suppose. But it's a poisonous habit. Before long you're overblown in everything you say. You can't even talk to your wife in simple terms. After a while you begin to think in these terms, then you're done. You're a caricature. Partly this happens, I guess, because you say the same thing over and over, thousands of times. And you seek variations in the way of saying it, or you embroider it with fancy words and phrases, which you store up until all your talk is fancy words and phrases, and no substance is left. Senators who reach that stage should be retired as partially disabled like the armed forces do."

"Well, you're far from that stage."

"Good. If I stray, nudge me back into line. Akers does. He resents the use of any word over two syllables."

"I'm looking forward to meeting him."

"Virgil is a good man. He lacks imagination, but his judgment is good, and he is a thorough. He is a second pair of eyes and ears for me, and that's invaluable when I'm not there. He is also one of the few people that I can categorically state is not interested in running for office. This makes him doubly reliable."

"He's never indicated an interest in it?"

"No. On the contrary, he has made it clear that he is not interested in office, under any circumstances."

"Why not?"

"I don't know for sure. I have some theories. Virgil is a cold person. He doesn't mind manipulating the controls from a booth somewhere, but he would abhor actually getting into the arena and rubbing sweaty-body with other human beings. He enjoys the spectacle, the unpredictability of it, the excitement, but he wants it vicariously. He was an engineer, you know. I think he sees people as little gear wheels, eccentric cams, and drive shafts. He's very interested in putting all of these little things together to make them work. Or, if they won't work, in tearing the machines down and putting them together again in some other form. In doing this, he never gets his hands dirty and he wears a snow-white shirt."

"Odd for politics, isn't it?" Sidney said. "I thought the human touch was necessary."

"Oh, he's human. One glaring defect saves him. He has a mistress."

"Really."

"Yes. Nice girl. Nothing cheap about her at all. Been having an affair with Virgil for fifteen years. She's very much like him. Rather cold and detached. All in all, it seems to me a rather dry relationship, but at least it makes Virgil a member of the human race."

"Isn't that something," Sidney said.

"No two are alike. You'll meet some strange and wonderful varieties in St. Louis. How do you like the wonderworld of politics, by the way, after, what has it been, two months?"

"It's the most fascinating thing I've ever done."

"I thought you had a taste for it."

"Working for you has been an education. And I stand in admiration of a really first-class political mind."

"Well, I see you've grasped an important principle of politics

You can flatter someone outrageously, and, though he will discount it somewhat, he'll still believe part of it, and he'll thank you for that."

"Aw now, Senator, I wasn't trying to flatter you. That's my honest reaction. I've never been in close daily contact with a . . . well, a great man."

"There you go again."

"What I mean is, the average man rarely comes in close contact with a man he considers great. The great man is somebody viewed from afar, some giant godlike being. But when he sees him in everyday life, human, sometimes irritable. . . ."

"When he pisses in the urinal next to yours, it's pretty hard to consider him godlike. That what you mean?"

"You're making this very hard."

"Sorry, I'll just listen."

"In a sense, you're right, with that earthy description. When you see him irritable, occasionally self-serving, sometimes unfair, your picture of him changes. You go through a period of disillusionment. But once that passes, you find a new and different kind of respect is building up. He's human, with all the limitations that that implies, but he's still the best we have to offer, and that's actually pretty good."

"Thank you."

"I mean it. It's a statement of fact."

"I know you do, Sidney, and I mean it when I say thank you. We, all of us, seek and covet this respect and honor that people like you are willing to pay to us. But, when we get it, it imposes a terrible burden, because people whose opinions we care about are watching every move. It's a force for bringing out the best in people, but it certainly keeps the pressure on. So often the choice is between what's honest and what's easy. I've certainly been forced, or thought myself forced, to take the easy way on a number of occasions. But I've never liked it. I've just closed my eyes to shut out the vision of all those people who really know what is happening and are saying over and over again 'shame,' without making a sound. Actually, being somewhat truculent by nature, I am muttering 'to hell with you' under my breath."

"Well, I for one don't begrudge your taking the easy course

once in a while, and I'll never stand in judgment when you do."

"Oh, you will, when it involves some matter of principle on which you feel strongly. Then you will not understand how I could do such a thing. You will feel that I am sacrificing all that is sacred."

"If I do, just remind me of this conversation."

"You may be sure I shall. And now, Sidney, I've enjoyed our conversation. I think I'll try to get a little nap, so that I can read your speech this evening with the proper spirit. Why don't you try to take one too?"

"I could no more sleep in an airplane than in a lion's den."

"All right," said the Senator. "Wake me up when we come in for a landing and I'll hold your hand."

A short time later the Senator was awakened by a change in the pitch of the propellers and a crackling of the loud-speaker system. Shortly thereafter, the stewardess announced: "We have begun our descent into St. Louis. We will be landing in approximately ten minutes. Please fasten your seat belts, and please extinguish all cigarettes."

The Senator yawned, groped about his rear for the elusive ends of his seat belt, and joined them over his waist. "Eternity ahead," he said to Sidney. "This is only the beginning. I fully expect to live long enough to be shot from one place to another on a rocket, with no pilot at all aboard."

Within a few minutes, they had touched down, bounced once, and then glided to a stop. "It leaves me the minute we touch ground," Sidney said. "No matter how many times it bounces."

"You survived. A remarkable display of courage."

"Hope you enjoyed flying with us, Senator," said the stewardess in her pleasant, unchanging voice.

"Fine. Fine. Slept like a baby."

"Wonderful, sir."

Virgil Akers was waiting for them at the bottom of the steps. "Hello there, Virgil. Good to see you. Virgil, this is Sidney Bronstein, whom I have mentioned on the phone." Virgil took a long, unabashed look.

"Glad to meet you, Sidney. You've certainly impressed the

Senator in the short time you've been with him, and I'm glad to meet you."

They climbed into Virgil's Cadillac. "State politics has its compensations, as you see, Sidney. Virgil makes four thousand a year as Clerk of Elections, and twenty thousand a year out of a hobby called insurance."

"You're high, Senator."

"Not much."

"Significantly," said Virgil, "I'm actually a poor man."

"Well, Virgil, what new enemies are about to beset us?"

"No new ones. The same old ones, plus a few dressed in sheep's clothing."

"Ross said anything further?"

Virgil eyed Sidney for a moment. "It's all right," said the Senator. "Sidney must know sooner or later all the ugly secrets of our little lives."

"Ross hasn't said anything further, but he has the air of a man who has made up his mind."

"And he's decided to run, I assume."

"I'd say so."

"I plan to have a talk with him," the Senator said. "I think that I'll have a pretty good idea of his intentions when I get through. I've known Ross a long time and I doubt if he could hide anything that important from me."

"Is Ross MacKenzie going to run against you, Senator?" asked Sidney.

"I would guess that he is, unless he can be scared off."

"What is the sense of that, may I ask, sir? Pitting two good men against one another."

"There is no sense to it. It's a matter of personal ambition, that's all. Mine as well as his. He wants to be a senator, and I don't want to retire yet."

"God, no," said Sidney, "you're at the peak of your powers."

"You see why I keep this boy around, Virgil. He bolsters my sagging confidence. He is also disingenuous and means every word he says. I plan to enjoy this quality while it lasts. What about the other characters in this drama?"

97

"Bill Milano is busily engaged in the investigation of State-chartered insurance companies."

"Good. Does he have any idea that he is on his way down a blind alley?"

"I don't think so. You know there's just enough hanky-panky in that mountain of material to keep him interested. He's sure that he'll strike a major vein of dishonesty if he just keeps digging. And when he does, he'll burst on the public mind like a Fourth of July rocket, so he thinks."

"Fine. If we can keep him at it another month or so, I think that he will be too late. The battle lines will be set, and he'll have no choice but to stick with us. Just make sure that Conner tips us off if Milano seems to be getting close to anything."

"He will. I've instructed him on that. But I can't imagine that Milano will find anything. I mean anything of consequence."

"Neither can I, but let's be damn sure we find out immediately if he does."

"We will, I'm sure. I hope you've got a good speech for tonight. They've sold a thousand tickets, and just about everybody is going to be there."

"The best. Sidney wrote it with his own hand."

"Ross will introduce you, of course."

"I thought he would. Make sure you tape his introduction, as well as my own speech. I want to be certain that we have a record of exactly what he says. It may come in handy later. You know, 'The hand that held the dagger . . .'"

"I don't think you'll have much chance to talk to him beforehand. We'll be going to the cocktail party."

"No matter. I won't get into the subject unless I have a good opening."

The black car rolled up to the canopied hotel entrance. The door was jerked open. "Been lookin' for you, Senator," said the Negro doorman.

"Hello, Dirgin. Delighted to see you. I wouldn't get out of the car if I drove up and saw that you weren't here any more. You look as trim as ever in that uniform. You haven't gone and done it, have you?"

"Oh, no, sir. Marriage is for other people."

"Still got the girls chasing you though."

"Very few, very few, Senator," said Dirgin.

"Thanks, Dirgin," said the Senator, handing him a dollar bill. "Wouldn't be home if you weren't here."

The Senator entered the lobby, and several people came forward to greet him, including the swallow-tailed manager of the hotel. "We're happy you're stopping with us again, Senator. I'll see you to your suite myself, if that meets with your approval."

"Oh, don't go to any trouble," said the Senator.

"That's all right, sir. It's no trouble. We're honored."

The Senator lingered a few moments in the lobby, talking with old friends, his arm clasping biceps, turning with delight to another, back to the first, away to a third. Finally he detached himself without haste and joined Sidney, Virgil, and the manager. An elevator had been held for him, and they rode in silence to the top. The manager briskly opened the door to the suite, gave a split-second piercing glance around the room to make sure that it had been prepared according to his instructions.

"This is fine," said the Senator. "I'm not accustomed to such elegance, but I'm certain that I'll get used to it in no time."

"Very good, sir. Is there anything else?"

The Senator dug into his pocket, fumbled for a moment, and pulled out a handkerchief. "No thank you, Mr. Richaux. You've been most kind to take care of us personally. I do appreciate it."

"You're most welcome, sir. The Chase is delighted to have you with us." He backed out of the room, as if he were leaving a king.

"What's the matter with him? Why is he so obsequious? I almost tipped him before I caught myself," the Senator said.

"You're a U.S. senator, and he's new on the job. Mostly, he's new on the job," said Virgil. "John, I'm going to run. There are a number of things I've got to do yet for this dinner. I want to make one last check. I'll see you at the cocktail party in the Continental Room at seven. Oh, one other thing. Here's a list of guests, with wives' names."

"The wives are current?"

"Current as we could make them."

"Virgil, either I'm not witty, or you lack a sense of humor. For reasons of vanity, I prefer to think the latter."

"Maybe so, but I think," said Virgil, grinning and tapping his temple. He shut the door.

"No arguing with that," the Senator said to Sidney. "Like an electric clock, never stops, never gains or loses a minute."

"This is pretty fancy," said Sidney, examining the room.

"This, my boy, is the Presidential Suite. That alone is enough to start a rumor that I'm available."

"Would you like to make the usual statement that you're not a candidate—however, if the people . . . ?"

"No," said the Senator seriously. "When I came to the Senate many years ago, I considered that possibility. I suppose every senator does. After all, it is likely that your party will choose its presidential candidate from among its governors or senators. That's only about a hundred possibilities. A large number of those are not really possibilities because of age, geography, or their records. So the field is actually rather small. But," he sighed, "my career didn't turn in that direction. Partly circumstance, partly my own doing." He turned to Sidney and changed the subject. "I'm going to take you along to the cocktail party with me tonight. You haven't been invited because they didn't know you were coming. The top people from the state will be there. Top businessmen, top labor leaders, state politicians. I don't want to make you nervous, but there will be a tremendous amount of power, influence, and money concentrated in that room. That's the reason I pressed you to turn out a really superior speech, which you have done. I'd like for you to stick close to me. I'll introduce you if I can. If I don't, please drift away. Talk, if you wish, but principally I want you to listen, carefully, to everything that is said. You have a good ear for intonations and inflections. Use it tonight. If anybody says anything that strikes you as particularly significant, find out who said it. If you didn't get the name, ask someone. All right?"

"All right. I'll do my best."

"That's plenty good enough, Sidney. Well, I think that I'll shower and shave in a vain effort to convince some of these people that I'm not really a Bolshevik."

"I'm sure none of them think that."

"You'd be surprised. In the meantime, I'd suggest you take

that nap, if being up in the air eighteen stories doesn't bother you. After all, this is just like an airplane, only it's larger and not moving."

"That makes all the difference. I can see that I'm never going to live this down."

"Yes, you will. You'll be a hero when you tell your grandchildren about how you rode in those old-fashioned, rickety propeller planes." The Senator threw a towel over his shoulders and went into the bathroom. "That list of the local aristocracy is there on the bureau," he said hollowly, "if you want to take a look at it."

Sidney picked up the list, went into one of the bedrooms and lay down on the bed. He scanned the list: Abernethy, Louis (Louis and Lorraine), President, Western Security and Trust; Artis, Peter (wife deceased), Chief Justice, St. Louis County Superior Court; Austin, Murray (Scoop and Esther), President, Austin Steel and Corrugated Iron Works; Averni, Leo (Leo and Mary), President, Local 1213, American Electronic Workers. . . ." An interesting mixture, thought Sidney. Banks and Unions. "Bain, Robert (Bob and Liz), Attorney, Chairman, Democratic Club of St. Louis; Baisch, Roberta (unmarried), *Post-Dispatch* society columnist; Bestovsky, Stanislaus (Stan and Irene), owner, Best Grocery Stores, Chairman, Democratic Fund Committee. . . ." Sidney studied them, trying to fix the pairs of names in his mind. He turned over page after page; it was hopeless. A thousand names.

"If you can learn the names of twenty-five of them tonight, you'll be doing well," the Senator said as he emerged from the bathroom, rubbing his pink form briskly with a towel.

"Do you know all of these people?"

"Yes, most of them. But I've been at it a few years. The real trick is to call the name when you turn around and see a man you haven't seen for a year. But I, like every politician, have ways of handling that situation."

"One thing puzzles me. These bankers and businessmen. This is a Democratic affair. I'm surprised that there are so many of them."

"More Democrats among bankers and businessmen than most

people think. And, of course, they play both sides of the street. Can't afford to be too far out of favor with the party that's in office. May I look at the list for a few minutes?"

He took it, sat down in a soft chair, with a towel draped across his bare middle, and for ten minutes briskly looked down a page, flipped to the next one, his lips moving constantly. "Well," he said, looking up, "that will have to do. We've got to be getting downstairs." While Sidney washed his face, combed his hair, and straightened his tie, the Senator dressed. When he emerged from the bedroom, he was in a tuxedo.

"Should I be wearing one of those?"

"No need to. The people at the head table will have them on, and some others, but plenty won't. You won't feel out of place."

"Good, because I don't own one. I hate the things."

"I used to, but I now look on it as a sort of uniform. You probably ought to get yourself one. When we get back to Washington, I'll put you on to a tailor who caters to us peons on the Hill. He has some ready-mades that are quite reasonable. Ready?"

They squished along the thick carpet, and went down in the elevator. As the doors parted, the Senator was immediately set upon by half a dozen people and swept away. Sidney politely snaked his way after him. The Senator was passed along, chatting here and there, the dual names flowing smoothly from his lips at every encounter. The room was crowded, and because of extended arms perilously holding drinks, progress was erratic. The Senator introduced Sidney from time to time. Once engaged in conversation, Sidney found it difficult to break off and follow the Senator. . . . Yes, Washington was fascinating, but so was St. Louis, from the little bit of it that he had seen. . . . The Government was quite large, perhaps too large, that's true, but there was much to be done, of course. . . . Yes, the Senator was a fine man, the best. Missouri should be proud to have sent so able a representative to Washington. . . . Yes, the labor bill was certainly the burning issue of the moment there. No question. The Senator was studying it and he could be depended upon to do the right thing. . . . Well, I do research mostly and drafting of speeches. The Senator, of course, insists on the final writing himself. . . . I'm not really qualified to speak on that subject, sir, since this is my first visit to Missouri. Yes, it is—it is a beautiful state. Excuse me. . . . Finally he caught up with the Senator.

"Sidney, I want you to meet Leo Averni, President of the American Electronic Workers local. The largest in the union, isn't it, Leo?"

"Pleased to meet you, Mr. Bronstein. Second largest. Pittsburgh's bigger. But we've got six thousand members in Missouri. With their wives, they add up to quite a lump of voters, don't they, Senator?"

"They do, and I've always counted on them."

"I want to talk to you about that, Senator. Ed Flowers called this afternoon and asked me to speak to you."

"Fine. You want to drop by the room tomorrow?"

"What time?"

"Would nine-thirty be too early? I'd make it later, but I've got to leave by eleven or so. I'm dedicating the bridge tomorrow."

"Right. Nine-thirty. We'll be there." He drifted off.

"Well, we know what that's about," muttered the Senator. "Another turn of the screw on the labor bill. . . . Well, well, Ross, how are you? Delighted to see you. Sidney, this is Ross MacKenzie, the Governor. Sidney Bronstein."

Ross flashed a smile, and gripped Sidney's hand strongly. "I had heard that John had taken a new man aboard. Your reputation as a bright young man has preceded you here."

"Thank you, sir."

"We're all delighted that you're with the Senator. You couldn't have a better teacher. I know. He taught me everything I know."

"I don't know whether I'll ever learn it all," Sidney said. They passed two more minutes in such conversation before the Senator drew Ross MacKenzie aside. Sidney shifted his eyes, and drifted unobtrusively away.

The Senator had made a quick decision. "Ross," he said, "I've decided to announce tonight. It would be very helpful to me if you would include some appropriate words in your introductory remarks. . . ."

Ross was obviously taken off guard. "Well, John, I . . . ah. . . ."

"Nothing elaborate, you know. All of us here hope that the man who has served this state so well can be prevailed upon—that sort of thing."

"I see," said Ross, slowly. "John, you know under ordinary circumstances I'd do it in a minute. It's just that I've worked up this introduction with some care. It's a little unusual, and, well, you know, to introduce new material into it at this stage. . . ."

"I understand. Let's just leave it this way. If you can gracefully do it, fine. If not, all right. . . ."

"Fine, John, good. Let's leave it that way." They parted, the Senator aware that he had the information he sought. He moved through the crowd, stopping to chat here and there, but looking for Herbert Shannon. Finally he saw him, standing austerely, talking to a man of equal social rank.

"Herbert, so glad that you could make it."

"Wouldn't miss it for the world, John." The three of them chatted for a short time until the opportunity arose.

"May I speak to you for just a moment, Herbert, before we sit down to dinner?"

"Certainly. Certainly, John. Would you excuse us for a moment, Tilden?"

They took a few steps into the corridor. "Herbert, I just wanted to mention this to you, as one of my oldest and closest friends. I thought you ought to know first. I'm planning to announce tonight."

"By George," said Herbert, "that's good news, John. I'm really delighted, old man."

"Thank you, Herbert. I've always relied on you for enthusiasm as well as advice. I wonder if I might ask this favor of you. . . ."

"Anything at all, John."

"I understand that you are the master of ceremonies for this affair."

"That's correct."

"Well, my announcement would be a little easier to make if it came in question form. Now it's possible that the Governor will make reference to it in his introductory speech. In which case, what I am about to propose will be unnecessary. If he doesn't, however, I thought that after I finish my speech and sit down, you might say something like: All of us here hope that the Senator will answer one question which he failed to answer, but one in which we are all vitally interested. Senator, may I ask you the direct question: Will you do this state the signal honor of representing her for another term in the United States Senate? Something like that. Would you be willing to do that for me?"

"Why of course, John. Be honored to. . . ."

"It would just make it somewhat more graceful if it came in the form of a question from you. The politician must create the illusion that he is being pursued, much like a young girl who wants her pick of suitors."

"In your case, John, not an illusion, a fact."

"Let's hope so." He reached forward and clasped Herbert by the hand. "Herbert, allow me to make a little speech, which will embarrass both of us. An apology. Sometimes I get a bit cynical. Or sometimes I get depressed. During those times, I think ill of people, downgrade them, sneer at them because of my own distemper. I've done it with almost everybody at one time or another. My wife, my closest friends—even you. I know that you never realized what my thoughts were, because I never uttered them. But they were there, just the same. And I would just like to apologize to you for them. Because there never has been a time that I have asked a favor from you that you haven't responded with good humor, understanding, and willingness. Well, I just want to tell you that I appreciate it, Herbert."

Herbert was obviously touched. "Why that's ridiculous, John. I consider that you're one of the most even-tempered, best-balanced men I've ever known. If you've had evil thoughts, they certainly were not apparent to me."

The lights were flashed, and people began to drift into dinner. The Senator was sought out by the chairman on arrangements, led to the head table and placed to the right of the rostrum. The Governor sat on his left; his partner on his right was the President of St. Louis University. They discussed Federal Aid to Education during most of the meal. The Senator ate lightly, as was his habit. Finally the dinner was over, and Herbert Shannon rose above its remains, and politely tinked a fork against a glass water pitcher. He made a short speech, introducing the Governor. Ross took his place at the podium, the picture of a firm and alert public executive.

"Senator Burnett, Honored Guests, Ladies and Gentlemen. In 1896, before the turn of the century, when Grover Cleveland was President of the United States, John Burnett was born in the little country town of St. Joe. I'm sure that no one then present realized that the oldest promise of our democracy would be fulfilled by that boy. He was the son of a farmer, and he grew up knowing the rich dust of the country roads before the automobile, the silence of the evening in the farmhouse before the telephone and the radio, the peace of the American land. He went to a country school, a one-room school which still stands, I am told. His father prospered on the land, through hard work, and John was able to go, as a scholarship student, to the university of this state, and thence to the law school, which was, as you all know, the first law school west of the Mississippi, having been chartered less than twenty-five years before John Burnett was born. He was an excellent student, a football player before the comfortable protective padding of the present day was developed, and a fierce debater, always seeking to take the weaker side in order to test himself and develop his powers. He was not long out of law school, trying to make his way in private practice, before he was sought to run for city councilman. At that time, the city of St. Joe was controlled by a powerful group, and a wise young man who wished to get ahead in politics didn't oppose them, he joined them. John Burnett, however, was not made of that kind of material. He chose to run on his own convictions—and he won that first election so many years ago. Who was this brash young fellow who won an office that outsiders had not carried in a generation of trying? They were soon to find out that he was no ordinary man —that he was, in fact, a man of paradoxes, of iron determination but gentle heart, a fierce champion of the right, a relentless pursuer of the guilty, but a man of compassion who defended the weak, the poor, the helpless—anyone who had no counsel. He became county attorney for Buchanan county, then deputy attorney general for the state of Missouri. In 1932, he went to Washington to represent the people of the sixth congressional district, as a part of the "Great Crusade," which was to minister to the wounds of our beloved country and rescue it from the depths of the Republican depression under the leadership of one of the greatest men this country has yet produced, Franklin Delano Roosevelt."

There was a burst of applause, and Ross took a sip of water from his glass.

"In 1934, President Roosevelt let it be known that he could use the help of this man in the upper chamber, and in that year he was elected to the United States Senate, polling 74 per cent of the total vote cast, a record which still stands in this state.

"Much of the noblest legislation of that time bears either his name or his imprint. The minimum wage law to protect the helpless, the Wagner Act, the Social Security Act, the child labor laws—all of these and many more in which he participated are the monument which John Burnett will leave behind. A record of public service unparalleled by any present senator, and equaled by few in history.

"Many of us in public life owe our success to this man who so willingly gave of his time and his wisdom to train us—so far as anyone can be trained for public life—and we stand ready to carry on the ideals, the traditions, the heritage which he so skillfully taught us by his own example, and which he, himself, in his integrity, so completely embodies.

"John," he said, turning to the Senator, "a suggestion was made a few days ago that this state should in some way honor her senior senator, a suggestion that was enthusiastically and unanimously accepted by all. It was realized that Missouri could not hope to present to you a gift which would measure in any way what you have done for her in your many years of faithful service in her behalf. Therefore, accept this as a token, a mere symbol of the affection of the citizens of this state for you. It is a pocket watch, which our agents ascertained was the type you prefer, gold, with this inscription which I will read, if I may: 'To John Burleigh Burnett, First Citizen of Missouri.'"

Applause broke from the audience as the Senator rose. It was clear why Ross had not wanted to introduce the subject of another term in his speech. The speech was intended to be a political obituary, and the watch a symbol of retirement.

"Governor, Distinguished Guests, Ladies and Gentlemen. I wish that my mother could have been here to hear that fine introduction which the Governor so graciously made." He paused with a slight smile on his lips. "Not only would she have enjoyed the ceremony of this occasion, but she would have believed every word of it."

The audience roared.

"It is not often that one who has been in the public eye as long as I have, is taken by surprise. But I confess, this touching gift has done so. I have no prepared speech to answer it, and the words come hard at this time. Let me just say this. I think the Governor was right when he spoke of this as a symbol. What really could be a more fitting symbol than a watch? A watch will last a man a lifetime if well cared for. A watch, carried through a lifetime, measures the triumphs and the defeats of the past; more importantly, it serves as a reminder of all of those things that need to be done now, before the hour hand makes another revolution; but most important of all, a good watch, well cared for, will run for years in the future, serving as a reminder of all of those things that remain to be done. Thus, I will cherish this piece, all the more because of its source, and it will remind me of some of the things that I have done in the past, some of the things that need to be done immediately, and it will remind me to keep in mind all of those important things that will need attention over the future years. It is some of those things," he said, moving smoothly into his prepared speech, "both immediate and future, which I wanted to talk to you about tonight. . . ."

He spoke for twenty-five minutes, giving a speech designed to highlight his experience in state, national, and international affairs, with passages to demonstrate his soundness, his reliability, his humility. Here and there a shot of humor punctuated the address. When he sat down, his experienced ear detected applause more than routine. Spirited, hard applause. He rose again and nodded to them, smiling. Herbert Shannon assumed the lectern, and after the applause had died out he spoke: "Senator, I am sure that I express the views of everyone in this room when I say that Missouri is privileged and fortunate to have a man of your caliber representing us in Washington. . . ."

He paused for another burst of applause.

"But John, there is one question which is of the utmost importance to all of us here, which many of us hoped that you might answer tonight, but which you did not answer. I wonder if you would undertake to answer it?"

"Well, Herbert, as an old friend, I can only trust that you're not about to ask me a question that will display my ignorance before this assembled multitude. All right."

"It is certainly an easy question as far as I am concerned," Herbert said. "In fact, in my judgment, it has only one answer. We'd like to know, all of us here in this room, if you can find it in your heart to serve the state of Missouri for another six years in the United States Senate?"

There was applause and laughter and cries of "Yes! Yes!"

The Senator rose, smiling, and slowly took his place at the lectern. "Well, Herbert, this is a night of surprises. When I agreed to answer the question, I certainly didn't think it would be that particular one." There was a ripple of laughter. "My friends, this is a very serious question, both for you and for me. I would be less than candid if I did not admit that I have thought about it. After thirty-five years in public life, one does begin to think of these things more carefully each time the possibility of another term of service draws near. One must balance personal considerations, perhaps militating against it, with other considerations. One must ask himself several questions: Is there anything else that I would like to do before I retire from life's stage? The answer is, inevitably, yes, there are many things, because no man accomplishes all that he would like to accomplish in his lifetime. The next question follows hard on the first: Is it necessary for *me* to do it? Cannot the responsibility be passed to others? This is the question to which I have given much thought over the past few months. After twenty-four years in the Senate, one moves up a bit in the ranks, one gains influence through experience, one is able to guide matters to successful conclusions and accomplish more than is ever possible in the early years of a career.

"I am now in that position. I am chairman of one of the most powerful committees in the Congress and a member of two more. I can see that in the next six years I might be able to accomplish more than I have in the previous twenty-six. Many things which need to be done for our state and our country, I can be instrumental in getting done. Many projects are already started which I will be able to guide to successful fruition. This is the challenge before me. And I'd like to give my answer here, among friends, the citizens of my own state, my people. Yes—"

A rising applause greeted the announcement.

"—if the people of this state would have me serve, I shall be proud to do so."

The entire audience rose and drew toward him, applauding. The applause lasted for several minutes as the Senator nodded, smiling benignly, and returned to his seat. Herbert took the microphone.

"Ladies and Gentlemen. I am sure you all agree that this most successfully concludes our evening's program. Thank you."

Most of the audience moved forward into a tight knot in front of the head table. Awkwardly, the Senator leaned across the water pitcher as they eagerly extended hands to be shaken. He smiled and repeated names from the bottomless barrel of thirty-five years of cultivated memory, thanking each in turn for wishing him well, thanking them for their backing in the past and in the future, thanking them, thanking them, thanking them. He passed through the clotted crowd, slowly, without haste making his way to the door. He declined several invitations to drink, and shortly he and Sidney entered the hotel room.

"Well, what do you think?" the Senator asked Sidney.

"I'm no Elmo Roper, but I'd say the applause was enthusiastic. They really seemed to warm up to you."

"That was my reaction. Got any reactions to Ross's reactions?"

"I watched him pretty carefully, but there wasn't much to see. Even when you announced, his expression didn't change, as far as I could tell."

"He was prepared for that. I asked him to do it himself. But, of course, he backed off from it."

"The only time I caught a flicker of unhappiness was when

Herbert Shannon was glorifying you. Then—and I'm not sure about this—I thought his lips tightened up a bit."

"I'm sure they did. They don't like to see anybody as powerful as Herbert in my camp. Even though Herbert doesn't know how powerful he is, they know that I know it and that I might try to use that power in a more active way, if I were pressed."

The door buzzer sounded. Sidney answered it. "Oh, hello, Mr. MacKenzie . . . Governor."

"Hello, Sidney. I just dropped by for a brief chat with the Senator, if he hasn't retired."

"No, he's right here. Come in."

"Hello, Ross," the Senator said.

"John, I didn't get a chance to talk to you. You were surrounded by such a large group of devoted constituents that I felt I shouldn't intrude."

"They're your constituents, too, Ross."

"Tonight they were yours. You had them in your back pocket."

"I hope so. Always hope so with a group like this. Lot of important people out there tonight."

The Governor's eyes flitted about uneasily, like a butterfly, lighting on the drapes, the lamps, the pictures on the walls.

"What can we do for you, Ross?" the Senator asked.

"Ah . . . I just wanted to tell you that I thought that your speech was excellent. Excellent. And I wanted to apologize for not providing that lead-in for your announcement. I guess you understand now why I was somewhat evasive when we talked before dinner. We had put this together, this little ceremony to honor you, and I was afraid we might spoil it if I tried to change it at the last minute. I hope you understand."

"I understand," said the Senator. He continued in a softer tone: "I certainly do appreciate the thought that you and all the others expressed. I was really quite surprised and pleased. I'll use that watch every day. I'll wind it at twelve noon sharp, when the Senate goes into session."

"Yes," said Ross.

"Besides, it worked out all right anyway, as things sometimes do. Herbert took me by surprise, as I guess was evident. I had decided to pass up the announcement tonight, since the graceful opportunity had not presented itself."

"It was most fortunate that Herbert was able to mention it."

"Yes, it was. Well, Herbert's been a friend of mine for so long that I guess he felt that he could take the liberty without clearing it with me."

Ross nodded. "John—I, all of us, were delighted with your announcement. Naturally. Most of us expected it and we're happy with it. There are going to be some problems. But I guess they will work themselves out."

"Oh . . . ?" said the Senator, drawing the word out to a fine point.

"I mean, there's some criticism, some dissension about. There always is. There's bound to be, when a man has been in office as long as you have."

"I see," said the Senator. "Criticism of what sort?"

"Well, John, you don't spend much time in the state. Of course, you can't, and you're not expected to, but you're not here all the time the way the rest of us are and thus you're probably not aware of some of the things that are said."

"Such as what?"

"Well, nothing really personal. Just a sort of dissatisfaction, not with you, but . . . well, perhaps they just feel the scenery needs to be changed a bit. . . ."

The Senator eyed him coldly, saying nothing.

"Well, you know the party. One civil war after another," Ross said.

"You had me worried for a minute," the Senator said. "You're just talking about the same bunch we whipped last time, aren't you?"

"Well . . . basically, yes."

The Senator gave a limp, deprecatory wave of his hand. "Nothing. Zeros. The least of my worries. Personally, I doubt if they'll get off the ground. They just don't have enough people with broad enough support to call themselves candidates. That means they can't even run a full slate. Oh, they can fill the slate with bodies, but I'm talking about real candidates with records to run on—not housewives and school teachers—and if they can't do that, they're dead, don't you agree?"

"Yes," said Ross reluctantly. "I see them as a more formidable force than you do perhaps. But I agree."

"Look at it this way: You and I stand together. Right?"

Ross gave a half nod.

"Bell is with us. I cleared that before I left Washington. You saw where Herbert Shannon stood, and most of the people in that room will stand in the same place. Our Congressional delegation is with us almost to a man. The majority of the State House of Representatives and the Senate is with us. So what do they end up with? A few dissenters from the General Assembly, perhaps a couple of congressmen, and a ragtag bunch of non-officeholders. Now I ask you as a politician, Ross, what chance have they got?"

Ross chewed his lip, and nodded.

"In fact, I would guess that one more disastrous try like the last one and they'll be finished in this state. Finished permanently as a force. And most of the people associated with them will be finished too."

"You may be right, John," Ross said. He stirred himself. "Well, old man, nice to have you among us again, even for this short time. I've got to be running along. I'll see you at the bridge at eleven o'clock."

"Bring your Horatius sword for repelling this ghost army you have visions of," the Senator said.

"Ah . . . righto. See you there." The door closed.

"Shouldn't have said that," the Senator said, "but I couldn't resist it. Well, my astute political analyst, what do you make of that colloquy?"

"He was so restless and uncomfortable," Sidney said, "it was a funny sort of a visit. He had something on his mind, but he didn't say anything important at all that I could see. I would guess that he was trying to get up his nerve to tell you that he was going to run against you."

"Precisely my feeling. But I think that in the presence of his political father he just couldn't quite get the words out. He was uncomfortable, because he really doesn't like what he is doing, would prefer not to do it, feels that it's a dirty business, which it is, but he still will probably do it. Such is the power of ambition. It's to his credit, I suppose, that he at least felt bad about it. He still has some shreds of conscience left."

"Do you think he'll run? He seemed to be quite depressed with the picture you painted of their chances."

"I think he recognized the truth of what I said. I exaggerated to scare him. And I think I succeeded. I hope I didn't overdo it. But I would guess that when visions of sugar plums dance in his head, namely my Senate seat, he won't be able to resist it. Well, I'm going to turn in. You can cat about if you like. See if you can find some doll out here in the hinterlands who will be impressed by the fact that you are from Washington."

"Not any more," Sidney said, with feeling. "I used to have theories that man was polygamous. But my wife brought that to a screeching halt, and I mean screeching."

The Senator laughed.

"We still have arguments about it from time to time," Sidney said, "but they are purely in the realm of the hypothetical."

"Every man has to decide that question for himself. Unless, of course, his wife has decided it for him. Good night, Sidney," the Senator said, going into his room and closing the door.

Promptly at nine-thirty the next morning, the door buzzer sounded. The Senator opened the door and greeted Leo Averni, of the AEW, and Steve Fields, President of the St. Louis Central Labor Council. Averni proceeded immediately to the point, without subtleties or preliminary amenities.

"Ed called me yesterday, John, and frankly what he said surprised the hell out of me."

"I see," said the Senator, "and what did he say?"

"He said that they weren't sure of you on the labor bill. Said you seemed to be wavering."

"Oh?"

"Well, I hope to tell you I was damn surprised at that. In fact, I wouldn't believe him. I told him he must be off base, but he insisted that we have a talk with you while you were here."

"Let's sit down," the Senator said, sweeping a casual hand

114

toward the chairs. "I'd like to talk to you about the bill. I'd be interested in hearing what you have to say about it."

"It's a goddam union-busting bill, that's what we think about it," said Steve Fields explosively.

"Granted it contains some objectionable features, which could be detrimental to unions . . . granting that, I'd like to know specifically the things that would hurt your unions and why, and what you might accept as substitutes for those things you can't live with."

"We won't accept nothing—nothing. That's all," Fields said.

"Is that your position, too, Leo?"

"It's the official position, isn't it?"

"Well, I'm not so sure," the Senator said. "That's what it started out to be, but I think that it's recognized at headquarters in Washington, privately, that the position is unrealistic. I think they've come around to where they would accept something."

"Who told you that?"

"Nobody told me. That's just my impression. They know that they can't make that position stick. So they're now getting the prepared positions ready to retreat to."

"Who says they can't make it stick?" Fields said.

"I think everybody says so. Congress just can't ignore the abuses that have been disclosed. They have to act. Mail is flooding in. The newspapers are editorializing on the subject. Magazines are full of articles about it. There are radio and television programs on the air all the time discussing it. The whole country is in an uproar, and the pressure is terrific. I think that the Federation was ill-advised to set an inflexible policy of accepting nothing. And I think they are beginning to realize it."

"Well, we won't accept nothing. That's final. We can take care of this matter ourselves. And we got the votes to do it. Most of those guys down there got labor support last time. They took our money. Now we want them to deliver. It's as simple as that."

"I can't agree, Steve, that it is as simple as that—just kill the bill, and that's that. It won't solve the problem. It's gone too far down the road. The Federation has sensed it and they're climbing back from that limb they climbed out on. They've been soft-pedaling that talk about accepting nothing. It's already gotten them in a box, as they should have foreseen it would. Labor has been pictured, successfully, as an arrogant, uncontrolled, evil giant. When you take the position that you will accept no controls, you are just strengthening that image. Making yourselves more enemies. I've been your friend for thirty-five years, and I don't intend to describe my activities in behalf of labor over that time. I shouldn't have to. You ought to know them well enough. So I speak as a friend when I tell you that some sort of controls are going to be imposed, and I think that the best course of action would be for labor to accept its responsibility by indicating that it will accept something. The important thing is to appear to accept some control. My personal view is that if you are willing to do that, the controls may not be so severe. They may not be controls imposed in anger. And it will give you much more negotiating room than merely to say, 'No, nothing, that's final.' If you do that, you abdicate the writing of the bill to someone else. This way, you'll have a hand in it. You can probably soften or knock out the really repugnant parts. And I think headquarters is recognizing its initial mistake. I think they are ready to negotiate a peace."

"Frank Raeder didn't give me that impression when I talked to him," Leo said slowly.

"I would imagine that this philosophy is not universally accepted as yet, and I think that Frank will be the last to accept it. But I think he will accept it in the end. I think that he will be forced to."

"Bullshit," said Fields, succinctly. "I can see what's going on here. I've talked to enough politicians to see what's going on. You're softening us up for the sellout."

The Senator cast a glittering eye on him and remained silent for a moment, looking at him.

"How many votes did you cast in the last election, Mr. Fields?"

"What?"

"How many votes did you cast? How many times did you pull the lever?"

"Don't give me that crap, Senator. I pulled it once. My guys pulled it fifteen thousand times."

"And they all pulled it for me because you told them to."

"Damn near."

"And none of them will pull it for me unless you tell them to."

"Look, let's cut out the quiz show. You know as well as I do that they voted for you almost to a man because we told them to. In fact, Mister Senator John Burnett, you can't be elected without these votes."

"I polled nearly a million votes last time."

"So?"

"So subtracting your fifteen thousand, I still got quite a few."

"So, we don't count for much, is that it? We don't swing enough weight, is that it? Well, listen mister, you just try to win without us. You just try—"

Leo Averni broke in. "This isn't getting us anywhere. Let's all just calm down."

"That's a good idea," the Senator said. "My fault. Let's just run down the major sections of the bill one by one. Now the bill of rights section, is that going to be impossible to live with? How much of a problem is it?"

"It's a real problem," Leo said. "It's going to make it damn difficult for a union officer to run his union. It gives every damn crackpot the chance to stand up and spout off whenever and wherever and at whatever length he wants to, and there's no power to stop him. Every back-stabber and malcontent will be able to keep the union in a turmoil. They'll use all those so-called safeguards to block everything. You'll never get anything done. You'll spend all of your time trying to be a peacemaker with this faction or that. You'll never be able to put up a solid front to management. In fact, it all but asks management to plant some trouble makers. We'll spend all our time fighting amongst ourselves, and we won't have time or energy left over to fight the people we should be fighting."

"This is going to sound pretty corny, Leo," the Senator said, "but that's democracy. Think about it. The problems you've described are exactly, exactly, the ones I have to face as an elected official. I grant you, it seems like a messy, inefficient way of getting things done. It would be a lot easier if you could be a strong

117

man who roped and tied the mavericks, and then determined these things without being bothered. And I admit, the trouble makers and malcontents make you think sometimes that there ought to be a better way, but I don't think there is. . . ." He raised his hand to keep Leo from speaking. "No, let's not argue this. Partly, I'm being the devil's advocate here. I just want you to think about them. Now what about trusteeships?"

"Well, John, there's nothing wrong with trusteeships. Locals get themselves in all kinds of messes, and the International just has to step in sometimes."

"And this bill would not prevent them from stepping in, provided they didn't abuse the privilege."

"But it would make it damn hard for them to do it."

"Still, how else are you going to control the abuses? How are you going to stop the Truckers?"

"Well," Leo said, "I don't know whether anything you do is going to stop them."

"You're not strongly opposed to this section then?"

"Well, I'm opposed to the whole goddam thing."

"Yes, but this particular section wouldn't touch your union, and it might clear up abuses in some others."

"Maybe."

"Now, what about the elimination of paper locals?"

"That ought to be stopped. That's plain crooked."

"O.K. Now what about the financial reporting requirements?"

"God, we'll have to hire a whole roomful of accountants. And whatever we do, somebody will dig some figure out of context and make us look bad with it. There's been no stealing in our union. Why tar us with that brush? I thought Congress was after the crooks. I thought they were supposed to legislate where a need was indicated. Well, there hasn't been any need indicated in our union. Nobody has ever pinned anything on us. Not one thing."

The Senator sighed. "Leo, for two years we've been hearing testimony about how the money of the workingman has been stolen by union officials and used to buy hundred-thousand-dollar houses, race horses, Cadillacs, women, and God knows what else. Loans have been extended which have never been paid back and carried no interest in the first place. Union officials have been getting a rake-off from pensions, insurance, medical payments, like they were the Government collecting taxes. This was clearly all just plain stealing. Now you want us to stand up and oppose this provision in the law. Leo, that's just stupid and foolhardy, and you as a politician should know it. It just can't be done."

"Well," said Leo slowly, "something could probably be done in this area."

"Ah, is that a retreat from the 'no legislation' position?"

"Something minimal, confined to those who've done the stealing."

"Now we're getting somewhere. You see the problem in at least a couple of areas, and you think something may be necessary."

"See what he's trying to do?" said Fields. "Chip away a little bit at a time. . . ."

"No, Mr. Fields, just trying to arrive at minimum acceptable legislation, on the off-chance that I'm right and some legislation does get through."

"Minimum acceptable legislation is no legislation. We've got the votes to kill it if we have to."

"I suggest that you do not have the votes and are not close to having the votes. That virtually nobody can or would support a 'no legislation' position."

"You mean you're about to run out on us, is that it?"

"No, that is not it, sir. I am not about to run out on you. I'm going to try to do what I can for you, as I always have. But neither I nor anybody else is going to be able to help if you refuse to compromise. Besides, this bill isn't going to be one hundred per cent bad. There are a number of things in it that you've been crying for since Taft-Hartley, and with a little luck and good horse-trading, I think we might be able to get a few more things, so that on balance the package might not be too bad. It won't be sweet, but it may be palatable. Steve, I've been around a long time. I was in the Senate when Taft-Hartley was passed, and the situation then has bearing on the situation now. We had a war, during which John L. Lewis called out his miners on strike for more money when our boys were dying overseas. People were ready to lynch him for that. And I suggest that in furthering their own selfish interests, the miners sacrificed the whole labor community. Then came the postwar period, when labor was legitimately striking all over the country to catch up on some of the benefits that had been frozen for four years. Strategically correct, yes. Reasonable, yes. But it ignored the fact that the American public, aching for all the new cars and appliances they had been denied during the war, resented it. And those people who hate labor, and always will hate labor, were lying in wait. They traded shrewdly on the public mood. They zeroed in on labor, which had grown fat and dictatorial. They'll rule the country, they said. Destroy all the things we fought for—wreck the system, destroy free enterprise, nationalize all business—you know what it was like. It was timely, it focused discontent, and it worked. We got a Republican Congress, and the Taft-Hartley Act, which I voted against. I thought it went too far. Then you all insisted on trumpeting about the country that it was a slave labor law. Which nobody believed, including yourselves. And now you, or at least some of you, seem determined to do the whole damn thing over again. Believe me, Steve, the country is aroused about this. Really aroused. I know that the labor-hating crowd has swung into action, and they're exploiting it, and that galls you. But they're just riding the crest. There is a terribly powerful undercurrent. Make no mistake about that. And frankly, it would be impossible to sweep the whole thing under the rug at this stage, as you seem to think. People wouldn't stand for it, and any politician who thinks otherwise will find himself back on the old homestead after the next elections."

"Senator," Fields said, "as far as I'm concerned, that's a yellow way of looking at the problem. Just roll over and play dead. Give up without a fight. Well, I ain't built that way, and neither are my guys. I've had enough of this." He rose and snatched his hat from the coffee table. "Leo, I'm leaving. There's no sense in talking to somebody who's already made up his mind to sell us out without a fight."

"Fine," said the Senator. "I don't see anything else we can usefully talk about."

"Just remember this conversation, Mr. Big. *We* will," Fields said. He walked out the door and slammed it without another word.

"Steve's a tough man," Averni said.

"A peach," the Senator said, rising and lighting a cigarette. "Leo, you ought to get rid of strong-arm guys like that. In the end they hurt you, and badly."

"Good suggestion. How do you go about it, especially if the bill of rights in the bill becomes law?"

"*Touché*," the Senator said. "I know. It's not easy. People like that have a lot of drive, and they scare a lot of people. But as long as the public has a glimpse of a man like that, he will be used as an example of the typical labor leader. It's about time the movement grew up. The thirties are over. The barricades are down. It's about time you started using your power with some finesse instead of like a blackjack, because if you don't stop it, you are going to lose it, and what's going on in Washington is a good example of precisely what I am talking about."

"All the battles aren't over yet," Leo said.

"No, of course not. But the battles of the future are going to be mostly diplomacy, instead of wars."

Leo Averni paced thoughtfully around the room, rapping his fist on the table, on the back of a chair. "Speaking for myself, John, God knows I trust you. If it were up to me, I'd say go to it. Get us the best you can, just as you always have. But Frank thinks we've got to kill it." He sat down again.

"Frank isn't the whole Federation. And, as I've said, they're not unanimous about this and they probably won't be. But they'll come around, after they've talked to enough people on the Hill. It's a slow process, especially when you're committed to something publicly. It's like turning the Queen Mary around in New York Harbor."

Leo got up. "John, I've enjoyed the talk. I don't agree with you in every respect, and probably won't. I'll think about some of the things you've said, if you'll think about some of my points."

"Fair enough. One of the purposes of my visit here was to talk to you, and it has been worth while."

Averni paused in the doorway. "By the way, before I go, let me ask you something: How well do you know Ed Flowers?"

"Oh, talked to him a few times. Why?"

"What do you think of him?"

The Senator pursed his lips. "Well, he's a personable and attractive fellow, and he seems to be doing a decent job, from my limited knowledge."

"Is he respected there in Washington?"

"Respected?"

"Yes."

"Well, I wouldn't say he was one of the union people that is relied on for detailed analysis of laws, or high strategy, but he's certainly liked."

"I see," said Leo. "Well, thanks. I'll be running along."

After Leo had left, the Senator sat down in a chair. "There you have it, my boy," he said to Sidney, "the world in miniature. The reasonable man and the unreasonable man."

"Fields is a son of a bitch," Sidney said definitively. "I'd like to have punched him in the nose, if he hadn't been so big."

"Don't try it. Not that I doubt your ability to land a fearful punch of righteous indignation. But the publicity aspects are terrifying to think about. Bullheaded bastard that he is, he carries a lot of weight with the radical union element in this state. Averni is typical old-line NFL—determined but reasonable. Not motivated by dogma and socioeconomic theories. Just out to squeeze as much as can be cheerfully squeezed out of management. Well, let's see who else is in line to abuse their chosen representative." He picked up the telephone. "Hello, operator, did you take any calls for me? May I have them?" He jotted down half a dozen names and numbers on a sheet of hotel stationery, thanked the operator, and hung up. "The next act," he announced, "immediately following the dedication of the bridge, will be the management team of Messrs. Murray Austin and William McClounts Morrow. It's called 'Will Miss America escape from the evil clutches of the villain Labor?'"

"I'm not sure I want to stay around for that," Sidney said.

"Come now," said the Senator. "You do want to hear the other side. There is one, you know."

Sidney, just back from Missouri, bounded up the front steps of his house, anxious to see his parents, who had arrived for a visit.

"Sidney, Sidney," said his mother, flying to him as he opened the door. She planted enthusiastic kisses on both his cheeks. "You are looking so good. Thin, but good. Mama will fatten you up while she's here. Some of your old favorites from when you were little." She stood back and contemplated him with pride. "Such a success now."

Sidney shook hands with his father and kissed him. He gave Sylvia a kiss and a strong hug.

"Well, well, Sidney. It's good to see you. You look wonderful. Syl looks good and the little ones too. Everybody looks fine."

"So tell us all about it, Sidney," his mother said, "now that you're such a big successful man here in Washington. We want to hear all about it. Everything."

"Absolutely," his father said, "the whole story."

"Well, it's a great experience, Papa and Mama. Even better than I thought it was going to be."

"And so does Senator Burnett ask your opinion about things? For advice and things like that?"

"Sometimes. I'm still quite new, of course. But I'm writing quite a few of his speeches. That speech he gave in St. Louis last week. I wrote every word of it, and he merely made a few changes to adapt it to his speaking style. Otherwise it was mine."

"Imagine," his mother said, clasping her hands. "And such a nice house. Not brick, but nice."

"So you're working for Senator John Burnett of Missouri," his father said, clamping his cigar between his teeth, throwing his coat back, and plunging his hands into his pockets. "I know of this man from a long time back. When for twenty-three years I worked as a cutter for M. Blustein, we heard of Senator John Burnett. He was a hero to us. He was for the workers, always for the workers. He was a true friend to us. A tried and true friend. Samuel Dubraska, president of our union, once said to me personally this: 'This man is the worker's hero of the twentieth century.' He told me that personally."

"He's a thoughtful man and a brilliant politician," said Sidney.

"That, yes, but he is also a very great man, Sidney, don't forget that. You should consider it a privilege to work with a great man like this."

"I do, Papa. And I'm personally grateful because he rescued me. I'll never forget him for that."

"Personally, yes, he did you a favor. But he is a giant. He is a man who fights for what he thinks."

"It's really a lovely house," said his mother. "So modern. How much did you have to give for this nice house, Sidney?"

"Twenty-one nine fifty, but we had some extras put in such as a larger refrigerator and the asphalt tile on the playroom, so it came to about twenty-two five."

"Such a lot of money they cost these days. Twenty-two thousand five hundred dollars," she clucked. "But it's nice. And nice neighbors. I saw that a doctor lives in the corner house."

"Yes. Doctor Willis Parten. We don't know them very well yet, but they seem very nice."

"I was always wishing for you to be a doctor, Sidney. A professional."

"I am a professional. I'm an economist, a labor economist. That's a profession," he said in mild irritation.

"M-m-m," she said doubtfully. "It's not the same though."

"Hush, Mama," said his father. "That's enough."

"I thought that while you were here, you might like to come down and meet Senator Burnett. I think I could arrange it, if you'd like to," Sidney said.

"That would be very good, Sidney. I would much like to meet this man, who I've heard so much about for so many years," his father said.

"Mama?"

"Lovely, Sidney. I will tell him how lucky he is to have Sidney Bronstein working with him."

"Now, Mama...."

"Well, he should know."

"I'm sure he does. After all, he hired me."

"Still," she said, "you should toot your own horn sometimes. That's the trouble with you, Sidney. You don't push yourself forward enough."

"Once I tooted too much, and I learned my lesson."

"Nobody else will do it for you," his mother said, "except me, your Mama, who knows what a smart boy you are. First in your class in high school. You should tell them that."

"There are other ways. If you do good work, it will be recognized eventually."

"It doesn't hurt to let them know though," his mother said doggedly.

"So, Sidney, things are pretty good with us too. Mama wrote you that I am now not just the Treasurer of M. Blustein and Sons, but the Secretary-Treasurer. How is that?"

"That's fine, Papa. Very fine. Yes, Mama wrote us that in her last letter, and we're very proud of you."

"No salary increase, but a nice title," his mother said.

"That will come in time," his father said. "The business wasn't doing too good for a couple of years there, but I think it's coming up now. Then, Blustein says to me, Oscar, when that happens, you will get what's coming to you. I'll take care of you."

"Papa," said Sidney, "it's so difficult to think of you as being in management. You were so identified with labor for so long."

"Twenty-three years a cutter, and for the last fifteen, shop steward of Local 1906, Garment Cutters and Seamers."

"Yes, and you were always so militant, such a crusader."

"It's true," his father said. "And I still represent the workers."

"As Secretary-Treasurer of M. Blustein and Sons?" Sidney said.

"Sure. The workers wanted me to continue on as their representative."

"Wait a minute here. I'm not sure I understand. You serve as Secretary-Treasurer of Blustein, and also represent the workers as their union representative?"

"That is right."

"But, Papa, that's illegal."

"So," said his father, "who's to know about it? Only M. Blustein, myself, and the six cutters. Who else?"

"And you see no conflict there?"

"There is no conflict, Sidney. You don't understand. I take care of the workers for themselves and for M. Blustein. It is to everybody's advantage. We give them good working conditions, the best—"

"But what about wage increases? What if a fight developed between Blustein and the workers concerning the amount of a wage increase, then where would you be?"

"Such a thing wouldn't happen. We give the same wage increases that the big houses give, minus five per cent differential that the union gives to small houses like us. The cutters don't ask for more than that, and we wouldn't give it anyway. If we did, we'd be out of business, and then everybody would be in a fix."

"What about grievances, then? Suppose some argument comes up about something? What happens then?"

"I listen to what the workers have to say. If they got a point, I give it to them, and I tell M. Blustein what must be done. If they haven't got a point, I deny them. That's final."

"And Blustein and the workers always abide by this ruling?"

"Of course. M. Blustein made me Secretary-Treasurer so I could handle these things for him. He's out selling every day. So I'm in charge. And the workers. Well, twenty-three years is a long time, and they know me very well. And when I tell them no, they know that no is the right answer."

Sidney laughed, shaking his head. "You're the missing link, the missing illegal link in labor-management relations."

"It works very nice for everyone," his father said. "Of course, we have our little arguments now and then, but then," he said craftily, "I apply a little balm in the right places. We get through it."

"Amazing," said Sidney.

"Thank you," said his father. "Now, enough about me. I want to hear more what you do. Do you talk about important things all day down there? About how the country and the world should be run?"

"In some ways we do. Everything is of such enormous magnitude. Every law that's considered affects millions of people, in ways you never think of. The economy is so complex that you have to investigate and research and hold hearings to be sure you know what you're doing when a law is passed. Otherwise it may have some unfortunate effect that you didn't think about. Now this proposed labor reform law. Before I went to work for the Senator, I had no doubts, no doubts whatsoever, that it should be defeated."

"Of course."

"But, when you study the matter, and listen to the hundreds of different points of view, if you really listen and try to think about them, you get a slightly different idea."

"What's this you're saying, Sidney? That such a bill should pass? I can't believe you're saying that."

"No, I'm not saying that. But I'm saying that it requires careful study. And that it shouldn't be taken for granted that it should be rejected."

"But it is a vicious, reactionary bill. It is bad. It seeks to put the workers back in chains."

"Now that's an exaggeration, Papa. It has some bad features, I admit, which ought to be eliminated, but it really isn't as bad as all that."

"I don't know, Sidney. You surprise me. I don't know about working for this man. Your ideas seem to be changed."

"They definitely have."

"But for the best? You turn against the workingman. You

turn against everything that was taught to you by me and your mama."

"No, that's not true. I'm not turning against anything. I'm trying to look at things with unbiased eyes, analytically, and to make up my mind on the basis of reason, not emotion."

"But this bill, Sidney. It is a terrible thing. A terrible step back. There is no question about it. There is no room here for doubt. About some things perhaps, but about this, no."

"I'm not so sure, Papa. It will stop some of the abuses."

"Yes," his father said. "It will do that. Those crooks and criminals maybe it will get. But at what cost? It will hurt all labor. Weaken us who have done nothing. That's the evil in it. That's why all of the big interests and the big money is for the bill. Why else?"

"That's true, and I know it," Sidney said, "but you can't escape from the fact that something has to be done."

"Did Senator Burnett put these ideas into your head? I refuse to believe that. He has been the workers' friend for twenty-five, thirty years. And he would not do that. I know it. . . ."

"He planted no ideas in my head. He . . ."

"But what does he think about this bill? He must be against it."

"Well, I can't speak for him. But I know that he is thinking awfully hard about it."

"I find it impossible to believe," said his father. "Impossible. John Burnett. Impossible." He paced up and down the living room with his hands behind his back. "Sidney, let me tell you this. If we come down to see him, I'm going to ask him about this. I'm absolutely going to ask him about it."

"Oscar," his mother said, "it might be a bad thing."

"So if you don't want the question asked, don't bring us down there," his father said.

"I don't mind," Sidney said. "I'm sure you'll find his answer interesting."

"Impossible," said his father. "But I will definitely ask. You can count on that."

"Dinner everybody," Sylvia said from the dining-room doorway.

128

"We'll see if Sylvia is taking care of our boy," his mother said. "Coming, dear."

Several days later, Sidney ushered his parents into the Senator's office. John Burnett rose and came around the desk to meet them.

"Senator, I'd like to have you meet my mother and father, Mr. and Mrs. Oscar Bronstein."

"Pleased to meet you," said Sidney's father.

"Charmed," said his mother.

"I'm delighted to meet you both. Your fine son and I have enjoyed a most rewarding relationship, and I want to commend you for producing such an excellent young man."

"So smart," his mother sighed. "Always first in his class, all the way through school. Even kindergarten."

"Ma . . ."

"So a mother can't say that about her own son," his mother said.

"Folks," Senator Burnett said, "suppose we eat in the Senate restaurant over in the Capitol."

"Oh, yes," Sidney's mother said.

They took the elevator to the basement and rode over to the Capitol on the monorail train, to the amusement of his parents, and went upstairs to the Senate restaurant.

"Senators only," his mother observed.

"The inner sanctum," the Senator said. "I recommend the bean soup," he continued, after they had been seated and given menus. "It's been on the menu for forty years. You really shouldn't eat in the Senate restaurant without having bean soup."

They ordered lunch. Sidney and the Senator chatted about a few matters while his mother and father observed the room.

"Very nice," his mother pronounced. "Oh, my . . ."

"What?"

"That fellow over there. He's somebody. Somebody famous that I know . . . but . . ."

"That's the majority leader, Senator Eldon Macefield of California."

"Of course," his mother said, "Senator Eldon Macefield of California."

"And he's eating lunch with somebody you ought to know too," Sidney said. His father peered at the other man. "Steinman. Irving Steinman from New York."

"Irving Steinman from New York," his mother said. "Of course, Irving."

"Right," Sidney said.

"We're old acquaintances," his father said, "from twenty years ago."

The bean soup arrived, and they all tasted it.

"Well, Mrs. Bronstein," said the Senator, "what do you think of our famous bean soup?"

"Very nice," she said, somewhat unimpressed. "Better than Campbell's," she added.

"So the labor bill is to be voted on before long," Mr. Bronstein said, launching boldly into the delicate subject.

"I think it will come to a vote shortly," said the Senator. "As soon as everyone gets the justification for his impending vote in the record. Probably sometime early next week."

"It has some good points," said Sidney's father in a conciliatory manner.

"I think it does," said the Senator.

"But overall it's bad," continued his father.

"Well. . ." said Sidney.

"Why do you say that, Mr. Bronstein?"

"Well, I'm no lawyer. The parts that stop the stealing of the workers' money, and the parts that make sure the workers can vote in who they want to vote in, they're not so bad. Something here is needed to protect the workers. All those things is O.K. I admit that. But those other parts. Like the part that says you can't picket somebody who's not paying the going wage. That's bad. Very bad. Because if we can't do that, how do we keep them from getting all the business, and the good employer who is trying to pay the going wage, he don't get any. So before long he goes bust. And after a while, there isn't going to be any going wage any more, and it's dog eat dog like it was before unions. That's a bad thing."

"I agree with you, Mr. Bronstein, and we're going to try to make sure that kind of picketing will continue to be permitted."

"And sweatshops," Mr. Bronstein went on. "I have been told that the boycott parts would not let us boycott somebody who is running a sweatshop and driving down workers' wages. So you're going to stop us boycotting. Impossible. You wouldn't let us boycott so one of the cheap chiselers couldn't flood the market with cheap goods produced by sweatshop labor? You're going to tell us we can't do that?"

"Well, it's a complicated subject," said the Senator. "Some kinds of boycotts are evil and should be forbidden, and some are healthy. Then the question of freedom of speech enters into the problem. We are trying to draw the line between permitting legitimate freedom of speech and outlawing the evil boycotts, and it's a very difficult line to draw."

"So don't draw it. I've been working in the garment trades for forty years, and I never seen a bad boycott. When they got boycotted, they deserved it."

"Mr. Bronstein, the garment trades have some special problems in this respect, and they have had very responsible unions. But some unions are not so responsible, and they've abused the rights of others. Remember, this bill, when it is passed, will apply to the whole country, not only to the garment trades."

"Senator, I want to ask you a very personal question. But you don't answer it if you don't want to. You've been with us for twenty, thirty years—I don't know how long. Fighting for our rights, fighting for the workers. I don't believe you're going to vote for this bill. I just don't believe that."

The Senator shifted uneasily in his chair. "It's a very complicated problem, Mr. Bronstein. Very complicated." He leaned forward intently. "I'll mention something to you, on the absolute understanding that it will go no farther."

"Absolutely not," Mr. Bronstein said.

"The problem is this. They're going to bring a bill to the floor, and my own feelings about that bill coincide almost precisely with yours. The union democracy and financial responsibility titles of that bill are, I think, necessary and good. The other portions I am opposed to as they now stand. We—that is some of

131

us here in the Senate who feel alike on the matter—intend to propose alternative language for those unacceptable sections, and we will attempt to amend the bill in those respects on the floor."

"Fine."

"But that's not easy to do. The vote looks as if it is going to be very close on the five crucial amendments we will offer. Maybe we will win them, and in that case there probably won't be much of a problem. We can all vote for the amended bill in good conscience. The problem arises if we lose. If we don't carry our amendments, and we are called upon to vote on the bill as it now stands, then how do we vote?"

"Against it," Mr. Bronstein said promptly.

"A very difficult thing for many people to do, Mr. Bronstein. Very difficult. That would mean, in effect, a vote against labor reform, because there would be no possibility of getting another bill through this late in the session. To vote against it means that you're voting to permit all these crooked things that have been uncovered by the committee to continue. You're voting to continue to permit these crooks and thugs to operate. A vote like that would mean that a lot of congressmen and senators, including myself, would go before the electorate with an albatross around our necks. Namely, that despite the exposures of the committee and the ample evidence of theft, bribery, and corruption in certain labor unions, we were 'owned' by the unions to such a degree that we were not permitted by them to vote for this necessary reform that the country is demanding. The more liberal your record, the more vulnerable you are to such a charge. And believe me, Mr. Bronstein, the country is aroused by this issue to a greater degree than any issue I've encountered in thirty-five years of political life."

"Hmmmmm," said Sidney's father.

"The other side, you see, is going to try to beat down our amendments, to force a choice between this bill or no bill. If they succeed, a lot of our people who will vote with us for the amendments will eventually go with them. Some because they believe that although the bill has some bad features, this messy situation has got to be cleaned up; and others for purely political reasons. Most people for a combination of the two."

"I still think," Mr. Bronstein said haltingly, "that such a bill as this . . . should be voted against."

"It's a very difficult question," said the Senator.

"Do what you think is right," said Mrs. Bronstein. "We trust you. And so will your people, if you do what's right."

"I hope that's so," said the Senator.

"Of course it is," said Mrs. Bronstein confidently.

The waiter cleared their table, temporarily interrupting further conversation. When he had finished, the Senator resumed it in another area. "Your boy Sidney is a great help to me. I don't know how I ever got along without him."

Sidney's parents nodded in perfect understanding.

"And he seems to enjoy the work, don't you, Sidney?"

"Love it."

"And I'm treating you all right?"

"Just fine."

"There you go, Mrs. Bronstein, what more could a mother ask?"

"Nothing," she said. "So exciting. To think, Sidney is right here in Washington, where George Washington and Abraham Lincoln were. All these famous people."

"I wouldn't doubt," said the Senator, "that Abraham Lincoln ate occasionally right in this restaurant. I think it was operating then."

"My," said Mrs. Bronstein in awe, "do you think so?"

"I wouldn't be at all surprised."

"So much history I can't absorb it all," she said. "You're a very lucky boy, Sidney."

"I know it."

The check was presented, and the Senator signed it. "Well, folks, I have enjoyed it. Very much. We'll have to do this again when you come to Washington."

"Our pleasure, I assure you," said Sidney's mother.

"Now I'm going to have to be getting back. Why don't you have Sidney show you around this old building? There are all sorts of things hidden away in the nooks and crannies." He bade them good-by and departed.

"I knew it, Sidney," his mother said. "I knew you had it, ever since you were a little boy."

"He's a good man, Sidney," his father said. "You're very lucky to be working for a fine man like that. Not many people have such an opportunity."

"I'm aware of that," Sidney said.

9

Ed Flowers drew on his cigarette and expelled the smoke with a feeling of great satisfaction. This evening at La Salle du Bois was the culmination of much thought on his part. With Barbara Merideth he had reached the threshold of conquest at their last meeting. His hands, after three months of restraint, were allowed the freedom of her body. Tonight, she was keeping the date, well aware of the outcome, for they would begin, later that night, where they had left off in his car two days ago.

He knew that she was troubled, but she was still coming to him. This did not disturb Ed, because at the climax of such affairs, a tender half love for whatever girl was involved welled up in him and assuaged his conscience. He was aware that the feeling was a detached one, which would comfortably abate with time.

He liked the La Salle. The silverware was heavy, the linen was heavy, the chandelier sparkled diamonds, and the waiters had French accents. Everything was quality, the best. The food was served with an air of casual waste. Only the hearts of steaks and artichokes were served. Tiny peas and tiny shrimp were eaten before they had achieved coarse maturity. Butter was cut from a mold in large slabs, rather than parsimoniously dispensed in small squares.

He saw her enter, in a shimmering white dress. As she stood in the elegant foyer, Albert greeted her with quiet restraint.

"Mademoiselle Merideeth looks particularly beautiful tonight, with that you must agree, Monsieur Flowers," Albert said, leading her to the table.

"With that I do agree," Ed said, taking her hand. "Two dry Martinis, Albert, if you please . . . particularly beautiful. A vision of loveliness."

"Something more original than that," she demanded.

"A mysterious and exciting woman."

"Bad," she said. "Our copy writers do better than that."

"A woman of the world."

"Hackneyed," she said, "but that's the general impression I was trying to create."

"But that is only on the outside," he continued, carrying on the arch mood. "On the inside still reposes the untouched soul of the country girl from Ames."

A grimace flickered across her face. "Hardly."

The Martinis, delicately frosted, arrived on a silver tray.

"Umm," she said, "they do make the best Martinis here."

"Beefeater's and Noilly Prat. The best there is."

"How are things at the office?" she said, withdrawing her hand, "not that I will understand a word of it, but I'll pretend I do. Are you still visiting senators and all those important people?"

"I visited John Burnett a while ago, to nail down his vote."

"Burnett," she said. "Now he's the one from Missouri?"

"Yes, one of the real great old-timers. A real scrapper. He doesn't look it. He's very tall and dresses sort of sloppily. He actually looks more like a college professor or a scientist. But, as I say, in spite of his looks, he's a fighter. I wouldn't want to tangle with him, I can tell you that. Sarcastic . . . boy, he can cut you to ribbons."

"He sounds fascinating, but I don't quite understand," Barbara said. "Why do you have to visit him? I thought he always voted labor's way."

"John does. But we don't leave any stone unturned. We have to be thorough. We're going to visit every senator on the Hill. Frank Raeder's in charge of the whole campaign, and he's a bug on thoroughness. They're a temperamental bunch, anyway, you know. You don't visit them, and pretty soon they get in a huff. They don't like you to feel that you've got them in your back pocket. For instance, Burnett asked me a lot of tough questions. A lot of people would have thought that he was against us, but I know him well enough to know that he's just trying to give the impression that he's independent, that he thinks everything over carefully, weighs every vote. You learn to take these things with a grain of salt when you've been at it as long as I have," he said offhandedly.

"And all the labor people are doing this?"

"Sure. We're trying to hit them from all sides. We've got to get heavy mail in against the bill. Got out a directive to the field men today on that. . . ."

"Directing them to what?"

"Directing them to get the members on the stick and get some mail in here opposing the bill."

"And what if they don't feel that way about it?"

"Well, it's their funeral."

"But you don't beat them up, or intimidate them or something, like all those people who've been on television before the committee."

"Oh, for God's sakes," he said. "That's what's happened in the whole country. Now everybody thinks that all unions do that. No, as I said, it's their funeral. If they don't believe us when we tell them that bill will hurt them, then they just don't have eyes and ears. Actually, that's not the problem. Most of them go along with what we tell them. It's just trying to get them to sit down with a piece of paper and a pen in their hand. Most of them haven't written a letter in ten years. And they have to do it on their own. We've tried form letters at union meetings, and petitions with a thousand signatures, but nothing gets through like the bumbling mistake-filled letter from the common man. So we just give them the idea, and let them express it in their own words."

"And senators and congressmen read all those?"

"No, but they count them, and they do read some to get the flavor. After all, that's the voice of the people. Nothing wrong with it," he said, sensing her silent disapproval. "Management does the same damn thing."

"Well, then, doesn't it cancel out?"

"Somewhat, but neither side can quit. And it certainly puts the senator on the spot. If you can ever get a man interested enough to write a letter, he'll watch what the senator does on that particular bill, and the senator knows it. We have to build up the volume, to counter management. It's like a hydroelectric plant. It takes a tremendous amount of fast-moving water to eventually light the bulb in your apartment. They get fewer letters in, but they're from more important people. A few years ago, it was their people with money and influence against our numbers. Now, of course, we have some money too. Of course, half the damn country is writing in on this bill. But more important than money, almost, we can offer them workers at election time. Door-to-door workers, precinct workers, telephone canvassers—and that's one of our great strengths. Management can't offer that kind of manpower. So," he said, concluding, "that's what we're doing, playing all the angles, just like management is."

"So you and a lot of other powerful people sit here in Washington, pulling the strings and determining what's going to happen."

He shrugged. "The race goes to the swift. That's enough about me," he said, conscious that he had run on about it. "How have you been?"

"Oh," she said, "so-so."

"Something wrong at the station?"

"Something's wrong with me, I guess. I'm bored. Restless. Television isn't exciting any more. Not for me anyway. I don't get the kick out of it I used to. When I first started to work there, I was so excited I could hardly wait to get to work every day. Now I guess I'm just sick of it. People who once seemed so fascinating now seem like phonies. And we just grind out the same old thing every day. But it's me. Occupational melancholia, somebody said. I seem to be the only one suffering from it. Everybody else seems to be running around importantly, still thinking that it's all so exciting. It must be me."

138

"It's probably just because of this new guy and all the un-certainty."

"No, I don't think so. I don't think I'll ever feel about it the way I used to. All the glamorous career business. I'm sick of it."

"Probably just temporary," he said. "You'll get over it."

"I know well enough what the problem is," she said as if talking to herself. "The problem is that I'm . . ." She paused.

"You're what?"

"Nothing. None of your business, Edward Flowers. Let's get off this dreary subject. I was determined that tonight I would have a good time. Live a little, as they say. So let's."

"Suits me," said Ed, slipping his hand over hers. She did not withdraw it. "Let's."

"Can we have another Martini," she said, "and then order? I'm starved."

"That's the spirit," he said. "We're off."

A few years before, Ed would have ordered a steak and French fries. Now he considered it something of a travesty to order such a meal in a restaurant like La Salle. He ordered veal, lightly touched with wines and herbs, and a wine that he had been told was both excellent and correct. For dessert, they had some Camembert and fruit, followed by brandy and coffee. He felt quite Continental and satisfied with himself. You've come a long way, he thought, as he looked at the sprinkling of sophisti-cated diplomats, slipping into their chesterfields and Homburgs. Before too much longer he must get to Europe. After the labor bill fight was over, and the damn Hillstrom thing. He watched the generals and admirals, trim and distinguished, and the others, casual, well dressed, accompanied by tastefully decorated women. He lit his pencil-thin cigar. His vested suit had cost one hundred and seventy-five dollars, and the girl with him was beautiful. And he was Edward T. Flowers, President of the American Electronic Workers. One of the chosen people, really.

"That was an absolutely marvelous dinner," Barbara said. "Just what I needed."

They lingered over coffee, feeling a light euphoria around them. The crowd was thinning out.

"Would you like to come over to the apartment and have a cup of coffee?" she said casually.

"If I have any more coffee, I'll be up until daylight," he said. "But fine, let's go," he added hastily.

They linked arms and walked slowly up the hill, saying nothing. They turned on S Street and walked in the spiny shadows cast by the trees. Barbara's apartment seemed warm and cozy.

"There's cannel coal in the grate. Squirt a little lighter fluid on it, why don't you?" He did as she asked.

"You really have a beautiful place here," he said, studying the low lines of the modern furniture, the camel saddle, the black primitive African masks on the wall.

"From my African period. Actually, I'm getting a little tired of it. Sure you don't want coffee? My tastes are changing, or something. It's not comfortable enough. Is that a sign of age, do you suppose?" Her muffled voice came from the tiny kitchen.

"Sign of a restless mind," he pronounced.

"I've got that all right. I'm never satisfied."

Ed was conscious that his mood had suddenly changed. "Nobody is. Look at me. I've got more than I ever dreamed I would. Yet I have those same feelings that something is missing. Or that I'm missing something. I always thought that when I had a good job with plenty of money, a couple of new cars, plenty of clothes, a nice house, I'd have it made. Well, I have it all. But it doesn't seem like so much now. What's the problem, doctor?"

"I respectfully refer you to the *Power of Positive Thinking*, and if no cure is effected, try *Peace of Mind*." She sat down beside him on the sofa. "I'm sorry. I shouldn't be so flip. You were being serious. But I don't know the answer. I wish I could find it myself."

She sipped her coffee, and leaned forward so that her young face glowed softly in the fire's reflection.

"You're beautiful," he said. "I think you're the most beautiful girl I ever . . ."

"Ever what?"

"Knew."

"Wanted to sleep with, I bet you were thinking."

140

"I said nothing of the kind, and I wasn't thinking anything of the kind either."

"Maybe I was being unfair," she said, "but being beautiful isn't the answer most girls think it is. I know lots of girls who could be called downright ugly, who are married and deliriously happy."

"Most of them would give their right arms to have your job, and live in glamorous Washington."

"Would they? I wonder. If they really knew what it was like."

"Oh, come on," he said, "you're just depressed."

"No, I'm not. I'm quietly exhilarated. You just don't recognize it." She leaned down and brushed his lips with hers. "I'm exhilarated because I'm with you. It's as simple as that."

He drew her to him and gave her a long, searching kiss. They fitted themselves to one another on the sofa. He kissed her, brushed her ears, eyes, chin with his lips.

"Hey," he said, "what are you doing?"

"I'm undressing you."

"Well, I'll be goddammed," he said in genuine shock. He leaned back and looked at her smug, amused expression with amazement. "This is one hell of a note. Why, after all this time? I guess I shouldn't ask questions," he added.

"No," she said, "you shouldn't."

"Do you know why I'm doing this?" she asked.

"You're seducing me, an old man of forty-six, for the sport of it. It's shocking what can happen to a boy in the big city."

"Be serious. Do you really know?"

"No, to be really honest I'm astounded. I'd given up hope."

"Well, little Barbara has thought it through, applying all that was taught her in Logic 101. After a lot of bawling and thinking about gassing myself in the oven. . . ."

"Oh, come on now," he said.

"It's true. You're married—" the thought was difficult for her to express "—but you don't love your wife and she doesn't love you. That isn't my fault. That happened a long time ago. Before I was ever around."

He nodded in agreement.

"But I do love you. Don't ask me why, but I do. And I can't have you the way I want you—married to you—so I'll settle for this, and hope for the best. A lot of women do, I guess."

"Don't sound so resigned."

"I didn't mean to. I'm actually happy, very happy. And my conscience doesn't hurt. After all, is this so immoral?"

"By most standards it is," he said.

"It seems to me that if I finally marry somebody I like but don't love and start sleeping with him, that will be immoral. If it's not, it should be."

"Let's stop all this deep conversation," he said.

They lay with one another for half an hour, saying nothing. Finally he took her, enjoying the laving softness of her, and her tense undulating body under his, the slipping softness of their skins, now hotly sensitive. He lay sprawled atop her, panting, then lifted himself off, and they lay beside one another. She left him with a brief kiss, without a word, and went into the bedroom to her own bed, leaving him on the sofa in front of the glowing coals.

The next morning, a knife edge of the sun awoke him, and for a moment he did not realize where he was. For a while, he lay thinking about things, mildly happy, mildly troubled about the direction things were taking. Presently he heard the comfortable sound of her in the kitchen; and the smell of frying bacon drifted in to him. He dressed, and they had a quiet, proper breakfast, speaking little. He bade her a lingering good-by, and left for the office.

The clean brightness of the morning drove out his remaining melancholy, his stride lengthened, and he found himself humming a vague, tuneless song. Ten o'clock, the clock in a barber shop chastised him when he stopped for a shave. At the office, the work was busily clattering on, unchanged.

"Mr. Harrack has been trying to reach you," Louise announced in mild reproach. "He seemed quite anxious."

"Put the call in," Ed said, more gruffly than usual. He had begun to glance through his mail when the call came through.

"Ed," said the muffled voice from South Carolina, "tried to get you earlier. . . ."

"So I heard," Ed said. "Had an appointment. What can I do for you?"

"Ed, I'd like to have you come down here."

"I see. What's up?"

"Well, this is going to be a close one, as we discussed. They're fighting us with everything they've got and they've got a smart lawyer. I think we'll win, but we've got to finish strong. I'm planning a sort of beer-party pep rally the night before the election. We've got the stadium at the fair grounds. They're trying to block that, but I don't think they can. Even if they do, we'll find someplace else. But what I had in mind was an appearance by you. It will be the type of thing that's made to order for you. Inspiring speech of fifteen or twenty minutes. It doesn't have to be full of facts, mainly the old 'go out there and win' type of thing."

"When is the rally scheduled?"

"Couple of weeks. The eleventh. That's a Thursday night. I hope your calendar's clear."

"Just a minute." Ed sat back and thought for thirty seconds. "All right, Don. I think it's a good idea. I'll probably fly down and get there sometime in the afternoon. We'll let you know. Any points you want me to cover in particular?"

"Yes, there are three or four things I hope you can get across. I'll get them down on paper and get them in to Washington. Only one thing—I hope it won't be a canned speech. I mean I hope you won't read it. I think it should appear to be spontaneous remarks. You're good at that sort of thing. Ought to be a snap for you."

All right. I'll plan on seeing you on the eleventh. Keep it up, boy. Glad to hear that it's going well."

"I wouldn't say that. It's a cat-and-dog fight. If we win it, we'll really deserve it." They hung up.

"Louise," he called, "would you shut my door? I want to get at some things for the next hour or so. If anybody calls, I'll call them back in a little while." The door closed, leaving him in the silence. He creaked back in his chair, loosely crossed his legs on the top of his desk, and lit a slim cigar. He congratulated himself. Well, well, well, he thought, after all this time she finally came around. He drew on his cigar. She really was a fine girl. The finest he had ever had. He smiled slightly to himself.

10

Paul Finch was packing his brief case with assorted papers. Most of the time he did not open it and he did not expect to this time, but after years of carrying a brief case, he felt undressed without it.

The telephone rang.

"You about ready, boy," the peremptory voice of the Judge rasped. "My hat will be full of quarters if you don't get down here soon."

"On my way," Paul said. "Just getting a couple of things together."

"You don't need all that crap, boy. You aren't a salesman, you know."

Paul hung up and took the elevator to the small lobby. The Judge was sitting in his wheel chair. Paul went ahead to open the glass doors, and then hailed a cab. The Judge was heavy on Paul's arm as he slowly eased himself into the back seat. Paul folded the light aluminum wheel chair, put it in, and got in himself.

"Damn nuisance, these pieces of tin from Detroit. Like trying to crawl into an upholstered sewer pipe. I'm going to have a cigarette," the Judge said. "That damn doctor says one after each meal. That's only teasing me. Can't exist on that."

"I have three or four pipes a day," Paul said. "Of course they last about half an hour."

"You ought to quit that too, boy. Pipes carry all sorts of un-fortunate connotations for different people. No sense in arousing the antagonisms of these people you talk to even before you open your mouth. People associate it with pomposity, universities, and slow thinking. You ought to cut it out."

"I've thought about it," Paul said evenly. "But I've about decided they'll have to take me as I am. For better or worse."

"Nonsense," said the old man. "You may cuss, but you don't cuss in front of the minister, do you?"

"I toe the line on important things. I ought to be able to have a few quiet vices."

"Have it your way. Hance asked me to bring you along to-day. I had some doubts about it, but he said you might learn something. So I am." He drew on his cigarette. "You weren't even planning on talking to Burnett, were you?"

"I had him at the bottom of the list," Paul said candidly. "There are so many people to see and not enough time to see them, so I thought I'd concentrate on the possibilities."

"Burnett wasn't on your list of possibilities?"

"No, frankly, he wasn't. His past record—"

"Past record, my ass. That's what comes of trying to figure out human beings by reading the newspapers and *Congressional Quarterly*. It takes experience, plus some horse sense of your own, not some warmed-over ideas of a reporter, who probably gets his ideas warmed over from some other reporter." He drew on his cigarette again and said: "Burnett is on the fence on this bill, boy, whether you know it or not. He should be on your 'definitely possible' list."

"That's hard to believe. Why would he go for a bill like this after all these years?"

"Believe it or not, it's true. The unions discovered it a few days ago, and it shocked the hell out of them. They figure if Bur-nett goes, how many others will kick over the traces?"

"I don't understand it. Why should Burnett vote against them on this?"

"Hard to say. People are complex. There are blind spots and odd quirks in all of us. Nobody ever does exactly what is expected of him all the time. We all occasionally surprise . . . I don't say he's going with us, mind you. I'd say our chances are less than

145

fifty-fifty. But that's a hell of a lot more chance than we've ever had before with him. And even more important, a few other fence-sitters might light on our side, if they see an old liberal like Burnett go for it. Covacks, Milton Deckler, Winthrop Whitmore, for instance."

Paul shook his head slowly. "It would really be something, after twenty years of militant liberalism. Vote for anything as long as he thought it was for the little fellow, for the underdog. Maybe some of these boys don't look so much like underdogs any more. If that's the case, then we have arrived at the millennium. If that's the case, I think the approach should be—"

"I'll take care of the approach. I've known Burnett for twenty years. Been studying him like a flea under a microscope. You just be quiet and listen. Might learn something."

Paul sank back into the cab, annoyed, and looked out the window for the rest of the journey. Neither spoke. At last the cab turned off Connecticut Avenue and down the lane of trees leading to the Columbia Country Club.

"Golf entrance, driver," Judge Russell said. As the car stopped, a Negro in a white coat opened it. "Well, Judge," he said, flashing a pink-and-white smile, "you goin' eighteen today?"

"Eighteen bourbons and water, Johnson. Better for you."

Johnson opened a cavernous pink mouth. "Sho is." He busied himself unfolding the wheel chair, and eased the Judge into it. "Men's Bar," the Judge ordered. "Senator Burnett in there?"

"Yas he is. Jus' come in. He's eatin' his lunch."

"Got anybody with him?"

"Yas, suh. One gentleman."

"Nobody you know?"

"No, suh, I don't."

Johnson rolled the Judge through the corridors, and Paul followed behind. They emerged in a smoky, paneled room. Two or three men lazed at the bar. One more was fixing himself a sandwich at the buffet. At two tables, men were playing cards. Two more sat desultorily in front of the television set. The Senator and Sidney sat at a table in the corner, next to the windows overlooking the swimming pool. Johnson wheeled the Judge over, with Paul following.

"Well," said the Senator, rising and dabbing his lips with a napkin, "the indestructible Judge." Introductions were made. Paul was introduced as a "fellow from my office who's going to take over some of the leg work."

"Sorry to bring you all the way out here," the Senator said, "but my schedule was tight and I had to be here on another matter, so I thought it might work out best all around."

"No trouble at all, John," the Judge said. "How do you like working for this fire-eater, young man?" said the Judge, addressing Sidney Bronstein.

"Fine . . . excellent."

"He'll work you to death. Man is a bear for work. Granddad on the rocks for me," he said to the waiter. "The Senator will have another. Sidney?"

"No thanks. I'm fine."

"Paul?"

"Scotch on the rocks."

"Judge," said the Senator, "I was sorry I didn't get out to see you while you were in the hospital. But they first told me that no visitors were permitted. Then I was out of town."

"Appreciate the thought, John. Nothing more useless than a broken-down lobbyist."

"Nothing more useful than a good one."

"Even if he never convinces?"

"Now, that is unfair. I have voted your way now and again. And I've always listened and learned a lot from what you had to say."

"You were merely probing the weaknesses of the enemy, I suspect."

The Senator laughed. "Well, I'm ready to be brainwashed on the subject of the labor bill. Why don't you boys begin?"

"Understand your mind is what might be described as open," the Judge said.

The Senator's eyes narrowed slightly. "Of course. Always."

"All right, John, I've never refused an invitation to talk yet. I think that you're in trouble down there on this labor thing."

"Why?"

"As I see it, stripping the whole thing of a lot of verbiage, false causes, and the rest, you've promised the country something that you're going to have one hell of a time delivering. For two years, you've had that investigating committee tramping up and down the land, trumpeting the evils of labor bosses, stirring up the people about labor crookedness. And they've done a good job. People all over this country are stirred up about this thing—really stirred up. The newspapers are crying for labor reform legislation. Now you have to give it to them and you've got a bear by the tail. Can you give it to them without politically destroying half the people in Congress and the Democratic party to boot? That's the question. I doubt it. On the one hand, you've got labor. They might be able to stop it if they dared, or if they were so stupid. Which I suspect they will be. I think they will stand to the last, bound and determined that no legislation gets through which is really going to hurt them. They'll *demand* that their congressman vote it down. On the other hand, out there in the countryside, in the congressman's district or the senator's state, people will be up in arms if there is no labor reform legislation this session. Any man who votes against it is going to be in real trouble. He'll be handing any opponent a great issue, and he'll be in a position which is too subtle to explain. The other guy will be tramping up and down the state saying: He voted for crooked labor leaders; he voted for the stealing and crookedness to continue. And he'll be making a few intimations as to why. How would you like to go out and campaign with that kind of black mark against you?" He shook his head. "As I see it, you are caught on the horns of a dilemma down there. A hell of a lot of people are going to be fighting mad, no matter which way you jump. I'm surprised to see that you let it happen."

"I think you're right, Judge. But I also think that the world is not that predictable. Nobody foresaw that it would turn out like this. Events have a way of shaping themselves, getting out of hand, just as they did here. . . ."

"I see this as a problem for you personally, John. You've got tremendous strength in Missouri. You're one of the great men of the Senate. You've always voted for labor, and you may this time too. But that halo is going to get tilted a little if you vote against this. You know that."

"Perhaps," the Senator said. "What you have said amounts to a good practical analysis of the problem. Now what about the other aspect?"

"What other aspect?" the Judge said.

"The simple moral question: In the best interests of this country, should I vote for or against this bill?"

"Oh, come on now, John," the Judge began.

"Politics isn't the only thing to be considered," the Senator said sharply.

The Judge leaned back in his wheel chair and eyed the Senator speculatively. "Well, I'll be damned, Senator. Do you mean to say you are entertaining thoughts of actually voting for this bill?"

"I didn't say that. I merely said there are considerations other than political."

"There always are. On every bill that comes up, aren't there? But you've never voted against labor on any important issue. Not that I can recall."

"Apparently I felt that the political and moral questions lay together," the Senator said. He turned to Paul. "How about you, young man? Do you see any moral question involved here?"

Paul was slightly flustered at being suddenly brought into the conversation. "Ah . . . well, yes, Senator, I do. It seems to me the question is: Has labor reached maturity to a sufficient degree to require them to obey the same laws that everybody else does? Is the period of protecting labor and tolerating labor's excesses, much as you do a child until it becomes grown—has that period passed? I think the answer is clearly yes."

"Interesting," the Senator said. "What do you say, Judge?"

"You know what I think, Senator. I think it's a good bill, a fine bill. It will bring democracy into these unions. It will put control of the unions back into the hands of the working people, and take it from the union bosses."

"And that's why you're for it?"

"Sure."

"You'll forgive me a little cynicism. But has Liberty Electric been all that concerned about the rights of the workers all these years? I must have missed some of your mailings."

"We're concerned. Sure we are."

149

"Judge, it's a little hard for me to believe that Liberty Electric is spending all this time and money out of some altruistic concern for the workingman. You run advertisements in the newspapers. You've got all your plant managers and your executives working on their local congressmen. You've mailed I don't know how many thousands of reprints of articles favoring the bill. You've formed committees. You've honored the sponsors of the bill at dinners. You've stirred up the Chamber and the NAM into a frenzy of action. Your company is working frantically day and night, as far as I can see, to push this bill through. Now all of this, you tell me, all of this is merely because you feel that the workingman is getting a raw deal."

"Partly, yes."

"Ah . . . partly. And what is the other part?"

"The other part is that we feel that the rest of the country— all of us—are getting a raw deal from these labor leaders. They have accumulated too much power in their own hands. They are dictators, little Caesars. They control the country. They control the movement of railroads, trucks, airplanes. They control the defense effort. They control the making of steel, automobiles, furniture, and everything else. We feel, simply, that the time has come to stop this. It is bad for our country to have men with such power. Fifty years ago, Congress recognized this same inherent evil in corporations, when it cut corporations down to size with the anti-trust laws. It's time the same thinking was applied to unions. If not, they will grow and abuse their power even more than they have, and that will be the end of this country."

"A slightly exaggerated presentation of the argument for my taste," the Senator said, "but you do have a point."

"Of course I do," the Judge said. "Senator, we've differed on almost everything that has been done over the last twenty years. But I've always respected you because even though you never voted my way, I thought that you had a view of things and you adhered to that view. But in all honesty, in all fairness, don't you think that the things I've just said are true?"

"As I said, you have a point."

"So," said the Judge, "the answer is clear, even though you decline to recognize it. This bill is in the interests of the workingman, and it's in the interests of the people as a whole. Clearly. What more can you ask?"

"Well," said the Senator. "I'd say there is one party in interest that needs a little more scrutiny."

"Who's that?"

"The Liberty Electric Company, and sundry other such organizations."

"We've mentioned them. I've told you. We're interested in the workers and in what's right for the country as a whole."

"But what's right for the Liberty Electric Company specifically, we have not touched upon. And that's the part that troubles me most."

"I don't follow you, Senator."

"Judge, the Liberty Electric Company has been in business for forty or fifty years."

"Fifty-seven."

"Fifty-seven. They opposed child labor laws because they could see nothing wrong with employing children of fourteen for ten hours a day, six days a week. They opposed the minimum wage law because they thought men should fight it out for jobs and offer themselves at the lowest possible price in order to get employment. They bitterly fought the Wagner Act, because their employees—who were at their mercy in matters of wages, discharges, or any other conditions they wanted to set—might not be so docile, might even fight back."

"Now, Senator. That's ancient history. You surely can't hold against us what happened twenty-five, thirty-five, or forty years ago. The men who did those things died years ago."

"And their places were taken, I suspect, by the same breed. Smoothed off, perhaps, but the same breed. Yes, I think I do have to hold it against Liberty Electric and the rest. When that opposition has followed one line and continues without abatement, perhaps even more violently, right up to now. What about public housing? I see it as an attempt to help the man at the bottom of the pile live a little better life. Not much better, but a little better. What does Liberty Electric think about it? Socialism. I think that unemployment compensation to tide over the family wage earner when he's out of a job preserves his self respect. What does Liberty Electric say? Socialism. Let him hunt for a job. He's probably a loafer or he wouldn't have lost it in the first place, and his empty belly will make him move a little faster. I think it might be a good idea if we gave national scholarships to deserving people, so that they could go to college, regardless of their income. I think it's criminal to deny this country the brains of those kids because they don't have money to continue their schooling. A criminal waste. What does Liberty Electric think about it? Socialism. It will give the Government control over the schools. I think a man who has worked hard ought to retire with a minimum income provided by Social Security, so that he won't be helpless and dependent in his old age. What does Liberty Electric say? Socialism. And so, when Liberty Electric comes around now and says we're spending all this money and all this time because we want to give the working class a fair shake, you'll pardon me if I am a bit skeptical. You know as well as I do that Liberty Electric has put everything it has behind this bill because it thinks that it will substantially weaken the bargaining power of the unionized worker. That's about it, Judge. Be frank."

"No," said the Judge. "We're interested in the country as a whole. We're part of it. We may not have been leading the liberal parade, but there were some important matters of principle involved."

"And those principles were, I suggest, the right of property to be amassed over the years and handed down through the centuries to people who never earned it, to permit them to live, not by the sweat of their own brows, but by the sweat of others. The principle of the right to amass enormous quantities of wealth, more than any one man could ever spend in a lifetime, while ignoring the plight of most of the people in the world."

"You're being unfair. I'm talking about the basic principles that this country was founded on. The right of a man to work hard, and through his own initiative, earn the rewards and enjoy them, without undue interference by the Government—"

"And to share his wealth only if he feels like it."

"Basically, yes. He earned it."

"Well, I hate to tell you this, Judge, but I think you lost that battle several hundred years ago when they wrenched from your

152

ind the right to vote even though they didn't own property. Now
f you had only confined that vote to property owners, you would
aave made certain that the status quo was preserved, and that
propertied people ran things. A really crucial error for your side."

"Senator, I really don't understand you. You've got me con-
used. A while ago you were listening with apparent interest to
our point of view, and you said, did you not, that our argument
vas pretty good. Now you light into me like I was the devil in-
carnate."

"I'll tell you why," said the Senator, leaning forward intently.
"You people make me angry. You've seized an unfair advantage
from these hearings, and you've thrown all sorts of things into
that bill that have nothing to do with the investigations. You
know as well as I do that you've tried to jam every anti-union,
union-busting provision in the book into that bill. You think that
because the country is aroused about corruption you can slip all
of these things through to cripple labor and pay off some old
grudges. Sock it to them when they're down."

"Well, now, John, aren't we getting a little holier-than-thou
here? They've done the same goddam thing to us time and time
again. They hung the whole goddam depression on us and they've
been slipping things through, as you put it, ever since. So what
exactly is so criminal about our present activities?"

The Senator expelled his breath in exasperation. "From your
point of view, nothing, I suppose. To me, what was done in the
thirties was a brilliant step forward, and what you are trying to
do here strikes me as a step backward toward feudalism. To you,
just the opposite seems true. We're just too far apart in our basic
attitudes ever to agree."

"Are we, John?" the Judge said softly. "Aren't you thinking
of voting for that bill because you recognize that the dirty business has to be, must be, cleaned up—that the country demands
it?"

The Senator eyed him coldly. "Don't bet on it, Judge."

The Judge sensed that he had pushed the Senator as far as
was prudent. He extended his hand. "John, we part friends."

"Of course," said the Senator, without warmth, grasping the
hand and dropping it.

"John, I may have said some things that irritated you. For that I am sorry. I'd just like to say that I consider it a privilege that you make yourself available to listen to people who may have different points of view. You'd be surprised how many politicians don't. They congregate only with their own, and, as a result, they lose touch with the outside world, or at least that segment of it that doesn't hold their own point of view. I thought you'd want to hear our point of view, even though you didn't agree with it."

"I did enjoy hearing it. I don't agree with it."

"But it's important to have this exchange, isn't it? Better than meeting at the barricades."

"We'll never do that in this country."

"Probably not, if we talk long enough. John, me and my sidekick here are going to be off. It was a pleasure seeing you."

"I'm glad to see that a little thing like a coronary hasn't dimmed the fire, Judge," the Senator said, with a trace of his cordiality returning. Paul wheeled the Judge out to the car, and the Senator and Sidney rose. The Senator signed the check, and he and Sidney went out to the portico to wait for the cab that had been summoned by the switchboard girl.

"Well, what do you say, Sidney?" the Senator asked.

"You know what I think about the bill."

"That I should vote against it. And nothing said today changed your mind about that?"

"No. If anything, it firmed things up. I was a little surprised at one thing though, Senator."

"What was that?"

"You seemed to be angry, really angry."

The Senator slapped his hat against his thigh in some agitation. "I shouldn't have been so hard on the old man, but I just get sick, tired, and disgusted with the human race sometimes, Sidney. Everybody trying to edge out somebody else. Nobody talks about that, of course. They all talk about principles, the public interest, what's good for the country. But they're all sham words. What they are all talking about is getting the edge." The taxi turned down the drive and made the circle in front of the portico. "I may have outlived my usefulness, Sidney. I'm beginning to doubt the essential goodness of man. That attitude is necessary for a liberal. Otherwise he's done." He slammed the door of the cab and immediately rolled down the window and said, "I'll be at the Mayflower tonight at the Missouri Society party, if anyone wants to reach me."

"Well, what do you say, Paul?" the Judge asked in a jovial mood as they drove back downtown.

"Obviously, the bill's troubling him, I'd say."

"Obviously, but is it troubling him enough to cause him to vote for it?"

"I doubt it. I think he sees what needs to be done, but I just don't think he will break the thinking habits of a lifetime to vote for it."

"Well, we shall see. We shall see," said the Judge, with some satisfaction. "A few more people will talk to him, and we may talk to him again ourselves before it comes up for a vote."

11

Don Harrack waited, lounging against the chain-link fence of the Spartanburg airport as the plane touched the earth smoothly, taxied along the runway, and cut its motors with four simultaneous bursts of blue smoke. The steps were rolled up, and the passengers, clutching coats and brief cases, made their way down.

"Don, my boy, how are you?" Ed said, extending his hand. "Everything under control?"

"Most everything," Don said. "It's going to be tight. Just like I've been saying all along."

"Don, I'd like to have you meet Miss Merideth."

Don turned to Barbara, his eyes wide with surprise. "Happy to meet you, Miss Merideth," he said, looking her straight in the eyes.

"I won't get in the way, Mr. Harrack. I'll just watch from way in the back somewhere."

"Miss Merideth has never seen anything like this before," Ed said. "I thought it would be an education for her."

They drifted toward Don's car, after they had claimed their baggage.

"You new on the staff?" Don inquired.

"Oh, heavens, I'm not on the staff. I work for NBC in Washington."

Don's eyes crinkled. "Oh," he said, "is NBC interested in this?"

"No. I'm just on my own. Because I'm interested. I produce a children's show on their Washington station."

"I see," said Don. "I thought we'd go to my hotel and talk things over for a while. You all had lunch?"

"Yes, on the plane."

"I thought if we could run down a few things for an hour or so, it would be helpful. This is going to be a pretty important speech, Ed. I planned to go over just what I've done so far. Miss Merideth might like to look around Spartanburg a bit, if she hasn't been here before. Not that there's a hell of a lot to see."

"I'd love to," said Barbara.

"Or she could join us," Ed said. "She's not a company spy, I can assure you of that."

"I'd really like to look around a bit," Barbara said quickly.

They reached the hotel. Barbara, armed with a folder entitled "Historic Spartanburg," agreed to meet them at five o'clock in the lobby. A slow elevator took them to Don's small room.

Ed stretched out comfortably on the bed. "Not exactly princely," he said, looking over the flowered wallpaper and the straight-hanging flowered curtains.

"Ed," said Don, standing at the foot of the bed. "What the hell are you trying to do? I know you're president of this union, and I'm just a guy way down in the ranks. But what the hell are you trying to do?"

"What do you mean?" said Ed, loosening his tie and slipping his shoes off.

"That girl. What do you think I mean? Look, Ed, your private life is your own business, not mine. But why bring her along? Why take the chance? What is there to be gained?"

"I don't see any problem," Ed said. "Nobody's going to know she's even here."

"But it's a risk we don't have to take. This goddam election is balanced on a knife edge. All it's going to take is a little push one way or the other. That's why I wanted you to come down here. You are going to be that push. Now, I don't know . . ."

157

"What do you mean, you don't know?" Ed said irritably. "Here I am. I'll make the speech and it'll be a good one . . ."

"I'm not worried about the speech."

"Well, then what are you worrying about? You're jumpy as an old lady."

"You're damn right I am. Ed, most of these people are country people. Baptists, Methodists. This is the Bible belt. Sure, they screw each other and hell around, but if a guy gets too public about it, they crack down. And I mean crack down. He's ostracized. And they're bringing their wives to tonight's meeting. They'll all be there in the stands, sitting in twos. The family unit. Now I ask you, suppose they find out the big man from Washington, who has a wife and two kids, has brought a playmate. Jesus Christ, Ed, this isn't New York, where everybody thinks a mistress trailing around is just the latest thing. It's death. I mean it. It's death. If they find out about it, we might just as well not bother showing up tomorrow. The ball game is over."

"Oh, calm down, Don. Nobody is going to find out about it."

"Maybe yes, maybe no. But it's a risk we don't have to take. Please, Ed, pack her up and send her back to Washington."

Ed drew on his cigarette. "Don, I think you're upset over this election. That is not meant as criticism. You've worked hard on it, and I know it. But I think it's warped your judgment a little. You're making a mountain out of a molehill. The chances of any one even knowing she is here are small. One in a thousand. She's got a room up on the tenth floor. I'm down on the fourth. There won't be any problem, take my word for it. Now," he said, exercising executive privilege, "let me tell you what I've done with those three points you thought ought to be made. See if they sound all right to you. . . ."

For an hour they went over the speech, with Don sullenly slumped in a chair, and Ed pacing four steps up and down the narrow room, running over the material.

"O.K. What do you say?" Ed asked.

"Fine. I never had any doubts about the speech. Great. It will do the trick. If . . ."

"Stop worrying. I've been through these things before."

"So have I," said Don. "May I make a special request?"

158

"Sure."

"I changed my mind about meeting Miss Merideth in the lobby, as we planned. Let her go to her room, and we'll meet a little later for dinner. I know a place out of town where we'll be relatively safe."

Ed laughed. "Don boy, you need a vacation. You're getting paranoid."

"With good reason. I've been through a lot of these."

"All right, we won't meet her. But who's going to let her know? She should be back any time."

"I'll take care of that."

"O.K., Secret Agent X-9. You do that. I'm going to my room. Give me a ring when you're ready to go eat."

Don's anonymous Ford bounced through the chuck holes, looking, as it was intended to, like any one of the hundred cars in the line inching forward toward the fair grounds, where the rally was to be held. Dust rose in an orange fog and dimmed the overhead string of lights, which disappeared over the hill as if they were a surrealist dream of moons. A circling flashlight mooned them into an orderly line of parked cars.

"Tight as you can git, man."

They got out of the car and walked across the dry grass, past the empty animal pens and the bleak boarded-up exhibition buildings and concession stands. Ahead of them was the typewriter shape of the grandstand.

"Looks like a college crowd going to a football game, doesn't it?" Ed said. Don looked at him in astonishment. As they turned the corner of the grandstand, they could see a small wooden platform facing it, draped with the worn insignia of the American Electronic Workers Union. Half a dozen wooden folding chairs had been placed on it. A thin microphone stood in front of the chairs. There was no railing or podium.

"Had some flags borrowed," Don said, "till the Legion found out what they were going to be used for. Barbara," he said, without looking at her, "why don't you take a seat in the stands, and meet us at the car afterward."

159

"All right." She detached herself and disappeared into th
darkness of the stands.

Don led Ed to a small group of men halfway between th
stands and the platform, and introduced him to them.

"These are the guys who did it, Ed, if it's done. They're th
ones that have been talking, arguing, writing letters, and gener
ally working their asses off to give us the support we need."

"I'm proud to meet you," Ed said, shaking hands, holding th
strong bony hands of the men, looking each in the eye. He wa
glad for his tennis calluses. "I'm proud to meet every one of you
We've been through this ourselves, Don and I, and don't thin
we don't know that it takes just plain guts to get out in front c
the pack like you guys have done, particularly down here in th
South. If the union gave Congressional Medals of Honor, yo
guys are the ones that deserve them."

"Appreciate it, Mister Flowers. You think we're gonna win?

"I do," said Ed. "I don't doubt it for a minute. Not that w
should get overconfident and let down now."

"I sure hope we do," added another, " 'cause they'll sure a
hell fire us all if we don't."

"They can't fire you for union activity," Ed said. "The righ
to engage in union activity without penalty is provided for by th
law. They can't do it."

"They done it to mah brother," said the man stubbornl
"Fired him two weeks later. They just laid for him till he mad
a slip, then they done it. You cain't work for too long withou
making a slip a some kind or other."

"Listen to me," Don broke in with a red, angry face. "I
they try any of that crap with you, you let me know. They thin
their smart union-busting lawyers can get them off the hook. Yo
just let me know. We'll get any man that's let go reinstated wit
back pay. We'll jam it down their throats if they try that goddar
crap. So don't start spreading that kind of scare talk around
You'll all be in a hell of a lot more danger if we lose this electio
than if we win."

"I ain't scared," said the man. "I'm in, ain't I?"

"I'm sorry, Turner," Don said. "I just get my dander u
when they don't pay any attention to the law. I ought to kno

better. Well," he said, surveying the crowd, "we filled up the park. We better get started, I guess." He led the small group up on the platform, where they all sat down—Ed, comfortably, with crossed legs; the workmen, uneasily, unsure of what to do with their hands and feet. Don went to the microphone and slowly raised his arms in a Y shape over his head. Slowly, the buzzing stands subsided into silence. When there was absolute silence, Harrack spoke:

"Fellow workers, I'm not going to make a long speech. We want to leave time for beer drinking and sociability. You've seen enough of me and heard enough of me in the last six months to last you all for a while. So the first thing I'd like to do is something that's probably unnecessary, but it's something I think you ought to do. Sitting here on the platform are four men. Not big shots. Not smooth talkers. Just four ordinary men. Men you know. Men who've worked beside you at the machines for many years. But look at them again. Look hard. Because they're really not ordinary. In fact, they're quite extraordinary. They're a breed of man we could use more of, but don't see enough of these days. Men of courage. It isn't easy to do what these men did. To stand up, all alone, and say, 'I'm for the union, I believe in the union, I'll work for the union.' That's not an easy thing to do, when management has connections at the bank that holds the mortgage on your house, the bank that lent you money on the car, and the bank that lends money to the merchants so they can give credit. That's not easy to do when they say, 'You're going to be blackballed and you'll never get another job in this town as long as you live.' It's not easy to do when management says, 'Spy for us and we'll take care of you after the election. We'll make you a foreman and if you don't go along, we'll fire you.' Or if management suddenly shifts you off the machine you know, and puts you on one you don't know, and says, 'If you don't make the quota, out you go, and if you make one mistake, out you go. Then where'll you be, Mister? Who's going to feed those four kids then, Mister?' I don't need to go on. You know the story better than I do. But I just want to leave you with this one thought. Not all the heroes were made on the battlefields in World War Two. It's no doubt harder to recognize a hero when he lives right next door. But there are some heroes, right here in this state, right here in this town, and they're four of them, right here on this platform. Right there," he said, turning and opening his hand toward them. "Turner Hawkins, Jesse Hussey, Coleman White, and Sam Pottinger."

The ripple of applause, which had begun with the first name, gathered and burst forth when he finished. Raggedly the people rose, clapped hard, shouted, and stomped on the wooden stands. The four men stirred uneasily. When the applauding was over, Don began again in a low voice: "Folks, tomorrow is the day of decision for all of us. Tomorrow we all go to the polls, the way we do in America, and we decide whether we will stand up against the tremendous power of management as one man, or whether we'll let them pick us off one by one. I've done all I can. So have Jesse, Turner, Coleman, and Sam, and many more. The rest is up to you. No one will ever know how you vote in that booth tomorrow. No one but your own conscience. And if you follow your conscience, you'll mark the big bold X in the Yes column."

A scattering of applause.

"Now folks, I asked a man of real importance to fly down here from Washington to talk to you. And he did. He did because he thought you were the people of real importance, and he felt the least he could do, on this crucial evening, was to let you know that you're not alone tonight, or tomorrow. The whole union movement is watching this election. Your brothers in Massachusetts and Michigan and California are with you. Now, I'd like to introduce Mr. Edward Flowers, President of the American Electronic Workers. Ed."

The union band, five strong, whose services that evening were dedicated to the cause without charge, struck up "Solidarity Forever." The crowd applauded, and some of them sang the few words that they knew.

"Thank you, Don. Ladies and Gentlemen. It sounds as if I put myself out a little to fly down here to talk to you folks and to be with you in these hours before we go to the election booth. But I just want to tell you that I didn't put myself out. I was happy to do it. I was proud to do it. You know, when this country was founded by men like yourselves almost two hundred years ago, the slogan they decided on was a simple one, 'In union, there is strength.' Those few men, John Adams up in Massachusetts, Tom Jefferson up in Virginia, and three men from your own state of South Carolina—Tom Heyward, Tom Lynch, and Arthur Middleton—knew that they could not stand up to the King of England alone. The King had all the money, all the soldiers, all the guns, and the government was in his hands. If they had tried to stand up to him one by one, they would have been picked off one by one, and tossed in jail. There was only one way to break free of the tyrant, and that was to join together. As one of them, Ben Franklin, said, We'd better all hang together, or we'll all hang separately. They took a big chance, those few daring men, because the odds were all against what they were trying to do. And yet they knew that in union, there is strength, and there was. Despite the tremendous odds, they won. They won. It was not easy. It was a long war; many lost their lives and their property. But they won something important. Something so important that it has been handed down in these United States ever since they won it two hundred years ago. It's something that they are handing to you tomorrow when you enter the booth. It's a very simple thing. The right to decide whether you will run your own lives or whether you'll turn that right over to the tyrant, King Peter Hillstrom the Second . . ."

There was laughter and applause.

"King Peter, I'm told, has been telling you all sorts of things. He hasn't said he'd hang anybody who voted for the union, but I bet he would if he could. But he's told you he might have to close up the plant. Now that's nonsense. He just moved here five years ago, and he designed that plant himself. It's his baby, and he spent a good chunk of the Hillstrom millions on it, and it's not an easy thing to pick up and move. No, Pete Hillstrom has too close a fist on that buck, ever to close that plant. What he means is, he'd like to punish you by closing the plant, but it would cost too much money, so he'll leave it open and cuss about it.

"He's also said he'd get the ringleaders of this union effort if it took his last penny. Well, folks, Peter Hillstrom is not noted for parting with pennies, and you can be sure he will make some trouble, but when it hits his pocketbook, he'll start wondering if it's really all worth it. Plenty of management people have said that before, but they find, after a while, and after they've lost a few pennies, that they might just as well live with the union. It costs too much to fight it, and since they're businessmen, they see this sooner or later.

"There's one thing I'd like to talk about and I'd like to face it square. The management has told you that if you vote for a union, you'll have to take Negroes in as equal members, and that before long you'll have Negro foremen over you. And that will lead to a lot of things that we don't even like to think about. I understand they've been circulating among you some juicy quotes, taken out of context, all of which are supposed to show that we're Yankees, out to make the colored people kings in South Carolina at your expense. Let me just explain this whole matter for a moment. If you choose this union, it will be your union. It will be your local and your officers. Your constitution and bylaws. The local will be made up from people working for the Airython plant, people who live right around here. And the officers for that local will be elected by the members of the local and they will be your people, your neighbors. And I'd like to say this: As long as I am president of this union, there will be no attempts to force down the throats of the locals or their membership, rules and regulations and ideas which the great majority of them wholeheartedly oppose. And if I try, or anybody else tries it, your local has the right to withdraw from the American Electronic Workers. So don't fall for this desperate, last-minute management scare campaign. It gives us a good indication of how worried they are when they resort to telling lies about us. Now you may say, what about all those mixed locals, and what about the picture they circulated, showing me with my arm over the shoulder of the president of one of our Northern locals, who happens to be a Negro. The answer to that is this: All our mixed locals are up North. They're mixed because that is the way the Northern members wanted it to be. We wouldn't consider forcing them to unmix if they like it that way, any more than we would consider forcing you to mix, even if we had the power to do so, which we don't. Well, I don't think I need to say any more about this, except this will be your local, and you'll run it the way you like. Just don't fall for this lying management attempt to destroy the union.

"I see that there are quite a few ladies in the audience, and I'd like to address a few words to them. We're all glad that you came, and I think we all know why you're here. It's simply because you know that although you won't be going into the voting booths yourselves, something very important will be decided in those booths tomorrow. Something that will directly affect you. And you're right. Tomorrow your husbands will be voting for more groceries and more money for the kids' shoes, that's true. But they'll also be voting something more important than that, for themselves. They'll be voting themselves the right to stand up and say what they think, and be certain that management will listen to what they have to say. That's important to a man, more important, maybe, than you think. How many times has your husband come home, mad and frustrated at some grossly unfair act at the plant, or how many times have you known that he was pushed around and had to keep his mouth shut about it 'cause he had to hang on to that job to protect you and the kids, so he blew off to you. Tomorrow they'll be voting for a union that won't let that happen, that will make sure they can stand up and have their say, that will force management to correct things that are unfair, that won't let them get pushed around. Don't you think a man that has these rights might be easier to live with than a frustrated, bottled-up man, angry at everything, even you? I think so.

"Let me say a little bit about economics. Now, economics is a long word that college professors like to use, but real economics is pretty simple. I want to talk about the laws of economics as applied to wages. When a man wants people to work for him, he advertises in the paper, or asks around if anybody knows people that would like to work. And when somebody comes in and asks him about a job, how much does he pay them for that work? Well, if he's a smart management man, he asks around to find out what other people are paying for such work, and what is the least he can pay and get people to come and work for him. The *least* he can pay for them and get them. No more than that, because if he pays more, he's just taking it out of his profits, and for no good reason except out of the goodness of his heart, and there's damn little of that in most management men. Excuse the swearing, ladies. So when you go in for a job, he says, 'Joe over there said he'd work for fifty cents an hour. I'm about to hire him, unless you can make me a better offer than that.' Well, maybe you're pretty hard up, need the money for food, so you say, 'I'll work for forty-five cents.' Then he says, 'Just a minute,' and he goes over and tells Joe. Then he comes back to you and says, 'Joe says he'll do it for forty cents. How about you?' That's how it works. Those are the laws of economics in operation, and in bad times, when a lot of people are out of work and looking for it, you can see how low that wage can be beaten down. That's the way it always was, until people decided they just couldn't stop this unless they banded together. And so they did: they formed unions. All the people that had acquired a particular skill over years of training banded together for their mutual aid and protection. Then they went to the employers and said: 'We're not going to bid against each other for jobs any more. We demand that you pay a living wage, and if you refuse to pay a living wage, well, none of us is going to work for you, and you just won't get any work done.' Well, folks, you can imagine what a stir that caused among the employers. They called these men every name you can think of. They tried to have them thrown into jail for conspiracy, or horsewhipped, and in those early days they succeeded. They passed laws, and they tried every trick in the book. But you folks down here surely know the old saying that you can lead a horse to water but you can't make him drink. They could throw those men in jail, but they couldn't make them work if they didn't want to. So, slowly, over the years, the unions gained strength, because people supported them and wouldn't cross their picket lines, and management couldn't hire enough scabs to do the work, or if they could, the scabs couldn't turn out the quality of work that a man trained for years in the trade could. Finally, gnashing their teeth, the employers had to recognize the union and the rights of their employees. But they never did it willingly. They fought it every step of the way; they're still fighting it, and they always will. Just the way Peter Hillstrom is fighting it. He wants to have it like it was in the old days. Low wages and high profits. Fire people after they've worked there twenty years if he gets out of the wrong side of the bed in the morning. Work them twelve hours a day, eighty hours a week if he feels like it. No wonder he hates the union; no wonder he's fighting it with everything he's got. He knows that the union will demand a living wage for every man in that plant and a fair share in the profits produced by the sweat of their brows; he knows he won't be able to fire people just out of whim; he knows that he will be forced to treat everybody fairly, or answer to the union of his employees; he knows the union won't permit unsafe conditions in the plant, or speed-ups, or sweatshop working conditions. He knows that when the union comes, the good old days for him will be over. So he fights. But he's going to lose. He's on the wrong side of the history book. History is marching right along with us and leaving Mr. Peter Hillstrom behind.

"Well, folks, you can see how I feel about this, and I think I've said about enough. I want to leave time for us to have a few glasses of beer, and I'd like to shake the hand of every one of you, if I can manage it. But before I sit down, I'd like to ask you to do something which may seem a little silly to you, but it's symbolic. I'd like to ask that each of you stand up and link your arm with your neighbor on either side, so that the whole grandstand full of people are linked together."

Self-consciously and awkwardly the people stood up and linked arms.

"Now each of you can feel the flesh and blood of the people on either side of you—the arms of your friends, your neighbors, your co-workers. This is the way we should march down to the plant tomorrow, if we could, to show Mr. Peter Hillstrom that he can't break us up, he can't come between us. What's good for one is good for all. We're united, joined together in this great effort to improve our living standards and demand the respect to which we are entitled as human beings as good as Hillstrom. And when you're there in the voting booth, alone with God, just remember how, a few short hours before, you were standing, arms linked, neighbor to neighbor, friend to friend, husband to wife. And if you remember this night, you'll know that there is only one way for you to vote. Ladies and gentlemen, by tomorrow night a new era will have begun, if you make it come. Thank you and God bless you."

12

For a moment after her eyes opened, Barbara thought that there was a strange man in the room. But it was Ed, standing barefoot, with his silk dressing gown hanging from his shoulders, staring intently out of the hotel window at the gray light of the dawn over Spartanburg. He was motionless; the only moving part in the scene was the smoke curling from his cigarette.

She contemplated him. His curly reddish hair uncombed and matted. The triangle of wrinkles at the corner of his eyes. The twin lines between his eyebrows that appeared when he was thinking, like quotation marks. His reddish beard bristles glistening in the first rays of the sun. His big hands, laced with the same fine-spun hair at the wrists, freckled underneath, shadowed with a network of veins. Those big hands that caused her to tingle when he laid one on the back of her neck, that caused a curious constriction in her loins when he held her breast. The writhing heat as one of them stroked her softly between the thighs. The searing touch of his finger in the quick of her. The gentle abrasion of his tongue against her swelling nipple.

"Hello," she said.

"Hello, angel, you awake? It's early yet."

"I've been watching you."

"You have? And what did you see?"

"I saw you were thinking hard about something. Worried about something. The election?"

"No. No sense in worrying about that. Nothing we can do at this stage anyway."

"Well, what is worrying you?"

"Us," he said shortly, grinding out his cigarette in the glass ash tray on the window sill. He sat down on the edge of the iron bed, which gave a screech of protest.

"I thought that was all settled," she said.

"So did I. But it's not. At least not for me." He turned his eyes to hers. "I'm in trouble. I want to marry you."

A tender smile was on her lips. "Eddie. . . ."

"I don't know how it happened. I was handing you a lot of sweet talk and malarkey, and suddenly I found out that I meant it. I love you like a silly school kid." He scrutinized his fingernails carefully. "But marrying you is easier said than done. There is a little matter of a wife of twenty years' standing, to say nothing of a couple of kids." He got up, jammed his hands in the sagging pockets of his dressing gown. "God knows I don't want to hurt anybody. I hate to hurt people. I've been married to Agnes for twenty years, and I have a great affection for her. I wouldn't want to hurt her any more than I'd want to hurt my mother. But I don't love her, and I haven't for a long time. For a while it worked out all right. I've been living my own life, and she hasn't asked many questions. Now you come into the picture and I'm caught up like somebody trying to swim in a flood. I've turned selfish. All I want is you. All I want to do is marry you. So what am I supposed to do? What do they want me to do? Forget all about you? Live out the next thirty years of my life with Agnes, pretending I love her? You spend only one lifetime on this earth, and I've frittered away more than half of mine already. Now I am supposed to spend the next thirty years in confinement. They try to trap you, box you in with moral pressure. And that's just the way I feel. Boxed in. I don't want to spend the rest of my life with Agnes. I want to spend it with you."

"What can I say, Ed? I can't help you."

"Nothing. Nothing anybody can say."

"I feel sorry for your wife."

"I feel sorry for her too. But I married her when I was twenty-six years old. Do I have to stick with that forever, even if it makes me unhappy and her unhappy and you unhappy? Till

169

death do us part. Don't they ever consider that people change? God, I'm a completely, totally different person from when I was twenty-six. Different standards, different objectives, different ideas. Everything about me is different. But they make no allowance for that. I'm supposed to stay in the same old mold, even if I don't fit any more. Besides," he gesticulated as if he were arguing with someone, "what kind of a life will she have if I do stay with her? We're never going to be happy together. Now I have no feeling for her but pity, but if I don't leave her, I'll resent her. And I'll show it. I know it. I can't be sweet and pleasant to her for the rest of my life when I secretly regard her as a ball and chain. I don't think anybody can do that. . . ." He stopped and looked at her questioningly.

"Ed, I just don't want to say anything."

"Don't blame you. What can you say? You want to get married and try to squeeze out a little happiness, but you don't like to hurt people either. It's just that you're once removed, so you don't feel this part so intensely. You couldn't be expected to." He sat on the bed, his ropy hands hanging between his knees. "I've racked my brain to think of some way to handle the whole mess, but there isn't any. I'm a coward about it, because I know how it will affect her. She has no place to go, and nobody to help her. We haven't been back in Fall River for seven years, and, besides, her people are all dead. She's never liked Washington, and never has made a lot of friends. And I kick her out, after twenty years, into a world she doesn't know much about. She won't be able to make any sort of a new life. I know her well enough for that. She'll just exist until she dies. You don't do that sort of thing easily. I've been trying to think of some way I could ease the blow, help her along. But hell, I can't think of anything. What can I do? There's money, of course. That goes without saying. She'll have plenty to live on. But I know how it will be. It will be like half of her has been amputated. Half her world, half her feelings. She's built her world around me and the kids. We're it. There just isn't anything else." He slumped down in the chair in despair. "Why does this world have to be such an utterly goddam stupid place to live in?"

She laid a hand gently on his arm. "Nobody knows the answer to that."

"Barbara," he said, turning to her, "do you really know what this has been all about?"

"Well, yes . . . maybe not. I don't know."

"It's the death rattle of my conscience. I'm going to ask Agnes for a divorce when we get back to Washington."

Tears welled up in her eyes. "All I can say is I love you, Ed. I didn't mean to do any harm, or hurt anybody."

He patted her hand. "This isn't your fault. I'm the one who got us into this. I made the advances. You didn't."

"I was interested, though, from the beginning. I knew I shouldn't be, but I couldn't help it."

"I have only one suggestion for the scientists of the future," he said. "If they want everything to go smoothly in the human race, they should breed out all emotion. All the rules and regulations are based on reason, but emotion rules the world. That causes a few problems. Anyway, this time I'm going to stick to it. The decision is made. I've been off and on about it so much that I thought I'd go out of my mind. This time I'll stick to it."

She said nothing.

13

The Senator sat in his library, methodically going through correspondence that his administrative assistant felt was more than routine. Some of it, which required personally dictated letters, he set aside on the floor; and on the rest he scribbled hieroglyphics decipherable only to Dick Goetz.

His wife opened the door quickly and startled him with a sharp "John! Leona's on the phone. She's terribly upset about something. She won't say what and she won't talk to me. She just keeps saying she has to talk to you."

He set his papers aside and came through the door. "Trouble of some sort for her to call at this hour." He took the phone and spoke noncommittally for a few minutes as his wife stood by, trying to piece something together from his remarks. He hung up.

"What is it?"

"Her son's in some trouble with the police. Rufus. Is that his name? Apparently it's pretty serious. Assault was about the only word I heard."

"Are you going down there now?"

"She wants me to. I guess I'd better."

"It's awfully late. The poor dear!"

He slipped into his coat and took his hat.

"Are you going to the police station?"

"No, her house."

172

She kissed him on the cheek. "Call me if there is anything I can do."

He left and caught a cab on Wisconsin Avenue. The cab made a U turn and raced through the empty streets. Finally, the cab slowed to a crawl.

"That it?" the driver asked. "Don't see no number, but it should be."

"I don't know," the Senator said. "Never been here." All the lights on the first and second floors of the house were burning. "I think this must be it." He paid the cab driver, and went up to the front door, which was flung open almost as soon as his finger touched the bell.

"Praise God," said Leona. "Oh, praise God you came."

"What's the trouble, Leona?"

"Oh, Mister Senator, it's bad. Very very bad." She burst into racking sobs.

"Why don't we sit down and you tell me about it?" He led her through the arch into the living room. It was filled with people. There was a Negro policeman and a white man in plain clothes, whom he took instantly for a detective. A Negro man sat in obvious fear on the sofa, and a Negro girl stood nervously smoking a cigarette.

"Detective Sheehy, Senator," said the white man, stepping forward and extending his hand. "This is Sergeant Brown," he said, indicating the policeman.

Leona sank in a heap on the sofa as the men shook hands.

"I'm Mrs. Smith's daughter, Ellie Mae," said the Negro girl. "This is Mr. Smith, my father."

"Well, suppose you tell me what this is all about," the Senator said.

They all looked at one another, but no one spoke. Finally, Detective Sheehy said, "Her boy Rufus, and another boy, Orton Carter, attacked a woman. Physically beat her up I mean, not sexually attacked. Sergeant Brown was making his rounds when he heard a scuffle and some screams. He lit out for the corner on the double, and this colored kid came around the corner and almost smacked into him. That turned out to be this Orton kid."

"Orton Carter," said Ellie Mae.

"So he yells for the kid to stop, but he don't. So he wings him. In the leg. Nothing serious. And he saw this other kid, this Rufus, running like sixty, but he was gone down the alley like a shot. That's it, isn't it, Sergeant?"

"That's right," the sergeant said.

"They beat up this woman pretty bad. About sixty years old. The doctors say she might die. They took her to the hospital. If she dies," he said, turning to Leona, "the charge will be murder, of course."

Leona gave a low moan.

"There was no cause to beat the old lady up, Senator. All she had was a purse. They could have grabbed that and run. A sixty-year-old woman wasn't going to take out after them. Anyway, Brown here had the presence of mind to scare hell out of this Orton kid. I guess the kid thought he was going to finish him off, and it wouldn't be no loss if he had. The Orton kid told us the name of this kid and where he lived. We staked out a man in front and back, and sure enough, he came sneaking in about two hours later, and we grabbed him."

Leona rose abruptly. "Senator, you got to help me. Rufus is a good boy. He never been in trouble before."

"How many times have I heard that?" the detective said.

"I'll do what I can, Leona. You don't have to worry about that."

"God bless you. You a lawyer and you can help. You know how to talk about these things. You can tell the judge."

"Well, Leona, we'll get you a good lawyer. But understand, I won't personally handle the case. I haven't been in criminal practice for thirty-five years."

"Oh, but Mister Senator, you got to. They'll listen to you. Please," she said, with tears running down her cheeks, "please Mister Senator. Please help me."

He grasped her by the arm. "I'm going to help you, Leona. But, you see, you'll want a man who's read all of the cases and knows criminal law in the District of Columbia. Believe me, he will do a better job for Rufus than I could do. It's not that I don't want to take the case and help Rufus. It's just that he'll have a

174

better chance if a practicing lawyer represents him. You just trust me, will you?" he said, giving her a pat.

"All right. Whatever you say. . . . Lawyers costs a lot, don't they? I haven't got much money. I mean, most everything we got is tied up in this house."

"Don't worry about that. We'll work that out somehow. Detective Sheehy," he said, "has the boy been arraigned?"

"I imagine so."

"Would there be any objection to my talking to him?"

"Well, I don't know about that," the detective said uneasily, "since you're not going to be his lawyer." He paused. "I tell you, Senator, let me call the station house and see what they say. This is a little out of my line."

"Fine."

He left the room quickly and began dialing the telephone in the entrance hall.

"What do you think they'll do to him, Senator Burnett?" asked Ellie Mae.

"Miss Smith, I don't know. The evidence does sound incriminating. But, of course, they didn't catch Rufus in the act. Brown didn't actually see him, as I understand it. Perhaps he didn't have anything to do with it. The other boy apparently incriminated him. Has anybody talked to Rufus?"

"No," said Leona. "We were all here when the police came for him. But he just clammed up and wouldn't say anything to anybody. We all went down to the station house, but he didn't say a word there either, except he gave them his name. Then they took him away. They told us we might as well come home, they'd let us know. About half an hour later they showed up and began questioning us."

"How old is he?" the Senator asked.

"Eighteen."

"Does that mean they goin' to say he's a man?" Leona asked.

"I'm not sure, Leona. I'm not acquainted with the laws of the District in that detail. I would guess from what the detective said that they will. Is that right, Sergeant?"

"Yes, sir, that's right. If he's eighteen or over."

"Captain says it's all right," said Detective Sheehy, entering the room. "He don't think you're going to get much out of him. He hasn't said word one to anybody. Then, of course," he added, "no senator has talked to him yet."

The Senator glanced quickly at the detective. "All right, I'll go down and have a talk with him. I'll call you, Leona, as soon as I'm able to."

"Can't I come? It's my boy."

"Leona, I just have an idea it would be better if you didn't. I'm afraid you'd have difficulty controlling yourself, and I think that it's much more likely that he'll talk if you're not there. I know it's hard for you, but I think it's best. Get some sleep if you can, and I'll call you."

"We'll run you down, Senator. Special service of ours for VIP's," said the detective.

The two policemen and the Senator departed together. They rode along in silence for a while, with the sergeant driving and the Senator and the detective in the front seat beside him.

"Nobody's asked me for any advice, but I don't know as I would get all involved in this if I was you, Senator. The boys did something and they ought to be punished for it."

"May I ask you, Detective Sheehy," the Senator said, "there was no sexual attack involved here, was there? You're sure of that?"

"Nope. That's right, isn't it, Sergeant?"

"Yes," said the sergeant. "They only seemed to be interested in robbing her and beating her up. Her clothes was torn up a little, but not like they was trying to rape her."

"It was a mean one, Senator. Beating up an old lady like that for no reason at all. They could have grabbed her purse and run. Maybe even knocked her down in the process. But it seems to me there isn't any defense for beating her up the way they did."

"What's your idea on why they did it, Sergeant?" the Senator asked.

The sergeant cleared his throat. "I don't know for sure, Senator Burnett. We see this kind of thing once in a while. Seems like they just lose their heads, forget where they're at or something. They seem to get kind of insane and strike out and slash like crazy people. I've seen it once or twice before."

176

"Was the old lady very badly hurt?"

"Seemed like it to me. I'm no doctor, of course, and sometimes blood gets spattered around from cuts that really aren't too bad. But she looked right bad off to me. They gave her a shot of something, and they was very careful getting her into the ambulance. . . ."

They arrived at the Sixth Precinct station house, and parked the car. As they entered the brightly lit charging room, a fat sergeant turned his swivel chair and peered at them over the huge book.

"This is Senator Burnett. Sergeant Murray."

The sergeant rose and came through the squeaking gate, from behind his little fence. "Happy to meet you, Senator. The Captain said it was all right for you to talk to the prisoner, even though you're not his lawyer."

"That's very kind of him."

"Only the Smith kid is here. The Orton kid is at the hospital. The bullet just cut the flesh a little, but they got to be careful, so they're keeping him there for observation."

"It was the Smith boy I wanted to talk to."

"He's in fourteen, Brown," said the desk sergeant, handing Brown a large ring of keys. "You better sit around the corner there, in case there's any trouble. You know this boy, Senator?"

"No. His mother is a friend of mine."

"O.K. Well, Brown here will be around the corner at the end of the cell block. Just sing out if he tries anything. We stripped him, so you don't have to worry about him having a weapon."

"One thing more, Detective Sheehy, if I may—"

The detective nodded.

"Have you talked to the other boy yet, and if so, what did he say?"

"Well, the Carter kid was right talkative at the hospital," Sheehy said. "Brown caught him dead to rights, so there wasn't much he could say. He said he grabbed the purse, but it was the other kid, Smith, who beat her up. That probably isn't entirely true. He seemed like he was lying to me. How about you, Brown?"

"I agree," Sergeant Brown said.

"As for the Smith kid. He wouldn't open his mouth at first. I

177

guess he figured that since we hadn't caught him in the act, we might not be able to charge him. But when I told him this Orton kid had incriminated him and put all the blame on him, he busts out cussing and crying and said it was Orton that beat her up. Take your pick. My guess is that they both did it. In a spirit of good clean fun. After that, he clammed up and he hasn't said a word to nobody since."

The Senator nodded wearily. "Well, let me go back and have a talk with him." Sergeant Brown unlocked the metal door to the cell block and tossed one of the keys to Sergeant Murray, who locked it after they had gone inside. Inside the cell block, the sergeant unlocked the gate in the bars, then locked it behind them. They proceeded down the block. Some of the cells were empty. A dark form was sprawled on the floor of one. Out of another a thin black arm reached out. "Lawd, help us," said its occupant. They reached number fourteen, and the sergeant peered in to satisfy himself that the prisoner was not in a dangerous position. He unlocked the metal door, and the Senator stepped inside. The door clanged shut behind him, and the key clicked promptly. The room was not lit, except for a small beam of light that came through the opening in the door.

"Rufus," he said.

There was no answer. He walked over and laid a hand on the form on the cot.

"Leave off me," said a voice.

"Rufus, I'm John Burnett. Your mother and I have been friends for many years and she asked me to come down and see you."

"Screw her."

The Senator paused. "Rufus, I don't need to tell you that you're in plenty of trouble. And it will go a lot harder for you if you won't let your friends help you."

"Go to hell."

"Rufus, I'm not interested in why you did what you did. All I'd like to know is exactly what happened. If we know that, then maybe we'll have something to go on in trying to help you."

"I don't need no help."

178

But the statement sounded as though he were on the verge of saying something else.

"Were you drunk?" the Senator persisted. "If you were, it might help."

"I'm done anyhow."

"Did you have anything to drink?"

Rufus looked at the Senator for the first time. "Me and Orton split a pint of lightning."

"When?"

" 'Bout nine o'clock."

"Then what? You wanted some more and didn't have any money," said the Senator, trying a random shot.

"I had a quarter. Orton didn't have nothin'."

"So you decided to snatch a purse and get some more?"

"Orton said we could do it easy. He said up on Butternut Street in Takoma Park mostly old people lived. They stayed there when colored moved in. And we could grab somethin' up there for sure, and they'd never catch us."

"So you thought you'd try it?"

"Yeah. We walked up there, and pretty soon we seen this old lady come outa her house. Orton say, 'She's goin' to the movies, so she'll have some money on her.' We followed her along for a while, on the other side of the street. Then when she come to a dark place, we jumped her."

"You jumped her? You mean you started beating her up right away?"

"Naw. I grabbed her purse, and she gave out with this goddam loud yell for an old lady. And Orton clobbered her one, but she keeps on screaming and screaming."

"And did you hit her?"

Rufus paused and turned his smoldering eyes on the Senator.

"I laid a couple on her," he said. "She was yelling her head off."

"I should have thought you would have run. But the police said that she was pretty badly beaten up. You must have kept at it."

"Somethin' caught on to me, and Orton too. There she was with her money, yelling, and Orton said, 'Shut up you old bitch

179

or I'll beat the piss outa you,' and she don't pay no attention, so he got mad and really began goin' after her, and somethin' caught me and I did too."

"You went after her too?"

"I was mad. Like I was crazy or something."

"Then what happened?"

"She fell down. She was knocked out and blood all over her face. Then we took off. Orton ran into the cop. I went down an alley and kept running for about half an hour. Then I laid down in this vacant lot to get my breath. Finally I got up and came home through the alleys where I could. I made it and I was just goin' up on my porch when this cop grabbed me. If that goddam Orton kept his mouth shut. . . ."

The Senator cast his eyes down into the darkness. No hope. No hope whatsoever. "Well, boy," he said, rising, "I'll see what can be done. We'll get you a lawyer."

"I don't want no lawyer."

"I'll get you one anyway. Just don't say anything more till he gets here. And don't start fighting with Orton and trying to blame each other for the whole thing. I'll be in touch with you. And your mother will be down to see you tomorrow. She was so upset we didn't think it would be advisable for her to come down again tonight."

"Tell her never mind," Rufus said. "I don't want to see her."

"She'll probably want to come anyway."

"I don't want to see her. Ain't I got any rights?"

The Senator rapped on the door. The key was inserted in the lock and the door swung open, admitting a shaft of light. He saw Rufus clearly for the first time. He looked no different from a hundred other Negro boys the Senator had seen. Bony. A haze of black hair which made him appear almost bald. The Senator stepped out the door, which Brown promptly swung shut and locked. He blinked as he emerged into the bright lights of the charging room. The detective was sitting in a chair which was propped against the wall, with the two front legs off the floor.

"Well, did he tell you he was walking down the street and everything went black and he don't remember a thing after that?" the detective asked.

"No."

"That's what he will be saying, after some smart lawyer tells him to."

"Senator," said Sergeant Murray, from behind his railing, "we talked to the hospital about the old lady."

"How is she?"

"She's on the critical list. That's all we could find out. I asked the doctor if she had a fifty-fifty chance, but he said that it wasn't his case and he wouldn't care to say."

The Senator shook his head, put his hat on, and started out the door.

"Senator," said the detective, "maybe this is out of line, but why are you concerning yourself in this case?"

"His mother is a friend of mine."

"And so you're going to try to get him off."

"No. The boy deserves to be punished. I'd like to make it easier for his mother."

"And so you're going to try to get him off," the detective repeated.

"I think he ought to get a fair trial. Besides, he's eighteen. Do we just give up on him and assume that he is going to be a criminal for the rest of his life?"

"I'm sure that's what some lawyer you hire for him will say. Plead temporary insanity or mental black-out and get him off scot free."

"He doesn't have a chance to get off scot free, you know that."

"Well, sixty or ninety days. That's scot free for what he did, isn't it?" He paused and examined his fingernails. "Tell me, Senator, how would you like it if that was your wife, face all smashed to a pulp, bones broken, on the critical list. Sixty or seventy years old. Old people's bones don't knit fast, you know. Sometimes they never do."

"I think the boy ought to be punished."

"But not too much. Why? Because he's colored, and he hasn't had the right opportunities, the right kind of family life. Things like that."

"Mike," said the cautionary voice of the sergeant.

"That's why I can't say much for these liberals, these bleeding-heart Democrats," he continued. "They're always so upset about the poor criminal and what society has done to him. They never give consideration to the victim. That's why I vote Republican, Senator. Absentee ballot, back in West Virginia."

"That's your privilege, Detective Sheehy," said the Senator. He tugged at his hat brim and walked out. He walked over to Georgia Avenue and caught a cab. He asked the driver what time it was. Four-thirty. He settled back in the darkness and closed his eyes.

When he got home, his wife snapped on the bed light as he came into the room. He told her briefly what happened.

"Terrible," she said. "What ever made them do it?"

"I don't know for sure. I was mainly interested in getting him to describe exactly what happened. He didn't have any reason that he could articulate."

"It was so senseless. So absolutely senseless and cruel."

"It's a senseless and cruel world to that boy." He slipped on his pajamas. "The detective down at the station house tabbed me as a bleeding-heart liberal. I guess he's right."

"What are you going to do?"

"Get him a lawyer. Leona was determined to have me act as his attorney, which is absurd. I tried to convince her that he'd be better off represented by someone who practices criminal law regularly, but I think that she just thought I didn't want to get mixed up in it."

"What do you think they'll do to him?"

"Dear, I just don't know District law. Partly it depends on the charge. I don't even know if he has any previous record. I'm pretty sure he'll go to jail, but for how long I have no idea. I'll know better after I talk to a lawyer in the morning."

He drew the covers over himself and pulled out the light. "If only they had just snatched the purse and run. . . ."

The next morning the Senator was up early. Leona would be awake and worrying. He hoped, wearily, to get a nap sometime later in the day. He slipped on his robe and went down to the library to call her.

"Leona. How are you feeling? Did you get any sleep?"

"Did you see him?" she asked.

"Yes. I had a talk with him. He didn't want to talk to anybody, but he finally told me the story. I thought I could call a lawyer friend of mine downtown, if that would be all right with you."

"Whatever you say."

"Fine, I'll do it when I hang up. One thing, Leona, has Rufus any police record?"

"No," she said vaguely, "I don't think so."

"Now Leona, you must tell me the truth. I'm trying to help you, and if he has a record, they'll have it at headquarters. You're not revealing anything."

"Nothing like this, Mister Senator. He was picked up once for taking a car and joy-ridin' around. They fined him and took away his license. And once they picked him up for stealing hubcaps, but they let him go because he wasn't old enough. I gave him a hiding anyway. But that's all, I swear to God."

"All right. How about this Orton Carter?"

"I don't rightly know, honestly. So far as I know, he's not been in any trouble since he came up here. But back in South Carolina, they said he was hard to handle. I wish to God he stayed down there where he belongs, 'stead of comin' up here and gettin' poor Rufus in this bad trouble." She was crying.

"Well, try not to worry. I'll do what I can. You can go down and see Rufus today. He may be a little nasty to you at first—I think you should expect that—but I think underneath he hopes that you'll come down to see him."

"I'll go."

"Fine. Well, let me call my lawyer friend. You'll hear from me."

"Mister Senator?"

"Yes."

"What they goin' to do to him?"

"I don't know, Leona. We'll know better after I talk to a lawyer."

"Is he going to prison?"

The Senator debated for a moment. "Leona, I think he well might. I think you ought to prepare yourself for that."

183

"Lord, Lord," Leona said. "I knowed it. How long will it be for?"

"I just don't know, Leona."

"Twenty years?"

"Not that long I wouldn't think," the Senator said, "but let me talk to the lawyer."

He hung up and decided to have breakfast, since it was only a little past seven and Alf Poole might not be up yet. Over breakfast, he read about the crime in the *Post,* and the report seemed reasonably accurate.

When he had finished breakfast, he called Alf and described the situation.

"I'll be frank with you, John," Alf said. "I'm not anxious to take the case. I've been turning most of my criminal work over to other lawyers. I've been moving out of that field, or trying to. There's nothing in criminal work but bad publicity and no fees. I hate to get back in it, particularly at this time when it will draw a lot of attention, the Negro problem and segregation being what it is right now."

"Alf, I called you because you're the best criminal lawyer I know, and this boy's going to need that."

"Senator, this case doesn't sound very complex. It's pretty cut and dried. You don't need the best criminal lawyer to handle it, and I'm not that anyway. . . ."

"Alf, I hate to put it this way, I really do, but would you take the case as a personal favor to me?"

There was a long pause at the other end of the line. "What can I say? Just keep me in mind when the next Supreme Court vacancy comes up," he said wryly.

"Thanks Alf, I really appreciate it."

"I'm doomed to be a two-bit criminal lawyer for the rest of my life, let's face it."

"What would you say are the chances?"

"Of what? Getting him off? Nil."

"How do you think it will come out?"

"Well . . . I don't see much to hang our hats on in what you told me. If you're thinking of temporary insanity, or one of those

184

defenses you read about in the newspapers, you can forget about it."

"What is the charge likely to be?"

"Did they have any weapon? Gun? Knife? Club of some kind?"

"Not as far as I know."

"Any previous record?"

"Took a car joy-riding once. Stealing hubcaps. Probably charged as a juvenile, but I guess he was released."

"Probably that's enough. It won't be a first offense anyway. What happens depends in part on what the U.S. Attorney charges him with, and he's been pretty tough lately. The papers have been on his back. They beat up this old woman pretty badly. It'll probably be assault and robbery."

"What kind of penalty does that carry?"

"If I had to guess, I'd say five to ten years. But it's hard to say."

The Senator thanked him, gave him the Smiths' telephone number, and asked Alf to keep him informed.

14

Ed Flowers rolled over, red-eyed from loss of sleep, to observe his wife lying in bed beside him. The night before, he had pledged himself that he would ask her for a divorce. He had conversationally circled the problem, as an animal circles a trap. Once he had been about to broach the subject when the telephone rang. He had started again, but one of the children had come in from a party. By the time he and Agnes were alone again, he just could not bring the words forth. He had settled behind the newspaper, pretending to read.

He rolled out of bed and went into the bathroom to shave. His brain was a dead lump of putty. He chewed his breakfast mechanically, and left for the office.

As he entered his office, the telephone was ringing.

"Mr. Harrack, from South Carolina," his secretary said.

He pressed the button. "Don?"

"Ed. Thirteen hundred forty-eight to twelve hundred seventy. We lost it."

"Oh, God, no. We lost it," Ed repeated, stunned.

"Seventy-eight goddam votes."

"Son of a bitch. Son of a bitch. That's impossible."

"It's a kick in the teeth. It's stupid. It's unexplainable. It's also a fact."

"Can we challenge?"

"We challenged as many ballots as we could. Fifty-two. But they won't be opened and counted, since they won't change the result. As far as challenging the election itself, we'll do it, of course. But I'll tell you, Ed, these guys had good legal advice, and they didn't make any serious mistakes. We ain't got the chance of a snowball in hell. I told you, Ed, that I thought it was going to be close. I always say that to keep everybody razor sharp on edge and moving. Frankly, I thought we had it. I was just wrong."

"Don't blame yourself, Don. You did your best."

"Hell, yes, I did my best. I been working my ass off night and day for the last six months, not counting all the time I put in on this outfit in Massachusetts. So what? My best wasn't good enough. I just wish some other people had done their best."

Ed paused. "What do you mean by that?"

"Nothing."

"You blame me? I gave you all the help I could. The money. The manpower. I flew down there. What more could I do?"

"You could have done less. Like not bringing that pussy down here with you. It was found out, Ed. Don't ask me how, and don't ask me how many people knew about it. Enough. We only lost by seventy-eight votes. If we had had forty of those, we would have been in. Some people just figured that you'd be using their dues money to buy that pussy fancy perfume and lace panties, and they didn't go for it. And the religious angle played its part too. They're death on that, I told you that."

Ed almost said that he was sorry, but he remained silent.

"I wouldn't be talking like this, Mr. Big, but I'm sending you a report, and my resignation is enclosed. I've had it."

"Now wait a minute, Don. Let's not be hasty. You're the best man we've got in the field. The most experienced and the most relied on by us to handle the really tough jobs. When you handle all the tough assignments, you got to figure to lose a few."

"Bullshit to that soft soap," said Don. "I'm quitting as of this week."

"Don, I think you ought to come on up to Washington, where we can talk this over after the dust has settled."

"No point in it. My mind is made up."

"Don, as president of the union, elected president, I'm requesting you to come up. Take a week off and go to Florida or something. Then come on up."

"Nope," said Don. "I've thought it all over very carefully, Mr. Flowers, and I just don't want to be associated with you or the kind of union you run. Is that plain enough?"

"All right. You're hot under the collar now, and I don't blame you. But I'm not accepting your resignation, and I'm not announcing it. As far as I'm concerned, you're on a leave of absence with pay. We'll send your checks wherever you want."

"Tear them up, or, better yet, don't make them out. They might fall into the wrong hands. I'm through, Ed. I'm through traveling around the countryside, like a tramp, trying to sell something that people don't want. Trying to sell it with no help from headquarters, and even being sabotaged from headquarters. I'll sell something that people want, like cars. But I'm through beating my brains out for you and the holy American worker, who's too goddam stupid to know what's good for him. And I'm also through talking to you. Do you have anything else to say?"

"Just think about it, that's all." The line went dead in his hand. Ed put the receiver back on the hook slowly. His buzzer sounded.

"Miss Merideth called. She seemed to be anxious to talk to you. Shall I get her?"

"No." He clicked off the intercom.

His lips half formed obscenities. Beaten. Beaten by that goddam, laughing, confident Hillstrom. He felt like crying, but no tears came. The whole NFL was watching that campaign. The *Federation News* had been playing it up as the current crucial battle for labor's army. Operation Spearhead. Operation Broken Spear. It would be a year before they could even try again, probably two, or even three, before it would really be practical. People would blame him. Hate him. Laugh at him. He wished suddenly that he were back on the bench. Soldering some electronic device, chatting with his benchmate, eating lunch out of a brown bag while sitting on the sunny side of the plant, his back against the warm bricks of the building, drinking a quart of milk out of a paper carton, drinking beer in the tavern in the evening, playing a little poker with the boys. Let somebody else do the working, sweating, making of decisions.

His buzzer sounded. "Miss Merideth on eighteen."

"What did you tell her I was in for?" he said furiously.

"Well, you didn't say—"

"I didn't say. You're supposed to be paid for having some sense." He cut her off. "Hello."

"Eddie darling. How are you? I know I shouldn't call you at the office, but I just had to know. Did you. . . ?"

"No, I didn't."

"Oh."

"Now get off my back. I'm going to do it, tonight. It just wasn't the opportune moment. We had interruptions."

"Ed, I'm so sorry. I don't want you to think I'm on your back about this. I know how hard it is for you, and believe me, I almost get sick, physically sick, when I think about your wife. I'm not pushing you. I just love you so. . . . Eddie," she asked wistfully, "is anything wrong?"

"No, I'll ask her."

"I mean is anything else wrong, at the office or something?"

"No, I'm just edgy. I'm sorry. I didn't mean to blow up at you. Least of all you."

"I sympathize entirely, and I'm an insensitive dope not to have realized . . ."

"It's not that," he blurted, "at least, it's not all that. We lost the election."

"Where? Down in Spartanburg? Oh, no. I'm so sorry."

"That's all right. It's not your fault."

There was silence on the other end of the line. "Was it, Ed? Was it my fault? Did they find out you brought me down with you?"

"No, no, of course not. You had nothing to do with it. We lost it fair and square. We just didn't have the votes."

"Are you sure?" she asked, with faint suspicion.

"Sure I'm sure. You had nothing to do with it," he said sharply.

She retreated. "Well, whatever the reason, I'm terribly sorry.

What's wrong with those people? Don't they know they have to have a union, otherwise they have no rights at all? After all, I'm a union member."

"So what's good enough for you ought to be good enough for an ignorant group of South Carolina mill hands," he said bitterly.

"I didn't mean it that way."

"Yes, you did, and you're right. But the answer is . . . God, I don't know what the answer is, unless it's just that they're too dumb to know better. That's the best answer I can give."

"Sweetie, I've got a show in eight minutes. Sorry I barged in, and I won't do it again. Love you."

She was gone.

15

For six weeks, Paul Finch had been working harder than he had ever before worked in his life. He was caught up in the tempo of activity which, like a saber dance, increased in speed and intensity almost beyond endurance.

In the last few weeks, the old man, Judge Russell, had faltered, then grimly thrown himself back into the fight, only at last to falter again. The crushing burden of work fell on Paul, who lived on sandwiches, coffee, and cigarettes, and worked late into the nights.

On the Hill, letters by the thousands were flooding into every senatorial office. The mail carts plied the halls of the Senate Office Building like tugs in a busy harbor, dropping bags at every door. In the offices, secretaries tended as many as half a dozen robot typewriters, which rattled out sterile but individual replies.

Paul walked miles on the marble floors of the Capitol and the Senate Office Building, retracing his steps dozens of times, waiting, idly chatting with secretaries in the senators' offices, or waiting in the crowded Senate reception room for audiences with senators. He had come to know the labor lobbyists who were traveling the same beat, sitting in the same waiting rooms, making calls to local unions all over the country, urging their members to send post cards, letters, and petitions to their representatives. Union and management lobbyists eyed each other with cold suspicion and mentally registered the name of the senator visited by the opposition. Senators were pursued with the relentlessness of bloodhounds, ferreted out, cornered in corridors, elevators, subways, and when getting into taxis.

He had been called and instructed by Rex Hance to cooperate with the effort being made by the electrical industry trade association. He spent hours at meetings of the Chamber of Commerce and the NAM, as those organizations attempted to coordinate the huge management effort and bring some order to it. In the NFL building on Seventeenth Street, similar shirt-sleeved meetings were being held, where speeches were written, television appearances arranged for, newspaper advertisements laid out and carefully composed.

He spent hours on the telephone, long distance, searching for the right people to talk with senators, briefing them on what to say. His lawyer assistant, Freddie Klinger, was red-eyed from analyzing substitute bills and amendments which might suddenly assume importance. Letters to editors had to be written, refuting unfavorable articles. Various diversionary tactics had to be exposed. The bill was labeled by a Washington columnist as a "civil rights bill in disguise." He said that it contained "sleepers" which would result in forced integration in unions. The Southerners, who had previously been for the bill, wavered until the bill had been closely examined on this point, and the allegation declared false. For three days and most of three nights, Paul had been working on a major speech to be delivered by a principal supporter of the bill.

With the vote only a little over ten days away, Paul was making a last-minute check on the effectiveness of the Liberty Electric Company.

"Mr. Abernathy from Seattle, Mr. Finch," Paul's secretary announced.

He picked up the telephone. "Horace? How's it going?"

"Pretty well, Paul," said the distant voice. "Pretty damn well. We're getting a lot of response from this thing. It seems like there was a lot of discontent out here looking for someplace to go. All they needed was to be told where to write and what to be for and what against. I bet we got a thousand letters or telegrams out of here in the last week. It's going like a house afire."

"That's great," Paul said. "If we just had a plant in every state, we'd have this bill through in no time. And Horace, one other thing—in getting this mail out, don't forget Shoten. Be sure he's getting some of it."

"You're not going to change his mind," Abernathy said.

"No, we're not going to change his mind. In fact, we're not trying to. We're trying to neutralize him, or at least take a little of the steam out of his opposition. That's almost as important as getting people on our side. You see what I mean?"

"I don't know as I do," Horace said, "but I'm a country boy. I'll leave all those strategy matters to you smart city fellers. You just tell us what you want done and we'll do our best to see that it gets done."

"We'll do that, Horace. You're doing a fine job. And you can be sure that New York is going to hear about it."

"Aw," said Horace, "you don't have to bother with that. It's all part of the job."

"The hell I don't," Paul said. "This is as important to the company as turning out toasters or whatever you make out there."

"Refrigerators. O.K. Paul, we'll be doing our damndest. You just let us know what you want done."

"I'll do that, Horace. Just keep the mail coming for another week. We'll have the vote in about ten days I'd say."

They said good-by and hung up.

"Mr. Martin from Texas on twenty-five, Mr. Finch," his secretary announced.

"Marty, how are you?" Paul said into the phone.

"O.K., O.K., boy," Martin said. "How are things going?"

"I think we're building up a head of steam. Down on the Hill they're saying that they're getting more mail on this bill than any bill since Prohibition."

"No kidding," Martin said. "Well, we're contributing our part. Even the men here in the plant are talking about it, and, believe me, it's something when they talk about something besides sex and baseball. Some of them are writing letters. Rotary had a report on it at the Thursday luncheon, and a lot of guys there said they would write. But listen, what I really called about was this. We got a connection to a big man down here. A millionaire in natural gas. He's a close friend of Senator Lucius Sears. In fact, this guy's son is working for Sears, right up there in his office in Washington." Martin paused, obviously waiting for an enthusiastic reply from Paul. But Paul was thinking.

"Well, what do you say, boy? How about that?"

"Marty," said Paul slowly, "we've got to be careful about this."

"Well, sure," Martin said, "of course we do and we will be. But we can't pass a thing like this up."

"Did this fellow contribute to Sears's campaign?"

"Oh, sure. He's a big supporter and he's loaded. I'm sure he kicked in a bundle."

"And has anybody talked to him yet?"

"No. I told them to wait till I called you. But that's the point. He's a friend of Roy Durst, the plant manager down here. You know him. They're big golfing buddies. That part of it is easy."

"I'd go a little slow here, Marty," Paul said. "We could get burned if this didn't go just right."

"Paul boy, here we got a pipe line direct to Sears. I think we should use it."

"It's a little risky. Sears is temperamental as hell."

"So it's a little risky. You've been living in the East too long, Paul. This is Texas. We believe in direct action."

"I'm not trying to hold you back, Marty. But I'm already in this thing up to my ears. Every place they turn there's Paul Finch and Liberty Electric, and I've got to watch my step or I'm going to end up in the *Congressional Record,* and it won't be in a flattering context for me or for Liberty."

"Paul—Durst and this guy are old friends. They've known each other for years. He isn't going to blow the whistle on Durst."

"Stranger things have happened. Listen, let's do it this way, Marty. Go ahead and make the contact with this fellow, but let somebody other than Durst do it. Somebody not at Liberty. Have Durst get one of his other buddies around town to do it. There must be plenty of other people in Fort Worth besides Durst who know this guy. I'd feel better about it if the contact came from somebody other than Liberty. Try to arrange it that way, and if it can't be done, give me a call, and maybe we'll be forced to take the other route."

"O.K.," said Martin wearily, "but this is the perfect setup."

"Trust me," Paul said.

"All right. You're calling the shots."

"Keep in touch," Paul said as he hung up.

"Do you want me to get Mr. Towell?" his secretary said from the door.

Paul glanced at his watch. "Let's try him again. I've got ten minutes before the Chamber meeting."

He spent a few minutes glancing through the carbon copies of letters sent to senators, which had been forwarded to him from various parts of the country. The call came through, and he exchanged pleasantries with Jim Towell.

"The reason I called, Jim," he said, "was that I was in Senator McComb's office today and they said their mail from Massachusetts wasn't too heavy on the bill. I just wanted to check the matter out with you."

"We've been a little slow getting started, Paul," Towell said. "We've had some problems here at the plant that have taken a lot of time."

"I'm sure that's true, but next week isn't going to do any good on this bill. It has to be now. And this is number one priority as far as New York is concerned."

"We'll get to it. But we've got a plant to run. That's where the profits of this organization come from."

"There's a lot of money riding on this bill too, Jim. A lot of money."

"I suppose so," Jim said. "I should have taken political science in school instead of engineering."

"That's all part of being an executive," Paul said. "You've got to develop the broad view if you're going to run the show."

"I'm not so sure I want to. I think I'd be better off just running the production line."

"That's un-American," Paul said jovially. "Give it a try, Jim, and see what you can do for us. We need your help."

"All right," said Jim. "I'll get on it. I suppose I can do it."

"Good," said Paul. "I'll be talking to you."

They hung up. Paul glanced at his watch and rose hastily to go. "Got to get going. I'm late," he said as he went by his secretary's desk. She got up quickly and trailed him to the elevator.

"Mr. Hance called while you were talking. He says that he thinks that the 'Today' show will take Senator Ruskin."

"Fine. Excellent," said Paul, pushing the elevator button. "Call Rex back and tell him that it should be the early part of next week if possible."

"The early part of next week," his secretary repeated.

"Yes. If he's on too soon, the unions will raise hell and they'll have time to get equal time. Tell him the best guess is that the vote will be about Wednesday or Thursday of next week. So Monday or Tuesday would be the best. See you later."

Paul stepped into the elevator, went to Connecticut Avenue, and caught a cab for the Chamber of Commerce. He entered the meeting room, which was well filled with about forty people. He entered quietly, since the meeting was under way. Wilfred Dann, who was presiding, noted his presence with a nod. Paul took a seat with the others at the highly polished U-shaped table.

"For the benefit of those who have come in late," Wilfred Dann said, "there are two papers circulating around the table. One is an order for our Chamber publication called, 'The Labor Monopoly Must Be Stopped.' Most of you have seen it. We're making copies available at cost—three and a half dollars a thousand. Just sign your name and organization and tell us how many you want. You can pick them up later today. The other blank is for reprints of Father Mooney's piece, 'Labor's Place in a Free Society.' These are available at four dollars per thousand, and we hope to have them here by Wednesday of this week. Just put your name down, along with the quantity you want. Now. We were just talking about the grass-roots campaign that is developing all over this country in support of this bill. I don't think there is any doubt at this point that the ball is rolling, and it is our task to keep it rolling. I don't think there is any doubt that the unions are doing everything in their power to stop it and reverse it—"

A hand was raised at the table.

"Yes?"

196

"I'd like to back up that statement, Will," said a man. "I just came from the Hill, and it's swarming with Truckers. Hundreds of them. You can hardly get through the halls of the Senate Office Building."

"They brought them in from all over the country," contributed a second man. "They had a battle meeting and laid out the plans over at the Truckers' headquarters yesterday."

"And they're not the only ones," the first man said. "The NFL has assigned all its vice-presidents to talk to every senator on the Hill. They're putting everything they've got into this thing."

"The building trades are out in force too," said another man.

"I think you can see, gentlemen, that we have our work cut out for us," Will said. "Let me just take an informal little poll. How many organizations are bringing people in to talk to their senators?"

A smattering of hands went up, mostly from trade association people.

"And how many are conducting a campaign to get their people to contact their senators by wire, or phone, or letter?"

Practically every hand in the room went up.

"And how many are talking to senators on their own?"

About two-thirds of the hands went up.

"All right. Fine," Will said. "That's not bad. But I think that we have to do more, gentlemen. I want to emphasize that I'm merely acting in a co-ordinating role here. You've each got to make up your own minds how to handle this, and I wouldn't presume to tell you what to do, but I think that this next week is going to be crucial. There are still a lot of uncommitted people down on the Hill, and I think that we can get them with us if we're really willing to put out the effort. But it really means putting out. I think we have got to infect our people with the urgency of this thing, and get them to infect others. If we do that, we'll win it."

The paper for ordering Father Mooney's booklet was passed to Paul. Paul signed his name, the name of his company, and in the "quantity" column he wrote fifteen thousand. He passed the paper along to the next man.

197

"My gosh," the next man whispered, "what are you going to do with fifteen thousand of those things?"

"We've got an opinion leaders list," Paul whispered back. "You know—professors, deans, newspaper columnists, presidents of women's clubs, people like that."

The man nodded in understanding.

"Sixty bucks, plus envelopes and postage. It ought to be worth it," Paul said. "It's a little late, but if we get them by Wednesday, we'll get them out."

"Will," said a man standing up in the rear of the room. "I was down on the Hill yesterday and they tell me that the mail on this bill is staggering. More than they've ever seen before. It's coming in so fast that they can't handle it all down there."

"That's it," Will said. "That's just what it's going to take to win this thing."

"Like everybody else, I've been down on the Hill all week too," said another man. "I picked this up and I just wondered if anybody else heard it. I heard that some of the liberals were preparing a series of weakening amendments. They plan to offer them and emasculate the bill so there's nothing left of it."

"I heard the same thing," said another man.

"That's what they're up to all right," chimed in a third. "I heard it on good authority."

"We heard the same thing," Will said. "Well, we just have to beat those amendments, that's all. Or we won't have anything." The circulating papers had returned to the front of the room. "Everybody got his name on these that wants copies?" He held them in the air.

"I'd like to add something here," someone else said. "I think these unions are confused. I don't think they're nearly so well coordinated as we think. Some of them are trying to get exemptions for their industries. And the railway and airline unions are trying to get themselves taken out and put under the railway labor act. And others are trying to get in all sorts of pet provisions. The left hand doesn't know what the right hand is doing, from what I can see. The Federation started out to oppose this thing all out. And now they seem to have changed their minds. But nobody seems to know what they want. Some of them are for some things and against others, and the next guy is just the opposite. I talked to a senator, and he was disgusted with them. Said they couldn't seem to make up their minds."

"Be that as it may," Will said. "We may have them on the run, but this is no time to let up."

"I didn't say we were supposed to let up."

"'But we shouldn't get the idea that we've got this thing licked. We've got to stay right on it until the last vote is counted," Will said, smacking his hands together.

"Amen," said somebody in the audience.

"All right," Will said. "I think that's about all we can accomplish today. I think another meeting is in order. How about Wednesday at ten? How is that with everybody?" There was general agreement.

"All right, Wednesday at ten it is. We should have the Mooney reprints ready for you then. Thanks for coming."

The meeting broke up, and Paul left quickly and hailed a cab for the National Press Building. He took the elevator to the sixth floor and entered a door marked, "Capitol News Services." Underneath, it said, "Jack L. Shankey, Pres." There was a painted insignia in the middle of the door—a hand clutching a roll of news copy. On the insignia was lettered: "News, Features, Editorials."

"Hi, Peggy," Paul said to the secretary in the tiny office. "Jack ready?"

"I'm ready," said the querulous voice from the adjoining office. Jack Shankey came out in his shirtsleeves and shook hands with Paul. "I'll get my coat."

He disappeared for a moment and came back, sliding his arm into his jacket. "Where to?"

"I don't care," Paul said. "Costins? Or the Willard?"

"Better make it Costins," Jack said. "I got a hell of a lot of stuff to get out this afternoon."

They took the elevator to the first floor. In the restaurant they got a corner table and ordered Martinis.

"You're really doing a job," Paul said. "The clipping services have picked up a whole raft of your stuff."

"Sure," said Jack carelessly. "You think I was shitting you when I told you I had two hundred papers?"

"No," said Paul. "But I'm surprised at the coverage. I'm just a babe in the woods. I always thought these papers wrote all their own editorials."

"Hell," said Jack contemptuously. "These little papers don't have anybody capable of writing editorials about national stuff. They got to get it from somewhere."

"I suppose that's right," Paul said.

"Sure. You think the paper in Tucumcari has a correspondent here?"

"Well, I guess not. I never thought about it one way or the other."

"They don't. The medium-sized papers do. I mean they have a man who strings for ten or twenty of them. I do that myself. But not these little jobbies." He took a long drink of his Martini. "You understand that I don't slant the news stuff I send out. You know that, don't you? That is straight reporting. But the editorials I do slant, because that is what an editorial is. An opinion. It's supposed to reflect a point of view. But I don't let that creep into the straight news. I take care that doesn't happen."

"I understand," Paul said.

"Some of these services write two editorials. One for and one against, and the guy can use whichever he chooses, but I don't go in for that. I get committed to one point of view or the other, and, hell, I can't write anything convincing the other way."

"Well, we're sure glad you're with us on this. You have a tremendous amount of influence out there."

"I know it. And don't get the idea you're buying me. I came to the conclusion that this was a good bill long before you ever came along."

"I know," Paul said. "Our clipping service picked up a couple of your first editorials."

"All right," Jack said. "Let's just be clear on that point."

"You don't have to worry about that. And besides, I'm not going around talking about this. Nothing is going to come from me."

"Good."

200

Paul reached into his brief case. "Here's a little background material I pulled together for you. Some of it is mine and some of it comes from other places. Read it over and use whatever you want to."

Jack took the material and studied it with mild contempt. "They should teach you boys how to write. This looks like the Government put it out."

"We'll leave that in your capable hands," Paul said.

"I'll have a look at it," Jack said. "There's probably some stuff here I can use."

"Fine," Paul said. "We're getting all your stuff. In fact, I think we might up our order to a dozen copies of each."

"All right with me, if you got use for them."

"And also, how should I make out the check? To you personally, or the Capitol News Services?"

"You don't have a hell of a lot of finesse, do you?" Jack said. "Make it out to me personally. And don't get the idea, Mr. Finch, that you're buying me or . . ."

"I don't have that idea," Paul said. "We just talked about this a minute ago, and I told you I don't have that idea at all. You've already established that you were for the bill before you ever laid eyes on me."

"Right. But here you are feeding me material and checks at the same time. I'm sensitive, that's all. A sensitive newspaperman."

"Come on now," Paul said. "All that is understood. Your opinions and mine happen to coincide on this bill. But next time we might be on different sides."

Jack eyed him. "That's right. We might, Mr. Finch. We well might."

"But as long as we're on the same side, why not make the most of it?"

"All right, all right," Jack said, impatiently.

"Jack, I've enjoyed the lunch," Paul said. "I've got to be getting back, and you've got a lot of things to do. Here, I've got it," he said to the waitress with the check. He paid her and shook hands with Jack Shankey. "Good to see you. Keep your fingers crossed."

"Righto, Machiavelli," Jack said with some amusement. Paul went out into the street and hailed a cab for the office.

"Hi," his secretary said. "You had some calls."

"O.K.," he said wearily. "What are they?"

"Senator Simms's office called. They thanked you for the material, but asked if you could at least work it up in rough form. She said the Senator said they were swamped."

"My God," he said, "can't they even write their own speeches? Who isn't swamped? All right. Call and tell them we'll do it. Tell Freddie to drop the other stuff and get on it. When do they want it?"

"You know. Yesterday."

He shook his head in chagrin. "All right. Tell them we'll have it down to them by close of business tomorrow. Why does everybody have to wait until the last damn minute."

His secretary shrugged her shoulders. She gave him the other calls. He put through the first of them, and called her into the office. "There's one other thing Simms's office wants. All those clippings. Can you put them together, paste them down in some order? In fact," he said, pausing, "paste them up by states. That's what will interest them. Quotes from their own newspapers. But there's one thing you've got to be very careful of, Susie, the editorials. You'll find that quite a few of those editorials are identical. And I want to be sure that no more than one editorial of a kind is pasted up for any one state. Try to pick the biggest paper, if there's more than one."

"Identical?" Susan said in puzzlement. "How does that happen?"

"They get them from an editorial-writing service. Between you and me."

"I see," she said wisely. "But isn't there a chance that they'll compare one state with another and see that some of them are the same?"

"Yes, they might. I doubt it, but it's a risk we just have to take. The way things are moving down there, I doubt if there will be much time for comparisons. Did the books get sent down?"

"Yes, thirty-seven of them."

"But under the senator's name?"

"Oh, yes."

"That's a crazy idea if I ever heard one. I can't imagine who is going to have a chance to read a five-hundred-page book in that chaos. But what the hell. Every little bit helps. When a professor from CCNY writes a book saying labor unions have too much power, I guess we shouldn't pass it up."

He retired to his office to look over the accumulated correspondence of several days. It was encouraging. People seemed to be on the move, excited, enthusiastic about getting the bill through. His secretary brought in a dozen letters for him to sign, and reminded him of his appointment.

"I'll be at the Statler. Suite 706B. I'm briefing a group of guys who are going to call on their senators tomorrow. I should be there until about six-thirty if you need to reach me." He leaned back in his chair and rubbed his eyes. "Boy, I am bushed! I wish they were going to vote on that bill tomorrow instead of next week."

"It seems like we've been rushing about frantically for weeks," she said.

"I can't remember when we weren't," he said. "Well, I better get on my horse. I'll see you tomorrow."

16

The Senator was a little late for breakfast as he hurried through the outer office and into the magnificent private office of the majority leader, Eldon Macefield, of California. Already there were Jack Shopper, of North Dakota, Winthrop Whitmore, of Massachusetts, and Bruce Willcox, of Ohio. Breakfast for five was set on one end of a long mahogany table under one of the great chandeliers.

"Sorry I'm late," the Senator said.

"I was about to drink your orange juice," the majority leader said, "even though it comes from that sandspit called Florida."

The Senator took the remaining chair.

"Since we're all here," the majority leader said, "we might as well get on with the business of the day."

"The business of the day is not conducive to the peaceful working of the digestive process," the Senator said.

"You can say that again," the majority leader said. He leaned back in his chair reflectively. "You know, I hate these goddam labor bills. Without a doubt they are more difficult to handle and more divisive than any other type of bill."

"Class warfare conducted by debate," the Senator said.

"Maybe that's it," the majority leader said. "I dread to see one of them coming up. It splits this body like nothing else. People don't speak to people for months afterward. And I'm not just talking about us, either. It's just as bad for the Republicans."

"It's true," the Senator said. "Remember the name-calling argument that Thompson and Flather got into over Taft-Hartley. They spewed fire back and forth at one another for five minutes. Pickett of Alabama was in the chair and he couldn't gavel them down."

"God, yes," said the majority leader. "Neither one of them would apologize, and Thompson came damn close to getting censured for it."

"And neither one of them spoke to the other unless it was absolutely necessary until after Flather retired," Whitmore said.

"Well, I hate to see another one coming, I can tell you," the majority leader said. "I'm the guy who has to pick up the pieces and rub oil into the wounds. It's damn near impossible to get anything else done for the rest of a session after one of these labor things. The Republicans hate us, and they hate the liberal Republicans, and we hate them and the Southern Democrats. It is a mess. Just a mess."

"That's why we elected such a strong and vigorous man for majority leader," said the Senator. "A firm hand at the helm, to guide us through these perilous seas."

"Nuts to you," the majority leader said. "Well, I suppose this problem is not going to go away, so we may as well get into it. John, why don't you give us a report?"

Each of the four senators had agreed to talk to half a dozen other senators about supporting the modifying amendments when they were brought up.

"Well, the bad news first, I guess. Steinman won't give us any help in rounding up votes, and he says that he will vote against the amendments."

"Irving is crazy. What's the matter with him?" Shopper said.

"He says that in his judgment there are enough votes around to beat the bill, and he's going to devote his efforts to that end."

"For God's sake," the majority leader said. "What is Irving thinking about? We can't beat the bill."

"Irving is a smart fellow," the Senator said. "He didn't say it, but I would guess his thinking is this: He is against this bill, strongly. If word gets out that he and a lot of other people are going to join with us to modify the bill, it means, in effect, announcing that there is no chance to defeat the tough bill on a straight vote, so the anti-tough-bill forces have retreated to the next line of defense. I think Irving feels that such a retreat will give aid and comfort to the enemy and encourage them to feel that they have all of us on the run. I think he is worried about the snowball effect it may have on the morale of the other side. And so am I, frankly."

Shopper shook his head. "I don't follow Irving's thinking on this."

"That's because he is starting from a different premise than ours," the Senator said. "He thinks there is an outside chance to defeat the tough bill on a straight vote, if no amendments or compromises are offered. Not a very good chance, probably, but some chance. Since he detests the tough bill, and doesn't like the modified form much better, he will take his chances on beating it completely."

"Well, he is out of his mind," the majority leader said. "Jack and I have counted a dozen times, and the votes are just not there to beat it."

The Senator spread his hands. "I told him that, naturally, but he just wouldn't hear of it."

"John, let me ask you this," the majority leader said. "Steinman is pretty far down the alphabetical list. If we come down to him and it looks like the amendments will pass, do you think he will go with us?"

"I just don't know. He says not, but I would guess—and this I emphasize is only a guess—that he would."

"He's off his head," the majority leader said. "If those amendments don't pass, the tough bill will go through as sure as we're sitting here. Well," he said, marking the list in front of him, "we'll put it in the doubtful column, and that's probably being optimistic. What about the others?"

"Albert and O'Donnell will go with us. In fact, their response was very positive, and I think that we could even count on them for some proselytizing."

"Who could they possibly influence?" Whitmore said shortly.

"Nobody, probably. I was just thinking that we could add their voices to what we hope is the swelling chorus. Create the illusion of a vast majority, marching along together invincibly," the Senator said.

"That's an illusion all right," the majority leader said. "What about Vince Austin?"

"Austin and Herkinson would fall into the category the opinion polls call 'leaning favorable.' "

"Fine. John, I'd advise you to stay with them right to the end, otherwise they may go wavering off."

"I shall."

"O.K. Who's left? Fellini?"

"Not much hope there, as you know. Labor elected him, and he carries a card in the Plumbers and Pipefitters. I talked to him at length, and I honestly think, Eldon, we are just wasting our time."

"I'd already written him off," the majority leader said, "but I didn't want to leave any stone unturned. Well, John, that's two positive, two leaning positive, one leaning negative, and one definite negative."

"Right."

"All right. How about you next, Winthrop?"

Winthrop Whitmore made his report, followed by Bruce Willcox and Jack Shopper, who made similar reports. The majority leader then reported his conversations with a dozen of his fellow Democrats.

"I figure I've got one, possibly two more," the majority leader said in conclusion. "I've got a couple of outstanding favors I can call, and I'm inclined to do it on this bill. I'm going to hold off until I'm a little surer that I would get a positive answer. Nothing is worse than to call a favor and get refused."

"Well, Eldon," the Senator said. "What's the count?"

"It's damn hard to make, I can tell you that. And let me say that, at least for the moment, I don't think this should go out of this room. We'll let them in on it a little later when we have the lay of the land a little better."

"Agreed," Shopper said.

"It's going to be another goddam cliffhanger," Macefield said. "Giving us all of the sures and leaning favorables, plus the two I referenced earlier, plus eight Republicans, I make it fifty-two."

Senator Burnett whistled lightly. "That makes it pretty clear we have our work cut out for us. We've got to hold absolutely every one of these, and we've got to rout them out when the vote is taken. We can't permit any absentees."

"Of course we may be able to pick up a couple more," Willcox said.

"Maybe you see them. I don't," the majority leader said. "I've been down that list fifty times."

"Well, we should keep on trying."

"Oh, sure. But I think our main attention should go toward holding what we now have, or think we have." He pushed his chair back from the table. "I think that does it."

The other senators left, but John Burnett lingered behind. "I'd like to discuss one small point, if I may, Eldon. In what order do you propose to call up the amendments?"

"Good question, John. I'm on the fence about it. If we call up the boycott amendment first, which is the most controversial, and it gets licked, then I think that all of them would probably go down the drain. If it passes, then of course it's strictly downhill from then on. On the other hand, if we call up the financial reporting thing, which is probably the least controversial, and it wins, we would probably build strength as we went along. My guess is that we'd stand a better chance of getting them all through. Of course, if the least controversial loses, then we're done."

"My thinking exactly," Senator Burnett said. "I would personally favor the latter course. I think our chances of getting the financial reporting amendment through are pretty good; and if it goes, I think it greatly increases the chances for all of them."

"My thinking is turning in that direction, John. I'm inclined to handle it that way."

The majority leader escorted the Senator to the door. "I think we have a chance, John. That count was just a trifle optimistic, but, hell, I've got to breathe some fire into the troops."

"We're making progress," the Senator said, "but the way things stand, we're not going to know for sure until the clerk totals the count."

The majority leader nodded.

17

As the vote on the labor bill drew near, Capitol Hill was tensely silent, like a battlefield before dawn on the morning of an attack. The lobbyists for both sides had withdrawn; telephones were almost silent; arguments which had been loud and wrangling a few days ago were now hushed and few. All that could be done, had been done. There was nothing to do now but wait.

The Senate debate on the bill had been going on for two days. On the first day, the Senate went into session at noon, as usual, and did not adjourn until one in the morning. On the second day, by agreement, the session began at ten in the morning and continued until nearly ten o'clock that night.

Now, with the debate in the third day, Senator John Burnett pushed his way through the crowded cloakroom and through the swinging doors. The roll-call vote on the first crucial amendment was about to be taken, and nearly every senator was on the floor. As he took his seat, his ears were assailed by the theatrical voice of Senator Wilfred Thomas, the fighting Wisconsin liberal whom he despised perhaps more than any other man in the Senate. Thomas took an emotional and usually hysterical approach to all legislation. Every bill was either the salvation of mankind or a vicious plot against the people. Even the extreme Republican conservatives were not as bad.

"Listen," Thomas was saying, with his hand raised ineffectually to still the buzz of conversation and his head tilted to hear the voices. "Can you hear the voices of the poor of this great country, the unprotected, the weak? Can you hear them calling? Stop! Ye know not what ye do. Can you hear them? Ye, who are about to cast them out. Ye, who are about to eliminate, in one slashing stroke, those rights so painfully accumulated through the years, yes, even the centuries, of battles. And for what reason? For the sins of a few. For the sins of a few you are about to inflict punishment on the many. Let him who is without sin. . . ."

"How long has he been talking?" the Senator whispered to white-haired Tom Farrington.

"Eternity. About an hour and a half. But I think he's winding up now, as you can tell by the increasingly hysterical tone of his voice."

"Anybody else scheduled before the vote?"

"No, I think he maneuvered the last spot."

"He would." Senator Burnett settled back in his seat, apparently listening to the strident comments of the senator from Wisconsin, but actually closing out the voice, and resting, with his eyes open. Sharp applause on his left told him that the speech was over. Spectators in the galleries joined in. The gavel pounded persistently and finally silenced all.

"The Chair must warn the galleries," said the Vice-President glaring upward, "that applause or any indications of approval or disapproval from the galleries may result in the clearing of those galleries, if it occurs again." He scowled at them fiercely. "A point of order has been made that a quorum is not present. The clerk will call the roll."

The quorum bells sounded in the cloakrooms, in the halls of the Capitol, in the committee rooms, in the offices of the Senate—an imperative, piercing sound, twice given.

The Senate buzzed with tense anticipation. The galleries, jammed to overflowing with lobbyists, relatives, staff members, and a few fortunate tourists, leaned forward for a better view of the pit. Even in the aisles of the galleries, people sat, giving the effect of a solid quadrangle of humanity above the floor.

The legislative clerks were rustling their papers, getting them in order. The reading clerk assumed his position, looked out over the Senate floor for a brief moment, then began his singsong reading: "Mr. Albert." "Here." "Mr. Allen." "Here." "Mr. Arleone." "Here." "Mr. Armistead." "Here." "Mr. Austin of California." "Here." "Mr. Austin of Vermont. . . ."

When the quorum call was concluded, several senators were on their feet. The Vice-President recognized Mr. Shopper of North Dakota.

Mr. Shopper called up the first of the crucial amendments. It was the least controversial and the most likely to pass.

"The question is on agreeing to the amendment offered by the senator from North Dakota. The clerk will call the roll," the Vice-President said.

"Mr. Albert." "Aye." "Mr. Allen." "No." "Mr. Armistead." "No." "Mr. . . ."

John Burnett listened sharply for two or three of the answers, and pressed his lips together. When his name was called, he voted to substitute the amendment. The clerk droned relentlessly through the remaining threescore names. After he had read the last name, he proceeded through again, calling the names of those who had not answered. After this reading, several senators, who had come to the floor late, were recognized, and voted. The clerks bustled through the count and the checking, and the result was handed up to the Vice-President.

"Ayes, forty-seven. Noes, fifty. The amendment is not accepted." He brought the gavel down sharply, amid boos and applause from the floor and galleries. On the Senator's left, labor's representatives sat, stunned, talking quietly, shaking their heads. On his right, Republicans jubilantly shook hands vigorously with one another and talked excitedly.

One after another the amendments were offered, and each was defeated by a slightly larger margin. When this was done, the chamber was almost silent, as the senators contemplated facing what many of them hoped would not occur.

"Mr. President," said the Chairman of the Labor Committee, "since there are no other amendments pending, I ask unanimous consent that this body consider S. 1976 as submitted by the committee."

"Without objection, so ordered. The question is on S. 1976.

The yeas and nays have been ordered, and the clerk will call the roll," the Vice-President said.

The ayes began to come thick and fast, piling on top of one another. It was something of an anticlimax. The bill would carry, and it would not even be close.

"Mr. Burnett."

"Aye."

There was a slight ripple of surprise in the chamber and in the galleries. A book on a desk to his left was slammed in anger. The Vice-President was presented with the count, and the gavel sounded three times.

"On the bill, S. 1976, the Labor-Management Reform Act, ayes, sixty-nine; noes, twenty-eight. The bill is approved."

The Senate and galleries rose as one. Wild cheering and back clapping were taking place in the entire room. Some made their way out of the chamber, heads down, silently cursing. The majority leader had gained the floor, and was making some procedural announcements. Within a few seconds, they had voted to adjourn. It was 11:50 in the evening.

John Burnett made his way to the cloakroom. Gene Zaboda of West Virginia, who had cast the last futile vote against the bill, gave him a look of piercing contempt, and did not speak. Several Republicans clapped him heartily on the back.

The cloakroom was chaos. Lobbyists and staff people had poured past the helpless guards. Newspapermen shouted their questions, and tried, amid jostlings and while off balance, to shorthand their answers. People were packed so tightly that almost no movement was possible. The Senator squeezed in back of Senator Ben Fellini, who twisted his head about and said, "You're a goddam traitor, Burnett."

"Senator. . . ." A spectacled newspaper reporter was waving a notebook at Senator Burnett. They squeezed toward each other. In the uproar, the reporter shouted questions, strained, and cocked his ear to catch the answers. Relentlessly, they were pressed together until the reporter's notebook rested on the Senator's chest, and the reporter had to crane his head backward in a vain attempt to see what he was writing. He thanked the Senator and was carried off by the crowd, turning his head, birdlike, from one side to the other, searching for more quotes.

A small man with a thin hand-microphone planted himself in front of the Senator. "NBC, Senator. May we have a statement?"

John Burnett nodded.

"This is Bob Hartley, your NBC Capitol reporter, now in the cloakroom of the Senate of the United States. All is chaos here, as I'm sure you can hear. This has been the culmination of perhaps the bitterest issue fought in these chambers in many years. I have here one of the leading liberal senators of our time, Senator John Burnett of Missouri. Senator Burnett surprised many when he voted for the bill today. Senator, I wonder if you would mind telling the radio audience why you voted as you did on this bill today?"

"Certainly, Bob, I'd be happy to. I don't regard this as a perfect bill. I don't think many of those who voted for it out there today think of it as a perfect bill. But I think that it is the best bill we could get, considering all of the interests here involved, and I think, read in the overall, it is a bill in the best interests of the people of the United States as a whole, because it will correct evils that all of us feel must be corrected."

"Senator, the margin by which the bill passed was a surprise to many of us who thought that the vote would be quite close. Have you any comment on that?"

"Well, of course the close votes came on the amendments, wherein a group of us tried to amend the bill in a way that we felt would improve it. We did not succeed in that attempt. Failing that, many of us voted for the committee bill because of our conviction that labor reform was necessary."

"How much influence, sir, would you say that lobbyists had in getting this bill passed? We heard that there was a lot of lobbying activity."

"The lobbyists were active for both sides, of course. And I, for one, am willing to listen to their arguments because, after all, they do represent important segments of our society. But lobbyists, of necessity, must neutralize each other to a certain degree. And that was the case here. I think that the overwhelming sentiment of the people, and their interest in this bill, was the crucial factor in the final passage of this legislation."

"Thank you, Senator. Ladies and Gentlemen, that was Senator John Burnett, the distinguished senior senator from Missouri, who today cast his vote with sixty-eight of his colleagues to pass the Labor Reform Act." He clicked off the recorder. "Thanks, Senator, it was a hell of a fight, wasn't it? Excuse me, I've got to get some labor guys. Two of them were so mad they wouldn't even talk to me." He moved through the crowd with his tape recorder held high like a passing quarterback about to be inundated by tacklers.

Sidney Bronstein and Dick Goetz joined him. They both solemnly shook his hand.

"Another one of those damn votes," Dick said. "Half the people end up hating you no matter what you do."

"They're the important ones," said the Senator. "Well, Sidney, what do you have to say?"

"I'm no use to anyone," Sidney said glumly. "I thought sure we'd carry those amendments. And when we didn't, I couldn't make up my mind. It still isn't made up. I'm in some sort of a state of mental paralysis. . . ."

"That's not surprising, Sidney. For most of your life you would have been against that bill without question or thought. It would have been an automatic reaction like a knee jerk. A conditioned reflex. Now you're undergoing a transition in your thinking. You'll probably fall in one camp or the other, sooner or later. Like a rocket, you either make it to outer space and don't come back, or you fall back to your earthly home."

"This indecision is hard on the nerves," Sidney said. "At this point, I think I'm heading for outer space."

"Senator Burnett," said a voice behind them. The Senator turned, and Paul Finch grasped his hand in an enthusiastic handshake. "Senator, I just want to thank you for what you did out there on the floor today. I think it was a courageous act. I know that Liberty Electric appreciates it, and I personally think that it was a fine thing, sir."

"That vote was not a service for the Liberty Electric Company," the Senator snapped.

"Oh, no, sir. I know that. I'm sorry if I implied that. I just meant that we were happy that our points of view coincided."

"Our points of view have never coincided, and probably never will, young man. The fact that the Liberty Electric Company was for this bill was the strongest reason not to vote for it, in my opinion. And let me tell you this, and you may—in fact, I request—report this back to the people who run that corporation. If you think that this bill is a license to destroy organized labor, you are wrong. Dead wrong. And if your company seeks to use the bill for such a purpose, I will crucify them. Many senators out on that floor today took their political lives in their hands to vote for that bill. And if it is used as a club, we will punish those who use it as a club. Tell them that, will you?"

"Yes, sir," Paul said.

"Nothing personal about this, Mr. Finch. But that company of yours has got to start living in the twentieth century, sooner or later." The Senator clapped Paul on the shoulder and they moved on. They strolled to the Senate Office Building, under the rustling trees, instead of taking the subway, which they judged would be crowded. The corridors of the building were knotted with groups discussing, in intense, hushed voices, the vote on the bill. The Senator went down the hall, nodding to the left and right, greeting them. He reached his office and paused for a moment to discuss the excitement with Mary, who had remained in case she was needed. He then went into his own office and closed the door. He sat in his swivel chair and looked out on the gleaming dome of the Capitol. So, it's done. Over and done. Recorded for all posterity to see, if posterity expresses any interest in the subject. There it is, an inconsistency on the record, for them to examine, explain. A mar on the record? Perhaps. He had no doubt that it would be judged so by many whose good opinion he valued. A foolish consistency is the hobgoblin of little minds. . . . Was that it?

The telephone rang.

"CBS television would like to interview you, Senator," Dick Goetz said. "They've got their mobile unit parked by the southwest steps. I told them I didn't know whether you would care to make a statement or not. . . ."

He drummed the desk for a moment. "When did they want me? Right now?"

"If possible."

"All right. Tell them I'll be down in five minutes or so."

He arrived shortly thereafter, and a young man introduced himself as the producer. "We're taping this Senator, so don't worry too much about fluffs. We can edit them out. This is Ray Carson, of the CBS news staff. O.K., are we ready to go?" He led the Senator over to the steps, along with Ray Carson. Four blinding lights flashed on.

"This is Ray Carson of CBS News, and I have here with me, Senator John Burnett of Missouri. It is after midnight here in Washington, and the Senate has passed the highly controversial labor bill. Senator Burnett voted for that bill. . . ." He sped on smoothly, and asked the Senator the usual questions. Why did he vote for it? Was it a good bill? Would it do the clean-up job that was necessary? Would it damage legitimate unions?

"Senator," he continued, "a few minutes ago we interviewed Senator Gene Zaboda of West Virginia. He was quite upset, and I think that I can quote him accurately from these notes. He said that 'this vote was a sellout to big business, and a sellout of the labor organizations of this country. It is a management-sponsored, union-busting bill, and no man who calls himself a friend of labor could have voted for it. The insidious coalition that foisted this piece of legislation on the American people was an unholy alliance of Republicans, Southern Democrats, and a few so-called liberals, who, by this vote, forever cast themselves out of labor's temple. The votes of such people as John Burnett, Tom Farrington, and George Wilkins are incomprehensible to me.' I wonder if you would care to comment on that, Senator?"

The Senator shot Carson a look of reproach for unfairly asking for an ad lib answer to such a statement. "That statement, by one of my colleagues, disturbs me. It is a time-honored custom of the United State Senate not to make personal attacks on other members or otherwise impugn their motives. I believe that Senator Zaboda, in the frustration of defeat, has breached that rule. And I deeply resent any implication that I voted any way other than my conscience dictated. Apparently, Mr. Zaboda feels that

216

anyone who takes a position contrary to his own should not be permitted to vote. I would just like to say this. The vote was difficult for many of us who actually thought about the matter. The bill is not perfect, but in my experience in this body, if one waited to vote for the perfect bill, one could go through a career in the Senate and never cast a vote. Most of us were shocked and horrified by the disclosures of the committee and were responsive to the demand that corrective legislation be enacted as soon as possible. The bill may perhaps contain some provisions which will prove to be too harsh in the course of time. In that case, the Congress will act to correct them. But I feel that the demand that no legislation be passed, which is apparently Senator Zaboda's position, is unreasonable. I'll just say in closing that I voted for the bill and that I will stick to my position, because I think that it is right. On the other hand, I will not criticize those who voted the other way, because I am certain that they feel, in the light of their own consciences, that they, too, are right. Thank you."

"Thank you, Senator." The lights went out, leaving them in darkness.

"You took unfair advantage with that question, Mr. Carson."

"Sorry, Senator. Didn't think you'd mind. Besides, I thought you gave a damn good answer."

The Senator nodded, shook hands around, and returned to his office. Sidney had sent Mary home, and the office had an air of messy abandonment.

"Senator," Sidney said, "you know I was all over the lot on this bill and then couldn't make up my mind. How did you make up your mind about it? If it's none of my business, say so."

"The student at work again," the Senator said. "Sure, I'll tell you. This is probably a bad case to learn any lessons from. It wasn't black and white. It was a close decision."

"The longer I work on the Hill," Sidney said, "the more I think nothing's black and white."

"Oh, some votes are. On some, you really haven't got any choice. As for your own vacillation, Sidney, I think part of the answer may be due to the fact that you didn't have to make a decision. I did. By this afternoon, I had to vote for it, or against

217

it, or absent myself, which would also be a vote. If you had been faced with that choice, you'd have made a decision too."

"Or had a nervous breakdown."

"I doubt that. When you've been in politics a long time, your mind more or less automatically sorts out all the arguments and assigns some sort of weight to each one. Then it's a matter of piling the arguments on the scale and weighing them, just like a butcher."

"How do you assign those weights?" Sidney said. "That's what I'd like to know."

"Instinct," the Senator said, "which is another way of saying experience. And it's not easy on a vote like this. You just instinctively weigh your constituents' various opinions, the party line, your career ambitions, your own conscience, and everything else which has a direct or indirect bearing on the matter. Then after this mysterious process has been completed, you shut your eyes, cast your vote, and hope that it's the right vote politically as well."

"It was the right vote politically," Sidney said. "You've seen the mail."

"Yes, I've seen the mail. The mail indicates that a lot of people were steamed up about it. Heaven knows, you'd expect it with all the publicity it has gotten. But I've seen this before. They're by and large a group of unorganized voters steamed up about this particular bill, and most of them will resume their places before the television set with the comfortable feeling that the problem has been taken care of. Oh, I'll get some votes because of it. But I wonder if they're all going to remember this in November and swarm to the polls in huge numbers to reward virtue. Because you can be sure our labor friends will remember it, and not kindly. That vote is going to take a lot of explaining to a lot of labor people."

"I can't believe the people won't remember, and that it won't get us a lot of votes," Sidney said.

"Maybe," the Senator said. "It's difficult to tell how it will look in November. Things have a disturbing way of looking quite different several months later."

"Senator," said Sidney gently, "you know you really haven't told me a thing."

"I think I've told you quite a lot."

"About why you voted for it, I mean."

"No, I haven't really," the Senator admitted. "It's such a complicated mental and visceral process it's difficult to trace down all the reasons, I guess." He paused. "The most important negative reason was the plain fact that the bill contained a lot of unfair things gotten into it by labor's enemies. A good liberal shouldn't vote against labor on so important a bill as this. My career goes back a long way, and almost everything I've done would have forecast a vote the other way. Yet, there I was, lined up with all of labor's old enemies. A deserter."

"But . . ."

"But," repeated the Senator, "I guess all the reasons boil down to one. Something had to be done. Business, government, the public, and most of all labor itself, need protection against the hooligans, the thieves, and the little Caesars. They will take over the unions and destroy them, given half a chance. And labor is so wrapped up in dogma they just don't seem to realize that. Sure, the bill has unfair things in it—and we tried like hell to amend it and failed—but it *is* needed. Nothing can obscure that naked fact.

"So, to summarize this long-winded political science lecture, the butcher's scales were tipped to an 'aye' vote. Very simple."

"Not so simple," Sidney said.

"No," the Senator agreed. "Not so simple, or it wouldn't have taken so long to arrive at it."

"Well," Sidney said, "I was interested in your reasons, because the war is on." He handed him a roll of copy torn from the Associated Press machine. It read:

(189) cont'd. Labor Bill comment
National and state officials commented throughout the country on the highly controversial labor bill passed by the Senate today. In Missouri, Governor Ross MacKenzie, rumored as a possible senatorial opponent of Senator John Burnett, made the following statement: "It was with deep regret that I noted that both senators from the state of Missouri cast their votes for this

highly restrictive, union-busting piece of legislation. I find myself in complete disagreement with their position. Our senior senator, who has posed as a friend of the labor movement, was apparently persuaded to vote for this bill by people in Washington. Certainly, the inspiration could not have come from the state of Missouri. I want to take this opportunity to reaffirm both my personal affection and regard, and that of the Democratic party in Missouri, for the thousands upon thousands of honest labor-union members and officials who will be unfairly punished by this bill. I think that it should be made the first order of business in the next session of the Congress of the United States, to wipe this unfair law from the books."

"Well, he had that one ready," the Senator said. "It's two in the morning out there. He wanted to hit the morning papers."

"Probably had two press releases ready," Dick Goetz said, "depending on how you went."

"I'm not surprised," the Senator said. "Ross has been looking for a handle, and I thought he would grab this one."

"The man is a disgrace," Sidney said.

"He's an ambitious politician," the Senator said, "but unless I miss my guess, he has this one gauged wrong. He's putting himself on the same side of the fence as the sinners, and I intend to make the most of that fact." He laid the roll of paper on the desk with a sigh. "Well, everybody had better get some sleep. The battle begins tomorrow."

Sidney glanced at his watch. "It is already tomorrow."

"In this job, it is always tomorrow," the Senator said.

18

Ed Flowers' secretary buzzed. "Mr. Raeder to see you."

With his usual air of urgency, Frank strode into the room, grasped Ed's hand, pumped it once strongly, and dropped it.

"Have you got a guy named Harrack working for you?" he asked.

"Yes and no," Ed said. "His status is sort of unusual. Harrack handled the Hillstrom affair. He was so disgusted and upset after we lost it that he wanted to quit. The whole thing took a lot out of him. He's a good man, so I told him to take some time off, take a rest, and then come up here and we'd talk about his next assignment."

"And you haven't heard anything from him?"

"No. He dropped out of sight and I haven't heard a word from him in a month. We've been holding his checks here for him. He'll show up eventually. I know Don."

"Do you know he's traveling around the country, stirring up the guys? Do you know that?"

"Don?"

"Yes, Don."

"Not exactly," Ed said.

"Well, it's more than idle rumblings, I can tell you that. Your communication with the field is very poor, Ed. You sit here in Washington, and you don't know what's going on out there. Harrack has been all over the country in the last month. He's played it very smart. He's contacted only his friends—people he knew really well and felt he could trust. People who wouldn't talk. That's why you haven't heard anything about all this. Now he's got a good strong nucleus of anti-Ed Flowers people, and they've begun to spread out and talk to everybody."

"That's impossible," Ed said, sitting down on the sofa, and rolling his cigar between his lips.

"Is it? When was the last time you were in Fall River or Canton or any of the other towns where plants are? Not New York, or San Francisco, or Miami, but the plant towns?"

"Oh, I get out there now and then."

"I bet you haven't been to any of them in a year."

"It's my union, Frank."

"Not much longer, maybe, unless you get on the ball. Ed, don't you realize what is happening? This is a full-scale revolt, and those guys are aiming to throw you out at the next convention this fall, and they're not going to settle for anything less."

"Oh, nuts! They haven't got the strength to do that."

"Dammit, Ed," said Frank, rising in irritation. He paced the floor and punctuated his remarks with smacks of the back of one hand against the palm of the other. "You don't seem to have the faintest idea what is happening. Your whole union was upset by the Hillstrom thing. Even I can feel that. You hammered away on Hillstrom week after week in your paper. How you were going to take them. How you were going to avenge all those people they fired or mistreated over the years. All that crap. Then you lost it. That was a real blow to a lot of people. Then came the labor bill, where we all looked like a bunch of dummies. Add those things to the fact that you already had people who didn't like you and are ready to plant the knife—and it's not a pretty picture. If you sit here with that attitude, you're going to be a retired president. And believe me, they're not about to set you up with a pension of twenty-five thousand a year. They'll cut you off right behind the ears. Remember that old saying: 'If you attack a king, kill him.' Well, they remember it, mark my words. They're not kidding."

"I still say Harrack can't do anything of the kind. Harrack, who's Harrack?"

"Harrack is apparently enough to persuade four locals, in which rests thirty per cent of your convention voting strength, to go along with him. Cahill and Minor are in with him. With Dan Gault, they practically formed those locals they're presidents of."

"Cahill and Minor are in with this group?"

"So I am told."

Ed cursed silently. "Well, that's a hell of a note. I can fire Harrack. . . ."

"I'd think that over very carefully. It might be a good idea and it might not. It would show them you have guts, and you're not going to knuckle under. But it risks making a martyr out of Harrack. And I don't think firing him will stop him. He'll get money from somewhere. Cahill and Minor could carry him easily. I think I'd string along for a while and see if I couldn't hang him. He'll make some mistakes. He's never done anything like this before."

"Frank," said Ed, "why are you so interested in all this?"

Frank paused. "Oh," he said, in a poor imitation of casualness, "several things. First of all, the guys who are in this are fragmentists, separatists, individualists—whatever you want to call them. They've all got their own little kingdoms, and they want to run them without interference. If they grab control of this union, the Federation will be that much weaker. And it's shaky as hell as it is. You're basically a co-operator. You go along. You've supported me on some key issues. Not the fighting kind of support, but you were there. These guys are a bunch of cat-fighters who would disrupt anything and everything the Federation tried to do. If we get many of these guys, they'll wreck it. I don't want that."

"And they might not support Frank Raeder for the presidency, if and when it ever falls open, whereas I would, because you helped me hang onto my job."

Raeder smiled uncomfortably. "Could be. But I'm not calling any favors yet. We'll see what happens when Ernie retires or kicks off. They'll probably want a smiles and sweet-talk guy. . . . Let's get back to the subject at hand: What should you do?"

"I'm open for suggestions."

"They're apparently planning a meeting sometime soon, in Chicago. A quiet get-together. It's supposed to take place at the time of the NFL convention here, so you won't be able to make it. They're playing it down as a low-level workshop session which won't require your presence. You need to get a man in there. Can you do it?"

"Ah . . . I'd have to think about that. Somebody not from headquarters and somebody I can trust."

"Right. Then we'll have something to go on. And I think you've got to get your fat ass on the road, and get out to some of those plants. Get in there where they're bargaining and get your picture taken. Get kicked around on a picket line. It would be the best thing that could happen to you. Blast a couple of senators, or the President. At least seem like you're doing something. That's why this whole thing has blown up. They think you're living it up, while they're out there in one-horse towns trying to please a bunch of hard-nosed members. The important thing is for you to look like you're driving hard. And another thing. Forget this divorce business."

Ed's eyes widened in surprise.

"I know about it. Sure, I know about it. Women talk, you know that. Elaine and Agnes have been over the whole situation a dozen times. So you want to toss the old lady overboard for some tender piece of fluff. All right, that's your business. But it can wait. All those members' wives out there are going to be saying, 'Ed Flowers went down to Washington and ditched his loyal wife of twenty years for some shameless bitch.' And your enemies are going to spread the story that you spend all of your time and plenty of union funds on such pleasures—such as trips down to South Carolina."

"You know everything, don't you, little man?" Ed said in irritation.

"Ed, I'm trying to help you. Such things may be irrelevant and unfair, but they are still used, and you might as well stop pretending they're not. Or getting mad at me for telling you so. They're painting you as a skirt-chaser who doesn't give a damn about the union. And if you ask for a divorce to marry that girl, it will prove the point as far as many of them are concerned. Hell, Ed, you're getting laid regular. What more are you going to get by being married to her?"

Ed turned on Frank as if he were about to strike him.

"*What?*" Frank said. "Think about it. *What?* Isn't everything to be gained by waiting a little, and nothing to be lost? We're only talking about four months and maybe less, if the thing blows over."

"I'll think about it," said Ed shortly. "But I can tell you right now, I'm not going to call off the divorce. It took a month and several drinks to get up my nerve in the first place. It was the worst scene I've ever been through, and I'm not going through it again."

"I'm not asking that," Raeder said. "All I'm asking you to do is postpone it."

"It's a hell of a strain, Frank, and I want to get it over with," Ed said, "but, as I said, I'll think about it."

"Good. Right now I think we need to get as much information as possible about this revolt. I've told you what I know, but I can probably dig out some more. If you dig some out yourself, we'll have a better idea of where we stand. The important thing is not to go off half cocked. I'll be in touch with you." He grasped Ed's hand, pumped it, and headed for the door.

"Thanks," said Ed, not rising from the couch. "I appreciate your help."

"We can whip them if we get cracking," Frank said.

Ed nodded.

"I'm not interested in being on the losing side, you know," said Frank as he closed the door.

Frank was obviously excited. The adrenalin was surging through him. He was stimulated by the prospect of conflict. Exhilarated by the coming battles. Already a hundred ideas for seizing the initiative and repelling the enemy were churning through his brain.

Ed did not feel that way. He sank back against the sofa until the Capitol dome in the window dropped from sight and the giant statue on the dome seemed to sit on the window sill like a small statue of Mary. The coming battle that so excited Frank seemed to him like an onrushing nightmare. His stomach twisted tightly, and he felt a little sick.

19

The Senator was in the library when Virgil Akers called from St. Louis.

"I thought I ought to call you, John," he said, "even though you'll be out here in a couple of hours. The Governor is going to speak to the state NFL at the Statler tonight, and rumor has it that he's going to announce. If he does, your plane will be met by a flock of reporters, because they know you're coming out tonight. I just thought you ought to know, so that you could prepare yourself."

"It was just a matter of time. Nothing to worry about. Thanks."

"He's picked a good forum, and the right time too. They're hollering for your scalp. I think they'll simmer down when this 'slave labor law' phase passes, but right now they're hot for blood. He's bound to get a rip-roaring reception, John. I think that you should expect that."

"I do, and I'll work out a few words on the subject coming out on the plane."

"Good. I think that's a good idea. We can't 'no comment' him to oblivion. After all, he is the Governor."

"I'm thinking of challenging him to some debates on the subject of the new law. He doesn't know the first thing about it, or about labor relations in general, for that matter. I could cut him into mincemeat. Not tonight, of course. I need to get some more statements out of him and push him into a corner before I challenge."

"Good idea. If we could coax him out on that limb, so he'd have to accept, I'd say it was bye-bye blackbird for Ross. I'll think about some means of doing it."

"Let's get going on campaign arrangements. It had better be a pretty extensive tour."

"I am. I'm scheduling it heavy, now that it looks as if Ross is definitely in. I've done my best to move us east to west in the northern part of the state, and west to east coming back in the south. But, of course, it didn't work out perfectly, so we'll do some hedgehopping."

The conversation ended, and the Senator noted by his watch that he still had half an hour before leaving for the plane. He poured himself a weak bourbon and water. He was annoyed and frightened, as are all politicians, at the prospect of opposition. It meant nearly three months of unceasing good humor, bone-bruising handshaking, speaking until his throat was raw and his voice a husky shout. Tramping from hotel dining room to cold auditorium, to radio and television studios, barns, tents, churches, schools. Three months of intense concentration, with no opportunity to relax his guard. And underneath it all, the flickering fear, carefully hidden from everybody, of losing.

He called a cab and picked up the small suitcase, their trunk having been sent two days before. Ellen was almost ready. She didn't dread it as much as he. It was a break in her routine. But after a month, her enthusiasm would flag. Inside, that is. No one but John would ever know it. How many times had she nodded smiling to the question: "It must be wonderful to be married to a fine man like the Senator." Yes, she would say, but, she would add with a touch of intimacy, everything was not as smooth as it appeared on the surface. There were problems, and it was demanding. Being in the public eye did have its disadvantages.

"Virgil just called. He says Ross may announce tonight, so be prepared at the airport."

"I just hate that boy, John. I know that is most unpolitical, but I can't deny it."

"Don't be too angry with him. We may be sponsoring him for a judgeship after he's licked."

Ellen clucked in uncomprehending dismay as she adjusted her hat. The cab driver rang the doorbell.

He knew the Senator by sight. He was a loquacious driver, and he dominated the conversation on the way to the airport. "No question, Senator, you did the right thing on that labor bill. I ain't saying that it may not lose you some votes, but there's lots of people around that ain't in unions that are getting pretty fed up with what they get away with, and nothing being done about it. And there's plenty in unions feel the same way. Besides, by next fall, they'll have forgot all about it, most of them. By that time, the Russians will have shot Khrushchev around the sun or something. People forget."

"I think that's an acute observation," said the Senator. "You're a student of politics, I see."

"I read the papers and I got my opinions. Then I hear a lot of talk in the cab, you know. It's like a poll, listening to everybody that gets in your cab. I know a lot of things before they ever break in the papers."

"I imagine you do."

"Sure. All kinds of things."

"Let me ask you a question, Mr. Scott," said the Senator, reading the man's name from his identification badge on the sun visor. "What has been the reaction to the labor bill by the people who've been riding in your cab?"

"On the whole," the driver said thoughtfully, "I think they been for it. Oh, I had a couple of guys, obviously labor leaders or something like that, that was fit to be tied. They were so mad they could have spit, both of them. But on the whole, I think that people are for it. You got to remember, though," he said, raising a cautionary finger, "the only people who ride cabs are the people with money. I don't have many fares that are laboring men, you know what I mean. They ride the bus. So that's a weakness in my polls. You got to take that into account."

"That's very true. Have you talked to any working people?"

"A few here and there. I'd say they were for it too. The ones that think about it. They feel like they been suckered when they see their dues money going for whores—excuse me, ma'am, that just slipped out—and for all kinds of things like that. Of course, a lot of them don't think at all. They just take whatever the union guy says as gospel. Still and all," he said, summing up, "I think you did the right thing."

"I hope so," said the Senator. "It was a hard choice for many of us."

They crossed the Key bridge, and headed down the George Washington Memorial Highway toward the airport.

Once the plane had left the ground, the Senator pushed his seat back as far as it would go and closed his eyes. He appeared to be asleep, but he was worrying through a statement to the reporters who would be waiting for the plane in St. Louis. Ellen leafed through a news magazine. She had him read a short article on some of his fellow senators. Those in the magazine's bad graces "snarled," "sneered," and "shouted" at those in its good graces, who replied "quietly," "firmly," and "forthrightly." The two hours passed uneventfully, and soon St. Louis appeared on the horizon, a sea of glittering light. The giant bird settled to earth, and as they came down the steps, someone shouted "Hold it there, Senator, please." He took Ellen's arm, and they both smiled. The flashbulbs popped. A knot of eager reporters waited at the bottom of the stairs. They were quickly surrounded and given contradictory orders about where to stand and what to do.

"The Governor has just announced that he is going to run against you in the primary," said an intense, horn-rimmed reporter. "Would you care to comment on that, Senator?"

"A little closer to the mike, Senator."

"First, let me say that I'm always glad to put my feet on the soil of Missouri again. There's something about this vital soil that sends energy through anyone who treads it. I'd just like to say that I'm glad to be back, I'm always glad to be back on my native soil. I suppose," he added with a sly smile, "that Mr. MacKenzie feels that way about his native soil of Pennsylvania."

The reporters guffawed.

"As for the challenge which you report has been issued to me by Mr. MacKenzie, I may say that I welcome it. A man becomes a man by responding to challenge, even the challenge of the young and inexperienced, because this is what keeps his mind sharp, keeps it from going soft. Not," he added, "that there is much chance of its going soft in the atmosphere of the United States Senate, where every word, it seems, is disputed. Mr. MacKenzie seems to feel that a law degree and an unfinished term as Governor qualify him for that body. I question whether he has tempered enough. We will test that out in the forthcoming campaign."

"Senator, the Governor was speaking tonight before the NFL. He told them that he would make it the first order of business to repeal the new labor law if he gets elected."

"I should think he might find that quite difficult to accomplish from the vantage point of the District of Columbia committee, to which, as a freshman senator, he would undoubtedly be assigned. But, perhaps with the wisdom of his thirty-six years," said the Senator, intentionally dropping Ross a year in age, "he will be able to change the minds of men like Lathrop Jones, Thomas W. Farrington, and Dewitt Lowell, and the others of the sixty-nine senators who voted for the bill, not to mention some three hundred members of the House of Representatives. He might be able to accomplish that, but then, of course, he might be overrating his persuasive powers a bit, you know. Overconfidence is a common fault in the young, I'm told."

"He got a big cheer from the labor boys on that, Senator. Does the possible loss of labor support worry you?"

"Boys, I'd like to be serious for a moment. Very serious. I'm sure that the American labor movement is upset about the bill. I know that it is. Many of them have communicated that fact to me. But a child who takes a dose of castor oil doesn't like it either, even though his mother tells him that it will make him well. It isn't until that child is giving his own kids castor oil, probably, that he appreciates what his mother told him. Now, the labor movement has just been administered a strong dose of unpleasant medicine, and they don't like the taste of it, and I don't blame them. But, in time, this will result in a stronger, healthier labor movement. The diseased portions will have passed from it. The sickness will have gone. And gentlemen, if I did not think that to be so, if I did not think that it would help the labor movement in the long run, I would never have voted for that bill. I don't apologize for that vote. I am proud of it, and I will trumpet it to the skies. And any thinking labor man need only look at my record and ask himself, 'Would John Burnett knowingly wound or weaken the labor movement?' There is only one honest answer to that question, and that answer has to be No."

It was a speech he would make, varied a thousand ways, said in a few words, said in several thousand, over the next three months.

The next morning, a light drizzle was falling as the Senator left the Chase for the ballroom of the Jefferson where he was to speak to the Democratic Women's Club of St. Louis. The ballroom was overflowing, and after a lunch of chicken à la king, of which he ate little, he gave the ladies what they were waiting for —his first public answer to the Governor. He strove to create the image of a man of wisdom, humor, experience, along with loyalty to his wife and family. He implied, rather than stated, that it was Ellen who most influenced him, who sustained him during periods of trial such as the present defection of a man both of them regarded almost as a son. Ellen was a trusted advisor with whom he discussed the important problems of the day, and she who gave him gentle guidance. He vaguely compared Ross to a man who deserts a faithful wife and runs off with a siren. He left them with the impression that the Governor was superficially charming, but recklessly ambitious and faintly disloyal. After lunch he stood at the door and thanked each one warmly for coming. It was a successful beginning.

He spent that afternoon in his hotel room with Virgil Akers, discussing job appointments with visiting state politicians. He pointed out to them that many of the appointments discussed would obviously not be made unless he were elected and could bring his seniority into play.

That evening he spoke at a small dinner at the St. Louis Country Club. There were about a hundred there, but they were influential far beyond their numbers. His record was faulty in many areas in which they were interested. Thus, he relied on personality and the labor bill. When he mentioned labor reform, he was greeted by a burst of applause, and half the audience stood. When the applause had subsided, he wondered aloud how Mr. MacKenzie would have voted on such a bill.

Herbert Shannon was there, of course, and he asked him to come back to his hotel after dinner. They talked for two hours, and Herbert agreed, although he doubted that he was the man for the job, to become finance chairman for the Senator's primary campaign. Virgil tapped out a press release on his battered portable typewriter, and the word was fed into the voracious ears of the waiting press. After Shannon had left, the Senator sat until past midnight, writing notes to carry him through the next thirty days of speechmaking.

Early the next morning, Virgil's Cadillac, bearing Virgil, the Senator, and Ellen, headed north toward Hannibal. At noon, he stopped to address a meeting of county agents in Bowling Green. He took another hour to tape an interview for the local radio station. They pressed on. The rain had stopped by the time they had reached Hannibal. He ate a small amount of fried chicken, and discussed the problem of flood control and farm subsidies. They sat until one o'clock in the bar, with a small group of flattered local politicians, and traded Midwestern stories on a first-name basis.

They arose early the next morning to make Columbia by noon. The Senator dined again, lightly, on fried chicken, and addressed the friendly, predominantly Democratic faculty of the university, on the subject of Federal Aid to Education. He was warmly received on that subject, but a coldness crept into the audience when he discussed the labor bill. He took a tour of the campus to see the new buildings which had been erected since his last visit. Later in the afternoon, Ellen had tea with the faculty ladies, and made an informal speech to them on juvenile delinquency and higher education. That evening, after dinner with the president of the university and his wife, the Senator addressed an enthusiastic but raucous crowd of students from the steps of the library. A group of the Governor's partisans heckled him from the vantage point of the library windows, but he dispatched them with humor. A giant bonfire was lit, and his name was awkwardly included in the school football cheers. A snake parade circled the quadrangle, and a ragamuffin effigy of the Governor was hung out of a dormitory window.

The next day, since they did not have to be in Kirksville until evening, they wound across the brown earth of Missouri at a more leisurely pace. Virgil had alerted friends in the towns ahead. They stopped for coffee, and the Senator shook hands and spoke for a few minutes underneath the hawklike visage of a Union soldier, who looked alertly toward the enemy to the south. In the next town, he took a ceremonial drink from the town spring. He shook the wiry hands of the farmers and local merchants and joked with them, but made no speech. At Moberly he dedicated a shopping center, which seemed gigantic and ambitious for the little town, and partook of the free Coca-Cola which was being distributed. They reached Kirksville about four-thirty, and he napped for about an hour. That evening he attended an arts festival at the high school, admired the water colors and sculptures, as well as the products of the more practical arts of carpentry and metalworking, and sat through a two-hour play, which was unbearable for all except those whose children were on the stage. Between the acts he was introduced, with appropriate flourishes of "Hail to the Chief," by the high-school band. That night they stayed at the home of an old college friend, who spoiled what they had all hoped would be a quiet breakfast and an unhurried start for Chillicothe the next day, by making breakfast a ceremonial occasion. Sixteen guests appeared at approximately eight o'clock for breakfast and an intimate discussion of politics.

Thus they were late in getting off to Chillicothe. Virgil had telephoned ahead to assure their hosts that they would arrive shortly, although they would be a little late and would, unfortunately, be forced to miss the meal. They arrived in time for apple pie and ice cream, which the Senator dutifully crushed with his fork in order to give the impression that at least part of it had been eaten. The next day they pushed on to Kansas City. There the Senator dwelt on that town as the true heart of the nation, where the culture of the East blended gracefully with the vigor of the West. He mentioned, of course, that Ellen had been born and brought up there, and that it was city of pleasant memories for him. It was a place to which he and Ellen liked to return, a place where they could get free of the multitudinous pressures of wicked Washington, where they could breathe the clear, fresh air of the Middle West, where men said what they thought and did what they thought was right, damn the consequences.

The next day was spent in talking to Kansas City councilmen, the mayor, the Democratic State Central Committee. Everyone he shook hands with assured him of their loyal support, although he knew that most of them were assessing their own positions, wondering how it would go with them if Ross MacKenzie won and they had backed the Senator, or how the Senator would deal with them if he won and they had backed Ross MacKenzie. Most of them had decided on a policy of watchful waiting, the cardinal principle of American politics. No need to jump one way or the other now. There was plenty of time yet. See which way the wind was blowing.

That evening, word reached them that the wind was blowing strongly in the direction of Senator Burnett. A St. Louis newspaper had published the results of its first straw poll.

If the primary election were being held today, which of these men would you vote for to be the Democratic nominee for United States Senator?

Burnett	67%
MacKenzie	29%
Don't know	4%

"Let's go back home, John," said Virgil, chuckling over the report. "Hell, it's all over."

"Wonderful, John, wonderful," said Ellen. "I knew he had no political appeal. They recognize him for what he is, an opportunist."

"It's gratifying," the Senator said. "It takes the pressure off a bit, but the most reliable adage in politics is 'always run scared,' and that I intend to do. Besides, the harder I campaign now, the easier it will be in the fall against the Republicans."

At Kansas City, the entourage was joined by Sidney Bronstein, his untidy brief case stuffed with notes, unrelated speech paragraphs, reports and pamphlets on Missouri by the U.S. departments of Agriculture, Commerce, Labor, and Interior, and the Missouri Chamber of Commerce. His foot locker, which could not be lifted by the strongest man, contained the *World Almanac*, the statistical abstract of the United States, the writings of Mark Twain, George Ade, and other Midwestern humorists, two books of famous quotations, a joke book, and assorted copies of the *Congressional Record*. It reposed in the trunk of the car and was not carried into the hotel rooms or the houses of friends where they stayed on the southern leg of their journey. Instead, Sidney would open it in the automobile trunk and thrash his way through it, trying to read notations by the tiny trunk light of the car. The Senator had an "all-purpose" speech—this required changing only the local facts—which he used in the places where the large metropolitan newspapers were not apt to pick up the speech in detail. But the local facts had to be correct, and they were checked by Virgil Akers with local townsmen. Nothing was deadlier than the mispronunciation of a local candidate's name or a place name, especially when the speech breathed long and folksy familiarity with the subject.

They moved east along the Missouri, stopping at the river towns, where the Senator shook hundreds of hands a day and made dozens of speeches. This was Virgil's territory, and he seemed to know the mayor and town councilmen of every town. Letters, of course, had been sent to them a month before, and Virgil spent his evenings talking on the telephone to the towns ahead, making a thousand small arrangements. The Senator dedicated a number of small bridges, additions to county courthouses and schools, strips of new road, a small airport, an ambitious industrial park, "close to all transportation, in the heart of industrial America, where labor is friendly and reasonable, and the tax and political climate favorable."

In the rural areas, he spoke to the farmers, the backbone of America, assuring them that their subsidies would continue, as indeed they must for the good of America. He was presented with innumerable bouquets from pretty little girls, and fancy scrolls from slicked-up little boys. In a single day, he made twelve speeches, ranging from ten minutes to thirty-five. He had dinner with the editor of the local weekly, or the owner of the radio station. When it rained, he spoke to small, sodden groups, in make-shift quarters. He pampered his rasping, protesting throat with box after box of honey cough drops, and, as he had learned in the early days of campaigning, took cat naps in the back of the car, in hotel rooms, in the bedrooms of friends' houses.

News arrived of the first poll taken by Kansas City's largest newspaper. The Senator was comfortably ahead, with something less than 63% of those polled favoring him for the nomination. Not quite as strong as the poll taken by the St. Louis paper, but still comfortable.

Word came also of the activities of the Governor. He was concentrating in St. Louis and Kansas City, believing that the labor vote in those industrial centers would go to him, if he hammered long enough on the Senator's "senile" sellout of his oldest friends, and his "political" motivations in so doing. After the publication of the polls, the Governor's attacks became more shrill and feverish, more and more reckless. Sooner or later, unless the polls turned, he must inevitably say something too irresponsible. The Senator waited patiently for this, carefully scanning the Governor's every word. There were things he said which could have been made to appear damaging, but the precise break the Senator was waiting for had not yet occurred.

Sidney was turning out paragraphs which would be integrated into speeches on the international situation, the farm problem, taxes and the budget, schools, roads, military preparations—and tying each of them to local problems wherever possible.

They all attended the fried chicken dinners, the fish fries, the pork barbecues, and corn roasts, eating little, while assuring the ladies, with a fond pat on an enormous arm, that it was a joy to taste home cooking again, and telling the proud husbands how lucky they were to get food like that daily.

They moved south into the Ozark country, "vacation head-quarters for the Midwest, where the accents of the south and the mountains blend." And finally they turned north, to make their way back to St. Louis, after a trip to Carruthersville, where the Senator demonstrated to a highly amused group of cotton farmers an almost forgotten ability to auction cotton.

When they got back to St. Louis, the Senator made a speech,

allegedly non-political, to the Missouri Historical Society. Often in Washington, he told them, he yearned for that great tawny river that was like no other. He yearned to sit on its banks in solitude and watch it majestically roll to the Gulf. Somehow, the old river washed away the trivial and the unimportant, leaving only the truth. More than once, on the banks of the Mississippi, he had worked out the answers to problems difficult for him. Did they know, those who lived on its banks and crossed back and forth over it every day, what a wonder of the world it really was? This touched them—and the Senator meant it, for although he had no enthusiasm for St. Louis, he had a great feeling for the river. A local newspaper the next day abstracted his remarks and printed them in a box on the front page. An editorial read, in part: "The Senator expressed, perhaps as well as anyone since Mark Twain, the way we feel about our mighty river. The American Midwest has sent forth many men who have become famous, but most of them, as attested by the simple elegance of Senator Burnett's tribute, never forget that awesome river that divides the East from the West."

Virgil estimated that on the tour they had shaken hands with seventy-five thousand, perhaps even one hundred thousand people, and had been seen or heard by two hundred thousand more. He gauged their reception among politicians as positive but not yet completely committed in the northern part of the state; positively committed to the Senator in the southern part; and in St. Louis and Kansas City, inclined toward the Senator but waiting watchfully to see how things were going. Under these circumstances, it was decided that a bold stroke was necessary to demonstrate that the Senator was going to beat Ross MacKenzie, and thus push the fence-sitters off the fence. The Senator, therefore, challenged Ross to a debate in the Civic Auditorium. "An old-fashioned method of exploring an issue and a method guaranteed to restore some of the old-time vibrancy and sense of urgency to politics, which has deteriorated to dull speeches of late." The topic suggested was "The Labor Question."

The newspapers seized the challenge and called for its fulfillment. Ross MacKenzie seemed at first to jump at the chance to pin the Senator to the wall on this, his chosen issue, and his lieutenants crowed quietly that the Senator had goofed badly, that he had misinterpreted the sentiment of the people. Then Ross began cautiously walking around the problem, examining it carefully for booby traps. His union advisors pressed him to go ahead and assured him that they would supply all of the help he needed to prepare the debate. Lawyers and economists would be flown out from the NFL in Washington. The St. Louis debate would serve to demonstrate to the country the infamy of those "hot-house liberals," who had failed labor at the crucial moment. But other advisors pointed to the Senator's reputation as one of the Senate's compelling debaters, a man who knew the forensic tricks that win arguments over better-reasoned approaches. There was talk that the audiences might be packed. Why not wait, they said. You have just begun your campaign. Perhaps it is going so well that you won't need to resort to exhibitionism such as this. If the next polls show that you are gaining, better leave things as they are and pursue a course which seems to be right, rather than take a risk on a chancy debate. And if the polls indicate that all is not going well, there will be plenty of time for debating later on.

Caution, in the end, prevailed, and Ross issued a statement that such "theatrics" were unseemly in a contest such as this. Abraham Lincoln did not feel them demeaning, the Senator replied. In the next week, the Senator continued his needling. How could a man who would not stand up for his principles before an audience in his home state be expected to conduct himself in Washington? And how effective would he be in the Senate of the United States, debating with many men, when he refused to stand up and debate with a single man?

Apparently the Senator hopes that a debate would give him a chance to explain his own flexible principles, Ross said. My principles are well known. They are clear and firm, and such a debate would only result in their being twisted beyond recognition by an opponent who is well known for such tactics.

Just what are these principles? the Senator answered. They are not well known to me, and I doubt if they are to most of the electorate. Is the problem, perhaps, that there are no principles, and thus the Governor has no fixed position from which to debate?

It seems to me that the Senator, answered Ross, is the man with no fixed principles. Now he is with labor, now he is against them. Blown from one side to the other by the winds of political expediency.

I am committed to the principles of personal honesty and integrity. I am owned by no one, as I think was well demonstrated in the last session of Congress. Can Mr. MacKenzie make such a statement in clear conscience?

A scurrilous implication that may warrant legal action, snarled the Governor. Typical of the falsities and malicious innuendo that my opponent is so skillful in spreading.

The Senator quoted from Benjamin Franklin: "It is hard for an empty sack to stand upright."

Nothing further is to be gained, said the Governor in a prepared statement, in attempting to answer the untruths of my opponent. I am confident that the people, in the privacy of the polling booths, will retire this old man, who demeans the dignity of the United States Senate.

With that he flew off to Hannibal, where, despite the fact that he had forsworn the contest, he continued the debate without surcease. The St. Louis paper released a second poll. The Senator's margin was five percentage points lower, and MacKenzie's four per cent higher. "The forces of liberality are gaining on the forces of reaction," shouted Ross. "The current is as strong as the Mississippi, and it is being felt at all levels."

The Governor appears desperate, said a statement issued by the Senator's office. The plain figures of the poll show the Senator with a little less than a two-to-one majority. We think that the figures speak for themselves.

The nation's leading news magazine said, in a capsule report on state primaries: "Canny John Burnett and youthful challenger Ross MacKenzie are slugging it out in typical Missouri Give-'em-hell Harry style. MacKenzie's charge of sellout on the labor bill has pulled in the liberals from the tall grass in left field, but the nod, on August 16, is still likely to go to old hand Burnett."

239

20

As the Senator traveled throughout Missouri, he hammered on the subject of a face-to-face debate. His speech subjects varied, but into every one he injected—sometimes with great seriousness or humility, sometimes with humor—a challenge to Ross Mac-Kenzie to debate "anywhere, any time," in the great American political tradition. Inevitably, the announcement of the grounded gauntlet brought a great round of cheers and applause from his audience. Radio, television, and the newspapers reported the successive challenges with great enthusiasm. Ross could feel his press going sour as he was repeatedly asked about a debate, and he refused to comment, or dismissed the idea as "undignified showmanship" or "worthless exchange." The press, always anxious for a good story, began to needle him. The columnists in the St. Louis and Kansas City papers began to remark about his caution, then his lack of confidence, and they began to hint that he was afraid to meet the Senator in open debate. True, they wrote sardonically, the Senator was a formidable and experienced opponent with whom no one would tangle without extended and careful thought, which the Governor certainly seemed to be giving the situation.

Finally, the Governor's reluctant hand was forced. He attended the state fair at Sedalia the day after the Senator had appeared there and had issued again his challenge to debate. The

Governor was to present prizes to 4-H Club winners. As he stood at the microphone in front of the stands, which were filled primarily by children and young people, a faint chorus sounded: "Fraidy cat. Fraidy cat. Fraidy cat." It was picked up with great glee by the entire group, and grew to a thunderous shout. For two or three minutes, the Governor stood, as if deaf, chatting with the embarrassed officials, as other officials frantically passed up and down before the stands, hissing and hushing down the youngsters. The Mayor of Sedalia shouted repeatedly into the microphone, "Stop that, stop that immediately," but the chanting continued. At last the fun began to wear itself out, as some youngsters dropped out of the shouting, until it finally collapsed into applause and laughter. The Mayor, tight-lipped and red-faced with fury, shouted into the microphone, "This is disgraceful behavior, and if I hear one more sound from anyone, these awards will not be presented and we'll never have a 4-H Club competition again. Do you hear that?" He waited for a moment in the silence. "I have never, in my years in public life in this state, heard of such a disgraceful insult to an invited guest. I can assure you that the question of whether 4-H Club competition will continue will be carefully studied after this shocking, rude behavior." He continued to lash them for two or three minutes. "I should not be at all surprised," he said, "if the Governor left immediately, and not only declined to make these awards, but refused ever to set foot at our fair again. I think that he would be perfectly justified in doing so. But apparently the Governor is willing to put aside this barbarous conduct, and make the awards. And, as at least partial repentance for our disgraceful behavior, I want every person in these stands to rise and give the Governor a round of applause." He glowered at them, and they, properly chastised, rose and applauded the Governor, then settled back to hear him.

"Mayor Meekins, Fair Manager Andrews, Members of the Awards Committee, and My Young Friends. After an exciting competition such as this one, there remains a certain residue of animal spirits, and I just want to say to your splendid Mayor Meekins that I certainly don't object to an occasional outbreak of such spirits, even if, as it seems, I am the goat. The prize goat, it might be appropriate to say. And I would like to propose to you gentlemen—and this is merely a proposal, a suggestion, because I would not presume to interfere with your authority in the operation of your own fair—that any thought of discontinuing this worthy competition be waived. Boys will be boys and girls will be girls. . . ."

Laughter and applause came from the stands.

He continued with the ceremony and presented a series of gangling youths and bright-eyed girls with the awards. He was politely applauded at the conclusion, and accepted with grace the repeated apologies of the officials.

A knot of admirers and handshakers moved with him across the infield to his car. The Governor and four of his party got into the car, and after he had shaken the last hand stuck through the back window, the car moved slowly off, but not before a mocking cry pierced the darkness:

"Fraidy cat."

One of the Governor's aides, who was riding in the front seat, spun around and said, "Did that bastard organize that, do you think?"

"I don't think so," responded another aide. "It seemed to start up so spontaneously. Some smart-aleck kid started it, and they all took it up. That's the way it looked to me. What do you think, Governor?"

"I'm not sure," he said. "Very difficult to tell. I wouldn't put it past the old coot, of course."

"I thought you turned it nicely," said the aide in the front seat, "proclaiming a general amnesty. Besides, half those kids didn't know what they were hollering about."

"Perhaps," said the Governor, pursing his lips, "but perhaps half of them did. And if that's so, then I'd say we can't ignore this any longer. If it's a general topic of conversation to that extent, then we have to move. I hate to give that bastard the satisfaction, but we may have to—"

"You're thinking of a series of debates?"

"No. I don't want to get into that. I'm thinking of some gesture, perhaps a single debate, that will get this monkey off my back. What I'm really after is something that will give the appearance of a debate, but won't be one exactly. . . ."

His aides listened in puzzled silence and offered no suggestions.

"Maybe a half-hour television show. He takes fifteen minutes. I take fifteen. That would give the appearance of face-to-face contest, yet I wouldn't get into this morass of debate with him."

The aides nodded.

"At any rate, let's wait and gauge the newspaper reaction. If it doesn't get much attention, maybe we can pass it."

"It'll get plenty of attention," said the aide in the front seat gloomily, "I think we can count on that."

He was right. The newspapers reported the embarrassing outbreak in great detail on the front page. The Mayor and other officials, when interviewed, deplored the incident and praised the Governor for his statesmanship. A 4-H Club official was highly irritated with the threat of a canceled program and lamented the tendency to punish his hard-working young farmers when they were blameless in the entire affair. The occurrence was discussed, dragged out, and referred to regularly in subsequent stories about the Governor's campaign. Finally, the Governor made an announcement, which was intended to be a *fait accompli*. He had, he said, arranged with the producer of a popular television show, "Meet the People," to appear in a debate with his opponent, provided that the Senator had not been bluffing about the whole affair. Not at all, answered the Senator blandly. He would consider it an honor to meet, as he had repeatedly said, "any time, anywhere," and he was certain that the electorate would benefit from having a chance to examine the two candidates in "free and fair debate."

In time, of course, the Senator became aware that the Governor did not have in mind a debate, but two separate speeches. It was an awkward problem. After his insistence on a debate, there was no possibility that the Senator could now cancel his own appearance on the technical ground that it was not a debate in the sense that he had meant. He had challenged the Governor, and the Governor had accepted. An argument over details would appear to be a trumped-up excuse to avoid the contest. Ross would obviously seize such an act, and accuse him of bad faith and bluffing. Finally, the Senator was able to win over the moderator of the show, a popular and wry news commentator. His role, under the Governor's plan, was merely to introduce the two candidates and to close the show. The Senator proposed, instead, that each of the candidates make a statement of seven minutes, and the remaining fifteen minutes would be devoted to debate on selected topics. This was rejected by the Governor's negotiators. A compromise was finally reached: In the final fifteen minutes of the show, the moderator would direct identical questions to each of the candidates. This was not accepted happily by Ross's group, but the moderator was strongly for it.

A week later, the two men met in the studio on the appointed date and took positions in easy chairs, with the moderator in the center, in the usual false library setting. Ross made his statement, which did not mention his opponent. It was serious and a little dull. The Senator began with a sly story, then made indirect references to the Governor's youth and inexperience, subtly contrasting it with his own career of the past thirty-five years.

The question period began without incident, after an announcement by the moderator that, although questions might at times appear to be sharp and intemperate, he was merely trying to clarify the issues.

"There has been one area in which you two gentlemen have persistently disagreed," said the moderator. "This is the area of labor reform. Senator, after a career of serving labor, why did you turn your back on her at this crucial time?"

The Senator took a few seconds to sort out the elements of the loaded and irritating question.

"Jack, I don't like the expression that I've *served labor*. It sounds as if I've been a lackey of labor. Owned by them. I'm sure you didn't mean it in that unfair context. . . ." He fixed the moderator with a cool eye.

"No, I . . ."

"I'm sure you didn't, but I just wanted to clear up any misconception that might arise. I have voted, it's true, to further the interests of the workingman. But that's quite a different thing, as I'm sure you agree. I've never served anybody or any group, except the people of Missouri and the people of the United States, and I make no apologies for either of those. As for the remainder of the question, I don't feel that I've turned my back on the laboring man. When a man has spent thirty-five years in public life, as I have, he looks back occasionally and asks himself: Just what have I accomplished? And when I look back over those many years, the single thing that I pride myself most on is the fact that I have tried to help the workingman. I bear the scars of many fights, because advocacy of such a cause naturally results in wounds. I think that my record has been one of consistent support for this cause, and I think that the vote I cast in the Senate two months ago was consistent with my record of thirty-five years. I cast that vote for a single reason and it is this: Labor will survive and grow stronger only if it is built on the solid foundation of honesty and service to the workingman. In this lies its ultimate strength. If the evils that we have seen exposed, continue to spread, they will ultimately poison, and perhaps destroy, the trade union movement in this country."

"Senator," continued the moderator, "you say all this despite the fact that labor itself is very much against the bill, and management seems to be very much for it. Does that mean you're siding with management?"

"I'm siding with the American people, and I believe, without question, the American people as a whole are in favor of the law. I am not for labor and against management, nor vice versa. I think that is essentially an immoral approach. That's a pressure-group approach to legislation, and I think it's clearly wrong. Further, if management professes to see in this law a license to destroy labor and attempts to pervert it to that end, I will personally introduce corrective legislation and use every resource to see that it is enacted."

"Senator, granting for a moment that something needed to be done in this area, why did the law have to be so punitive? Why did it have to cut so deeply into the good to destroy the bad?"

"Jack, I'm not at all convinced that the law, in practice, will be so upsetting as many people think. I don't view it as punitive. I would never have voted for it if I had. I view it as corrective, and I have no doubts that it will prove to be so. Let me say this. The law is not perfect. No law ever is. Certainly, some disabilities will develop, and I think that you can rely on the Congress to amend the law, when and if it is found that certain provisions are in fact imperfect."

"Now I would like to turn to the Governor, and cover this same ground with him," the moderator said. "Governor, what specifically are your objections to the new labor reform law?"

"Jack," he said, addressing the moderator in a friendly manner, "the laboring people of this country need the help and assistance of the Government. The single laboring man is helpless before the assembled might of money and power of the large corporations. His only salvation is in his right to organize and bargain collectively—and to be protected in that right."

"And your objections?" asked the moderator.

"I'm coming to that, Jack," said the Governor, evenly. "I feel that the enemies of labor have seen their opportunities and seized them, and in so doing have duped the unwary. They have seen labor's troubles and have rushed in, in an attempt to sever labor's jugular vein, while she is weak."

"You feel, then, that the bill is all bad?"

"Much of it," the Governor said. "In fact, most of it I think is bad. The limitations on labor's right to picket, for example, seem to me to be evil. A step backward. In fact, there is evidence indicating that this particular section was dreamed up by the National Association of Manufacturers."

"But where that picketing is used to intimidate workers and employers and force them to join unions they don't want to join . . . ?"

"This should be discouraged, of course. But I think that labor itself, given enough time, could have cleaned up its own house."

"And you feel they are cleaning up their own house?"

"Yes," Ross said, "I think they have shown a high degree of responsibility. They have made an excellent beginning."

"Beginning?" said the moderator.

The Governor colored, and began in measured words: "Mr. Tream, I have not said that I countenance the evils that have occurred. I have stated that repeatedly and I state it again, so that there can be no mistake about it. I say merely that we should not use a meat ax where a scalpel is required."

"As I understand you, Governor, and I may be misinterpreting, and please correct me if I am, you feel that labor should be permitted to clean up its own house."

"I do. And they are doing it."

"And that in the meantime we should hold off on legislation?"

"In the future, if they don't do the job, something further may be required. . . ."

"But right now, no legislation is necessary."

"That is correct," said the Governor. "No legislation is necessary right now."

Thus, John Burnett got the break he was waiting for, and Ross MacKenzie lost any chance of winning the race for Senator. The next morning, editorially, the St. Louis paper spoke: "With over two years of investigations behind us, and almost daily exposures of crime and corruption by a certain element within the trade-union movement, we find it incredible that the Governor should make the statement, as he did last night on a televised program in which he appeared with Senator Burnett, that 'no legislation is necessary.'

"We feel that the recently passed labor reform law is, in some respects, too harsh and perhaps will require amendment. But the major thrust of the law, which attempts to protect the workingman against the stealing of his money and his birthright as a union man, we think represents a necessary step forward. We have been told that every politician is against sin. Perhaps our Governor has not been in politics long enough to be aware of that maxim. We recommend it to his attention."

Across the state, Kansas City's principal paper said indignantly: "The plain facts of the case are that corruption was beginning to take over the labor unions, rather than an eradication of corruption by the unions. Without the protection of the new law, a predatory labor leader would be able to operate, using the methods of beatings, bribery, and intimidation. The united labor movement ejected the Truckers from the Federation, yet the Truckers did not collapse; in fact, they gained new members at a faster rate than the Federation itself. We suggest that this indicates that the Federation, with all of its good intentions, cannot handle the problem itself. When the Governor states that 'no legislation is necessary,' we wonder just where he has been for the last few years. To suggest that the present law may be inadequate or may be too strong is one thing; to suggest that nothing is needed, flies in the face of several hundred volumes of testimony taken by the investigating committee. Such a position may gain the Governor applause from his coterie of union backers, but it will not gain him many votes from sober-thinking citizens who have even cursorily examined the facts."

The newspapers in Jefferson City, St. Joseph, Hannibal, and other towns began to take similar lines. A number of radio stations and several television stations editorialized on the subject. Senator John Burnett, of course, made the Governor's statement the subject of a number of speeches, and never failed to mention it.

"I don't think my opponent," he would say magnanimously, "is an evil man, nor do I think that he countenances evil. I think perhaps that he spoke out on problems with which he had little acquaintance. And perhaps that small and intimate circle of 'advisors' who appear to be telling him what to say placed a hand over his mouth, his eyes, and his lips, so that he resembled the proverbial monkeys who could 'see no evil, hear no evil, and speak no evil.'"

Ross fought back, but the battle was lost. The statement was misinterpreted, he said. That part of the law devoted to clearly criminal activities he would support to the hilt. It was only those parts which sought to weaken the union movement that he objected to. As for the question of evil, one had only to look at his record as chief administrator of the state. A record unblemished by a whiff of scandal. That was his answer to those who would drag this campaign for high office to the level of a mudslinging contest.

As the campaign went into the final week, the Senator moved more rapidly, appearing in public, shaking hands from seven in the morning in the barbershops, until eleven at night in the hotel lobbies. The newspaper polls showed that Ross was a clear loser, and he became angrier in his outbursts, while the Senator remained calm. Audiences listened to the red-faced Governor with interest and mystification as he shouted for twenty minutes, without variation in pitch or modulation. He attacked the Senator shrilly, stating that his vote was a pay-off to the National Association of Manufacturers and the Chamber of Commerce. But few listened to the desperate voice. Most minds were made up, and when August 16, primary day, arrived, sweaty people stood in line to enter the suffocating voting booths. By nine o'clock that evening, television was blaring the results. John Burnett was the nominee of the Democratic party by a margin approaching three to one. They also announced that Roger Carpenter, who was unopposed for the Republican nomination, would be the Senator's opponent.

21

The flight from Washington to Providence seemed long. Ed Flowers stared tensely out of the window at the wing as it cut through the cold mist. A cloud of depression had settled on him.

Goddam Agnes. And her stinking, rotten mess of a squabble over money. Fighting over support payments for the kids. Trying to make him feel like a war criminal. Teamed up with that lawyer, trying to bleed him white. Punishing him because he didn't love her any more. Sitting through the whole thing like a sad Madonna while the lawyers were snapping and biting over the dough. Bitch. What was he supposed to tell her? That he just outgrew her. That he made a mistake twenty years ago. That he just couldn't face the same dull life with her for the next twenty years. What was he supposed to say? Look, Agnes, here are the six reasons I want a divorce.

And goddam Barbara. When will it be over, Ed? When will she go to Alabama, Ed? Pushing him. Pushing him, pushing him, pushing him to get it over. Frank was pushing him too. And Harrack. Everybody was pushing him.

A column head in the newspaper lying on the seat beside him caught his eye. He picked it up.

"Senator John Burnett drew large crowds in Hannibal and St. Joseph as he kicked off his campaign against the Republican nominee, Roger Carpenter," the story began. "Burnett defended his labor record and stated, 'I firmly believe that the true liberal, who is usually on the side of reform, was on the side of reform here.'"

Ed dropped the paper in disgust. The traitorous bastard had beaten MacKenzie. Goddam John Burnett too. Goddam everybody.

He had an hour's layover in the Providence airport before the connecting flight left for Fall River. Then a long cab ride to the DeSantos'.

As he sat in the DeSantos' living room, Ed was conscious that he was very tired, but his bitter mood was gone.

Although he had not seen the living room for three years, it remained the same, a mismatched collection of Bronx Renaissance. Pete DeSanto lived in the same house, with the same living-room furniture that he had had when Ed had been president of the Local and Pete had been secretary-treasurer. Now that the DeSanto children were grown, time seemed to have stopped in the old frame house. Typical of Pete, Ed thought. Plain, honest, straightforward. Right up the middle. Ed yearned for the old days in Fall River; they had been full of success and good fellowship, free of the press of fighting and responsibility and decisions that seemed to be his present lot. Pete held aloft his glass of wine.

"To the continued success of the American Electronic Workers, Edward Flowers, and the DeSantos." Ed nodded and raised his glass.

"And how is Agnes?" asked Alma DeSanto, attempting to ease the gap of years.

"She's fine," Ed said, but he decided that he might as well get it over with. "Actually, she really isn't so fine. We've decided that it might be better, in view of the fact that we've had a few problems, if we . . ." he strung out the sentence with unnecessary words ". . . went our separate ways."

Both the DeSantos' great Italian eyes opened wide with astonishment. "You've decided to separate?" Pete said, in open disbelief.

"Yes," Ed said, "we have. It's no secret that there hasn't been anything between us for a long time."

"It was a secret to me," Alma said.

"It's been a very difficult thing on both of us, but we've talked about it, and it seems like the best thing."

"It's impossible to believe," Alma said. "Everything seemed to be fine when you were up here. Did something happen when you went to Washington?"

"Not exactly. Nothing in particular happened. It just became apparent that it was just a sham, living together."

"Stay apart for a while, I think," said Alma. "Think things over and get your bearings and probably in a week or two, everything will work itself out."

"It's too late for that, I'm afraid. We have already decided that Agnes will file for divorce."

"Divorce," said Pete.

"Yes, actually we're just trying to work out a property settlement with our lawyers. Once we agree on that, then she'll go down to Alabama and get it."

"So quick?" Alma said.

"It can be done this way if both parties are in agreement, so that nobody contests it."

"Eddie," said Alma, with tears in the corners of her eyes, "what are you doing?"

"It's a very hard thing to explain, Alma, as I said. Sometimes two people decide that they'd be happier going their own separate ways."

"But after twenty years . . ."

"That makes it hard," Ed said. "But you finally wake up to the fact that you're forty-six and there's no sense in living the rest of your life in a way that makes you both unhappy."

"Agnes feels this way?" Alma said.

"Well, I don't think she's been very happy either."

"You were always so much to her, Ed, you and the kids," Alma said. "That was her whole life. Now, *pfft*, it's all gone. All over in a second."

"I know, Alma. I know it all," Ed said, "I've thought it over a thousand times. Believe me, there's no other way."

"Are you sure?" Alma said. "Maybe a little waiting might make things different. What can it hurt?"

"I've waited as long as I'm going to wait," Ed said. "I'm not getting any younger."

"What will Agnes do?" Alma said.

"She'll be all right moneywise. We're still arguing about some things, but her lawyer is making damn sure of that. She is going to be plenty well taken care of. She'll be able to live without working. Which is more than I can say for myself."

"The poor little ones."

"That's the worst, of course. They're not so little any more, Alma. Ed Junior is seventeen, and Anne is fifteen. It's hard for them. It's hard for everybody."

"You interested in somebody else, Ed?" Pete asked.

Ed took a long sip of his wine. "That's part of it, yes."

A wounded look crept into Alma's eyes. "Someone young, I guess."

"Somewhat younger."

"It's a sad thing," Pete said.

"I know it."

They sat for a full minute, looking at one another, or staring at the convoluted patterns of the imitation Oriental rug on the floor.

"Actually," Ed said at last, "I came to see you, Pete, because there's some trouble brewing in the union. You may know about it. May know more than I do about it."

Pete nodded. "I heard a few things."

"Some people apparently want to kick me out."

"I haven't heard much, but I did hear that. They don't talk about it much around me because they know we're friends."

"Don Harrack's the ring leader. He apparently feels that I didn't do as much as I should have in the Airython campaign. And he's got some other grudges. Feels I'm not militant enough, like Frank Raeder. Feels we sit around in Washington, spending the dues money and doing nothing."

"Blowing it on women, he says," Pete added. "This thing about this girl, that's gotten around. I'm just mentioning it because it plays a part."

Ed pressed his lips together. "People are such damn busybodies."

253

"In your job, Ed, you got no secrets. Face it."

"Well, it's none of their damn business."

"Maybe, but they think it is," Pete said, "so I guess it is. And I think you ought to keep it in mind. What else do you think is causing all this?"

"Oh, the labor bill, of course. That has them all discontented. They blame us for not stopping it. I don't know what all is involved. You get one troublemaker like Harrack, and all the other troublemakers gather around him."

"Have any of them talked to you?" Pete asked.

"No. They haven't been near me. Although they must know that I'd hear about it sooner or later. It's a funny thing. After we lost the election at Airython, Don was upset, and I told him to take a month off. Go down to Miami and relax, and we'd send him his checks. But he just disappeared. Never called for his checks. Never even picked up his last two-weeks' pay. We went ahead and made out his checks for three or four weeks, and held them for him, then we stopped."

"Checks don't mean much to Don."

"He's an oddball. I always thought so."

"A good man, though," Pete said. "Too bad if we lose him."

"I'm not so sure," Ed said. "We can't be forever pampering the egos of a bunch of prima donnas who think they're God's gift to the union movement or something."

"Maybe not, but I think you ought to get in touch with them. See what's on their minds."

"Get in touch with them, hell. Let them get in touch with me."

"But if they don't? Then I don't see that you hurt yourself to swallow your pride for the good of the union."

"If I did that, they'd think they've got me scared."

"Well, don't they, a little bit?"

"Sure, between you and me, yes. But you don't go around advertising that fact. You don't give them that satisfaction."

"I don't mean, of course, that you would have to do it personally. Somebody else could do it. A middleman."

Ed eyed him. "You volunteering?"

Pete grimaced. "I don't like the idea much. But I'm the one's been talking up the good of the union. I guess I would, if you got nobody else."

"All right," said Ed. "I buy the idea. You'll have to travel around a good bit. The International will pick up the check on that."

"Better not. Better I manage it from here. Let me handle it."

"All right," said Ed. "We've been friends a long time. I don't know anybody I'd trust more. See what you can do. I'd sure as hell like to do it this way, rather than have the whole thing blow up at the convention."

"My idea is this," Pete said. "See what the gripes are. Not what they say they are at first, but what they really are underneath the surface. And see if they might go for a deal, if they got at least part of what they wanted. When we know that much, we can talk. It's the same thing as dealing with companies. You need to find out what the real gut issues are, then you got to probe around for a deal."

"I agree. With this local as a base, we've got a good start."

"If we have this local," Pete said. "If."

"This is my own local."

"Was. Seven years ago it was."

"For Christ's sake," Ed said, rising and kicking idly at the rug. "If this local isn't with me, I might as well quit right now."

"I didn't say it wasn't," Pete said. "But there's troublemakers in this local just like all the others. I've had my feelers out, and I know who they are, and I don't think there are very many of them. But there are some. I haven't sounded off on the matter till I got the lay of the land. These things come and go, and it might be all over in a month. So lay low and see what happens, I say."

"My own local. God, that's hard to believe."

"Don't be so upset. There's nothing to believe one way or the other yet."

"Well, let me ask you this. If you had to send delegates to the convention right now, how many would be with me?"

"I told you, Ed, you can't say. You'd get a majority. Maybe eighty, ninety, ninety-five per cent. But you can't tell. There's a big body of guys that will hold off to see who's going to win, so they can end up on the winning side. Those guys will come with us, if they don't think the Harrack crowd has a chance. Other-wise. . . ."

"Harrack's going to be strong on the coast. He organized the aircraft out there, and he's thick as thieves with them. But in Cleveland he won't get very far with Hager, unless I'm badly mistaken."

"We don't know nothing yet, remember," Pete said. "Let me get out and talk to a few people before we start jumping to con-clusions."

"Fine, Pete, I sure do appreciate it." He put his arm around the wiry Italian's shoulder. "You know who your friends are when something like this happens."

"You should know them any time," Pete said.

22

John Burnett had come back to Missouri, the newspapers speculated, to patch up the Democratic party. It was true. In the several months of the primary campaign, a large number of Democrats had come to dislike him more and more, and finally to hate him. For weeks they had dwelt on his weaknesses, his follies, his duplicity, and his trickery. All of the hate talk of the last three months—that votes had been bought and paid for, that scurrilous lies had been circulated, that unconscionable deals had been made, that people had been duped by craft or frightened by coercion—had to be denied or explained, and all those who had believed such talk must push it into a far corner of the mind and enter the new world of morality where bad had become good. Now they must turn about, under the general political rule that any Democrat was better than any Republican, and fight for the hated John Burnett. It was a difficult transition, which only experienced politicians were able to manage easily. These amateurs, who made up such a large part of the party, were emotionally committed to the Governor, and they would find it difficult to slide out of one set of emotions and into another, like a snake shedding its skin. Ross's help would be necessary.

The Governor, his bright dream tarnished, showed his disappointment only for a moment as the Senator entered his office doorway. But for an instant his face was contorted.

"John," he said, rising from his desk and extending his hand, "again, congratulations from the vanquished to the victor."

"I don't look at it that way, Ross," the Senator said, settling comfortably into the chair in front of the Governor's desk. "As I see it, it was a spirited contest between two good men, if I may be so immodest in the sanctity of your office . . . and one man, because of small circumstances, must be given the job. The other man isn't a loser, because they both had a share in making a better and stronger party, and because the loser, if you will, lives again to fight another day."

Ross smiled tightly. "A pretty speech, whatever it means."

"It means this, Ross. We had a knockdown, dragout, and things got pretty mean and bitter, as they always seem to, despite the best of intentions. But to use the old analogy, it was a family fight. You may fight with your kids, but you don't throw them out of the family; you form a solid front in dealing with the world."

"Come now, John," said Ross, strolling over to the window. "What do you think I'm going to do, back the Republican candidate?"

"Of course not, but you and the fine organization you built up might not give their enthusiastic and unreserved support to me, and the result might be the loss of a Democratic Senate seat for Missouri."

"Oh, nonsense, John, Carpenter doesn't have a chance. You have nothing in the world to worry about."

The Senator paused. "Let me give you a short lecture, from my vantage point of thirty-five years in politics, in the privacy of this office, Ross. Carpenter does have a chance, and a good one. He's going to run well in this state. It's apparent he's going to take his half of the road out of the middle. And now that the Old Guard has seen that he's not a New York liberal, they're falling in line. The younger people in the party are wild about him. There is a Republican tide running. I can feel it the way old men can tell by their bunions that a storm is coming. If you wanted me to, I could sit down and list a thousand little manifestations of it. And don't think that I'm running scared, like all politicians. I am certain of this. Now, I don't think that the Carpenter tide is strong enough to carry Missouri against a united, hard-working

Democratic party, but I do think that it is possible, if half of the party sits on their hands or gives lukewarm support. It's not only possible, but likely. So I'm pointing this out to you, Ross—you lost the primary and I won. But in a real sense, you won because you hold the key to whether I win the general election in November. . . ."

"I think you're exaggerating."

"No, sir. If I'm anything, I'm a political realist. I took a few opportunities to watch Carpenter in action during the primary. He isn't one of these boneheaded, stiff-necked Neanderthal Republicans that we're used to. He's smart and quick; he's good looking and mildly progressive; and he exudes honesty and integrity. You add a good candidate like that to a tide running and a split Democratic party, and I think that I am not exaggerating when I say we have something to worry about."

"John, there's no question that we'll support you. No question at all."

"The question is: How and how much, Ross? I'm not just talking about a declaration from you that you support me. I mean some real campaigning on your part, and what's more important, some private talks with some of your key supporters. Some real hairy-chested talks that lay down the law to them. Most importantly, with the labor people who broke away from me to support you . . ."

"That's not easy, John. They worked up a real hatred for you, mainly because of the labor bill. They feel you betrayed them."

"I know that. I tried to reason with them, but they were determined not to listen. It was the old case of having their minds made up and not wanting to be confused by the facts."

"As you said earlier, things got pretty emotional before we were through," Ross said.

"True, but I think that you can help me with them. And you can help in the northern part of the state. You come from there, and you ran well up there. Your organization was superior to mine. I need your help there. And third, I need money. I'm not asking you to turn over your principal financial backers to me, even assuming that you could. But I need some help in raising money, and you have access to some sources that I don't."

"You have Herbert Shannon."

"I do, but Herbert is not enough, and he's already contributed heavily to the primary."

The Senator watched Ross MacKenzie closely as he spoke. He judged that he could ask the delicate question. "Actually, I had high hopes that you might serve as chairman of my campaign committee. It's the traditional method of sealing the breach that primaries bring about."

The Governor looked at him without a change of expression. "I don't know about that," he said slowly. "I'd want to be sure it was the right thing for you as well as for me. Let me think about it."

"As you wish."

Ross strolled back to the desk and sat down in the Governor's chair. "Now let me ask the sixty-four-dollar question, Senator. What's in this for me?"

"Anything," said the Senator. "I regard your ability highly, and I would certainly support you for any post that I can think of. If you want to run for Governor again, or for Congress, I'll back you to the hilt. I'll campaign hard for you. In short, I'll do for you exactly what I'm asking you to do for me. If you're interested in a judgeship, and I think that you are well qualified for that, I would guess that with my seniority and my generally good relations with the other side, I could swing it for you. An ambassadorship—that takes more money than you or I have, and I'd say that it's doubtful, unless you would be willing to take some less desirable post. But you name it."

"Suppose," said Ross, tapping a pencil on his desk blotter, "suppose I wanted to run for Bell's seat next time."

The Senator was ready for the question. "I think that there is a good chance that Bell will want to run for Governor when his term expires. In that case, I would, of course, back you, if you wanted it."

"And suppose he doesn't. Suppose he wants to continue in the Senate."

"Well, let me say this, Ross. I will do everything in my power to get Bell to move out of the Senate seat at the end of this term, and there are a number of other things that might be attractive to him, and I think the chances of his taking my advice are fairly good. However . . . however, if Les Bell wants to run for the Senate again, I am committed to help him. I gave him that pledge when he agreed to back me in the primary."

"I thought as much."

"Look, Ross, I could have lied to you and made promises to back both of you and worried about it when and if the time ever came. But I'm trying to be honest with you."

Ross glowered at his desk calendar. "So I am to be limited to the state, then, is that it?"

"No, there are other things."

"Well, I can tell you right now that I am not interested in being a freshman member of the U.S. House of Representatives. And I'm not interested in being a cookie-pusher someplace in Southeast Asia. And I'm not much interested in running for Governor again."

"And the judgeship?"

"Retire to the bench at thirty-seven, with one chance in a thousand of making Appeals Court, and one in a million of making Supreme Court. Thanks for nothing."

"I'm sorry you feel this way, Ross."

"I'm just being candid with you. I suppose these leavings are the rewards of a defeated politician."

"Ross, I think that you have a great future in politics, in this state, and at the national level, if you manage things right. Most of your life is ahead of you. You've already come a long way in thirty-seven years. You've got a lot of drive, but a major part of the art of politics is waiting and grabbing the main chance. You've tried to grab too soon, but that doesn't mean that you're finished. All sorts of opportunities are going to open up, and as the ablest young politician in the state, you are in an unequaled position to take advantage of them."

"Those are pleasant, vague words. We've run over all the possibilities, haven't we? And I don't see all of those opportunities you cheerfully paint."

"Well, not right now, not right at this moment, but things change, and rapidly."

"Things can change for the worse as well as for the better."

"So," said the Senator, "that's always the case in politics as well as anything else, isn't it?"

"They seem to run one way or the other sometimes. Luck, good and bad, runs in threes, they say."

"Well, Ross," the Senator said, rising to depart, "if you're going to roll over and play dead after one defeat, I can't help you. But let me say just one thing. If Carpenter should beat me, and carry a few of his cronies into office with him, control of this state will be in jeopardy, and it may take years of shoring up to repair it. If you let me go down the drain, you will just be cutting off your nose to spite your face; you'll be imperiling your own political future."

"I've already told you, John. We're going to back you."

"But back me as I outlined, really effectively?"

"Of course."

"With our labor people, and in the north, and with your financial people?"

The Governor sighed. "I'll do my best."

"That's all I can ask for," the Senator said, extending his hand. "I'll be in close touch with you, Ross." Ross shook the hand unenthusiastically.

The Senator went to the door and turned back. "Think over that business about being campaign chairman. I'll be interested in hearing from you." He passed through the door, and it clicked behind him.

The Governor sat for a moment staring at the door, and then walked to the window and looked at the small dome of the Missouri capitol.

23

The Senator, Sidney Bronstein, Virgil Akers, and Ellen Burnett began the laborious retracing of their route of a few weeks before. The late August heat on the plains of central Missouri was intense. During the long days, the sun relentlessly pursued them, trying to dry them out like crackly leaves. Buildings of the little Missouri towns shimmered in the waves of heat rising from the soft asphalt. The dusty caravan wandered to the north. Every morning, after a sticky night, they reluctantly climbed into the car and set off, with the windows turned wide open and the oven-hot breath of summer blowing in on them.

It seemed as if the primary had never happened. The short interval between the Senator's primary victory and the beginning of the general election campaign now seemed like a cool, almost forgotten moment as day after day they shook hands, smiled, and wiped their dripping faces with handkerchiefs. Nearly every day, the Senator's entourage held off-the-record meetings with the local Democratic officials, trying to get old enemies to forget their emotional commitments of a few weeks before, trying to infuse friends with enthusiasm, trying to prevent retaliations by the Senator's supporters against the supporters of the Governor. There was rarely a day when the Senator did not breakfast with one group, lunch with another, and have dinner with a third. Sometimes Virgil Akers, or perhaps Ellen, and occasionally Sidney, had to carry the Senator's greetings to some group. The Senator showed them a handshake he had developed to keep his hand from being reduced to a pulp by a thousand other hands which gripped it in various enthusiasms. The succession of hotel rooms, motel rooms, rooms in the houses of friends became an amorphous memory of flowered wallpaper.

Sidney was charged with the responsibility of scanning all publications which reported what Carpenter had said. He abstracted and typed for a special file anything which might be useful.

In rural areas, the Senator hammered on the Republican weakness on farm supports; in the larger towns, he reviewed his long labor record, defended his vote on the labor bill, and warned the union men that the bill would have been much worse had the Republicans in Congress prevailed.

One evening in the "Presidential Suite" of a small hotel, the Senator had removed his shoes and propped his stocking feet on an adjacent chair. He sipped a light Scotch and soda. To Sidney, he seemed gray and tired, suddenly old.

"Gentlemen and ladies assembled," he announced, "this is my last campaign. I've said that before, but I never really meant it, as evidenced by the fact that I never said it publicly. Politics is a game for wise old men, but campaigning is for young ones." He wiggled his toes. "Like an athlete's, a politician's legs go first, and mine are about gone. Yes, sir, six more years and I'm going to retire. Retire to what, I don't know. Everyone else seems to have a peaceful old family homestead, or a flourishing high-level law practice. Ellen, how would you like to spend your declining years, which seem to be upon us, in London or Paris?"

"Fine, John," his wife answered.

"Maybe I could get myself appointed Ambassador to the Court of St. James. Sidney could come along and be the chauffeur, and Virgil here could buttle."

"I'd like an inside job, if you don't mind," Sidney said.

"Sure, plenty of them. We'll put you in charge of the upstairs maids. I'm sure they could use some looking after." He took a quick draught of his drink. "Pleasant dreams. I've contributed time and energy to the party, but I've never been in a position to contribute money in large quantities, because, primarily, my father was not astute enough to make it in large quantities. The expenditure of time and energy for thirty-five years does not equate, in this day and age, with the recent expenditure of thirty-five thousand dollars."

"I see you as a judge," said Sidney, "somewhat in the image of Learned Hand."

"A little late to begin a judicial career."

"I don't know," Sidney said. "Michelangelo didn't paint the Sistine Chapel until he was seventy years old."

"He had been practicing for some time, however," the Senator said, speaking through his glass.

"Well, six years from now, who can tell what the situation will be?" Virgil said. "Let's concentrate on the present. Like, how do you think it's going, for instance."

"All right," said the Senator. "Reception is generally enthusiastic, as far as I can tell. Most of Ross's people seem to be coming around."

"The labor people seem to have cooled off. That's the major thing," Virgil said. "I think they realize that it would be downright silly for them to put Carpenter in office, just to punish you."

"Oh, I think they'll come around all right. What worries me is lack of enthusiasm. They certainly won't vote for Carpenter, but they are still mad as hell at me, and I'm afraid this may induce the deadliest political malaise of all—indifference."

"You know what surprises me," Sidney said. "With the exception of a few people, nobody seems very concerned with the issues involved. I look out at those people when the Senator is talking, and it's obvious they are mostly interested in how he looks, in the jokes he tells, how he demonstrates his knowledge of the state by mentioning places and people, and how he tears into the opposition. But nobody seems to pay much attention to what he actually says about the important issues of the day. It annoys me, because I labor over getting those things just right in the speeches, and then they stand oxlike, only appreciating the sarcasm, the jokes, and the references to familiar things."

"Democracy in action," the Senator said. "Nothing new about that, Sidney."

"I suppose not," Sidney said. "I'm just surprised no one is interested."

"I agree," said the Senator. "It is a tragic waste of time. This country is wrestling with the most serious problems in its history, and in the middle of everything the U.S. Congress picks up and leaves for a few months, to engage in handshaking, plowing contests, and hoedowns. The world can wait. People will tell you that in a democracy the people's representatives have got to keep in touch with the people. But nobody has told me just how shaking hands with a farmer, letting him feel the firmness of my grip and see the size of my smile, actually accomplishes anything. Sitting down and talking about his problems, sure. But on a campaign, you never have a chance to do that. It's just one long receiving line with about a hundred thousand people in it. I've often thought it would be a good idea for all the candidates for an office to send every voter a one-page rundown on his background and record. Let them read it and make up their minds."

A bellboy rang and delivered a bundle of newspapers.

The delivery boy reminded Sidney of something. He snapped his fingers. "By the way, Senator, when I talked to Dick this morning, he said to tell you that Rufus Smith got five to ten years. He's your maid's son, isn't he?"

"Yes," said the Senator. "Too bad, too bad."

"Five to ten years is kind of stiff."

"I wasn't thinking so much of Rufus as Leona. Leona's a good human being, and it's just a damn shame things have turned out this way. She's caught up in this thing, and it's wrecking her life, really through no fault of her own. This conviction and all that publicity is liable to mean more trouble. As for Rufus, he's only eighteen or so, but I'd say he's gone. He'll come out of prison three or four years from now a defeated, sullen subhuman, and it won't be long before we electrocute him for murder or rape or something. That's modern, advanced criminology." He shook his head in incomprehension. "Sidney, what's in those newspapers?"

Sidney laid them on the table and began to turn the pages, picking out things that would interest them and reading them aloud. He set one paper aside and turned to the next. Suddenly, he bent down intently to read something.

"What is it, Sidney?"

"The first poll. The head is:

Burnett in Front in Race for Senator. The percentages are as follows:

Burnett	52%
Carpenter	42%
Don't know	6%

Sidney looked up at the Senator. "How does that sound?"

"Not too bad," the Senator said, after a pause. "Depends, of course, on whether or not there is a trend, and in which direction the trend is going."

The next day, the caravan resumed its journey, joined now by the Governor, Ross MacKenzie, who had finally agreed to serve, in name at least, as the Senator's campaign chairman. Ross was to stay with them for two days, for a dinner in St. Joseph and another in Kansas City. He was falsely buoyant, but no trace of bitterness was detectable in his friendly smile. Contact with the voters stimulated him; he had not yet come to regard it as drudgery. Ross, like all politicians, was partly actor. He had enjoyed the center of the stage: the adoring glances of the girls and women; the respectful attitude of the men; the turning of eyes when he entered a room; and the clustering of people who always seemed to follow him. But now, as a defeated candidate, he quickly noted a decline in people's interest, and it was difficult for him to sit on the platform, as the second attraction, with the man who had beaten him, but he tried hard to give no outward evidence of it.

The steamy warmth of early September gave way to rain. At one stretch it rained for five successive days. The farmers came in along the back roads in muddy-wheeled cars, and in the auditoriums the reek of steamy rubber rose from the inevitable pile of rainwear on the tables at the rear. Finally the rain ceased but left in its place unseasonably cold weather. Events were still scheduled for the outside, and doggedly carried through—events for which the Senator had to be prompt, or risk facing a half-frozen, annoyed audience, which would mumble and stamp its feet throughout his remarks, or, worse, drift off to the warmth of their automobiles.

In all of this time, the Senator never saw his opponent, except occasionally on television. No pictures of them jovially shaking hands were taken. No debates were proposed. To Sidney it was like shadowboxing. You could never tell when a thrust had gone home and hurt, and you never had a chance to size up the other fellow—see how he was bearing up and whether he really thought he was going to win.

The polls were inconclusive. A second poll showed an insignificant one per cent rise in Carpenter's column, a one per cent loss in the Senator's. Other polls showed the Senator's margin as somewhat narrower, but all of them indicated that he would win. Finally, it was no longer possible to deny among themselves that Carpenter appeared to be gaining somewhat, if the polls could be trusted, which was doubtful. It was disturbing but not unexpected, for when Carpenter began his campaign, he was not nearly as well known as the Senator. Although he was bound to gain somewhat, the margin was still ample.

Dick Goetz had reached the Senator by long-distance telephone, just before he left St. Louis for Washington. In the short time they had for conversation, Dick told him that there had been another incident involving the Smiths. A homemade bomb of some kind had been thrown onto their porch, but, fortunately, had failed to explode. In the newspaper account, the Senator had been named as Leona Smith's employer.

"It's a damn unfortunate development," the Senator said to Sidney on the way to the airport. "My own fault. I should have told Leona not to mention my name. It just didn't occur to me."

"I suppose they'll latch on to this," Sidney said.

"Sure, they'll use it wherever they think it will help them."

"They won't be able to make much of it, I don't think, Senator," Sidney said. "So you employ a colored maid who happens to buy a house in a mixed neighborhood, and she's involved in a controversy. How does that touch you? I mean, in any significant way. They'd be drawing a pretty long bow, wouldn't they?"

"Well, first of all they'll say I put the idea into her head. And secondly, that I probably put up the money for the house. I'm a liberal and therefore I'm for mixed schools and mixed neighborhoods and mixed marriages. And further, they will probably engage in rhetorical questions about my trying to help her son, which is bound to come out soon. Why does he do this? Why does he try to interfere with the course of justice? Why his *great* interest in this woman who was regularly at his house? Is it not strange that he takes such an unusual interest in this boy who is the son of his colored girl?"

"Oh, for Christ sake," Sidney said, "that's disgusting."

"Innuendo," the Senator said. "The most difficult of all attacks to combat. You defend yourself against a charge that has never been specifically made. If you deny it, you merely give it added currency. If you don't, well then you take your chances on its effect."

"How do they get away with that sort of thing?"

"Well, what can you do? If you can advance some method of preventing it, we'll all be grateful. But in the meantime, we have to live with it. And it worries me, frankly. I don't like to see all these negative matters piling up this way."

"What do you mean all these?" Sidney said. "What others are there?"

"Nothing. Just a few small things," the Senator said. "Nothing important, really."

The Senator found out how much the incident at Leona Smith's home was to touch him when his plane landed in Washington a few hours later.

The Washington reporters met the plane and began to ask questions at once.

"May I take a moment to familiarize myself with the details," the Senator said, taking the newspaper from the hand of the nearest reporter. "I just got off the airplane, and I haven't had a chance to look at the paper." He read the article quickly.

BOMB IS THROWN AT NEGRO HOME

A gasoline-soaked bomb was thrown on the porch of a Negro home in a predominantly white section last night. About midnight, a can of gasoline, wrapped in gasoline-soaked rags, was lit and thrown on the porch of the home of Mr. and Mrs. Arthur Smith, 6705–7th Place, N.W. The Smiths are Negroes. The gasoline rags charred a portion of the porch and blacked the asphalt siding which covers the house. The can of gasoline failed to explode. Damage was estimated at $250. A hammer head with a note attached was thrown through the front window. The note urged their departure from the predominantly white neighborhood into which they moved six months ago.

Mr. and Mrs. Smith told reporters that their neighbors had been "very polite, but not too friendly." Mrs. Smith said that the family had no warning that such a thing might happen. She said that she "couldn't think of anybody who would want to do such a thing." Asked if she was considering moving from the northwest neighborhood, she said that she did not think so but that she wanted to talk with her husband before arriving at a decision.

Police disclosed that the Smiths are the parents of Rufus Smith, recently sentenced to five to ten years in prison, along with Orton Carter, 19, Negro, for assault and robbery. Smith and Carter were convicted of beating up Mrs. Lillie Livesay, 62, white, of Takoma Park, D.C., and of robbing her of $1.35 for "beer money." Police theorized that bad feeling might have arisen out of the assault conviction. A neighbor, who preferred to remain anonymous, conceded that the assault conviction against young Smith might have touched off the bombing. "Feeling is very high against them," he said. Police said that the investigation is continuing.

"All right," said the Senator, "what is it that you want to know?"

"We are told, Senator, that Mrs. Smith has worked as a maid for you for several years. Is that true?"

"Who told you that?"

"She did."

"Yes, that is correct. She has worked for us for a number of years. I would have to consult Mrs. Burnett to know exactly how long. And I will make this statement for the record. In our years of association with Mrs. Smith, we have always found her reliable and completely honest. She has enjoyed our complete confidence for years, and she will continue to do so, in the foreseeable future."

"Senator, we understand that you have been active in trying to get her son off from this assault charge. Is there anything in that?"

"The statement is incorrect as it is stated," said the Senator. "I have been a friend of Mrs. Smith's for many years, and I am also a lawyer. When her son became involved in this matter, she came to me for advice. I assured her that I would do all that I could to see that he had adequate representation, and that is the extent of the matter."

"Did you feel that he would not get adequate representation without your intervention, Senator?"

"I merely told her that as an old friend I would help her through the matter. . . ."

"You're considerably more active in the case, Senator, I would take it, than just helping out with advice?"

"No . . ." said the Senator.

"We have a report, sir, that you hired the lawyer to represent Mrs. Smith."

"Again, that is incorrectly stated. She was not well versed in matters of this sort, and I offered to contact a reliable lawyer for her. And I did so."

"Are you paying the lawyer, sir?"

"No . . ." said the Senator at first, not knowing how much they knew, "not as such. I made a small contribution to Mrs. Smith, and perhaps she may have used it to pay the lawyer. She does not have large funds at her disposal."

"Is there any chance that you will act as courtroom attorney if the case is appealed, Senator?"

"There is no chance whatsoever. I haven't been active in a courtroom for thirty years."

"Senator, is there any possibility that you supplied Mrs. Smith with some of the money for the house, or that you assisted her in any way in obtaining it?"

"All right," said the Senator, "now I want you both to listen to this answer. No. Absolutely not. Categorically not. No help or assistance of any kind, in any manner. Now that's an honest answer, and I think honest reporting of the matter would be to print neither the question nor the answer."

"Why not, sir?"

"Just this. It raises a lot of questions in many minds, and no matter how much I deny it, the rumor will persist in some quarters. Since it has no foundation whatsoever in fact, it is unfair for you to stimulate it as rumor. Do you see my point?"

"Not entirely."

"Well, if I do have the right to ask it, I ask that you print neither the question nor the answer."

"Senator, in view of your voting record in the Congress, I wonder if you have any statement to make on this matter of integration as related to this particular case, where a friend—and a person you have known for some years—is involved?"

The Senator pursed his lips. "Boys, I am going to decline to comment on that matter because I feel that any comment from me at this time might serve only to further confuse an already confusing situation. Just say that I hope that the matter can be solved peaceably among neighbors, and in a Christian manner, and, further, that it will not become a *cause célèbre*, which will make it impossible for the people involved to settle it themselves."

"Senator, does the fact that you're not making any comment have any connection with the fact that you are running for re-election, and this subject is a rather hot one in your home state?"

The question stung him, but he kept his temper and gave no sign. "Fellows, I want to say this off the record, and I want it clearly understood that it is off the record. This is not merely a question of a Negro family moving into a white neighborhood. The whole matter is inextricably bound up with this robbery conviction against Mrs. Smith's son. Her son committed a most repellent crime. Only if the old lady had been raped could it have been worse. It is a crime which, when read about, brings emotion, hatred, and choking gorge into another matter entirely. It was a terrible thing, but it does not have anything to do with the basic question of integration."

"The neighbors seem to think so, sir. They claim such things follow inevitably after Negro infiltration. Certainly, the available statistics would seem to indicate that. A tremendous increase in the crime rate follows wherever they go."

"Well, of course it does," said the Senator, irritated at the reporter for trying to goad him into a statement, "but not because they're Negroes. Because they are on the bottom of the economic heap. That's the point. Give them a chance. You can't dress up a Cockney and expect him to be comfortable in court and follow all of the rules of protocol of that court. But you recognize that knowledge of the rules is a matter of environment, not heredity. That's the point."

"I wonder, sir, if we might have permission to quote just that last bit."

The Senator considered it. "I think not. I don't want to be dragged into this particular controversy any further than I have to be. I think we had just better let the matter rest with the original statement."

The reporter looked disconsolately at his sparse notes. "Thanks for nearly nothing."

The Senator smiled. "Well, you got something. I didn't intend for you to get anything at all."

24

At precisely nine o'clock, Paul Finch walked into the executive offices of the Liberty Electric Company in New York. Rex Hance was not yet in.

"That Rye train is probably late again," his secretary said. "Why don't you go into his office and I'll bring you a cup of coffee."

Paul thanked her and went into Rex's office. It occupied a large corner, with a view to the south of lower Manhattan, and a view to the west of the Hudson and New Jersey beyond.

"We love the view," said Rex's secretary, entering with the coffee. "Though I don't know how long we'll have it at the rate they're building skyscrapers around here. There are some magazines there on the table, if you'd like to look at them." She smiled winningly and left.

Just the kind of doll you would expect Rex Hance to have for a secretary.

Paul looked at a couple of issues of *Electrical World*. In a few minutes, Rex Hance walked in. They talked for a while before Rex said, "Well, let's go upstairs. The new president wants to have a look at you."

"Oh, my God, Rex," Paul said, "why didn't you tell me?"

"I thought you'd want to be surprised," Rex said, grinning.

"Besides, you look fine. Dark suit. Shoes shined. Fresh haircut. What else could you do?"

"I could have prepared myself mentally," Paul said. "Three days of meditation in a monastery would have been about right."

"No time for that in the modern business world," Rex said. "Let's go."

They rode up in the elevator, and when they emerged, Paul saw the early-morning mists of Manhattan swirling outside the window. "Are we in heaven?" he said.

"We're on the fifty-second floor," Rex said. "You're making nervous conversation."

"Wait till you hear me in a few minutes."

"I'd advise listening," Rex said.

Rex's secretary had called and announced that they were on their way up. One of the president's secretaries ushered them into Briggs Christy's office.

"Rex," he said jovially, extending his hand. He turned and shook hands with Paul also. "Paul, I don't believe we've seen each other since we met in the Judge's office."

Paul could not restrain a look of surprise. "I'm pleased to meet you again, sir, and I must say I'm amazed that you could remember that. You met about ten people in ten minutes that day."

Briggs Christy crinkled a smile at him. "Sit down, won't you." Paul noticed for the first time that the office had no desk. It was a tastefully furnished living room, and not a single business paper was apparent anywhere. Rex took a wing chair and Paul a straight chair. Briggs Christy lounged on the sofa.

"The first thing I want to do, Paul," the President said, "is to congratulate you on the work you did in the labor bill fight. We've had reports from a number of sources, and they are all in agreement that you did a really first-rate job. First-rate."

"Thank you, sir."

"You more than justified the faith we had in you. All of us here wondered how we were ever going to replace the Judge, and I'm confident we've got the right man. A little experience under your belt and you'll be as good a man as the Judge. Better. How is the Judge, by the way?"

275

"I believe he's coming along all right, sir. He still has the old spirit. I think he'll always have that."

"A vigorous fellow. And respected down there, wouldn't you say?"

"Absolutely, sir. Very much so."

"And how are you finding it? Enjoying yourself?"

"I am, very much. It's challenging and demanding, but I'm enjoying it."

"Good. Well, Rex has a great deal of faith in you, and so have I. It's interesting. You know, I sit on top of this vast empire, but I wouldn't last a minute without the loyalty of my top people. No executive would. There's only so much I can do. The number one job of a good executive, I'm convinced, is to pick good associates. That's what makes him or breaks him."

"It has to be a team operation in a big organization like this," Rex said.

"That's right," Christy said. "That's exactly what it has to be. I sit here at the summit, so to speak, and co-ordinate and make policy. I've been doing a lot of thinking about what those two terms mean since I took over the presidency, and they're not easy to define. Make policy. What does that mean? It sounds fine to say it, but what does it mean? It means, of course, making some of the major decisions on pricing, financing, and things like that. But that is only part of it. It means, I think, setting the whole tone of the organization. A company is known by the president it keeps. Just as Liberty Electric was an extension of the personality of Ralph Clore. He was a vigorous, strong-minded man, who came up from the manufacturing end. His main objective was to manufacture the best-engineered, most respected product in the electrical industry, and he saw to it that this company did just that. He had strong opinions on many things. And for fifteen years, Liberty Electric *was* Ralph Clore. Isn't that right?"

"Very true," Paul said.

"And so Liberty Electric must necessarily take on aspects of my personality. Not instantly, naturally, but in the course of time. Image is all-important these days. In Ralph's day the emphasis was on production. Turn out a first-class product. The best value for the money. And that's a major objective yet, I don't mean to say that it isn't. But the world has gotten more complex since he took over this company. The job of a corporation executive has become so much broader, it seems to me, in the last decade. It all began, I suppose, with the New Deal, and it's been getting more so ever since."

"No doubt about that," Rex said.

"So, whether I like it or not, it's my fate to cast my shadow throughout this organization. And I intend that it shall be a creditable shadow. I intend that the image of this organization shall be, in all of its complex aspects, a symbol of Ralph Clore's old vigor and concern with excellence, but I intend that that excellence shall be carried into many phases that he . . . that were not as necessary in his time. Do you follow me?"

"I think so, sir," Paul said.

"All of this foreshadows some change, as indeed I think that it must. This is where I would like to ask your help, Paul. You and Rex and all of the other executives of the company are absolutely necessary in the building of the right image of Liberty Electric and in projecting that image. In fact, it cannot be done successfully without you."

"I'll be happy, of course, to help in any way that I can," Paul said.

"Good. You can. You can do it in the image you yourself project. Now I don't mean that you must think exactly as I do and feel exactly as I do about everything. But I do think there should be some rapport. There should be a general agreement among us as to what we are trying to do. I can't oversee every act of every executive. That would be impossible and undesirable. But I think that we should make some effort to be on the same wave length. One thing I'm going to do, Paul, is to put you on my private list to receive my top-management letter. The entire list consists of only twenty people, and I'll be frank to tell you that everyone on the list, with the exception of yourself, is one of our vice-presidents. I want to do it because of the key position you hold in the organization. In many ways, it's more important that you reflect the proper image, dealing as you do with powerful people, than almost anyone in the organization with the exception of myself."

"I'm flattered, sir."

"Just read it carefully. It's for your own consumption alone, and should not be shared with anyone. I might also suggest that you read my speeches with some care. I am sure that they seem long and boring, but I think that if you will give them some attention, you will find in them some examination of the road ahead of us as I see it."

"I read them now, of course," Paul said, "but I'll give them more attention in the future."

"Good. Paul, I hope that you are in accord with my ideas on this subject. I'm not trying to brainwash you. That is the last thing I would want to do. An organization will wither and die if the men in it have no original ideas of their own. But I do think that it's important that we keep in close touch, and this seems to me to be one method of doing it."

"I think it's a good one."

"I think we've got a great job to do," the President said. "A challenging job, that won't be accomplished overnight. The Liberty Electric Company is thought of as the producer of an excellent product. We have Ralph Clore to thank for that, and we intend to preserve that image. But it's also thought of as anti-government, anti-labor, anti-progress. That's the image we've got to get to work on. That's the image we've got to change. I don't mean by a massive, expensive public relations splash, but by our daily conduct. By an accumulation of activities that over the course of time will bring about a change in attitude on the part of the public, the Government, and even the labor unions. I've got the Public Relations Department thinking through a co-ordinated plan, which we will eventually adopt on a company-wide basis. But, as always, Washington is somewhat different. It requires a little different treatment. Thus I'd like to ask you, Paul, to give a little thought to the matter. What are the ways we can work on this problem from the Washington point of view? Set down your thoughts in a memo and send them directly to me. Send a copy to Rex, of course. Do you think you might do that?"

"Sure," Paul said. "I think there's a great deal in what you say, Mr. Christy. I'll get my ideas down on paper and shoot them right up to you."

"Very good. I'll look forward to receiving them. And you can be sure that I'll read them with great care. One thing more you might want to give a little thought to, Paul," Christy said casually, "is getting yourself some first-class help there in Washington. You've got junior men, of course, and we had hoped that the Judge could serve in a loose advisory capacity, but it doesn't look as if that is going to be quite practicable."

"I don't quite follow you, sir," Paul said.

"Oh, I'm thinking," said Christy, as if he were just now thinking through the idea, "of somebody who could give you a hand on some of the tough questions. Maybe somebody older than yourself. A sort of senior counselor. . . ." His voice trailed off apologetically. "There I go," he said, "making decisions. I shouldn't. But you think it over and let me know what you think about it. Well, Paul, I'm so glad you were able to drop in to see me. I'm glad we've had an opportunity to chat." He rose, as did Rex and Paul. As they walked toward the door, Briggs Christy put his hand on Paul's shoulder. "This is a big job I'm trying to hold down. I can only do it with your help, which consists of doing a first-rate job down there in Washington. Washington is a great opportunity, Paul. It's a nerve center in an organization the size of ours. There's a great opportunity there. A great opportunity to do an important job, and to grow personally. And I'm satisfied that we have picked the right man for it. I'll be watching your activities with interest." He gave Paul a parting clap on the shoulder. "And I know I won't be disappointed."

Paul and Rex entered the elevator, but there were two other passengers so they did not talk until they got off at Rex's floor.

"Did you enjoy yourself?" Rex said.

"That's not exactly a situation where you enjoy yourself," Paul said.

"You did all right," Rex said. "You said yes and no in just the right places."

"It was enlightening."

"Enlightening. That's a good Washington word," Rex said. "What does it mean?"

"Well, I think you have to translate everything he said. He hinted here and implied there without stating things outright."

"It's his way. In fact, it's the way of most top executives. It gives them maneuvering room. If they want to change their mind, they can always claim that they were misunderstood, that they never said it. Not that I'm saying that Briggs is that kind. It's just a trait I've noticed."

"The message was pretty clear, though. One. Ralph Clore is no longer running this show. Two. I'll be running things differently from the way he did. Three. The new look will not be as severe as the old. Liberty Electric has been concentrating on modernizing its equipment. Now it will concentrate on modernizing its image. Softening it, if you will. Four. Stick with me and be loyal to me and help me with this, and there'll be a vice-presidency in it for you. If you're careful and remember from whom all blessings flow."

"Very good for a first-year student," Rex said.

"And one other thing," Paul said, "just to keep your ulcer percolating, we're going to give you some competition. A senior advisor. So that we'll have somebody to move in if you kick one."

"That's life in the executive suite, my boy," Rex said.

25

Ed Flowers listened to the muted sounds of the hostess welcoming people aboard the plane. It sounded almost as if he were under water. In a few moments, the door would clang shut, and he would be inevitably headed for another series of meetings, at which he would be forced to maintain false high-pitched joviality with people who hated him and were trying to cut him down. Suddenly, he made the decision. He pulled his small bag from under the seat, where he had stowed it for the flight, and seized his topcoat from the rack above the seats. He plowed into the latecomers who were blocking the aisles as they surged aboard. He desperately squeezed past them with no apologies.

"We'll be taking off in a moment, sir," the hostess said, in smiling puzzlement.

"Not going," Ed muttered. He ran down the ramp of stairs and hurried into the corridor of the airport. He hurriedly made his way, swimming against the stream of passengers, into the babbling main lobby, and upstairs to the bar. There he sat on a stool, and relaxing for the first time in several days, he watched with great satisfaction as his plane's door was shut, the motors turned over, and it headed to the end of the take-off runway. He watched the plane with detachment. The moment the wheels left the runway, he felt a sense of relief. He sipped his drink, savoring it, making it last. He had another lingering drink, but not a third, for the decision not to go was a sensible, rational decision, and he did not regret it. Outside, he caught a cab and went back to his office, making a stop to pick up a pint of bourbon, which he tucked away.

The elevator doors opened, and he strode past his secretary with a nod.

"Well, for heaven's sake," she said as he went into his office and shut the door. A few seconds later there was a light knock, and she opened the door wide enough to admit her head.

"What happened? Did you miss the flight?"

"No. I decided not to go."

She was bewildered. "You mean you just decided not to go?"

"That's right."

She worried her next question. "Well, won't that cause some problems? I mean, shouldn't I notify some of those people?"

"I don't care," he said airily. "Do as you choose."

"Well," she paused uncertainly, confused by his strange behavior, "I guess I should, don't you?" She half withdrew her head. "Should I tell them you were taken ill or something?"

"Anything. As you wish."

The door clicked. Ed sat drumming his fingers on the desk, then he remembered the bourbon. He poured himself a third of a tumbler of bourbon, dropped in two ice cubes from his small refrigerator, and added some water. He dragged a large easy chair around facing the window so that he could sit and look out over Capitol Hill. He sipped the drink, in easy, gentlemanly fashion. The long rays of the sun lit up the Capitol dome, as if it were floodlighted. A shadow crept gradually up the dome. The Taft Memorial chimes sounded five o'clock. He fixed himself another drink and sat as darkness fell and lights began to come on all over the Hill. The throb of traffic increased, and outside he could hear the police whistles and the roar of cars and buses.

A gentle knock sounded on the door beside him. He leaned around his chair without rising. Louise put her head in tentatively. "It's five-thirty, Ed. I was going. . . ."

"Go," he said.

"Is there anything else you might need me for?"

"Nothing that I can think of."

282

He had turned around to the window again, but he was conscious that she had not yet gone.

"Is there anything wrong, Ed?"

"There's nothing wrong. Everything's fine."

There was another pause. "Well, good night."

"Good night. . . ." Now he was conscious that she was gone. He mixed himself another drink. In the distance, he could see the blinking red-and-white lights of the airliners as they seemed to run down a hill to landings at the Washington airport. He decided that he would go over to see Barbara.

He got his car from the garage, drove over, parked, and went up the narrow stairway to the second floor. He could hear her moving about inside. He knocked.

"What are you doing here?" she asked.

"A fine greeting."

"Well, I'm just surprised. I thought you were going . . ."

"How about a kiss?" She complied perfunctorily.

"That was a minimum."

"You've been drinking."

"Now, don't say it like that," he said. "I've been drinking. I have had a couple of drinks, but I am not drunk. I just decided that I did not want to make that trip today, and everybody seems to be in a sweat about it."

"Well, I just wasn't expecting you . . ."

"You make some other plans?" he said narrowly.

"No, but it's just that I don't have any food in the house. I was just planning to have a bite and spend the evening reading."

"Well, I'll just have a bite with you."

She paused. "All right. Weren't some people expecting you?"

"The hell with them," he answered, going over to mix himself a drink. "I don't have to go running out there hat in hand. It's a confession of weakness. Frank talked me into it in the first place, and I shouldn't have let him do it. I can handle them. And I don't have to go running out there to do it. I'll order them to come here, if I want to see them." He was scowling, and she hesitated to ask him more questions for fear of worsening his mood. She changed the subject and asked about the divorce.

"It's about wrapped up, thank God. The lawyers probably

283

closed the deal this afternoon. We're going to give in, and give them their goddam money."

"At this point, I just want to get it over with."

"They tried a little blackmail which, I must admit, worked."

"Blackmail?"

"You know, 'You wouldn't want to see that poor girl's good name dragged through the mud'—that sort of thing."

She went rabbit-faced with fear. "My name wasn't even going to be mentioned."

He waved her down. "Don't worry. It won't be. There is a small price attached to their silence, but it won't be."

She nervously put her fingernails to her teeth. "They couldn't do that, could they? I haven't done anything wrong. There isn't any law against . . . I mean it's your own damn business."

"I don't know if they could do anything or not. He says they could, claims to have witnesses, and. . . ."

"Witnesses. Witnesses to what?"

"Witnesses to me coming and going from the apartment, and spending the night, I suppose."

She looked as if she were about to cry.

"Ed, I can't have that. I just can't. If it ever got back home, it would be awful. Really awful. And if it got around to the station, and to some of my girl friends, I just. . . ."

"It won't," he said coolly. "But I thought this was the great romance. Love for love and let other people be damned."

"Yes, but you don't go about broadcasting it where it isn't necessary."

"And if it is necessary?"

"If it is necessary, then all right. We'll face up to it if it comes. But where it isn't necessary, well then . . . and besides, do you want it all to come out in the papers? How about your work, and your friends, and your kids? Are you anxious to publicize it all around town. . . ?"

"No, but . . ."

"Well, then you shouldn't criticize me for not wanting to."

"I'm not criticizing you," he said in irritation. "I just don't like the idea of treating this as a dirty relationship that we're both ashamed of." He took a large punctuating swallow of his drink.

284

She stared at the floor in front of her chair for a long while. "It isn't easy for the woman, you know, Ed. Men don't get criticized for this sort of thing. But a woman gets talked about in ways she feels, sneered at in polite ways, insulted and cut, made to feel that she's nothing but a slut."

"Nuts to people," Ed said, draining his drink. "Who needs them? Another?" he said, pouring himself a second drink.

"No, thank you."

"Let's forget the whole thing," Ed said thickly. "I'm willing to pay the price. Only it just annoys the hell out of me, her grabbing at the dough that way. She's trying to punish me, you know that. She's trying to rake off so much money that we'll have to live like pigs. Then she'll gloat. That's what's so odd. I lived with that woman for twenty years, and I never thought she would do a thing like that. Vindictive, you know. The hell with them," he said abruptly, with a gulp of bourbon and a wave of his glass. "Agnes, lawyers, Harrack, the whole goddam bunch. Who needs them? I'll whip them. Frank and Pete and I will whip them. Would you still love me if we didn't, and I was out of a job?" he asked her with glazed eyes, and with no particular attention to her answer.

She paused for a few seconds. "Of course."

" 'Course you would," he said. "You're a good girl. I love you, did you know that, Barbara? Every square inch of you, if I may be so lewd."

"Fine," she said, rising and patting him on the hand. "It's about time we had some dinner."

"Dinner," he roared. "We had dinner."

"No we haven't, hon. Quiet down."

"We haven't had dinner? You're crazy. 'Course we have. I distinc-tally remember it. It was steak," he announced.

"No . . ." she began.

"It's a stinkin' life, you know, Barbara. I don't ordinarily use that word stinking. I broke myself of it. You probably don't. You're young. It probably seems all exciting and nice to you, doesn't it? It is, for a while. I can remember when it was that way. When I was on my way up to being the big success I now am. Har-har," he said grotesquely. "Think it, for a while. It won't

285

hurt you. Think it while you can. . . . Excuse me, honey, but whatever it is you're cooking out there is making me feel sick." He lurched to his feet. "I don't want any dinner. Thas terrible, after you worked and cooked it, and I am very sorry for that. I truly am."

"How about some coffee? I've got some hot."

"No," he waved her away. "I'll just lie down, and in a very short time, I'll be fine. Then I'll get up and eat that veryfine dinner that you're cooking." He wove his way to the sofa and rolled onto it, with a great expiration of breath. "If I go to sleep," he said, "wake me up in fifteen minutes." He was asleep. She walked over to him, still holding a large spoon in her hand, and looked at him carefully for a couple of minutes. Then she got a blanket and spread it over him. When her dinner was ready, she set it out and sat down to eat it. The room was silent. The electric clock hummed on the kitchen wall, her coffee cup clinked in the saucer, and from the living-room couch came the alcoholic wheezes of Ed Flowers.

26

The Senator and Herbert Shannon entered the hotel room to find
Virgil Akers, Sidney Bronstein, and Dick Goetz staring at them
glumly.

"I never saw three more downcast faces in my life," the Senator said. "What's the matter?"

"Everything," Virgil said.

"Carpenter has just announced a razzmatazz election finale,"
Dick Goetz said, "and Ross MacKenzie is trying to stick the knife
into us."

"Sounds like a typical day in political life," the Senator said.
"Let me make a call before we get into this."

The Senator stepped to the telephone and put in a call to
Ernie Kane at NFL headquarters in Washington. Kane was not
there, and the Senator left word for him to return the call.

"There isn't any chance Kane himself will come?" Virgil
asked.

"Unfortunately, no," the Senator said. "I'm hoping Frank
Raeder can make it."

"What's this?" Sidney asked.

"A call for reinforcements," the Senator said. "We're just not
moving these labor boys and we need some help. I asked Kane to
come out, but he begged off. Frank Raeder is my next choice.
Ernie was supposed to get back to me yesterday, but he didn't

do it. He's taking his own sweet time about it. I'm going to have a drink while listening to this dismal recitation of yours. Will anyone join me?"

Herbert and Dick Goetz wanted a drink. Virgil and Sidney declined. "I'll fix them," Dick said.

"Well, let's hear it. We might as well begin with Ross. Who has the facts?"

"I guess I have as many as anybody," Sidney said. "Ross, as you know, made a speech in Kansas City last night to a group of labor people. All Kansas City people. I forget what they call themselves. League for Political Action or something like that. They're a creature of COPE, and they consist of labor people who seem to be more interested in politics than labor. At any rate, they're a group that knows the score—"

At that moment Ellen came in. They all rose and greeted her. Dick hung her coat in the closet, and she took a seat with the group.

"We're just finding out, dear, about a speech Ross made last night."

She nodded.

Sidney continued: "In the speech there was a reference to your vote on the labor bill and your feelings about the whole matter. I briefed Ross on this, because we all agreed that this is a touchy subject, and the party line has got to be adhered to. I told Ross how sensitive it was, and he agreed. I'm sure that he understood exactly the permissible limits on this subject."

"Did you write the speech for him?" Senator Burnett asked.

"No, I gave him a rough draft and told him that he was free to adapt it to his own style, of course, and I asked him to let us know if he was going to depart substantially from it or introduce anything new that would require discussion."

"And he understood that?"

"Absolutely. So I didn't think anything more about it. Ross has made a half a dozen speeches, all of which have been fine. Then Virgil got a call late last night from Kansas City. Virgil, why don't you tell them what the guy said?"

"He said," Virgil replied, leaning forward intently in his chair, "that Ross said that he felt that you had some 'second

288

thoughts' and perhaps some 'regrets' about your vote on the labor bill, and that after seeing the law in operation you might be interested in substantial changes in it, maybe even repealing it."

The Senator rose, went to the window and stared out. "Damn him. That's a goddam awkward thing for him to say."

"It sure is," Dick Goetz said.

"I should point out that there's some doubt as to what he actually did say," Virgil said. "The newspaper reports say that he expressed his own view that some parts of the law were 'regrettable.' The problem is that nobody is quite sure what he actually did say, and we haven't been able to find out. The morning paper had a copy of the speech, and they scanned down through it for me while I was talking to them on the phone. There was nothing in the prepared speech like this. It was apparently an ad lib."

"That's some help," said the Senator.

"The problem is that some Kansas City radio station is reported to have taped the speech. I'm trying to get hold of the tape, but I haven't been able to get one yet."

"I have never trusted that boy, John," Ellen said. "Call it woman's intuition or what you will, but I think that it was a deliberate attempt to embarrass you."

"I'm afraid I agree with Mrs. Burnett," Sidney said. "I emphasized to him that this was a delicate and touchy area. I don't see how he could have done this without malice aforethought."

"Perhaps," said the Senator. "But all of us here know Ross. He strives to please, above all things. And when he got in front of this audience, I can see where he might decide innocently to make one of his friendly, off-the-cuff sallies. When he started out, he probably didn't know what he was going to say, but in an effort to say something that would please this particular audience, he fell back into the old terminology that he used in the primary campaign."

"You're the last man I'd accuse of being naïve, John," said Virgil, "but I think you're bending over backward to exonerate Ross. He may be young, but he has been in public life a long time, and I can't help believe that he knew what he was saying, particularly on this point."

"My feeling exactly," Ellen said.

"Have we had any newspaper queries on this?" the Senator asked. Each in turn shook his head negatively.

"They're bound to come though," Virgil said. "I don't know why we haven't heard by this time."

"Maybe we won't," Sidney said. "Maybe it will pass if we don't mention the subject."

"I would doubt that very much," said the Senator. "Conflict among politicians, especially of the same party, is good copy. Of course, we won't say anything if we are not asked, but we must work out some sort of an answer in case we are. The first step is to find out exactly what he said. We can't do more without that. Sidney and Virgil, I'm going to charge you with getting the text as soon as possible, if it exists. . . ."

They both nodded. "Let me see if the evening papers are out," Sidney said, and departed.

"Actually, we can handle the statement that after seeing the law in operation I might be interested in voting for changes in it. That goes without saying, and I can legitimately defend that. In fact, I said in a television interview the night it was passed that I did not think it was a perfect bill and that it might have to be amended if certain parts of it did not operate as we anticipated. So I don't see any great problem with that part of the statement. But as far as regretting it and having second thoughts about my vote on it, or now advocating repeal, that hurts. It makes me sound as if I'm sorry, because the vote now poses political problems for me. As if I had just now realized that it was going to cost me a substantial number of votes, and I am scrambling to get some of them back by saying that I'm sorry I voted for the bill in the first place."

"You can deny it outright," Dick said.

"It's not actually the statement so much," said the Senator. "It's that it gives him the initiative. Carpenter can tramp all over Missouri pounding away on this issue, and I have to trail him about, trying to explain. More than one political campaign has been lost this way. The truth never catches up. And it's not nearly so interesting." He grimaced and rapped his knuckles repeatedly on the back of the chair as he stood behind it. "Yet it's risky as hell to ignore it. If he sees that I intend to do that, he'll demand and keep on demanding an answer all over the state."

Sidney entered the room, awkwardly closing the door with his elbow as he tried to scan the paper. "No text of the damn thing," he said, "but a blast from Carpenter." He laid the paper on a table and began to read from it.

"Roger Carpenter, Burnett's opponent for the Senate seat, branded the statement as a 'weak-kneed attempt to play both sides of the street. Senator Burnett's vote for the bill in the first place,' Carpenter said in a prepared statement, 'was a blatant kowtowing to what my opponent felt was prevailing sentiment at the time. Now he feels that sentiment has changed and the vote will hurt him. Thus, with the ease of a practiced chameleon, he changes his colors. The statement, made by my opponent through his lackey, who was strongly against the bill when he was running against my opponent, is an attempt to confuse the voters, and nothing else. To those who think the new labor law is good, the Senator will smile sincerely and say, "I voted for it," and to those who think the law is bad, he will smile just as sincerely and say, "I'm for getting that bad law off the books." The electorate will not be confused by such a two-faced attempt to curry favor in order to get votes.'"

"He's not exactly temperate, is he?" the Senator said. "He's one of the few Republicans who can recognize the jugular vein when he sees it. Well, Sidney and Virgil, get right to work and get the statement exactly as it was uttered. I'll try to reach Ross on the phone. Does anybody know where he is?"

"He was staying at the Hilton," Sidney said.

"This fellow Carpenter is really a despicable individual," said Herbert Shannon. "He seems completely undisciplined in his language."

"Oh, I don't know, Herbert," the Senator said. "I might go after him with just as much vigor if I had him over the barrel."

"But John, I think I can state that you would not depart from the common precepts of decency."

Senator Burnett smiled. "Perhaps not. Now, what was this other thing about Carpenter planning a great finale for the campaign?"

"Television spectaculars," Dick Goetz said. "Fifteen minutes for four successive days before the election, seven-fifteen to seven-thirty, and a one-hour show the night before the election. In St. Louis and Kansas City."

The Senator frowned. "Paid for, I assume."

"Sure," Virgil said. "We figure it's going to cost them between ten and fifteen thousand. And they've already spent a pot of money on this campaign."

"Can't we demand equal time?" Sidney asked.

"We could ask for it and get it, but we'd have to pay for it, Sidney," the Senator said. "The stations are required to give only equal opportunity. If they give it to him free, then they've got to give it to me free, but if he pays for it, then the only requirement is that I may also get the time if I pay for it."

"That's unfair," Sidney said.

"Like many laws, I've found it favors the well-heeled over the poor but honest," the Senator said.

"We've got to raise some money, pronto," Virgil said. "John, we just can't let this kind of a thing happen in the last week of the campaign without combatting it. Maybe we can't match him, but at least we can do something."

The Senator turned to Herbert Shannon. "Herbert, as the wealthiest citizen in this room, you may suspect that we have staged this little drama in order to extract some more money from the Shannons. I assure you that we did not, and furthermore that I won't accept any more money from you. You've already been too generous. I just want you to be at ease in this discussion."

"Nothing was further from my mind, John. I'm as concerned at the news as all of you are. I think that we must, as Mr. Akers says, do something. And I'll . . . well, I'll bend every effort, including the financial. Not the sum mentioned, but I can certainly do something."

John Burnett waved his hand. "Thank you, Herbert, as always. But we've been to the well often enough. And besides, this is not tax deductible, and that makes it a real bite."

"It does rather," said Herbert, "but I'm still willing to do what I can to help."

"Maybe this is just rationalizing," the Senator said, "but I'm

292

not so sure that tit for tat is called for here. This televised series in the stretch may not be all that Carpenter expects it to be. It's two hours of Carpenter, and I'm not sure that people won't be bored to death with him at that point. He doesn't have that much to say, and he's bound to repeat himself about half the time. Secondly, I think that we can make an issue of the money being spent here. Electronic vote-purchasing, a new technique in campaigning. We can ask rhetorical questions about where all of this money came from so suddenly, and we can paint them as rich slickers and ourselves as impoverished but determined."

"One other thing might be important," Sidney said. "People seem to resent having their programs pre-empted by candidates. I checked, and in St. Louis he'll be ousting two Westerns, a kiddie cartoon show, and some kind of a courtroom documentary. In Kansas City, much the same. And he'll be kicking something else out for his one-hour show on election eve. I think that might build up quite a lot of resentment."

"It's possible," the Senator said. "There's always some protest over these pre-emptions. People are always doubtful that what we have to say is so important that it should take precedence over 'Dennis the Menace.' "

"All this is fine," Dick Goetz said, "but there's no use sitting around here and pretending this isn't a blow, and dismissing it as unimportant. It isn't unimportant, and we all know it. We can hope it will backfire and we can hope that this will happen and that will happen, but we've got to take some positive steps."

"I agree with Dick," Virgil said. "Let's hope it flops and let's do everything we can to help it flop, but let's also do something positive."

"How about a monstrous parade and rally," Sidney said, "climaxing with a great show at the ball park? Admission free. Get movie stars, baseball players, football players, colorful politicians, night-club entertainers, college presidents. Then get them to televise it free. I bet they'd be glad to do it, if we had a really good show."

"It's not a bad idea, Sidney," the Senator said. "But it's late to plan something like this. I've been connected with a couple of similar things before, and it takes long lead time to produce a show which will have the intended effect. It's very easy for it to be a fiasco. The weather at this time of year is very chancy too. In the balance, I just don't think this is quite the answer." He paused. "An idea has been forming in my own mind. Let me try it out on you. After each of Carpenter's programs, we purchase the little short announcement in the period that follows. In this period, we make the statement that at eight o'clock or eight-thirty, whatever it is, the Democratic candidate, Senator John Burnett, will answer *specifically* any charges or arguments made by Carpenter in the program they've just heard. Then we'd buy five minutes, and put together a hard-hitting answer."

"Damn good idea," Virgil said. "How about it, Herbert?"

"I fear it's going to be a problem getting the time," Herbert said. "You can probably get the announcement after Mr. Carpenter's program, provided that they have not signed a contract with him guaranteeing him against something of that sort. But the five minutes will be difficult. You see, the station will be carrying the network at that time, and they would be very reluctant to cut five minutes from a network show. I think that they would refuse to do it."

"They might if we brought sufficient pressure to bear," said the Senator.

"In that case . . ." said Herbert.

"Are there any time periods which would be feasible, Herbert?" asked the Senator.

"Well, the network feed begins at seven-thirty," Herbert said, "and he has taken the time immediately preceding. You could probably get some time before his show, or after the network goes off at ten-thirty."

"It's not as good, of course," the Senator said, "but we might go on the air just before he did, to answer his calumnies of the previous night and ask what new ones will be uttered tonight."

"That would build up an audience for him," Sidney said.

"True," said the Senator. "There seems to be some disadvantage to every possible course."

"How about some of those little short announcements scattered throughout the day?" Dick said.

294

"If you have very many of them, they'll add up costwise to about the same as the fifteen-minute show," Herbert said.

"Dick, I think we need more exact information," the Senator said. "Why don't you go over to the station and sit down with some sympathetic soul and find out exactly what we could do and how much it would cost. Are there any Democrats over there with your competition, Herbert?"

"Oh, yes," Herbert said. "A good many."

The phone rang, and Sidney answered it. "It's Kane," he said, extending the phone toward the Senator.

The Senator took the phone. "Ernie?"

"Hello John. I wanted to get back to you earlier on this thing, but I just couldn't do it. Listen, I'm going to send Ed Flowers out to give you a hand."

"Oh, for God's sake, Ernie," the Senator said. "I mean, I don't want to seem ungracious and I do appreciate your willingness to help out, but . . ."

"I know you wanted Frank Raeder to come out, John, but I just can't spring him loose now. I need him here. We've got some problems coming up, and I just can't send him. If you don't work full time on it, this Federation would come apart at the seams."

"Isn't there somebody else besides Flowers?" the Senator asked.

"John, Ed will do a good job for you on this. He's well liked out there and he's got a couple of big locals. Real big locals. He's smooth. He's just the guy to go around oiling the squeaky wheels, and that's just what you need."

"How about Johnson or Battalone? Leach? Any one of them would do."

"You're hitting us at a bad time, John. We allocated our manpower for this election a long time ago. Leach or Battalone might be able to make a couple of phone calls for you, or maybe fly out and appear on a platform for one night. Something like that. But you need somebody to stick with you for ten days or two weeks. You need somebody to circulate among these fellows and lay on a little grease. And Flowers is the guy for you, I'm telling you."

The Senator reluctantly agreed and hung up.

"Who's he sending?" Virgil asked.

"Despite my best efforts, Ed Flowers."

"Ed Flowers!" Sidney said.

"I was looking for somebody with a little status," the Senator said. "I'd almost rather not have anybody. Well, we'll just have to make the best of it. He may do us some good. I'll have to depend on you, Sidney, to gently inject into his head an idea or two. He can't just go around smiling and charming people. He's got to be able to get in there and argue and win a few points against some tough boys."

"I don't see Flowers winning too many," Sidney said.

"You make the best use of what you have," the Senator said. "That's all you can do." He rubbed his eyes wearily. "Well, I don't like to break up this pleasant gathering, but I think we've got to get moving on these things. Virgil, why don't you check out the facts on the Ross speech? I'll get in touch with Ross myself and we can compare notes. Dick, why don't you and Herbert see what can be accomplished on the television front with a small expenditure of our meager campaign funds?"

After they had all left, the Senator fixed himself a bourbon and water.

"You're worried about this, aren't you?" Ellen said.

"Of course. I always run scared. You know that from past campaigns."

"More than usual though. That's your third drink."

He looked at the offending glass in his hands. "Yes," he said, "I am. But hell, I don't know. I've been worried and tense in every campaign. And I'm worried and tense about this one. But I'm also six years older than I was last time."

"Every time we go through this, John, I wonder if it is all worth it."

"And every time we win, you're sure that it is," he said.

"I suppose so. But I just wish that it didn't have to be a vicious fight every time. It has been from the time you started as a county attorney. This time we've had four solid unpleasant months of fighting with Ross, and now we have two more months of vicious fighting with this awful Carpenter man."

"The political scientists call it the power struggle," the Senator said. "Power is neither gained nor relinquished without a struggle."

"It just seems wrong to me," she said. "So much time and energy are expended on fighting and so little on getting together and trying to get things done."

"I feel that way myself."

"John, what are you going to do with Ross?"

"A very difficult question," he said. "First, we've got to find out what he said, and whether, as best we can tell, it was deliberate or unintentional. If it was unintentional, then I guess we'll just have to impose a written script on him every time he speaks and not permit him to depart from it. If it was intentional—"

"Which I think it was . . ."

"I don't think so. But if it was, well, we'll just have to get rid of him, and the dangerous part of that is that while we can get rid of him, we can't stop him from speaking. I just hope, and believe, that it was unintentional. Ross just doesn't have judgment and, I fear, never will."

"I hope you're right."

He picked up the telephone. "We'll see." He put in a call to the Hilton in Kansas City.

27

Sidney approached the Senator, who was chatting with three people in the lobby of the Chase. He plucked the Senator's coat sleeve. "I'm sorry to interrupt, but could I see you a minute?"

The Senator excused himself and joined Sidney on a sofa in a corner of the lobby.

"I just heard something I think you ought to know about. Did you know that there's a big fight going on in Flowers' union? A power struggle?"

The Senator's eyes flicked up in concern. "Where did you hear that?"

"I was talking to a labor union guy and I mentioned that Flowers was coming out to do a little campaigning for you, and he told me about it. It's a regular civil war. They're going to try to throw him out at the next convention."

"Damn it," the Senator said. "What's it all about?"

"Well, they've finally got around to finding out what a nothing he is. Then, apparently he lost a big election at some big plant in South Carolina that they've been trying to organize for years. Also a messy personal life. Some girl."

The Senator slumped back against the sofa and sat staring straight ahead for a few moments. "I'm going to call Kane. We need to know a little bit more about this." They went up to the suite, and the Senator put through a call to Washington. Ernie

298

Kane was finally located in the NFL building and came on the line. "Ernie," the Senator said quietly, "I've just come by a little intelligence that I find worrisome. I hear that there's some trouble in the American Electronic Workers."

There was a pause. "Oh, sure, a little. Same type of thing I deal with here every day."

"I was told it was more serious than the usual insurrections. That this was serious. That it might succeed in unseating Flowers."

"No," Kane scoffed. "Not a chance. Tempest in a teapot."

"Ernie, I've got some evidence that it's damn serious. That it may split that union wide open. And that comes from a good source."

"Well, Flowers is in a little trouble, but he'll ride it out."

"Goddam it, Ernie, why did you send him out here like this without telling me what was going on? You know I'm in a real fight. What the hell were you trying to do?"

"John, you asked for help, and Flowers was the best man I could break loose. And besides, I figured it would help you both out."

Now the Senator paused. "Oh, you figured that I could shore Flowers up while he's giving me a hand."

"Sure. It'll help you both."

"Ernie, I just want you to know that I'm surprised that you would do a thing like this. Maybe you just didn't think about what you were doing."

"Think about what, for Godsake," Ernie said.

"You know damn well that I'm already having my problems with your boys in this state. Fields and several others are sitting on their hands. Now you send out a guy like Flowers, who's about to get tossed out of his own union on his ear for general ineptitude, malfeasance, and whoring around. He can only hurt me. That's what I mean when I say what the hell were you trying to do."

"You're just edgy about the election, John."

"You're damn right I am. Thanks to you and some others."

"I don't see this line of reasoning," Ernie said.

299

"Well I do. And I don't want Flowers stumping for me. Now, are you going to tell him or shall I?"

"This puts me in a hell of a position."

"We can do it one of two ways. You can put in a rush call for him to come back to Washington on some vital project, or I'll dream up some reasons that won't hurt his feelings and tell him myself. Which shall it be?"

Ernie thought. "I still think you're off base, but it's your campaign. Why don't you do it?"

"All right," the Senator said. They bade one another short good-bys and the Senator hung up. "Sidney, we may as well get this over with right now. Would you put in a call to Leo Averni and tell him we'd like him to join us at Flowers' hotel? I'll call Flowers, and if he's there we'll go over right now. We'll meet Leo in the lobby."

Flowers was in his hotel, and Sidney reported that Averni would meet them there in fifteen minutes. Sidney and the Senator put on their jackets and left. Flowers' hotel was a short distance away, and they walked.

"I had no idea this would upset you so much, Senator," Sidney said.

"I shouldn't have lost my temper that way with Ernie, but that was a hell of a thing for him to do."

"I don't quite see where Flowers' being here is all that harmful."

"Put it down to political intuition. I just think his presence here will lose me votes. In his own union, which is not inconsiderable in this state, all of the people who are against Flowers will also be against me if he goes around actively supporting me. Not all of them, but enough to worry about. Secondly, Steve Fields is smoldering at me, as you know. And he thinks Flowers is an ass and also incompetent, as he has stated several times. I just worry that if he sees Flowers out stumping for me, he'll fly into a rage and do some real damage. I just can't afford to take the risk on either count. I'd rather let the labor thing lie and take my chances with it than take this kind of a risk."

They arrived at Ed Flowers' hotel and waited a few minutes

for Averni. When he arrived, the Senator outlined the situation to him.

"I thought it was kind of funny that they sent Flowers," Averni said. "I thought you knew all about this revolt in his union or I would have mentioned it."

"Didn't hear a thing about it until an hour ago," the Senator said. "Sidney picked it up and fortunately recognized that it might be important. I'm going to tell Ed that we can't use him. He may get pretty annoyed, but I think we can handle him. I'd just like you to pitch in with a couple of sentences at the right time to convince him, Leo. All right?"

"Sure."

They went up in the elevator and knocked on Flowers' door. He opened the door in his bathrobe. He had been drinking, and his eyes were bleary, but he seemed alert. They spent a few minutes on trivia, and all three permitted Ed to fix them a drink.

"Ed," the Senator said finally, "I'm in a little jam, and frankly this is damn awkward and embarrassing to me, but since we're old friends, I thought the only way to handle the matter was just to bring it right out into the light."

"Shoot."

"Well, this campaign has taken a little different turn than I expected it to. You know how these things go. It's very difficult to predict in advance just what the right strategy is going to be."

"Sure," Ed said. "You have to play it by ear."

"That's right. You have to adjust your strategy, as things you didn't expect come to the surface. And, after much thought and consultation with Sidney, Dick, Virgil, and Leo here, we have about decided that the best way to handle this labor thing is to play it down. It seems to us that we are taking the risk of stirring up the animals and we might be better off to ease up on it a bit. In our judgment, some of the animosity is wearing off."

"That ain't the way I hear it."

"I think it is, Ed," Averni said. "It's getting pushed into the background. Don't you think so?"

"Oh, I dunno. I guess. But there's still a hell of a lot of feeling there."

"At any rate, we've decided to hold off, at least temporarily.

If it doesn't seem to be wearing off, then we'll probably go back to our original strategy of trying to bring about some unity in labor."

"So?"

"So we don't think we'll try to talk the thing through with the labor people. We're not going ahead with that idea." The Senator paused.

"You mean you don't want me to get out in the field for you," Ed said.

"Not don't want you to," the Senator said. "We'd love to have you do it, believe me. But our collective judgment indicates that it might not be the best strategy."

"Well, that's a hell of a note. Why didn't you tell me this before you got me all the way out here from Washington?"

"We would have if we could, Ed," the Senator said. "But this was something that we finally decided on only this morning."

"So I'm no good to you, and you want me to go back home."

"No. I think you're looking at it in the wrong way," the Senator said. "We wanted you. In fact, we specifically asked Ernie if he could arrange for you to come. It's just that the facts have changed since we made that original judgment. It has nothing to do with you personally."

Ed looked at the Senator skeptically.

"Believe me, if we were going to have anyone working for us, it would be you. We were all agreed on that. But don't you see the situation?" the Senator said.

"I suppose so," Ed said. "You're the politician. You must know what you're doing."

"It was hard for us to do this, Ed," the Senator said. "The only reason we could do it was that we knew that you'd recognize the merit in the whole thing, even though it has been a personal inconvenience to you."

"I think it's the right thing to do, Ed," Averni said. "My reading of the situation agrees with the others."

"O.K. O.K.," Ed said. "Far be it from me to intrude myself where I'm not wanted."

"It's not that you're not wanted," the Senator said. "It's just that we don't think the timing is right."

"All right," Ed said. "You're calling the shots."

"Fine. I knew you'd understand. Now I suppose that I've got a lot of nerve in asking a favor, but I'd like for you and Sidney to have dinner together tonight. I'm making a little speech, otherwise I'd be there. I'd just like you to fill Sidney in on your thinking about what's going on in the labor area. That all right, Sidney?"

"Sure. Fine."

"You don't seem to need anybody to tell you what's going on in the labor area," Ed said.

"Oh, yes, we do. This is only a tentative decision. And if you think that it should be changed, or you have any other ideas, we'd like to have them. We're always looking for ideas, and this course is not necessarily final. We may change our minds at any moment."

Ed agreed, somewhat reluctantly, to go to dinner with Sidney. They departed, and as they left the elevator the Senator asked, "Do you think he believed all that?"

"I don't think he did," Sidney said. "I think he knew he was getting the brush-off."

"It's a small deception I suppose," the Senator said, "but it troubles my conscience. Flowers is so defenseless."

"He'll be all right," Averni said. "Just give him a big boozy dinner and arrange for a babe, and he'll wake up tomorrow morning with only the kindest feelings toward everybody."

"That's a good idea, Sidney," the Senator said with a smile.

28

Frank Raeder's fist slashed the air as he paced up and down Ed's office at the end of a depressing afternoon. He was giving a fight talk in the American tradition—an attempt by a manager to put a bit of tiger into his fighter, or a football coach to send the adrenalin surging through his boys' systems so that they would not feel the pain, or falter from exhaustion. Harold Berg and Al Horwitz were caught up in the hypnosis and seemed on the verge of rushing out the door, with a wild rebel yell, to do battle. But Ed withdrew into himself, closing his ears and lowering his eyes until Frank's thin voice seemed to be coming from a great distance. He hated Frank for driving him this way, yet he could not let him go. Frank was contemptuous of Don Harrack and his ragtag brigade. They weren't much; they could be handled. Frank was sure that he would win, overwhelmingly. Frank was sure, because Frank would make it so. By working all night, Saturdays, Sundays, and holidays—every moment. Intimidating, cajoling, and joking in his awkward way, he would beat Harrack or anyone else, by swamping them with an energy that no one could match.

Now that they were out in the open, Ed had heard what they were saying about him. A playboy, who had never been a real workingman, who threw away great sums of union dues in liquor, parties, women; who failed in leadership; who let employers walk all over him; who sold his members down the river by failing to organize the unorganized, and thus threatened the wage standard of all of them; who was a wishy-washy zero in the councils of the NFL; who made the union a laughingstock because he himself was a laughingstock; who rewarded highfalutin, prissy friends with cushy jobs at headquarters.

For several weeks there had been a paralysis of fear at AEW headquarters. The staff knew that the fall of Edward Flowers would mean their own fall. A few became spies for the opposition, seeking to ensure their own survival in the case of an insurgent victory. But they said nothing to anyone, hoping to survive if Ed won. They were staff men, suppliers of facts, analyzers of opinion and argument, and they waited quietly to be given instructions. No instructions were given, and for several weeks there were guilty, frightened conversations in the halls, over lunches, and with wives at home. But nothing was done.

Then Frank Raeder laid out a plan for Ed. First, it was the prerogative of the president to name the city in which the convention would be held; and it would be held in Washington instead of Chicago. Second, the staff would set about preparing an elaborate presentation of slides, films, and printed argument, glorifying Ed's term as president of the union. Third, the President of the NFL would be prevailed upon to address the convention. He might protest, since there was a factional fight taking place. But Frank thought he could persuade him to make the opening address, and thus lend Ed prestige. A booklet outlining Ed's career would be prepared by a commissioned newspaperman. It would be paid for, not out of union funds, but by Ed's loyal friends, and also, although unannounced, partly by Ed himself. Before the convention delegates were selected, each union member would receive a personal multilithed letter signed by Ed. Some reliable, prestigious Congressional friends would appear on the platform and speak obliquely in his behalf. . . . Thus, Frank's mind spewed forth ideas as each day passed, and they were carried out by the headquarters staff, relieved to have something to do at last. The office came alive with activity and excitement. Harold Berg ordered buttons in the shape of sunflowers, bearing the inscription: "Win with Flowers." They were loyally worn by the entire staff.

Frank told Ed to stop drinking until the convention was over. He did, when things seemed to be going well, but when a period of depression overtook him, he locked his office door and sat solitary in the shadows, with a drink in his hand.

Frank was sure they were going to win. Harold Berg was certain of it. The office girls absolutely knew it. But Ed doubted.

Frank tried to persuade Ed to make some trips into the troublesome areas. Once he did this, but finally he refused to go any more. Instead, some of the more reliable staff people were sent on the road, to drum up votes for the cause.

With the convention now only ten days away, Frank, in a fury of excitement, paced Ed's office floor, as he did almost every afternoon. Ed was relieved when the session ended. He assumed an air of jaunty confidence when they were in his office, agreeing with all of them that he would win. When they left, he turned the latch, poured himself a strong whiskey, and strolled about the office, viewing everything for the first time, like a tourist—the rich, real leather chairs, the paintings on the walls, the books in the bookcase, the new Oriental rug. Finally he called Barbara.

"I'll be over in an hour or so," he said.

She was slightly vague and evasive, and it angered him.

"Not tonight, Ed," she said finally.

"Why not?"

"Well, I just have some things to do. Quite a lot of things."

"Well, can't I sit there while you do them? If you've got ironing or something, I'll talk to you."

"That wouldn't work out too well, Ed. Actually . . ." she said in measured tones, "I'm busy."

He puzzled over the word. "Busy?"

"Yes."

"Well, all right," he said at last, "I'm damn disappointed."

There was a long, aching pause as he waited for her to say something. "Ed, I didn't want to tell you this way, over the phone . . . but I think maybe . . . well, it might be better for both of us, if we . . . well, if we stopped seeing each other." The last words came with a rush.

He closed his eyes in swirling darkness. "What did you say?"

"Oh, Ed. . . ."

306

"You don't want to get married?"

"No," she said softly, "I don't."

He let the receiver flop in his lap. After a moment he picked it up and said, "You stay right there. I'm coming over," and he hung it gently on its cradle.

For three hours they fought. She alternately cried and became hysterical. He accused her, called her filthy names, then was tender, pleading. She seemed to sway for a moment, to come to him, then she receded from his arms. He wanted to beat her with his fists, force her to love him, force her to marry him. Finally she rejected his last exhausted compromise proposal—that they not see each other for a while, until they had both settled down. She listened as if she were deaf. She did not love him. She was terribly, terribly sorry, and she had thought of killing herself she was so sorry, but she did not love him. And there was nothing more to say. It was a terrible thing, and she knew it, but there was nothing more to say.

He took his hat and left.

Two days later, at 7:15 A.M., Frank Raeder received a telephone call from Agnes Flowers. Within an hour he had picked her up in his car, and they were on their way to the hospital. When they arrived, they were asked to wait. Frank paced up and down the floor, got several drinks of water, glanced at several magazines and cast them aside, and smoked numberless cigarettes. Agnes sat on the uncomfortable wooden bench, stiffly, without speaking. Shortly before ten, Doctor Holly, who introduced himself as a psychiatrist, asked them to come into a private room.

"What happened?" Frank Raeder asked before the doctor could begin.

"Mr. Flowers was found by the police, sitting on a curbstone near DuPont Circle about 3 A.M., two nights ago. The police assumed that he was intoxicated, and in fact he had been drinking. But he behaved abnormally, so they brought him here to the hospital . . ."

"Is anything wrong with him?" Frank asked.

"It appears so. His mental status appears to be abnormal. He was given a physical examination when he was first registered, but the results of that were somewhat in doubt because of the presence of alcohol. But subsequent examinations have confirmed the original diagnosis. I have given him a psychiatric examination which, you must understand, is to be regarded as preliminary. He continues to exhibit some of the symptoms which he showed on Monday night, but they seem less intense."

"What were the symptoms?" Frank asked.

"Stuporous. Apparently he was able to hear and he appeared in command of his physical faculties in carrying out what was asked of him. But he did not appear to hear anything else that was said. Nor did he know who he was or where he lived. Or perhaps he did not want to answer. That's difficult to determine, this early. As I said, he shows some improvement this morning. But I'm just mentioning these things, Mrs. Flowers, so that, if possible, you won't exhibit extreme emotion if he should not recognize you."

"I don't care particularly," she said.

The doctor looked at her uncertainly. "I believe you indicated that you and Mr. Flowers were separated and that a divorce suit is in progress. Has this upset him, do you think?"

"I don't think he has any feelings," she said. "Besides, I haven't seen him in two months, and then only at the lawyer's."

"He's been under pressure in his job, Doctor," Frank said. "He's been fighting a dissident group, and it's been unpleasant for him."

"I see," said the doctor.

"The annual union convention is only a week off. It begins next Wednesday. There was quite a lot of pressure building up there."

"I see. Did he feel that he would be criticized?"

"Oh, he will be criticized, no question about that. He thought that they might throw him out."

"You mean, out of the presidency?"

"Yes."

"I see. Is there anything else you can think of that might have contributed to this apparent breakdown? Does he drink excessively?"

"He didn't used to. Only once in a while," Agnes said.

"More lately," Frank added. "He was feeling the pressure."

308

"I see," said the doctor. "Well, let's have a talk with him. Please try to be as normal and relaxed as is possible under the circumstances, and don't ask too many questions."

He led them down the corridor and opened the door. Ed was lying on the bed, which had been partly raised. He had a hollow, haunted look about his eyes.

"Hello, Frank. Hello, Agnes," he said cordially. They exchanged greetings.

"How are the kids?" he said to Agnes.

"Fine."

"Eddie Junior get the jalopy running yet?"

"Well . . ." said Agnes. Eddie had sold the jalopy several months ago.

"You're looking fine," Ed said.

"Thank you," said Agnes.

"I guess I owe everybody an apology," he said. "I guess I had a little too much to drink last night. Don't know when to stop, Doctor."

"It happens to all of us from time to time," the psychiatrist said.

"Sure it does," Ed said. "Everybody goes out on a bender once in a while." He laughed weakly. "I really tied one on. You'll forgive me for that, won't you, Agnes?" he said with a smile.

She nodded.

"Very forgiving woman," Ed confided to the doctor. He winked. "Couldn't get along without her. Listen, Agnes, you got enough money? I left some on the bureau yesterday. Fifty dollars."

Agnes tried to answer.

"I guess you're going to keep me here a couple of days, Doctor?"

"For a little while," the doctor said. "We'll want to make sure you're completely recovered."

"I won't be home for dinner then, Agnes. You think you and the kids can make out all right for a couple of days without me?"

Tears coursed down Agnes' cheeks. She gave a stifled sob and rushed out of the room.

"Upset," Ed said. "I'm damn sorry to upset her that way."

309

"She's just worried, Ed," Frank said.

"Sure," Ed said. "Seeing me in the hospital this way."

"She'll be all right," the doctor said. "I think it might be a good idea if you got some rest, Ed. Do you feel tired?"

"A little," Ed said. "I probably could use a nap."

They turned to go. "Frank," Ed said. "I haven't said one word to you. How's tricks?"

"Fine," Frank said.

"Good. Look in at headquarters and see that they don't goof off while the boss is away."

"Sure thing."

"You could bring me that Airython file too, next time you come. Couple of things I want to look at."

"Well, Ed. . . ."

"Goddam tough nut that Airython. Put a lot of time and money into that damn thing. One other thing, when is the next convention, Frank?"

Frank looked at the doctor.

"We'll talk about that a little later," the doctor said soothingly. "You just concentrate on getting a little rest now." They left the room and pulled the door closed behind them.

"Nurse," said the doctor, "will you give Flowers six milligrams of Trilafon, repeating every six hours."

"Yes, sir."

"What's that?" Frank said.

"An anti-depressant drug," said the doctor. Frank strode along beside the doctor, worried. "Retrograde amnesia," the doctor said. "Erasure of some events. He appears not to recall the divorce, or the upcoming convention."

Frank grimaced. "Is he . . . is this permanent do you think?"

"Recovery has been experienced in the great majority of cases. Prognosis for temporary recovery is good. For permanent recovery, prognosis is questionable. That depends on many factors, of which the minimization of stress situations is the most important."

Frank digested that. "Doctor," he said, "it would be damaging if reports of Ed's hospitalization got out at this point, especially if the reason were known. We'd greatly appreciate it if you

310

could keep quiet about this. Particularly if you're approached by reporters. I'm hoping that you won't be approached, because if they get wind there is a psychiatrist involved, the cat will be out of the bag pretty much."

"Of course I'm bound by hospital regulations, Mr. Raeder. And I must act always in the best interest of the patient. But I assure you I will not reveal any information beyond what is absolutely necessary."

"Thank you, Doctor. May I keep in touch with you?"

"Certainly, by all means. He may be close to normal when he wakes up this time. With some rest under his belt, he may come around. It often happens. But we can't be sure."

The doctor and Frank parted, and Frank joined the haggard Agnes in the waiting room.

"I'll run you home," Frank said. "Agnes, I think it was swell of you to come, considering the circumstances. The doctor doesn't think this will be permanent. He thinks he will come around."

"I really don't care," said Agnes. "It's punishment he deserves. All I care about is that he keep out of my life and the children's lives. I don't care whether he lives or dies."

"You're upset."

"I won't change my mind about that."

They drove out to the suburbs in silence. When they reached the Flowers' house, Frank said, "I'll be in touch with you."

"You can if you want to," Agnes said, "but it's of no importance to me. I have no feelings on the subject one way or the other."

"Well, I'll call you anyway."

"Have it your way," she said carelessly. He waited, watching the squat, middle-aged figure slowly climb the steps and enter the house without looking back.

He pressed his lips together and began to think. He realized that for a period of time at least, Ed Flowers would be incapable of making any decisions or taking any action. There was no one in the AEW who could do it. Decisions would have to be made, and action would have to be taken by Frank Raeder. He would have to come out into the open more. It was risky. They would resent him if he got heavy-handed, and he was aware of his limitations in that respect. He would have to give them all the idea that he was just helping Flowers, as a loyal friend. It was a tricky course. The whole thing might blow up in his face. But there was no other course to take.

29

Paul Finch took a satisfied sip of his after-dinner brandy in the living room of Judge Russell's large house. The Judge had never before invited them to his house; it seemed to Paul that this visit was significant. At last, perhaps, the tough old man was going to admit that he was through.

"We've been looking at some property out beyond Potomac," Jean said to Mrs. Russell. "We haven't found anything yet that we like, that we can afford. But we've got the bug, no doubt about that."

"It's lovely out there," Mrs. Russell agreed. "What type of place are you looking for?"

"An old barny house with fifteen or twenty acres," Jean said, "off the main road."

"You're crazy," said the Judge.

"I always thought I'd like to do that, but I couldn't budge Robert from the city," his wife said. "He always felt that he had to be on call twenty-four hours a day. Someplace where he could get down to the Hill in twenty minutes."

"Of course," the Judge said. "You have to. You're crazy to live out there. Crazy."

"It's not so far, Judge," Paul said. "It only takes fifteen minutes longer to get out there than it does to get where we live now. And outside of rush hour, even less."

"You're out of the heart of things out there, boy. Those people out there aren't concerned with Washington. They're local gentry. They're not concerned with the Federal Government."

"That's one of the things I like about it," Paul said. "They're involved in something besides the Federal Government. So that when you get out there at night, and get active socially out there, you're moving in an entirely different world. And I think that's healthy."

"Well, I don't," said the Judge. "If you're going to take this job, you ought to give yourself to it, and not try to run away to the peaceful country every night. Washington isn't a peaceful place, and that job isn't peaceful either."

"Exactly," said Paul. "And that's why I need a break from it. To get away and think."

"Nonsense," said the Judge.

"But Judge," said Jean daringly, "don't you think a man should be able to get away from the job sometimes?"

"Of course," said the Judge. "But every night is a luxury. You try that and some young feller will have the job. Like you did me."

"Now, Judge, that's not—"

"No, it's not," the Judge said, "and I take it back. It was the stroke that got me, pure and simple. You had nothing to do with it. But I might as well tell you what I brought you out here to tell you. I'm getting out. Entirely."

"Oh?" said Paul.

"I just don't have the physical strength to do it any more. That's the only thing that would stop me. Wheel-chair-bound the way I am, I can't go running around and sitting in people's offices for hours. I can get around the Capitol with the ramps, and the House and Senate Buildings, but that's about it. I can make two or three calls, and then I'm pooped. Can't do any effective work on a schedule like that. Besides," he said, "my sight is failing some."

"Oh dear," said Jean.

"Sorry to hear that, Judge," said Paul.

"Eyes will probably last longer than I will, the doctor says.

But I can't do the amount of reading that I used to, and that cuts down on what you know."

"Well, Judge, if I can help in any way . . ."

"You can't. Except for one thing. You might drop out, or give me a call, from time to time, and fill me in. I'll be interested. And I might be able to give you a little advice. Which you probably won't take, due to your pigheaded tendency."

"I sure will, Judge. I'll be glad to. Make a point of it."

"All right. Now there's something else I want you to do. Want to get a little air before I go to bed. Think you're up to pushing the chair around the block?"

"Sure," Paul said. They slipped their coats on, and his wife threw a blanket over the Judge's legs. He said he didn't need it, but allowed it to remain, and they went out into the cold and frosty night.

"I'm sorry to hear about this, Judge," Paul said. "I liked to feel that you were there to ask for advice if I felt I needed it."

"You asked for damn little, boy. You spent most of your time trying to shoulder me out, but that isn't why I got you out here away from those women. I want to talk to you about something."

"O.K."

"About this crazy idea of moving out to the country. Forget it. The travel isn't so bad, if you're so crazy about the country, but I know what you're thinking about. You've seen how the other half lives and you've been thinking how nice it would be to live out in the horse country and hobnob with the upper crust. Well, I'm telling you, stick to your knitting. You think that you can break into society out there—or your wife does—by buying a house and getting involved in the horse shows and dog shows and the Hunt Balls, and being nice to everybody. But I can tell you right now that you won't. You will always be on the fringes, and you will know it. They will see to it that you know it. Remember, you're a lobbyist, than which there is nothing lower in Washington, and you might as well give up any ideas you have of going society. These people out there—I mean the real society, not the hangers-on—will pull back their skirts so they won't touch you. And if you try to keep quiet about what you do, they'll find out sooner or later. You're bound to get your name in the papers at some time or other, and it won't be in a flattering context—it will be as an influence peddler or a fivepercenter. And that little wife of yours will just die, and not be able to show her face outside the house because of the disgrace. And while I'm at it, I may as well tell you you're not going to be government society either. In government society, you're nobody, but nobody, unless you're in government. And even if your personality is so scintillating that they all like you, they're not going to take the chance of hobnobbing with a lobbyist. That leads to a bad press. In fact, the only consolation in the job is that it pays well. I'm just telling you this for your own good, boy."

"Well, I appreciate it," said Paul, who was a little winded from the slight uphill grade.

"I'm telling it to you because it happened to me. Not that I gave a damn about it personally, but Martha did. Women always do. And she was hurt by it; she was made miserable. You know how women can do those things to other women. My advice is: Live a nice, upper-middle-class life, and don't fret your life away trying to climb into the next bracket, because you ain't going to do it—and it's not worth it anyway, trying to keep up with those people and doing everything they do. Take my word for it."

"I'll think about it," Paul said.

"You better. You're carried away now, because your salary is going up fast, and it's likely to go up a good bit more, so you think you can buy anything with it. Well, this is one thing you can't buy, because the only protection they have is that they don't sell it for money. You'll just be beating your head against the wall for nothing. If you're thick-skinned enough to hold this job, you probably won't mind it too much. But your wife will."

Paul realized that the Judge was probably right, but he did not want to accept what he had said. He pushed the chair along in silence.

"Now it's my turn," Paul said. "There's something I want to ask you about before we get back to the house."

He related the story of his visit to New York and his audience with Briggs Christy. "Why is New York doing this?" he finished. "If they wanted another man, a more senior man, why didn't they drop him in the slot when they could have done it easily?"

The Judge did not reply immediately. "Things changed, boy," he said at last. "They were figuring that I'd be around to keep the train on the track. This is too important a job to turn over to a man no older or more experienced than you. A serious mistake in that job could really damage Liberty."

"I know that," Paul said.

"So I was to keep you from making any serious mistakes. But now I'm out of the picture, so they want somebody comparable to me."

"To compete with me and undercut and second-guess me," Paul said bitterly.

"You're looking at it the wrong way. Hell, you're a fair-haired boy in New York's eyes. They picked you for this job and they're willing to bring you along. Honest to God, I don't know what you young fellows want."

"I'd like a little peace of mind and a little freedom to do the job," Paul said.

"Look boy, you're forgetting something. From what you told me, Christy is willing to let you pick your own man, subject to his O.K. Is that right?"

"That's the impression I got."

"Well, what are you so worried about then? You control the situation. Pick a man who won't be a threat to you."

Paul nodded. That was good advice.

"They want a senior man," the Judge continued. "Give them one. Get a guy who's sixty-five and part time. They're not going to move a guy like that over you. In a couple of years he'd be too old. Keep the reporting reins in your own hands. Use your head and keep your elbows out. This is a competitive society, you know."

"That's being impressed on me more every day," Paul said.

"Won't hurt you a bit," the Judge said.

They had reached the house.

Paul rolled the wheel chair up the ramp. "You're no featherweight to push around, Judge."

"Getting fat," he said. "Get no exercise. I eat like a bird, but I'm still getting fat."

They entered the living room and Paul waited while Jean put on her coat. The Judge rolled off down the hall, with a quick good night.

As they drove home, Paul said: "Maybe we ought to think about that country place."

"Why," Jean said, "I thought it was all settled. What did the Judge say to change your mind?"

"The Judge?" he said. "Nothing. We didn't talk about that."

Jean looked at him through narrow-slitted eyes. "I bet he did. Why are you suddenly changing your mind?"

"I'm not changing my mind. I merely said that maybe we ought to think about it a little bit more."

"I know what that means. That means you're not going to do it."

"Not necessarily. Not at all. I just think we ought to know what we're getting into before we jump, that's all."

"He said something," she accused.

Paul did not reply.

30

Sidney paid the cab driver, walked up to the large stone house, and rang the bell. A maid opened the door. "Mister Bronstein?" she said. "They're in the library." She led the way down the old-fashioned stucco hallway and opened half of the double door to the library. Virgil Akers and Dick Goetz were seated; the Senator was standing in front of the fireplace. "It's my fault," Dick was saying as Sidney entered.

"Come in, Sidney," the Senator said. "Sit down."

Sidney nodded to all of them and took a chair. They returned his nod without a change of expression.

"Sidney," the Senator said, "I want you to tell us exactly and precisely about your relationship with the International Peace Foundation."

Sidney felt as if a bucket of ice water had been dashed over him. "What?" he said, playing for time. "What do you mean?"

"I think the question is clear. Begin at the beginning. How were your first contacts made with the organization?"

"Senator . . ." he said.

"At the beginning, if you please, Sidney. And omit no details."

Sidney squeezed his hands together and looked down at them hollowly. "No serious relationship. Just went to a few meetings."

"Sidney," the Senator said, "we're not trying to convict you of anything, but this is a serious matter. We're trying to protect you and ourselves. Now begin at the beginning, if you please."

Sidney licked his dry lips and plunged in. "In college, at Columbia, I knew a couple of guys and a girl. They were very interested in the movement. They said it was a discussion group that was interested in exploring the causes of war and how those causes might be removed from the modern environment. It was just like a lot of groups around the campus—on most campuses, I guess. Liberal, wild-eyed, rejecting all the old ideas because, in their judgment, they had failed. Seeking new ones."

"Like the Soviet form of government?"

"No, not exactly. I mean their ideas and approach were studied along with all the others, and they were analyzed in a friendly way. The materials used were usually Soviet government documents, so they were obviously friendly to the Soviet way of doing things. Some of the group were Communists—at least they thought they were. What does an eighteen-year-old kid know about it? They were mostly blowoffs, inflated with their own sense of importance at being daring and different. We had a few rallies to support and raise money for the Spanish Loyalists. I think we raised about seventy-five dollars or so once. And we condemned the Fascist governments."

"Were you ever an officer in this organization?"

"No. I wasn't enthusiastic enough. I was generally considered to be a limp rag."

"Did you ever sign your name to a membership card or to a petition?"

"No. There was no such thing as a membership card that I ever heard about. The only petition I ever signed was to give aid to the Loyalists when a bill was pending in Congress. . . ."

"That is the only document that you ever put your name to?"

"Yes, sir. As far as I can remember. That was twenty years ago. But I think that's right."

"Think harder, Sidney."

"I don't remember any more."

"Did you ever contribute money?"

"I never had much money to contribute. I think I gave five

bucks once to Spanish War Relief. And once I remember I gave a couple of bucks for Abyssinia."

"Was this recorded?"

"The five dollars wasn't. That was just tossed in a hat. I don't remember about the other."

"Then what happened?"

"Well, that's about all. I graduated from college, and I went to a few meetings after that, saw a few of these people socially. Then the war came, and I went into the service. I didn't see any of them for several years. After the war I saw Lila Stern. She got married not long after that. Now she's a housewife with four kids. And her husband is a capitalist who owns a big supermarket out in Manhassett. She lives in a big house and worries about taxes and getting her kids in socially acceptable schools. So you see," he added, "the group was not all that subversive."

"How about Isaac Gold? Do you remember him?"

Sidney cast his eyes down. "Yes."

"You're aware, then, that he was a Communist when you knew him, is still a Communist, and is now in a federal penitentiary, convicted of attempted espionage?"

"Yes, sir, I am aware of that."

"So it isn't all quite so rosy as you make it seem, is it, Sidney?"

"When did you last see Gold?" Goetz asked.

"Sometime after I got out of college. I never saw him after I went into the Navy.

"You haven't seen him, then, in about twenty years. Never laid eyes on him, is that right?"

"That's right."

"Well, thank God for small favors," Dick Goetz said.

"Sidney, let me ask you this," the Senator said. "Since shortly after you graduated from college, you have not seen any of these people. You have not written to them. You have not sent them money or contributed money to any cause of this sort. You have not visited any of them. Is that true?"

"Yes, except for Lila Stern. I have seen her two or three times. My wife knows her, and we have stayed with them on Long Island twice when we visited New York."

"And did you talk about this organization?"

"Only in a joking way."

"Is there any possibility that she had continued to be in touch with them?"

"God no. She's gotten very stuffy about things. She wouldn't sully her hands. She's working to break into upper-class Jewish society on the Island."

"Sidney, are you sure?"

"That's one thing I'd bet my life on."

"One last question, Sidney. Is there anything you haven't told us? Is there anything you're holding back? We're all in this boat together, and we're trying to save our collective skins, and we have to have the truth. All of it," said the Senator, towering over him as he sat in the chair.

"I've told you everything."

The Senator pulled out a cigarette, lit it, and sank into a chair. "I'm sure you realize what has happened, Sidney. They've gotten wind of this matter. We don't have any idea how much they know. But it doesn't take much. All they need is a fact or two to protect themselves from a suit, and they can hint the rest. In fact, they can make it far worse."

"They don't have any right to destroy a person's life," Sidney said.

"Don't be stupid, Sidney. They're not after you. They don't give a damn about you. They're after me. I'm the one they want to crucify, not you. If you had told us about this, we wouldn't be in this mess."

"I didn't tell you because I would never have gotten the job, Senator. And I needed that job desperately. I am sorry that I did not, but I just didn't think there was a chance it would ever come up after twenty years."

"In politics, everything comes up."

"I know that now, but I didn't then. In any case, I'm offering you my resignation. I'll get out of here, and nobody will find me until after the election." He rose and extended his hand to the Senator, who did not take it.

"I will make that decision, if you please, Sidney." He turned to the fireplace and flicked his cigarette carelessly. "Sidney, I'm going to be honest with you. It may come to this. I may have to accept your resignation. It may be necessary to sacrifice you. We will know in a few days, I suspect. In the meantime, I want you to continue. They don't have much time left, and if they're going to get started with the tarbrush, they'll have to get started pretty soon. They may not have anything but a smell of a lead. If that's the case, we may be able to ride it out. I am warning you, how-ever, that we may not. Now I want you to keep quiet about this. Say absolutely nothing. If the press ever questions you, there is only one answer I will permit you to give: 'No comment.' Not one other word. Don't let them bait you or get you angry or get you to answer questions that sound innocent. Call your wife tonight and give her exactly the same instructions. Can you be certain that she will follow them?"

"Yes."

"And your parents. Did they know of the connection?"

"I don't remember. I suppose they did."

"All right. Call them and give them the same instructions. Only two words: 'No comment.'"

"Yes, sir."

"There are others, I assume, but we can't call everybody. The more people we have keeping a secret, the more likely it is to get out."

"Yes, sir."

"I wish to God I knew where they picked this up. Nobody's been able to find out?"

"Not yet," Virgil said.

"Well, let's keep our ears open and let's keep our fingers crossed. I'll see you in the morning." He held out his hand.

"I'm sorry, Senator. That sounds inadequate, but I'm sorry for myself and I'm sorry for you."

"I'm not going to say, Sidney, that it's all perfectly O.K. Something like this could pop my political career like a balloon at this critical stage, if the other side handles it right. Fortunately, they usually take out like a pack of wolves after something like this, and the public begins to sympathize with the rabbit. But we can't count on it. Good night, Sidney, and keep your mouth shut."

Sidney nodded to all of them and left.

"Well," said the Senator, "that's a hell of a note. One more faggot to throw on the merrily burning flame. They're riding the hell out of the Leona Smith thing. God knows what effect that's going to have. Ross is wavering all over the lot. Now this, with Sidney."

"Jews that lived through that period almost always have something like that in their background," Virgil Akers said. "I would have bet on it before I heard him say a word."

"I should have picked it up somewhere," said Dick Goetz, "but I checked his background pretty carefully."

"The reason you didn't pick anything up," said the Senator, "is because there isn't anything there, for Christ sake."

"You'll never have a chance to prove that, if the question is raised," Virgil said.

The Senator nodded wearily.

31

The faces of the Senator, Virgil Akers, Sidney Bronstein, and Dick Goetz were tense as they watched the television set in a St. Louis hotel room. Roger Carpenter would be making his appearance on the small screen in two or three minutes. They had all seen him often enough to know what was coming. Mildly progressive views stated with great vigor and decisiveness, resulting in the impression that he was at the same time an aggressive fighter and a safe, sound middle-of-the-roader. He came over the screen as young but able, tough but sensible, honest but practical. It was a disturbing image.

When station identification appeared on the screen, Sidney got up and turned on the tape recorder which rested on top of the television set.

"Good evening," the announcer said. "We are happy to bring you this evening, through our facilities, the Republican candidate for the United States Senate, Mr. Roger Carpenter. Mr. Carpenter."

Roger Carpenter appeared on the screen, sitting behind a desk, with an easy smile on his face.

"Good evening, friends," he said. "It is certainly a pleasure to join you in your living rooms tonight, through the marvelous medium of television. My wife, Marcia, and my children, Roger

Junior and Deborah, were so excited about it they demanded to come, and they're sitting here in the studio."

The camera panned to a pretty, conservatively dressed woman, who smiled at the audience and then at the two children beside her. "Hi, Daddy," the children chorused.

Carpenter smiled fondly at them. "Friends, I want to talk to you about two things this evening. One of them is of primary concern to our city dwellers, and the other is of primary concern to our rural people. Though both of them are very important to all of us. The first is the question of labor reform, and the second is the matter of our farm program. . . ."

The Senator smiled slightly. "Hot dog," Dick Goetz said, "he's bound to go on the rocks on these."

Sidney and the stenographer who had been hired for the evening were taking notes.

For ten minutes, Carpenter spoke smoothly. On the matter of labor reform, he was, of course, a great admirer and supporter of labor unions. They would look far to find as militant a champion of their rights as he was. But, of course, he was against intimidation, coercion, and threats, as practiced by a small element which had wormed its way into legitimate unions. The passage of the labor reform act was necessary and good. It would root out the evil and let the good remain.

"The son of a bitch is stealing your thunder, John," Virgil said.

Carpenter found it most interesting that his opponent had voted for the bill. He was surprised. In fact, everybody was surprised. And why was that? It was because his opponent had never before voted against the interests of labor, whether the bill in question was good or bad. The reason for Senator Burnett's vote was really quite simple. His vote was actually indicative of a cynical contempt for the voters of Missouri. The election was coming up. He thought that the voters would be taken in by it, would now believe that he was not unduly influenced by crooked labor leaders, and would forget his previous record. "He must think of you as simpletons and nincompoops," Carpenter said. "He thinks this one lone vote will make you forget the years that he has been associated hand and glove with these people. If you

326

return him to office for six years," Carpenter asked, "do you really think he will be a changed man? Do you really expect him to vote against labor evils ever again? Or, once elected for six years, do you think he'll go back to his old cronies of thirty years? I know what I think."

"He's improved," Sidney said disconsolately.

Carpenter was now into the subject of the farm program. He viewed the mountainous farm surpluses with incredulity and humor. Several slides were flashed on the screen, showing immense warehouses full of grain and corn. Rotting and useless, and profited on unconscionably, he said. Next, a slide appeared on the screen, of small, almost naked children, whom Carpenter alleged to be living in rural Missouri, near starvation. Could anyone defend this as sane and sensible? Could anyone possibly defend the waste, the sheer idiocy of encouraging production and then deliberately letting millions of tons of food rot away? A thousand pounds of food for each and every family in the state of Missouri every year. This was efficiency? This was management? These demonstrated incompetents were the people we were going to permit to run the country?

The Senator was listening hopefully to hear Carpenter advocate the cutting or abolishment of subsidies, but he did not fall into that trap. Instead, he praised the farmer, and maintained that these people, engaged in the most basic of all human activity, were entitled to the security of a predictable income. He wound up with a militant pledge, delivered with ringing sincerity, to bring down the prices of food dramatically for the city dwellers while maintaining the subsidy program and eliminating the surpluses.

The program closed with his wife and children at his side. He gave her a kiss on the cheek and patted the head of the engaging little girl who clung to his trouser leg.

When the program ended and the announcer was reading his closing lines, a burst of conversation began in the hotel room. Then, suddenly it ceased.

"Stay tuned to this station," the announcer was saying as a picture of Senator John Burnett appeared on the screen. "Just fifty-five minutes from now, at eight twenty-five, Senator John

Burnett will answer specifically the allegations of his opponent for the United States Senate, Roger Carpenter, whom you have just heard."

Sidney snapped off the television set and the tape recorder.

"Virgil and I will take the labor reform, and you and Dick take the farm stuff," the Senator said quickly to Sidney. The Senator and Virgil went to the other side of the room, spread papers on the coffee table and set to work. Sidney sat down at the typewriter. "I just want to get this down here while I remember it," he said to Dick, his typewriter starting to clatter. After a couple of minutes he stopped. "Dick, over there is the *Agricultural Yearbook*. That thing he said about food prices. I think we can nail him on that. There's a table right there at the beginning." He began to type rapidly again as Dick searched for the reference. He found it, and they incorporated it into the script. Dick read the page in the typewriter over Sidney's shoulder and made several suggestions. They argued about a point, and both went to the tape recorder. The machine gurgled and squeaked as they ran it backward to locate the point in Carpenter's speech they sought.

"Turn that goddam thing down," Virgil shouted from the other side of the room. "We can't hear ourselves think."

The Senator was scratching rapidly on a yellow pad, listening and nodding to Virgil at the same time.

Sidney had removed his coat and pulled his tie down as he typed rapidly. Suddenly he stopped to curse. "Dammit. Dammit. I can't get this in four hundred words. I can't do it." He got up and walked rapidly to the other side of the room. "Are you going to use all your four hundred?" he asked the Senator and Virgil.

"Hell, yes," Virgil said.

"We may need some of yours," the Senator said.

"Christ," Sidney said. "It can't be done."

"Concentrate on the solar plexus," the Senator said. Sidney hurried back to his typewriter.

"I've cut this," Dick said, "and added this phrase here. We cover the same thing and save three lines." Sidney nodded. Dick glanced at his watch. "Ten of eight already."

"Ten more minutes," Sidney said. "Who's writing the close?" he said suddenly, spinning around in his chair.

"You are," Virgil said.

Sidney turned with a curse and began to type rapidly.

Dick Goetz sat on the sofa, reading Sidney's first page and editing it with his pencil. "Miss Gelter," he said, motioning to the typist, "can you read all this?" He indicated his penciled words and the tortuous lines connecting them to the text. She puzzled over it and nodded her head.

"Up, Sidney," Dick said, as he stood behind Sidney at the typewriter. "She's got to get going." Sidney tore his paper out of the machine, and the girl slid into his place. He and Dick sat down on the sofa to finish in longhand.

"It's almost eight," Dick shouted to the Senator and Virgil.

"Our first page is ready to go. Second will be ready in a couple of minutes," Virgil said.

Dick took the first page, written by the Senator and Virgil, and began to work on a transitional paragraph. Sidney shoved the second page they had been working on in front of him with a great expiration of breath. Dick read it intently. It was too long, and he cut it while Sidney groaned.

The typist called for help, and Sidney read one of the meandering scribblings to her. He gave her the second sheet. The clock moved past eight. Dick departed to make sure the cab was waiting. The third and fourth pages were given to Miss Gelter, and they checked over the two pages she had completed. Sidney and Virgil waited nervously as the typewriter clattered on. The wait seemed endless, and time seemed to be racing by. Finally she finished and handed them the sheets. The Senator sorted out the originals; Sidney and Virgil each took a set of carbons.

The Senator glanced at his watch. "Let's get going." The elevator seemed slow, and they hurried through the lobby into the cab, the door of which was held open by Dick Goetz. All of them crowded into the cab.

"Whose crazy idea was this anyway?" the Senator said.

"Who knows at this point?" Sidney said. "If it was mine, I must have been out of my mind."

"May we leave the dome light on, driver?" the Senator said. "I have something I must read."

"Not supposed to."

329

"We'll take care of any fines and pay you five bucks," Virgil said. They all tried to be silent as the Senator studied the text. Here and there he awkwardly penciled in a change.

"I hate to do it this way," he said. "I'd much rather have no prepared text, but you've almost got to if you're going to get everything in, in a little over four minutes."

The cab arrived at the station and they got out and hurried down the long corridor to the studio. They were greeted by several of the staff; and the Senator, now accustomed to the procedure, took his place at the table and began to go over the script intently. From a long boom, a microphone was lowered over his head. Last-minute changes were made in the angles of the lights. The director of the show refreshed the Senator on the hand signals that would be given him.

"One minute," somebody shouted.

The Senator adjusted his chair, his tie, and his jacket. He looked into the camera.

"Ten seconds."

In a few seconds he heard the voice of the announcer, elsewhere in the studio, introducing him. The red light on his camera came on, and he began.

"Good evening, everybody. About an hour ago many of you heard my opponent make some strange and wonderful statements over your television set. . . ."

In the dark rear of the studio, Virgil Akers and Dick Goetz, motionless as statues, stood watching the monitor television set. Sidney paced nervously back and forth, with his eyes half closed, listening to the words as the Senator spoke them. Here and there he wished the Senator had laid the emphasis a little differently, but the moment was irretrievably gone, and several hundred thousand people had already heard it.

The Senator was leaving the whimsical and humorous and was now approaching the stinging climax. The floor manager was circling his hand in the speed-up motion.

"Thank you very much," the Senator was saying. "I'll bring you the truth again at this same hour tomorrow night." The red light on the camera went off, and the Senator leaned back in his chair, rubbing his chest with the palms of both hands.

Sidney, Dick, Virgil, and the floor manager all surrounded him at once and assured him that it had gone well. The best yet. They all moved slowly out of the studio, ducking their heads to avoid overhanging equipment, and placing their feet carefully to avoid the black cables snaked across the floor.

Dick decided to take a cab back, while the Senator, Sidney, and Virgil decided to walk at least part of the way. The air was cold after the heat of the studio.

The Senator seemed to be slowly relaxing. "These really are trials by fire," he said to Sidney. "They're so concentrated and so short."

Sidney nodded agreement.

"I've never been comfortable with television," the Senator said. "Carpenter is pretty good at it, let's admit it, and he's getting better. He's been raised in an age where television is an accepted part of the campaign. I've had to adapt and I fear I haven't made an entirely good job of it. I have, with practice, been able to reduce the flamboyance of my expressions and gestures, but I still have the feeling that I'm something of a caricature. I've noticed that actors from the legitimate stage have the same difficulty."

"Oh, I think you've mastered that problem. You're fine in that respect," Sidney said.

"God knows I've tried to. But the thing that really troubles me is the sense of coldness in the studio. They say: 'Just look in the camera and talk to it as if you were talking to a voter.' That's easy to say, but difficult for me. I can't hear their response to my jokes or sarcastic barbs. There's no applause. There's no way of knowing whether you're carrying them with you or not. Just that damn glass eye staring coldly at you."

"I thought you were the best tonight that you have been," Sidney said.

"Perhaps," the Senator said. "Who knows? I know what John Gilbert felt like when talking movies came along." He sighed. "At any rate, the damn thing is almost over. Shall we catch a cab?"

They caught a cab and returned to the hotel. The hastily abandoned room was a shambles. Virgil Akers roamed restlessly around the room until Sidney left. When the door finally closed, he said what he had been waiting for several hours to say: "I'm worried, John."

"So am I," the Senator said.

"I mean really worried. That damn labor bill is dragging us down. It's going to cut into our vote as sure as I'm standing here." Virgil sat down on the edge of a chair, leaned forward, and said intently: "Some people are swallowing Carpenter's line that you just voted for that bill to mend your fences. Tried to buy their vote, if you will."

"That isn't the thing that's really worrying me," the Senator said. "What's really worrying me is the labor boys themselves. For months they've been brainwashed by Ross that I sold them out. I'm not worried about their going over to Carpenter. They're supporting me, so they say. But their hearts aren't in it. There's no real enthusiasm, no real gritty determination to get every living body out to vote for Burnett. We're not moving them. And we're going to lose some votes there. That's my real worry."

He rose and began to pace up and down the room. "We tried to get Ernie to send a man out here, and we ended up with Flowers. That came to naught. I have only one other idea. Let me try it out on you for size."

Virgil nodded.

"I think I'll give Ernie Kane another call at the Federation and get him to make some phone calls. Eight or ten calls to the right people in this state." He cocked a quizzical eye at Virgil.

"It's not the greatest idea I ever heard," Virgil said.

"Have you got any others?"

"No," Virgil confessed.

"I would hope he would be able to convince some of these hardheads that the Federation is with us all the way. He could talk to them in a way you or I can't."

"O.K.," Virgil said. "We've got to do something. I haven't been able to come up with any better ideas. I don't see that it can hurt us, and it might help. Ernie might turn us down, but nothing's lost. Let's try it."

"I'll call him."

"All right. Item number two," Virgil said. "The Bronstein thing."

"I've heard," the Senator replied. "I've got a pinko at my elbow, giving me advice on how to deliver the United States into the hands of the Communists."

"Pretty potent charge, even these days."

"Pretty tough charge to handle," the Senator said. "Any thoughts?"

"Only one. Charge them with anti-Semitism. Indirectly. You know, you're shocked that anti-Semitism has entered the campaign under its common guise of accusations of un-Americanism. Maybe get Bronstein's parents out here on a couple of platforms. They'd wring a lot of immigrant hearts in St. Louis."

The Senator thought for a while. "Negative. Something about it doesn't hit me just right."

"It might convert the whole thing into an argument over whether they were anti-Semitic or not. Put you on the offensive," Virgil said.

"Maybe," the Senator said. "I'm going to hold off a decision on what to do about this one for a little while longer."

"I don't see any great risks for you in doing it." He paused, seeing that he was not going to move the Senator. "O.K. Item three. Leona Smith."

"I know," the Senator said. "They're circulating the word through the political underground. They're using Leona Smith as a vivid example. Burnett bought her a house in a white neighborhood to further his liberal ideas. Burnett paid her lawyer to get her son off scot free. Burnett contributes to the NAACP." He paused again to think. "Virgil, I just don't think there's any way I can combat this. I'm not going to get trapped into denying I bought her the house, denying I contribute to the NAACP. Telling them her son got a stiff prison sentence. I'd be answering charges that a lot of people haven't even heard. I'd be giving them more currency, and I'd look like a damn fool to boot."

"It's going to hurt in the rural areas, and maybe in the city suburbs too," Virgil said.

"I know that," said the Senator in mild irritation. "Sometimes the right thing to do is to do nothing. Unless you have any brilliant suggestions, I'm going to ignore the matter."

Virgil stared at the floor. "No. But they're bastards."

333

"That's news," the Senator said.

"Well, there is one thing we can do something about and that's Ross. He keeps acting like he wishes he were someplace else."

"I've tried to get Ross moving," the Senator said, "but he's obviously just going through the motions. Ross is such an egotist that he really can't get enthusiastic about anything that doesn't involve his own immediate progress in the world."

"Can't we promise him something?"

"I've tried that. But there's nothing in my power to promise him that he's interested in except my job."

"That's so stupidly shortsighted," Virgil said.

"I'm going to risk one more try. Let him make a major speech before a big crowd. Maybe he'll get caught up in the spirit of the thing."

"If he doesn't come around, John, I'd get rid of him. Drop him. He's a dead weight at this point."

The Senator nodded. "You haven't mentioned one thing," he said. "The most important thing."

"What's that?"

"Carpenter himself. He's surprised me, surprised the Republicans, surprised everybody except, I suspect, himself."

"He's not bad," Virgil acknowledged.

"And getting better. Republicans in this state have never really had the instinct to hit you where it hurt. They've always wrapped themselves in the flag and talked a lot of generalities about the free enterprise system, creeping socialism, and the precepts of our forefathers. Carpenter doesn't. He hammers away on a lot of down-to-earth issues that they understand. He's scoring some points. There's no denying it. And he's getting sharper as he goes along. He may not have any background and damn little experience, but he has instinct. And he has sense enough to follow it."

"Pretty goddam black picture," Virgil said.

"Charcoal gray anyway." He clapped the downcast Virgil on the shoulder. "You know what this reminds me of. Remember my second campaign for the Senate. You and I sat in a hotel room just like this, on the night before the election, and pronounced me politically dead."

"The Towson campaign."

"Yes. Towson had cut into the labor vote, and the women were mad for him. And Walter Decker had defected and said he'd vote for Mussolini before he'd vote for me."

"Walter died last year, you know."

"Yes. He told me once he was sorry about that statement."

"Remember when you grabbed that microphone over in Lexington," Virgil said, "and it was wired wrong and you couldn't let go of it. You stood there with your eyes bulging and your hair practically standing on end. I thought you were having a seizure."

The Senator laughed. "I've lived sixty-two years, and I will state flatly that the sensation of electricity running through me was the single most memorable moment of my life."

Virgil chuckled. He rose and gave his hand to the Senator. "We've had a lot of good times."

"Now, just a moment," the Senator said. "If that isn't a remark signifying the close of a career, I never heard one."

"And we'll have a lot more," Virgil added. "Don't take me too seriously, John. You know I get jumpy about everything when we're coming down to the wire. This isn't any different than I've acted every time. You know me. I'm always surprised that you win."

"I've got a few more good races in me yet," the Senator said. "Besides, we haven't even discussed what we have going for us. Registrations in our favor, better organization than they have, a good record. A lot of favors done. A name, if I may be so immodest, that is a household word."

"We'll take them," Virgil said.

"I'll offer you a sporting proposition, young man," the Senator said. "One hundred dollars that my margin is not less than one hundred thousand." He extended his hand to be shaken.

Virgil put his hand in back of him. "I won't take that bet."

335

32

Frank Raeder was not a psychiatrist, but he was a practicing psychologist. As it became apparent that Ed Flowers was drifting back to a vague, detached kind of normality, Frank began to work on the psychiatrist. His argument was simple, and it could have been right: Ed Flowers had thrown away his wife and had lost the girl he loved. Now his last rock in these troubled seas, the presidency of the union, was about to slip out from under him. Then, truly, he would have nothing. The effort required to hang onto the presidency could certainly physically be held to a minimum. If the doctor thought it necessary, Flowers could limit his appearance to a single short speech, but that much, at least, was required. It was a risky thing, Frank admitted to the doctor, but was it any more risky than letting the presidency go by default and breaking the news to Ed that he had been deposed? The doctor admitted that customarily the patient was permitted to live his usual life, providing that undue stresses were eliminated. Frank argued that losing the presidency would be the greatest stress Ed could experience. Finally, reluctantly, the doctor gave his consent for Ed to attend the convention for the single and sole purpose of making a speech. He was not to be kept away for longer than two hours, and Frank was instructed to take all necessary steps to remove conflict situations from the experience. Frank agreed to the terms.

In a Washington paper, on Thurday morning, a columnist wrote, for the benefit of the assembled delegates who were to begin deliberations within approximately one hour after reading the paper:

Ed Flowers, much assailed President of the American Electronic Workers, is in Doctors' Hospital, where he is "under observation," this columnist learned yesterday. Obviously, there have been attempts to hide the fact that Flowers is in the hospital, and further, to hide the reason for his being there for fear of hurting his chances of re-election. Hospital aides confessed that they had been instructed specifically not to talk to any member of the press by Dr. Barton King, chief of the hospital staff. Flowers has been under severe attack by an insurgent group which claims that he has been playing hanky-panky with union funds, and shows no leadership.

Frank Raeder scrutinized the column and concluded that the columnist did not quite have the whole story, but that he was close to it—or perhaps he was waiting to break it until the next morning, the day on which the balloting was to take place. The use of the term "under observation" was worrisome. The implication was clear.

Shortly after 9 A.M., the officers of the American Electronic Workers filed onto the stage of the hotel ballroom and took their seats. On each seat was a glossy booklet which described the growth of the union, with many pictures and a greeting by Ed Flowers on the first page. It mentioned "the loyal men and women without whose untiring efforts and dedication the union could not have achieved its present standing in the forefront of the American labor movement." The center seat at the head table, Ed Flowers', was left vacant. A small delegation from the musicians' union played a lively march as the officials came on stage, some comically trying to keep in step with the band, others shuffling, ignoring it. A minister stepped forward, unfolded a crackly paper before the microphone and gave the invocation. The band then struck up "The Star-Spangled Banner." Everyone sat down, and a hush fell over the audience.

Pete DeSanto stepped to the microphone. "Delegates and Brothers: Welcome to the Twenty-fifth Annual Convention of the American Electronic Workers. One of us is missing this morning, our respected President, Edward T. Flowers. President Flowers wanted me to tell all of you how disappointed he was that he could not be here this morning, and to assure you that he will be here tomorrow. I think that the newspaper story which appeared this morning needs to be commented on, because it is largely false. Mr. Flowers went to the hospital last week for routine tests, which have taken longer than any of us anticipated. It is not a serious matter, and, as I said, he will be with us tomorrow. Until he arrives, Ed asked me, as a personal favor to him, to chair the convention, which I assume will be satisfactory to this body . . ." In the single second, before Pete DeSanto said, ". . . and now I would like to call for a report from our Secretary-Treasurer, Al Horwitz," the insurgents glanced quickly at one another, but the moment was past, and Al Horwitz was in front of the microphone, reviewing the financial status of the union.

Thus, the opening of the convention got smoothly under way. The morning and afternoon sessions of the convention droned with reports of the organizing committee, the legislative action committee, the inter-union co-ordinating committee, the committee for political education. At five o'clock, the cocktail party, to be followed by a dinner, began. Frank Raeder circulated with his glass of ginger ale, flicking his eyes here and there. Don Harrack caught his arm. "I understand Flowers is pretty sick," Harrack said mockingly.

Frank sipped his ginger ale. "I hear he's going to be O.K.," he said. "I understand the tests were negative."

"What were they testing for?" Harrack said.

"Well, Ed's pretty closemouthed," Frank said, "and I didn't want to push the matter too far, but I assume they were testing for a malignancy of some kind. So we were all relieved to hear the tests didn't turn up anything."

"He's been under a lot of pressure lately," Harrack said. "I suppose that could have affected his health."

"Pressure doesn't produce malignancies," Frank said.

"True," said Harrack, "but I suppose it could cause you to imagine you had a malignancy."

"Apparently the doctors themselves weren't sure until they had explored," said Frank. "I doubt that three or four doctors could be fooled."

"They might be," Harrack said. "Funnier things have happened. Nice to see you, Frank." Harrack drifted away, and Frank studied his back. Apparently they had a glimmering of what had happened, but they were not sure. In time, of course, they could find out—through a nurse, a technician, or a porter. Fifty or a hundred dollars would bring the story out of the hospital. His only hope was that it could not be done before the balloting on the following afternoon. He left the party and went to the hospital.

Ed seemed to be in good spirits, pleasant and vague. Frank handed him a short speech which he himself had written.

"The staff put this together for you, Ed. It's not too long—about twenty minutes of reading time. It's a shame that you can't get over there and join all the fun and festivities. Everybody's asking about you and saying that it doesn't seem like a convention without you around."

"Good," Ed said. "Like to be there. Hate like hell to miss it."

"Well," Frank broke in, "you've got to pay attention to your doctor. He said that it was all right to go over for a short time tomorrow. But he doesn't want you to tire yourself. Besides, there'll be plenty more conventions."

A shadow passed across Ed's face. "Is Harrack there, and that bunch?"

"Oh, sure," said Frank casually, "they're there. But they're behaving themselves."

"You don't think they're going to kick up a big ruckus?" Ed said.

"Not a chance," Frank said. "They're discredited, Ed. The guys just don't buy it. They're loyal to you."

"Sure," said Ed. "They know me. I know practically every one of them on a first-name basis."

"Of course," said Frank. "It's a love fest over there. Smooth as cream."

"I'm glad to hear that. Very glad. I didn't like the way things were going. It's going to be O.K.?"

"Sure," said Frank. "You get some sleep, and I'll be over tomorrow to pick you up." As he left, he met the nurse, bringing the sleeping pill.

Frank returned to the Sheraton Park just as the dessert dishes were being cleared. Shortly thereafter the lights were turned out and the forty-minute movie on the history of the American Electronic Workers began. It was a skillful job, which had been put together by a public relations firm for twenty-five thousand dollars. Ed Flowers' name was only mentioned twice, and then in offhand references, although he appeared many times, unidentified, in pictures. In one, he had a young boyish grin and stood at Dan Gault's left hand on the picket line fifteen years before. The conclusion of the movie left the delegates saying to themselves, as it was intended to: This is really a great group of guys, a great union, and we've come a long way.

On the following morning, Frank noted with relief that the newspaper columnist had said nothing further. Various committees met on Friday morning to draft resolutions and proposals for action. The organization awaited an attack in the committees—resolutions attacking Ed Flowers, or perhaps some juggling of the organization of the union to, in fact, make Flowers a figurehead. But nothing came. The committees worked on innocuous projects, arguing, within parochial limits, about various subjects. But not about the subject that was most on all their minds. To the incumbents, the silence was unnerving. It became apparent that the insurgents were going to stake everything on the vote. They were going to attempt to take control in a single series of votes: for the president, vice-presidents, secretary-treasurer, and the five at-large members of the executive council. Before lunch the various committees reported their morning's activities and offered their resolutions, which were either accepted unanimously, or tabled for further study. At noon they adjourned for cocktails and lunch. When they seated in the vast ballroom of the Sheraton Park, Ed Flowers made his entrance, accompanied by Harold Berg. As he moved in back of the head table, those on the floor caught sight of him and began standing to applaud. Ed made his way down the table slowly as everyone extended a hand to him. The applause was vigorous, and died away as he sat down between Harold Berg and Frank Raeder. As Ed ate his lunch, chatting with Frank and Harold and a few others, those on the floor watched him like birds. After a few minutes, many of them performed the same gesture—turning back to their lunches and shaking their heads. Clearly the rumor was wrong. Ed Flowers was not off his rocker. He was up there laughing and smiling just like always. He looked fine. Anybody could see he was all right. A pretty crummy trick, a McCarthy trick, to spread that kind of rumor about him. A cheap trick, trying to put one over that way.

A great clatter of dishes arose as the waiters cleared the tables. Several hundred delegates lit cigars, cigarettes, and pipes, and settled back to hear their president. The introduction had been entrusted to a reliable member of the executive council. Frank had persuaded him to delete a couple of phrases which might have brought boos or hoots of laughter. It was a short, dry, safe introduction, and the councilman read it in a workmanlike manner. Ed stepped to the microphone. Many in the audience had risen and were cheering wildly, but many remained seated, glowering at him. Ed gazed over the heads of the audience with a glazed expression, and waited until the cheering died away.

"Delegates and Brothers: I am prouder and happier than usual to be standing before you at this twenty-fifth convocation of our beloved union. I say prouder and happier than usual, because it was not until yesterday that I was sure that I would be here at all. I won't bore you with the details of my operation, as old ladies do. Suffice it to say that I went into the hospital for a checkup and tests, and it seemed for a while as if I would have to remain there for some time. Yesterday, they informed me that I would be able to come over here for a while today, provided that I returned to the hospital promptly so that the series of tests could be continued. All tests to date have proved to be negative, and I am confident that they will continue to be so. My health is good, and while my youthful vigor isn't what it once was when I worked on the production line twenty years ago, I think there is enough of the old zip left to do an effective job for this union, which is, as all of you know, the work of primary importance in my life. . . ."

Ed then read, smoothly, the rest of the prepared text, which, in optimistic and glowing terms, painted the future of the union, under his guidance. Part of the way through, one of the delegates, who had been drinking, rose and began to abuse him from the floor. Ed paused. Sweat appeared on his upper lip, and his lips continued to mouth words, although no sound came forth. Finally the miscreant was clawed to his seat.

"Go ahead, Ed," Frank said. Ed ran a nervous tongue over his lips, bent his head, and plunged ahead. He read the dramatic and emotional closing paragraphs vividly, and at the close, most of the audience stood to applaud. He broke into a smile and raised both of his hands above his head. Harold Berg arose and shook his hand, followed by Frank and several of the councilmen. Ed made his way along the raised platform, with Frank trailing behind. As he left the rostrum, Ed paused, smiled, and waved confidently. He and Frank got into the black Cadillac and were driven back to the hospital.

"It was fine," Ed said. "I knew it was going to be fine. Harrack and those bums. . . ."

"Couldn't have been better," Frank said. "You'll be re-elected unanimously."

"I think so," Ed said. "I think I probably will." He laid his head back against the seat, and in a few minutes he was asleep. When they arrived at the hospital, the driver got out and opened the door.

The doctor was waiting for them. "Oh, my God," he said. He put a hand on Ed's pulse.

"He's asleep," Frank said.

"No, I'm not. Just a cat nap," Ed said. He stirred slowly and allowed himself to be helped from the car.

"How are you feeling?" the doctor said.

"Fine. Just a little tired." The doctor ordered that Ed be put to bed, with a sedative, while Frank waited, pacing the cheerless waiting room. Presently the doctor returned.

"I shouldn't have done that," he said. "It was against my better judgment."

"It worked out fine, Doctor," Frank said.

"I shouldn't have let myself be talked into it," the doctor said. "It was my sole responsibility and it was a terrible risk."

342

Frank clapped his battered hat crookedly on his head. "There are a lot of risks in life, and how would he have taken it if we had to break the news to him that he was booted out of the union in disgrace?"

The doctor sighed. "Well, it's over, and he seems to be all right. It might be worse if he doesn't make it . . . I mean if they don't re-elect him."

"Don't fret about it, Doctor. We took a pretty close nose count yesterday, and we had the votes to win. And after the speech, I'll bet he got most of the fence-sitters, and probably brought over a good bunch of Harrack's guys." Frank glanced at his watch. "In fact, it's probably all over by now. It was first on the agenda after lunch. Look at the paper tonight, Doctor, and you'll be sure you did the right thing."

Frank left the hospital and rode back in pleased silence. He got out at the hotel and slipped into the back of the great ballroom. The room was noisy, people were walking around, and the floor was littered with paper.

"For the office of Secretary-Treasurer . . ." Pete DeSanto was saying. Frank caught the sleeve of a large man at a rear table. "What happened?"

The man withdrew a wet cigar from his mouth. "Flowers got re-elected."

"What was the count?"

"Geez, I dunno. It was a walk." He grasped the shoulder of another man at the table. "Mike, what was the count on Flowers' election?"

"Four eighty-six to . . . somewheres around two hundred. Two hundred something."

Frank patted him in thanks as he spied Don Harrack sitting at a table in the middle of the room with half a dozen of his lieutenants. They all sat in identical, surly positions, glowering at the rostrum.

"Local Sixty-seven . . ." Pete DeSanto was shouting from the platform.

"Thirty-two votes for Horwitz. No votes for Smith," a man from the floor answered.

Frank snaked his way to Harrack's table and crouched beside his chair. "Don, it was a good race. I congratulate you." Harrack looked at him with disdain.

"Fuck you."

"I'm not being sarcastic, Don. I mean it."

"Drop dead," Harrack said, putting his cigarette back into his mouth and turning his attention to the platform.

"Listen, Don, and listen carefully. You've been licked good. Horwitz is going to win, and our vice-presidential candidates are going to win, and we're going to sweep the council. We're going to shut you out. Now you can goddam well see that's true."

"Bully for you," Harrack said.

"We'll have all the cards. Every one of them. And we'll have four years in office. Four years to root you and every one of your guys out of the union." A sneer appeared on Harrack's face, and his big hand doubled into a fist. Frank laid a hand lightly on the the fist. "Unless . . ." he said.

"Unless what?"

"Look, it's taken twenty-five years to build this union, and none of us wants to tear it apart. It's going to be a pretty messy fight, if it has to be a fight. But we're dealing from strength. We'd win. You know that, don't you?"

Harrack didn't answer.

"This union ought to fight the people it's supposed to fight over the next four years, and not fight each other. Ed wants you to stick with the union . . ."

"Thanks, but no, thanks."

" . . . as an officer," Frank continued. Harrack's eyes widened slightly.

"What as?" he said. "Third assistant janitor?"

"As a councilman."

"For Christ sake, as one of five councilmen," Harrack said. "You're just looking for window dressing."

"I'm looking for a future president."

"You're outa your mind," Harrack said.

"Far from it. Ed can't last in that job forever."

Don Harrack's eyes were now unmistakably caught in interest. "Don't tell me something is wrong with Flowers, after that

344

big show you put on to convince everybody that everything was hunky-dory."

"I didn't say that. Now what do you say. . . ?"

His voice was drowned out with cheers and clapping as Pete DeSanto announced that Al Horwitz was re-elected as Secretary-Treasurer by a count of four hundred thirty-six to two hundred twenty-five.

Harrack considered the proposal. "Why not?" he said at last. "But if you're trying to make a fool of me"—he waved a horny finger under Frank's nose—"I can play rough."

"It's a deal," Frank said. "Let me see what I can do." He rose and started to leave.

"I thought that Flowers was president of this union," said Harrack mockingly. Frank wound his way to the edge of the room and along the wall, crowded with men standing, to the exit near the rostrum. He beckoned Harold Berg, and the message was relayed to Pete DeSanto, who promptly called a twenty-minute recess. Berg, Frank, Pete, and half a dozen trusted loyalists assembled in a room across the hall from the ballroom. Frank told them that Ed had asked him to make the offer to Harrack in the hope that the breach could be sealed. Berg objected.

"Is Ed nuts? Christ, Harrack will cut him to pieces if he gets on the council. And he'll have a base to build on. He'll have all the inside information. It's crazy. We've licked them, now let's clean them out. For good. I refuse to go along with any such crazy idea as that, even if Ed did say so. . . ." Several others nodded. "He's right."

"Ed's thinking is this," Frank said. "If we go through four years of infighting, we'll be in a constant state of turmoil. We won't be able to act in concert on anything. Strikes or anything else. Everybody will have the knife out. And some of the guys are going to get sick and tired of it. Some of them already are. And they're going to start looking around for some other union— and there are plenty of unions that are itching to get their hands on the skilled trades. Before long we'll be fighting a civil war in the union, and fighting off other unions, and fighting employers. Now that's going to be one hell of a mess."

"So we purge them," Berg said. "It's as simple as that."

"How are you going to purge the presidents of those locals that supported Harrack?"

"We'll put up candidates against them and lick them. And we'll starve them for money. There are plenty of ways."

"Sure there are, and they all lead to war. Why not do it the easy way? Forgive them, and weaken them. Work quietly within the framework of the union, and wean away Harrack's supporters. No fight, no fuss, no bother. But when Harrack looks around for the troops, he finds they are all lined up with opposition."

"Harrack isn't going to let you do that," one of the councilmen said. "He'll be in there chipping away at Ed and all of us. He's not going to sit still for that kind of crap."

Frank played his trump card. "Remember this: Any councilman can be removed by a vote of the council, the president, and the secretary-treasurer *any time*, when it's in the best interests of the union. They don't even have to have a reason. So, we play along with Harrack, try to weaken his support, and if he gets to be a problem, we remove him. By taking that course, we have it both ways. We try to beat him quietly, and if that doesn't seem to be working, we declare war. And hell, he's got them stirred up and raring to go now, but they're going to cool off in a month or so, particularly when they see who's in the saddle. Time is on our side. Ed thinks it's the thing to do. Now what do you say?" The men in the room glanced sidewise at one another. "Is anybody against it?"

"I'm against it," Berg said. "You've got a point, but I still say, let's go after them now while we're hot."

"I think we ought to go along with Ed," Pete DeSanto said.

Frank paused. "Is everybody else agreed?" The rest of them nodded their heads and spoke reluctant assent. "Good," said Frank. "Why don't you pass the word and get the job done. I'll phone Ed and tell him that everybody's willing to go along with him." They filed out of the room, and Frank sauntered down the hall. He put a dime into the telephone and dialed.

"Good afternoon," the voice said, "the latest Weather Bureau forecast for Washington and vicinity." Frank spoke a few words into the phone, but he was not paying attention to what he was saying. He was wondering whether Don Harrack could be honed down. He was a tough nut, but hell, that's the way the cards fall. And he wondered how much time he would have, because he was sure that Ed Flowers was on the way down. It was just a question of time.

33

At six o'clock on the evening of election day, Roger Carpenter was lovingly editing his acceptance speech in his house in a fashionable suburban section of St. Louis. He read the speech with some satisfaction. Within a few hours he would know whether his aching need to win had been satisfied. The speech promised idealism tempered with common sense. Progress and growth, but without waste, financial irresponsibility, and inflation. The solution of domestic and foreign problems by the application of sound, practical business principles, not by professorial theories. The speech contained no principles, no guiding philosophy. It promised only that what was right and good would be done, and what was evil would not. Carpenter was actually an ambitious man with few firmly fixed principles except the single principle that success was the object of life, and it came more easily when everybody liked you.

It had been quite a successful principle. As a young businessman, he had pleased his bosses by joining the Republican party. When his prospective father-in-law had objected to his daughter's marrying Carpenter, he had won over the rich old man by carefully, though not servilely, reflecting his views. His marriage had brought him a fair amount of money, a blonde wife, and two photogenic children. His business career had brought him the presidency of a sizable company at the age of thirty-four. He was a compulsive joiner and at one time had belonged to twenty-five organizations. His business permitted him to build a political career in a non-political way, using community work with St. Louis libraries, hospitals, and schools to establish his reputation as a civic leader.

All of the clear-eyed building—his marriage, his successful business and public career—had come to fruition when Carpenter, at forty-three, and the younger members of the Republican party finally persuaded the Old Guard to accept him as a candidate for the U.S. Senate.

The Old Guard had reluctantly given its assent, feeling that he would have little chance against John Burnett. But the boy had proved to be vigorous and aggressive. He was enthusiastic, and people liked him. He was causing quite a stir. The Old Guard nodded to one another in surprise: the boy was a good choice.

He set aside the ten-page address and started on the distasteful task of constructing a statement of defeat in the event that it should come. It would, of course, be much shorter. Perhaps a page in length. It would begin on a note of hope—that the benighted voters would ultimately see the light and would return to the politics of their forefathers, the politics of freedom and integrity. The creeping hand of government bossism from Washington must ultimately be stayed, and it was his profound hope and prayer that it would happen before we woke up, one bright morning, to find ourselves enslaved. There was a short, one-sentence commendation of the incumbent Senator, and wish for luck.

In his hotel room, John Burnett was thinking only of the turnout. The television set was blaring that the turnout was heavier than expected in the rural areas, and not as heavy as expected in St. Louis and Kansas City. They speculated over whether this was a protest vote, or a heavy Republican turnout—discussed it lengthily, and concluded nothing.

The first scattered returns came in from the small towns, which vied to get the results in early: 28 votes for Burnett, 2 for Carpenter; 14 for Burnett, 5 for Carpenter; 140 for Burnett, 171 for Carpenter. As the television commentators said over and over again, desperately attempting to fill time, there was nothing in yet which would indicate a trend one way or the other. Returns from the East came in as the station switched back to the network, and it was clear that the Republicans were running a strong race. There had been one upset for governor, and two Democratic senators were running dangerously behind. In Massachusetts, New Jersey, and Maryland, the Republicans were obviously going to make some gains. On the other hand, in New York, the Democrats were holding their own, and perhaps stood to gain two seats in the House of Representatives. At eight o'clock, the station switched out of the network to give the local returns. The count stood at 34,314 for Carpenter, 30,868 for Burnett. The television commentators assured the audience that this was as expected. These were rural returns, where the Republicans were expected to run strongly. The large city returns, which were normally Democratic, had not reported yet in any substantial numbers.

"Well," the Senator said to his wife, Sidney Bronstein, Dick Goetz, and Virgil Akers, "let's go down to headquarters."

"I don't like the looks of it, John," said Virgil, biting his lip. "It's too close for comfort."

"Too early to tell," said the Senator.

"That margin in the rural areas is disturbing."

"Let's not give extreme unction just yet. Let's all put on our smiling best faces and come along downstairs."

Outside his hotel room, three reporters and two television cameramen had set up. The blinding lights were turned in their faces.

"Statement, Senator."

John Burnett gave a large and confident grin. "Not just yet, boys."

"Are you conceding, Senator?"

The grin did not flicker. "Not on your life."

The little group pushed its way through the knot of reporters, who quickly snapped their notebooks shut; and one of the cameramen capped his camera and slung it over his shoulder. The newsmen followed them, like wolves trailing prey. The elevator let them off on the ballroom floor, and as they entered the brightly lit ballroom, a cheer went up. Other Democratic candidates for office pumped the Senator's hand and assured him that victory was certainly his, and theirs. Several television monitors were set up on tables. Tables were scattered around the room, pushed out of line from their original geometric arrangements, and were littered with papers and hundreds of paper cups, half filled with beer or Coca Cola. Giant pretzel dishes, some empty and overturned, studded the tables. The Senator and his retinue settled in a row of straight chairs at the front and watched the national returns. The national pattern had now become apparent. The Republicans were making gains. Those hopeful places where the Democrats were running well were the exceptions. At nine o'clock, the station left the network for the state returns. A familiar, pompous TV commentator flashed onto the screen. "An upset victory may be in the making in the Missouri senatorial race," he began . . . and continued for some time, exhibiting his knowledge of Missouri political affairs. Shouts of "Returns!" and "Shut up!" came from the ballroom. In back of the commentator, returns were being chalked up on a board, but they were tantalizingly unreadable. "Now," said the commentator, "let's have a look at the board." A small cheer went up in the ballroom. "In over-all total, Carpenter, 85,004; Burnett, 74,846." The room settled into chastened silence. "Now, let's look at it on a county-by-county basis," the commentator continued. The cameras slipped down the counties one by one, revealing that only a small fraction of the big-city vote was as yet in. The Senator drew his chair close to Virgil Akers, and they put their heads together.

"Ten thousand votes," Virgil said. "If that margin continues—"

"I'm not interested in those," the Senator snapped. "What do you make of the St. Louis and Kansas City returns?"

Virgil shrugged. "They're probably suburban returns, so his total is inflated, percentagewise. No way to tell if they are from the industrial districts."

"Maybe," said the Senator. "Why don't you try to find out?"

Virgil slipped away, and the Senator resumed his emotionless vigil before the set, which was again spewing forth national returns. A few returns were coming in from states west of Missouri. The Republican trend was not apparent there. In fact, if anything could be gleaned from the scattered returns, it seemed to be a Democratic trend.

"See that," Dick Goetz said, leaning across Ellen. "West of us things don't look so bad, and we're more comparable to them than New England. Hell," he said with bravado, "Massachusetts is fifteen hundred miles from here."

The Senator nodded without comment. He stood up and took a long stretch. People shook his hand and slapped him on the back and assured him that the returns were fragmentary. Wait until St. Louis. . . . All over the hall, people were saying, Wait until St. Louis comes in. It had become almost an inaudible chant. Virgil slid into the chair beside him.

"They're wild as March hares down there. They shout something at you and leave the phone hanging for five minutes. Some of those are suburban returns, John, but," he added apologetically, "some of the industrial districts are in—couldn't find out how many, but I got a couple." He thrust a wrinkled piece of paper into the Senator's hand. The Senator studied it. "We haven't got the margin," Virgil said, "but, hell, it's a couple of districts." The Senator set his lips, but said nothing. "John, you don't suppose they been giving us the knife there?" The Senator shrugged.

"Let's not kid ourselves, Virgil," he said. "It's all over." He set his face in a complaisant expression and turned once more to the television set. The national returns included those from Missouri, but they were behind those that they had just heard. The hands of the clock were moving toward ten o'clock. When the long hand reached the top, John Burnett knew that the secret would be out.

"Carpenter is claiming victory in the senatorial contest," the commentator said. "He leads John Burnett 365,666 to 324,784, with approximately forty-six per cent of the vote counted. We have been trying to reach Senator Burnett for comment, but as of this moment we have not been able to do so. . . ." A second commentator was called on the scene, and he made the definite prediction that Carpenter had won.

John Burnett rose slowly from his seat and made his way up the packed aisle. As he turned and climbed the three or four steps that led to the small stage of the ballroom, the sound was turned down on the television sets and the room settled into expectant silence.

"Fellow Democrats: I think it is obvious to all of us from the returns that the people, in their wisdom, have seen fit to retire me from public office." There was a protesting roar from the audience. "I have spent thirty-five years in public life, and I have been a politician, that curious mixture of private and public interests. And I will not try to tell you that I always tried to do the right and the just, that I always made the honorable decision, even at the cost of votes. Because that is not true. Often my decisions have been dictated by passion, vindictiveness, and expedience. For public officials are not judicial gods; they are merely men, sprung up from the people. If they are good men, they are merely trying to do their best within the limits of practicality. If they are bad men, they are merely trying to promote their private interests while appearing to be acting in the public interest. If they are men who never waver from the path, then they are prophets, and there are few of them, and they are usually martyred in one way or another. But most men in public life—and I include myself—hope that in the summing up they have succeeded in some small way in pushing back the darkness. When, over my grave, some of my good-intentioned friends are eulogizing me as a man of absolute integrity, I'll be off somewhere, looking on and chuckling a little to myself, but I will hope that some of what they say, at least, is true.

"To those of you who have worked with and for me in the years past, I can only use the inadequate words 'Thank you,' and hope that each of you will accept those words as a personal tribute. I am told that men who have been under the shadow of death in battle together feel no need to communicate emotions. Indeed, it seems profane. And it seems profane here."

Senator Burnett gave a quick nod and descended the stairway to the floor. The room rang with cheers and applause, and as he passed down the aisle, shaking hands, laying a hand on a shoulder here and squeezing an arm there, he made his way to the exit. A number of the women were crying, and one moved forward to kiss him on the cheek.

The reporters and television cameras laid in wait for him,

with the blinding lights of half a dozen small suns. He stood against the wall, like a man in a police line-up.

"Senator," said a reporter, "do you concede, sir?" A pause fell on the group.

"In view of the substantial margin which my opponent enjoys over me, with a substantial part of the ballots counted, I concede defeat." There was a scurrying among the group, and several reporters dashed off with that single line in their notebooks. There were more questions, but he brushed them off and pushed through the crowd. Virgil and Dick opened a way through the crowd for him, and he squeezed into Virgil's Cadillac. Ellen and Sidney managed to get into the front seat. They drove off, with a dozen cars in close pursuit. No one spoke as they drove over to Republican headquarters. When they arrived, they found it a delirium of noise. The senator-elect from Missouri was brought to him, and they were herded again in front of the cameras. They repeatedly shook hands, smiling, to satisfy the insatiable photographers.

"To what do you attribute your victory?" a reporter asked Carpenter.

"To the good sense of the people of Missouri," the senator-elect said, "who recognize that it's time to put our Federal Government on a sound, businesslike basis." The Senator was asked to what factors he attributed his defeat. He was expecting the question and was thinking about the answer, but there was none. At least there was none that he could glibly roll off in a sentence.

"I'll just answer that question with a quote from a favorite poem of mine, if I may: 'The moving finger writes; and, having writ, moves on: nor all your piety nor wit shall lure it back to cancel half a line, nor all your tears wash out a word of it.' "

Slowly, the Senator and his thin file made their way from the hall. On most of the faces staring at him there was an expression of mild contempt. The Circus Maximus, he thought. A small boy rushed into his path and splattered his tongue out at him before he was yanked back by his embarrassed but amused mother. Finally they reached the door.

"You want to go home, or what?" Virgil said.

"How about a drink?" Dick Goetz said.

"I think you should get some rest, John. You're awfully tired," said Ellen. He bore it for a few moments, then he shouted at them: "Leave me alone. Get away from me. I want to be left alone." He advanced at them fiercely, and they, as a group, retreated a step. "Leave me alone," he muttered, and turned his back on them and lumbered down the stone steps to the street. In a moment, he turned the corner, away from the worried, piercing glances that penetrated his back. For the first time in many months, he was on a quiet street, alone. The sound of his footsteps bounced hollowly against the dirty granite buildings.

"Election returns," the old man at the corner said, proffering him a paper.

"No, thanks."

"Burnett got beat," the old man said after him. He walked for several miles on the concrete of the city that had rejected him, which lay over the soil of the state that had rejected him. At length, he sat down on a slatted bench in a small deserted park in a city square. Newspapers scudded past him, turning over and over slowly in the wind, making erratic progress. The graceful complex of delicate black branches drifted against the dark sky. A solitary man hurried past him. For an hour, the Senator thought in a drifting, disjointed way about his life, now over. Then the cold of the bench penetrated his bones, and he made his way slowly back to the hotel.

"Sorry to see you wuz beat, sir," the elevator operator said. He nodded. He fitted his key into the lock and went inside. Ellen came over to him and gave him a light kiss on the cheek, but she said nothing. It was a labor to hang up his coat and hat. He sank into a chair and did not speak for a while.

"Well, Ellen, that's that, as they say."

She waited for him to say more.

"Executed," he said finally, "not for any major crime. Just a lot of little things . . . a couple of votes . . . for getting a little old and pompous . . . because of a few enemies made here and there . . . because of young men's ambition . . . a lot of little things that add up to capital punishment."

"Maybe it's for the best," she tried.

He looked at her from under heavy lids. "For whose best?

355

The country's? Now that I have mastered the problems, and have some influence. To turn it over to that empty-headed dunce. Mine? Trained in politics and government for thirty-five years to the point where I have a great store of facts, and have, I hope, acquired some judgment. Now I find myself trained for nothing, usable for nothing, useless. That's for the best?"

"I'm sorry," Ellen said. "I was just searching for something to say."

"I think that I'm being realistic when I say that there is no comparison between that idiot Carpenter and myself. To think that the people of Missouri could have elected him in my place is just . . . incomprehensible." He rose and began to pace the floor. They let him run because they didn't think he would have a chance." He looked at his wife in pain. "He's handsome. He has a pretty wife and two picture-book children. He smiles. He's vigorous. He exudes confidence that he has the answer to every problem. But he stands for absolutely nothing. Absolutely nothing. Whatever anybody thinks, he thinks. Is that what they want, Ellen? Is that all they want?" He stopped and opened his hands to her.

"I don't know," Ellen said. "I don't know." And for the first time since she had realized that he was beaten, tears welled up in her eyes.

34

Ten days after his defeat, John Burnett walked down the long corridor of the Senate Office Building to his office. He dreaded the moment. He laid his hand, for a few seconds, on the doorknob, but did not turn it. The sign on the door read:

Senator John Burnett, Missouri

Welcome — Walk In

He turned the knob, and the animated conversation that had been going on, abruptly ceased. Four pairs of eyes were fixed on him, as if he had risen from the dead.

"Good morning, ladies," he said loudly. "The vanquished has returned." With that, Mary, who had been with him for fifteen years, burst into tears. Other tears, set off by this outburst, coursed down Estelle's cheeks and welled up in Frances' eyes. Clair sat, slumped and sad-eyed. "Now, now, girls," he said. "It isn't the end of the world, you know. We're all still alive and we have not been atomized."

"Oh, Senator," Mary said, "when I heard the news, I just couldn't believe it. I just couldn't. And I said to George, 'They must have made a mistake. They must be reading the wrong line or something.' I said, 'I just know that is not true, it just has to be

357

wrong.' But it wasn't," she wailed. The Senator laid a hand on her shoulder and gave her a gentle pat.

"It tests your faith in democracy," said Clair, his bright Radcliffe graduate.

"It does mine," the Senator agreed. "And it is found a little wanting, I'm afraid."

"Only idiots could put a man like that in the Senate instead of you," she continued hotly.

"Now Clair," he said, "we mustn't say things like that, even if they are true."

"I've always believed in universal suffrage," she said, "but this is just too stupid. Maybe we do need a benevolent autocracy."

"Just figure out a way to keep them benevolent, and I'd say you've got something." He hung up his hat and coat. "I'm going to talk to each of you privately and individually this morning. You girls first, then Dick and Sidney. I'll call you in a moment, Frances."

In his office he sat for a while in his chair, thinking about nothing, looking at nothing. His buzzer sounded. Paul Finch, Frances said, was there to see him. Reluctantly, he told her to send Finch in.

"Well," said the Senator, "it's good to see you, Paul. I assume we are well enough acquainted by this time for me to call you Paul."

"By all means, Senator. Except that I'd like to continue to call you Senator."

"You may if you like, though I'm not sure how long the designation applies. Until he takes the oath, I suppose. Then I'm Mister Burnett. That will take some getting used to . . ."

"Oh, I suspect you'll be Senator for the rest of your life to most people." Paul paused. "Senator . . . I was terribly . . ."

John Burnett waved him into silence. "Thank you, Paul, but no more post-mortems. What's on your mind?" Paul sat down in a comfortable leather chair. "Cigarette?"

"Well, sir," said Paul, beginning uneasily, "over the last few years the Liberty Electric Company has followed your record with great interest. . . ."

"I'm sure that's so."

"And with great admiration most of the time, I might say."

"That's surprising, if true," the Senator said. "Judge Russell was always belaboring me to vote his way on matters, and I rarely did."

"But you listened to him and considered his views."

"I hope so."

"And this interests us. The fact that you have an open mind."

The Senator looked at him with amusement. "Paul, I'm sixty-two years old, and about as set in my views as I'll ever get. I could hardly be described accurately as having an open mind."

"That's an unfortunate choice of words on my part. What I really mean to say is a far-ranging mind, willing to examine all the facets of a question before making up your mind. . . ."

"An illusion," said the Senator. "I usually knew in advance."

"Well, we're interested in you, sir," Paul struggled on, "in a professional way. As you know, Judge Russell, who was here in Washington for Liberty Electric for so long, is just about out of it. He remains on a consultant basis with us, but for all practical purposes, he is no longer active. Now it has occurred to us that it might be very valuable for the company to have access to a man who had been around Washington for a long time and who knows just about everybody there is to know. Somebody who has access, in a confidential way, to all the doors, some of which are now closed to us. Our idea was that this man would be carried as a consultant, to advise us on policy here in Washington, and also to make high-level contacts. What we had in mind, sir, was that perhaps you might be interested in such a proposition. We'd be very proud to have you with us, if you would consider it."

The Senator rose to his feet, jammed his hands deep in his pockets, and gave a dry laugh. "Well, well, well, I certainly never expected anything like this, never in my life. . . ."

"As you know," Paul plunged on, "I'm in charge of the Washington office here, and you would be working with me. Not for me, you understand. But on a co-ordinating basis. It wouldn't have to be full time. In the area of compensation," Paul hurried on, "we had in mind a retainer arrangement of some sort, and the figure we had in mind was in the neighborhood of fifteen hundred dollars a month. I think these things are usually handled on a yearly contract arrangement. I don't know whether that will be important in your decision, but I did want to mention it."

"I apologize for laughing, Paul. I didn't mean to imply at all that this is a laughing matter. It's just that I am astounded by this offer. Flabbergasted. That's the only way to describe it. Why, in God's name, should the Liberty Electric Company be interested in hiring me? I have fought everything they have stood for for the past quarter of a century."

"Well, sir, I'd like to be completely honest with you. There's been a change of command in New York. You've probably read about it in the papers. The old President, Ralph M. Clore, has moved up to Chairman of the Board, and we have a new President, Mr. Briggs Christy. Naturally, his ideas are somewhat different from Mr. Clore's, particularly in the labor field and . . ."

"Ah," said the Senator, "so I am to become the instrument for putting a new public relations face on the Liberty Electric Company."

"Not exactly, Senator. I would say that the Liberty Electric Company has moved its position sufficiently so that it feels that a man of your views could represent them."

"That's one hell of a move. I hate to be a cynic, but I doubt strongly if they've moved that much."

"Well, sir, I was consulted about this matter, and I was very flattered to be, and I suggested your name. Frankly, all hell broke loose, and it took a bit of selling, but I think it's fair to say that they've all come around to my way of thinking. Well, almost all."

"What arguments did you use, if I may ask, to sell me?"

"This will probably be as embarrassing as hell for both of us, Senator, but I'm going to tell you. I said that I thought that you had one of the best minds in the Senate, and further, that there was no one on the horizon who could touch your broad knowledge of the labor field, and that your contacts on the Hill were second to none."

"Very flattering," said the Senator, "but it omits my attitude. What did you tell them about that?"

"I told them, first of all, that you were not a captive of the labor unions. That you did not jump to do their bidding, like some of them down here, as evidenced by your vote on the labor bill. And I told them, further, that I felt that while you had participated in the writing of much New Deal labor legislation, you were no longer the flaming liberal that you used to be. That you had seen, as many have, the inherent danger in a government that becomes monopolistic or too powerful. Perhaps I should not be this frank, but that is exactly what I told them."

The Senator sat down in a companion chair to Paul's and shaded his eyes, as if from a bright light. "That's not a very pretty picture, young man. I hope to God you're not right."

"There's nothing to be ashamed of there, Senator, that I can see. A man doesn't grasp one set of opinions to his breast at eighteen and carry them for the rest of his life. I think that it's a tribute to a growing mind."

"Is that how I'm to be looked upon? A deserter from the cause?"

"The cause did a lot of good. Very few people will deny that, Senator. It filled a need, but it doesn't seem to me that you need to consider yourself a traitor to it, just because times have changed and a different course of action is called for. As I say, I think it's a tribute to a mind that can adjust."

"I have never liked adjusting minds," the Senator said. "Minds that adjust are usually minds in which there really aren't any principles. Just the appearance. Most great men, I think you'll find, did not have such minds."

"Great men are in history books," Paul said.

The Senator idly moved the corner of the newspaper on the floor with his foot. "I suppose that's true." He clamped and unclamped his lips several times. "Paul, I want you to know that I am flattered that you, and your company, thought enough of me to consider making this fine offer. It was most unexpected, and I'm most appreciative. And you have been most flattering in some of the compliments that you have paid me. However, I'm afraid that I must decline."

"I'm very disappointed to hear that, sir. Could I just ask you . . . that is . . . is the money not enough, perhaps?"

"No, the money is perfectly adequate."

"It's just, then, that you would feel that . . . well, that you couldn't be comfortable with us?"

361

The Senator smiled. "Something like that."

They chatted for five minutes more, then Paul rose to go. He grasped the Senator's hand firmly. "Senator, we probably won't be seeing much of each other . . ."

"Oh, let's get together occasionally. I am now unemployed and I will have plenty of time. We can have lunch on some park bench, play a game of checkers."

After Paul had left, the Senator considered the conversation, somehow so depressing.

Finally he rang for Frances. She brought her dictation book, in case, but he told her to lay it aside. He told her that as of noon on the third day of January, he would no longer be able to carry her on the payroll, and that, of course, there was no possibility of the new senator's employing her. Frances was easy. She was getting married in the spring, and a January dismissal would make little difference in her plans. Estelle was offered a place in the office of Les Bell. Clair wanted to stay on the Hill, and he told her that he felt that he could place her on a committee. She glumly agreed. Only Mary was a problem. She was his friend and servant, almost a second wife. She had handled his social engagements, arranged his complicated travel schedules, tended his children, and had, at times, acted as tailor, seamstress, grocer, shoeshine boy, and even, once, barber. She was not really attached to the Senate, or to the Hill, but personally to John Burnett. Her typing and shorthand were only mediocre, but her loyalty was great. She was not much younger than he—fifty-five. He had hoped she would say she was going to quit work, but there were no children at home, and her husband had not been financially successful, so she did not offer.

Dick Goetz was cheerful. He had been busily ferreting out other work. He had had one offer which he was attempting to hold in abeyance, to see if he could do better. He had talked to several other groups—a newspaper, a labor union, and two or three corporations. He had worked for the Senator for five years and had thought he would attempt to move himself up a notch in the world after the re-elected Senator returned to Washington. The defeat only moved forward his timetable.

Last, the Senator buzzed and asked Sidney Bronstein to come

in. The door opened, and for a moment Sidney stood silhouetted against the bright light of the outer office, a picture of haggard dejection.

"Come in, Sidney," the Senator said gently.

"Senator . . ." he began. "Senator . . . when I realized I was the one who . . ."

"Don't take the whole weight of the world on your shoulders, Sidney," the Senator said. "You're talking a lot of nonsense. Dramatically satisfying, I'm sure, but nonetheless nonsense. Sit down."

"I knew you'd say something like that," Sidney said.

"It's true," the Senator said. "The sport of Red-hunting has declined in popularity."

"Still," said Sidney, ramming the fist of one hand repeatedly into the palm of the other, "it had a detrimental effect. Some unmeasurable detrimental effect."

"Some," the Senator said, "but it was the labor bill that killed us. I have no complaints. I went into it with my eyes open. Oh, there were other things. Leona Smith. The charges against you. Ross's listless performance, Carpenter's spectacularly good one."

"Why didn't we see it coming?" Sidney said. "That's what I can't understand."

"We didn't see it coming for the very good reason that it was an upset," the Senator said, "and the very definition of an upset is that you don't see it coming. You would think that we would have seen enough upsets in politics to expect them, but we never do."

"But you must have seen it coming."

"I saw the signs. I was very worried. But you know how silly all of us human beings are. We discount the bad, emphasize the good. It's very difficult, when you've been around as long as I have, to force yourself to believe the signs. Delusions of immortality are very strong at my age."

"If you were worried, you certainly kept it to yourself."

"I tried to," the Senator said. "There's one thing a politician must never be and that's a sinking ship." He turned in his chair slowly and looked out the window. "It was the confluence of a lot of things, all coming together at a particular point in time. A few thousand votes lost because of one thing, a few hundred because of another. A few thousand gained by the other side because of something else. It doesn't seem fair that these things should end a career, but they have."

Sidney stared straight ahead of him, as if he were in a trance. "It's so goddam unfair that all of these things had to come together right at this particular point."

"Many generals and premiers and presidents, and many senators too, I suppose, have said that before, Sidney. At least, I hope that I have convinced you that your youthful indiscretions were not wholly responsible, damaging as that may be to your sense of tragedy. Anyway, I owe you an apology, too, Sidney. When you came here a few months ago, I should have gone into more detail about the occupational hazards of working for a senator, but frankly, I just did not expect this. I should have, but I did not."

"Don't worry about it, Senator. I said when I shook your hand and agreed to come to work for you that I considered myself the most fortunate man in the world. I meant it then, and I don't regret it now. If I had stayed at the Department of Labor, I probably would have been committed to an institution by now."

"I'm sorry, though, because it seemed to me that you liked this work so much, and you were so well suited to it. Good judgment, sympathy, an excellent skill at writing. I'm sorry to see you cut off this way, in mid-career—cut off from something you do so well and enjoy so much."

"I feel the same way about you, Senator."

The Senator flushed. "It's unfortunate for me, but I'm hardly at mid-career. I am sixty-two and I have a good many years to look back on. I can't start over now. I have no choice but to live out the remaining years of my life in some fashion. But you have to start over. You have no choice about that."

Sidney nodded.

"So the question is: What would you like to do? I'm willing to give you all the help I can, though God knows, I've found out this week that a defeated senator doesn't have much influence. To be frank, Sidney, I think there is very little chance that I could swing a job similar to this with any senator that you would care to work for. I've run through the list in my mind, and unless there are some unexpected resignations, there are just no places. I've talked to a couple of new senators, but, as usual, they're bringing along men from their home states. They have more people crying for jobs than they can take care of."

"Thank you, Senator, but no," Sidney said. "I don't want you to do this."

"Don't be absurd, Sidney. You have a wife and children and you need a job. Let's try to find you the best one we can."

"Well, needless to say, it's a question I've been thinking a good deal about. I . . . well, I haven't come up with anything for which I am qualified and which I would really be interested in."

"That's the trouble with politics," the Senator said. "It qualifies you for absolutely nothing. You have to retrain your mind from thinking big to thinking small."

Sidney clasped his hands in front of his chin. "Senator, I do want to thank you for thinking of me, but I just can't think about it now. I've tried and I just can't do it."

"Of course," said the Senator. "Just don't wait too long. These things take a little time to arrange, and as I said, I find that my influence is waning rapidly."

Sidney nodded. He extended a warm, moist hand for the Senator to shake. "Senator, I can't say a lot of things that I should say."

"No need, Sidney. We have worked closely enough together so that I think I understand your feeling. And I reciprocate it completely."

"Well, I'd just like to say, Senator, that I consider you a great man. Certainly the greatest man I've ever known."

"Thank you, and I know you mean that. But I'm not."

"Yes, you are. To the people who really know you." Sidney withdrew his hand and awkwardly left the office.

The Senator stood in the center of the room, alone. He had been twenty-four years in this dark, paneled office, surrounded by the mementos of a lifetime. He strolled along as if he were a leisurely visitor to an art gallery, looking over the pictures. There, as a young man, with Franklin Roosevelt, in the traditional young congressman's picture . . . there, with Harry Hopkins . . . there, with Harry Truman . . . there, with Adlai Stevenson. And in each, looking older and more like a senator. With successive governors of Missouri, including a smiling Ross MacKenzie . . . with senators from his state, the last being Les Bell. With fierce old General Hugh Johnson . . . Brandeis . . . La Follette. Even Robert A. Taft. "To a good man in the wrong party," the inscription said. About as close as Taft got to humor. There were many more—pictures of the retired, the defeated, the dead. Hardly a man on the wall was still alive and fighting. People must always feel this way when they get old, he thought. Alone in the world, the last of a generation, now pushed aside to make room on the crowded planet for successive waves of young men. Books stood silently behind the glass, old friends that he had relied on many times: The Bible, several books of quotations, two books of humor and jokes, *Rules and Regulations of the United States Senate, Robert's Rules of Order, The World Almanac*. Plaques, laboriously elaborate. Awards. A piece of petrified tree from the Ozarks. Half a dozen donkeys made of various materials. A vial of Mississippi River water on a plaque. An ash tray turned from a shell casing from a Missouri defense plant. A gavel from his term as county judge thirty-five years ago. A piece of wood, on a plaque, from Mark Twain's old house. A motley and pointless collection. Many things were missing.

He lit a cigarette and glanced at his watch. "To John Burleigh Burnett, First Citizen of Missouri." He slipped it into his pocket and left his office. His door clicked loudly as he gently pulled it shut. His footsteps echoed in the deserted corridors. He walked toward the Capitol, a shiny hemisphere against the darkening sky. He crossed the street into the shadow of the building and walked along the side of it to the back terrace. He walked to the balustrade and looked down the magnificent mall toward the Washington Monument and the Lincoln Memorial beyond. It was early evening, and he drew his topcoat more closely about him as he felt the first chill wind of loneliness.